Readers Love *The Last Straw*

'An excellent and intriguing detective story'

'An excellent story with many twists and turns'

'Exceptionally good detective story'

'A real page-turner for me'

'Looking forward to more'

PAUL GITSHAM started his career as a biologist working in the UK and Canada. After stints as the world's most over-qualified receptionist and a spell ensuring that international terrorists hadn't opened a Child's Savings Account at a major UK bank (a job even duller than working reception) he retrained as a science teacher.

Also by Paul Gitsham

No Smoke Without Fire
Blood is Thicker than Water
Silent As The Grave
A Case Gone Cold
The Common Enemy
A Deadly Lesson
Forgive Me Father

The Last
Straw

Paul Gitsham

ONE PLACE. MANY STORIES

HQ
An imprint of HarperCollins*Publishers* Ltd
1 London Bridge Street
London SE1 9GF

This paperback edition 2020

2
First published in Great Britain by
HQ, an imprint of HarperCollins*Publishers* Ltd 2020

ISBN: 9780263917581

MIX
Paper from
responsible sources
FSC
www.fsc.org
FSC™ C007454

This book is produced from independently certified FSC™ paper
to ensure responsible forest management.

For more information visit: www.harpercollins.co.uk/green

This book is set in 11/15.5 pt. Minion

Printed and bound in Great Britain by
CPI Group (UK) Ltd, Croydon, CR0 4YY

*For Nana. You never got to read it, but
I think you'd have enjoyed it.*

Prologue

Blood.

Everywhere. Across the walls, over the desk, even splattered on the glowing laptop computer. The human heart is a powerful, muscular pump and a cut artery bleeds out in seconds, spraying red, freshly oxygenated blood across the room like a fire hose.

Tom Spencer removes his gloved hands from the dead man's throat and rubs them down the front of his lab coat, leaving bloody trails across his chest. Hands shaking, he picks up the blood-covered telephone and presses 9 for an outside line, followed by another three 9s.

"You are through to the emergency services. Which service do you require?"

Spencer's voice is shaky, his breathing rapid. "Police. There's been a murder."

FRIDAY

Chapter 1

Detective Chief Inspector Warren Jones slid to a halt with a faint squeak of tyres outside the main entrance to the University of Middle England's Department for Biological Sciences. Fifteen minutes had elapsed since he'd received the call and he doubted he could have done it much faster with blue lights and sirens. He switched off the engine and the sat nav on the dashboard beeped then went silent.

Two weeks into this new posting and the freshly promoted DCI was still reliant on the little device to get him around his new patch: the small Hertfordshire market town of Middlesbury. By driving everywhere with the device in map mode and where possible leaving for appointments early to take the most circuitous route, he was slowly building up a mental map of the local area. Although it was costing him a fortune in petrol — he felt guilty about passing on that cost to the force — it was the best way he knew to learn his way around.

The call could have been better timed, he supposed. He'd just finished pouring a bottle of Chilean red and was in the process of toasting his mother-in-law's upcoming birthday when his mobile had rung. The temperature in the freshly decorated lounge had dropped precipitously. Bernice had never been impressed that her eldest daughter, Susan, had married a police officer — she felt that she and her monosyllabic, hen-pecked husband, Dennis, had raised their children to aspire to greater things. Private education and all the accoutrements of a wealthy middle-class upbringing in the leafiest part of Warwickshire had led Bernice to expect her daughters to marry well. That being said, she grudgingly acknowledged that Warren was a nice enough man and at least he was a Catholic.

Mumbling his apologies, he'd slipped on a jacket and left the house as quickly as possible.

Now that he was here, the familiar singing in the blood had started, mixed with a tightness in his gut. He took a few deep breaths to steady himself, whilst rummaging around for a breath mint. He'd only had a sip of the wine, and had abstained completely at the restaurant so that he could drive, but the last thing he wanted was for somebody to smell alcohol on his breath. Not on his first big case. A murder. This was what he'd joined the force for — and even more importantly, what he'd trained as a detective for. For the past fortnight, he'd overseen his small team as they dealt with the endless tide of robberies, burglaries and low-level violence that plagued any society — a job that he was proud to do and that he knew was important to the public. But a murder was different. A murder was what got you known. A murder could make your career. It could also ruin your career before it really started…

Clambering out of the car into the hot, breathless, summer night, he scanned the largely deserted car park. Adjacent to the entrance, an ambulance was parked up next to two police cars. At the other end of the car park, a silver BMW sports car sat alone in the dark. The ambulance's blue lights were off, but the rear doors were open, light spilling out into the night, throwing shadows across the thick black tarmac. The paramedics stood by, chatting and smoking, relaxed, not expecting to have to do anything for a while. According to the call that Warren had received, the victim was beyond their help and they were now little more than a glorified taxi service to the morgue.

The front of the building was mostly glass, with two large sliding doors leading into a well-lit reception area. As Jones strode briskly towards the building, a young, uniformed police constable with a clipboard stepped out of the dark shadows to the side of the entrance.

"I'm sorry, sir, I'm afraid I can't let anybody enter the building at the moment."

Jones reached inside his jacket for his warrant card. "DCI Jones." Where the hell was his wallet? Bugger! He'd been in such a rush to leave, he'd grabbed the nearest suit jacket to hand. Unfortunately, it wasn't the one he'd been wearing to the office during the week and so the pockets were empty.

The young constable clearly didn't recognise either him or his name. Not for the first time, Jones regretted his forgettable surname. The PC flushed a little, clearly realising there was no way out of this awkward impasse without loss of dignity for one or both of the two men.

Fortunately, or unfortunately, the day was saved by a booming Essex voice.

"Don't you recognise the new boss, lad?" Jones suppressed a sigh. Great, his first big case and the DI first on the scene had to be Tony Sutton, the man who many believed should be the one wearing three Bath stars on the epaulettes of his dress uniform, rather than this outsider, parachuted in from the West Midlands Police to clean up their mess.

Turning, he saw Sutton walking towards them, a barely

concealed smirk on his face. Like Jones, he was dressed in a smart suit, although he wasn't wearing a tie. But there the similarities ended. Where Jones was a slim six feet one inch, Sutton was a short, squat bear of a man, his pugnacious features and crooked nose a reminder of his days on the force's rugby team. He was six years older than Jones, and most observers had expected him to be promoted when the previous DCI, Gavin Sheehy, retired. Unfortunately, Sheehy hadn't made it to retirement and although Sutton had been fully cleared of any involvement in Sheehy's disgrace he was nevertheless seen — rumour had it — as too close to the shamed detective to be given such an important role. At least not yet. Hence Warren's sudden and unexpected appointment.

"Sorry, sir." The young lad was blushing now.

Jones patted him on the shoulder encouragingly. "Never apologise for doing your job, son."

Son? Bloody hell, when did he get so old that he called twenty-year-old constables 'son'?

Putting aside his discomfort, Jones walked to join Sutton, who led them through the front doors into the lobby. Inside was a large reception desk with a computer and a bank of telephones, behind a reinforced glass screen, rather like a bank teller. To the right of the desk, two large double doors were held open by another uniformed PC. A swipe-card lock flashed red and an angry-sounding electronic alarm buzzed insistently, no doubt triggered by the door being held open so long.

"What have we got, Tony?"

"Nasty one, guv. White middle-aged man, identified as a Professor Alan Tunbridge, throat slit right open and head bashed in, sitting in his office."

Sutton led Jones up a flight of stairs to the right of the entrance, before proceeding along a wide-open corridor deeper into the building.

"Who found the body?"

"A young man named Tom Spencer, apparently one of the late professor's students. Claims he was working late, came back to the lab and noticed the prof's office door was open and the lights on. Figured he'd pop his head round and say 'Hi'. Found him in his chair, blood everywhere. Reckons he took his pulse but couldn't find anything, then phoned 999 on the office phone."

"What state is the crime scene in?"

"Untouched, except by Spencer. Two uniforms were first to respond and were let in by campus security. They took one look and figured there was nothing they could do for him. Paramedics arrived a few minutes later and agreed, pronounced him dead at the scene, probably from loss of blood. Yours truly arrived just after the paramedics. Scenes of Crime are on their way."

At the end of the corridor, Jones and Sutton turned a corner. "Here it is," said Sutton somewhat unnecessarily.

The corridor was crowded; two pale-looking uniformed constables were standing guard either side of an open office door. A couple of middle-aged men wearing blue woollen jumpers with 'Security' stitched in white writing on the left of the chest leant against the opposite wall, looking decidedly shaken. Standing awkwardly, answering questions to a uniformed sergeant, and looking like the demon barber of Fleet Street, stood a young man in a bloodstained white lab coat. His hands were covered in white latex gloves, also smeared with blood. A surgical face mask, rather like the ones worn by carpenters or DIY enthusiasts, hung on an elastic band around his chin. His shoes were blood-spattered and crimson footprints led from the open office door to him.

Slipping his hands into his pockets and moving as close to the door as he could without stepping in any blood, Jones peered into the office and almost wished he hadn't.

As a detective with many years of experience, Jones was used to the sight of blood, of course. But this broke new ground. It looked as if every last millilitre of the life-giving red liquid had been forcibly ejected from the man's body. The pasty, greyish-blue tint of the corpse's skin confirmed the observation. He could see why the responding officers hadn't felt the need to contaminate the scene by checking his pulse. The Scenes of Crime team would have to check with the paramedics to see if they had touched the body.

The late professor had been a man in his fifties, with a shock of grey, unruly hair. About average height and weight for a man of his age, he was clad in brown corduroy trousers and a white polo shirt. That was about all that Jones could make out amidst the blood. The man was slumped to one side in a comfortable-looking padded leather office chair, pointed halfway towards the office's only door. The seat was a swivel chair, positioned so that the occupant could easily operate the laptop, answer the phone and reach the various pieces of paper that were piled carelessly on the remaining surface of the desk. A selection of different-coloured ballpoint pens was scattered across the workspace. A clear area to the right of the laptop suggested a space for a mouse.

The professor's throat had been slit, clearly by something very sharp. Whoever had wielded the blade had done so efficiently. It looked to Jones' eye as if the blade had managed to sever both carotid arteries. If that was the case, it put a different complexion on the attack. Contrary to Hollywood movies, cutting the throat of a surprised man wasn't a simple affair. The victim would almost certainly have struggled. Looking closer, Jones could see that, aside from the cut throat, the back of the professor's head — facing away from the doorway — looked to be a bloody mess. On the floor next to the chair sat what appeared to be a large lump of granite rock on a pedestal, blood and matted hair covering a particularly prominent edge. Jones could just make out the words "Boulder, Colorado" stencilled on the base. A souvenir perhaps? Significant or not?

Jones turned to Sutton.

"First impressions, Inspector?" he asked quietly. Jones was already formulating a theory himself, but he liked to see what others had to say first.

"I reckon he was sitting at the desk, probably working on his laptop by the looks of it. Whoever did it came up behind him and whacked him over the back of the head with that bloody great lump of rock. That probably stunned him enough for his attacker to slit his throat."

Jones nodded. "The question is, why didn't he turn around? It looks as though he was facing away from the doorway when he was hit. And then, did his chair turn around after he was hit or whilst his throat was being slit?"

"Well, either the attacker sneaked up on him, or he knew his attacker was around and wasn't surprised by their approach."

Jones nodded his agreement.

"And what about the angle of his chair?"

"Too early to speculate."

"I agree, let's not second-guess Scenes of Crime." Jones was pleased with Sutton's response. He was always a little wary of officers who jumped to conclusions without all the facts. Good detectives, he felt, tempered their deductive reasoning with caution and were honest enough to admit ignorance, rather than stretching the evidence beyond breaking point.

With nothing else to be gained from the bloody office, Jones turned away from the carnage. He glanced at his watch: 11 p.m.

You were complaining how bored you were, Warren. Well, you know what they say — be careful what you wish for.

It looked as though Susan and the in-laws would have to finish the wine without him.

SATURDAY

Chapter 2

The alarm clock buzzed angrily. With a groan, Warren swiped the OFF button. Prising an eye open, he saw that it was six-thirty. His head felt mushy and his mouth was dry. It seemed as though he'd barely closed his eyes. That wasn't a huge exaggeration, given that he'd arrived back home at well past 4 a.m. Resisting the urge to indulge himself in another ten minutes' sleep, lest he didn't awaken again, Warren swung his legs out, planting his feet on the woollen rug that covered the floor by the bed. Behind him, Susan grumbled in her sleep and rolled over.

Ordinarily, when Warren worked night shifts or Susan stayed up late marking, the night owl would take the spare bed in the guest room to avoid waking the sleeping partner. With the in-laws visiting that wasn't an option this time. It hadn't mattered though. When Warren had tiptoed into the bedroom, Susan had been flat on her back, her comatose status testimony to the sedative effect of red wine. Indeed, Warren had noticed a second empty bottle on the coffee table in the lounge. He smiled to himself, glad that he wouldn't be here in a few hours when his slumbering wife awoke. Never a morning person at the best of times, Susan also wasn't a big drinker and he suspected she would wake up grumpy and feeling a little the worse for wear.

He padded quietly into the bathroom, passing the guest room

on his way. Through the closed door he could hear strident snoring. He wouldn't like to put money on who was the culprit, Bernice or Dennis.

Warren showered quickly and brushed his teeth. The elderly pipes in the house groaned, reminding Warren that he still hadn't called a plumber, but the rhythmic noise from the guest room didn't miss a beat. By now, Warren was feeling marginally more human. As he shaved, he stared at the familiar face in the mirror. Aside from a little redness around the eyes and a couple of faint dark smudges beneath them, he didn't look too bad. He still had the good looks that Susan claimed had attracted her years before; a firm jaw and eyes that could switch in an instant between friendly and hard, a trick he'd learnt during his earliest days on the force. His dark brown hair, just this side of black and still neat from his trip to the barber's prior to starting this job, had yet to sport its first grey hair, although he was under no illusion that it would be long before his new position changed that.

Creeping back into the master bedroom, Warren slipped on the previous night's suit and tie, remembering this time to retrieve his warrant card from his other jacket. Pausing to look at his slumbering wife, he risked a peck on the lips, tasting the wine on her breath. Still asleep, she nevertheless smiled.

Outside, the sun was already up although it had yet to chase away the night's chill. Warren had grabbed a banana from the fruit bowl before leaving the house, and now crammed the remains of it into his mouth as he unlocked his car. The birds were singing loudly, but the rest of the street was quiet. Most of Warren and Susan's neighbours worked regular office hours, so few would be up and about at 7 a.m. on a Saturday. Similarly, the roads were quiet and Warren pulled into the small staff car park at the rear of Middlesbury Police Station barely ten minutes later. A few cars dotted the tarmac, most noticeably a brand-new Mercedes. Warren felt his stomach contract; his boss, Detective Superintendent John Grayson, was already in.

Middlesbury Station was something of an anomaly in Hertfordshire. Most of the county's detectives now worked out of the joint Hertfordshire and Bedfordshire Major Crime Unit based in Welwyn Garden City. However, a combination of the distance from Welwyn and the rapid growth of Middlesbury meant that the town's police station sported several custody cells and despite the budget cutbacks had retained its small but fully operational CID unit. Many of the other towns in the local area had to make do with a reception desk manned nine-to-five with an emergency telephone connected to Welwyn for out-of-hours emergencies.

Swiping his access card and keying in his pin number gave Jones access to the building and he headed directly for the largest of the incident rooms. He had scheduled this morning's meeting for 8 a.m., timing it to catch the day shift as they came on duty. He glanced at his watch: seven-fifteen. Plenty of time to go over his briefing notes and set up the chairs. As he approached the room, he spotted that the door to the superintendent's office was ajar. It would be rude not to pop his head in, he decided, plus it wouldn't hurt for the boss to notice how early he was in.

He rapped confidently on the door, his knock answered immediately with a curt, "Come in." Stepping in, Jones stopped in surprise. Sprawled in a large, comfy-looking visitor's chair, sipping a cup of freshly brewed coffee, was Detective Inspector Tony Sutton.

"Ah, good morning, Warren. Tony was just filling me in on last night's discovery."

So that was how it was going to be, thought Jones, pushing down a sudden flash of annoyance. His first big case since moving here and already Sutton was trying to muscle in on his territory, ingratiating himself with the boss.

Sutton smirked. "Just the juicy bits, guv. Thought I'd leave the details to you."

"So kind, Tony," commented Jones. If the super noticed the tension crackling between the two men, he gave no sign of it.

"This is a big case, Warren. A murder is a nasty business at the best of times, but this one could be especially problematic." The superintendent leant back in his chair, rubbing his eyes wearily. "The vice chancellor of the university phoned me at six this morning, 'to express his concern' and emphasise the need for a 'speedy resolution'. If I ever find out which bugger gave him my home phone number, they'll spend the next twelve months telling primary-school kids not to talk to strangers.

"Either way, we do need to solve this quickly and decisively. A murderer running about the campus could be disastrous for the university's reputation, especially with next month's Controversies in Science conference. The guest list for that event looks like a who's who of shit-stirrers. Richard Dawkins and the President of the British Union for the Abolition of Vivisection are some of the less controversial speakers. If they think we can't guarantee their safety, the organisers may well cancel the conference or, worse, up sticks to bloody Cambridge."

Sutton grunted. "Rumour has it, King's College wanted to host it, but Channel 4, who are footing the bill, reckoned it would seem too elitist. You can bet they'll be the first in line to offer their facilities again if we lose the conference."

Jones tried to hide his puzzlement. They seemed to be taking this whole thing rather personally. During his time in the West Midlands, Jones had worked dozens of serious cases linked to the region's several universities. The reputation of the university in question hadn't been a huge worry. As far as the police were concerned, a crime was a crime and it would be solved with no more or no less vigour than an offence occurring anywhere else on their patch. Seeing Jones' lack of comprehension, Grayson leant back in his chair, assuming a professorial air.

"Look around you, Warren. Middlesbury is a small market town, with bugger-all local industry. The decision to turn the technical college into a university forty-odd years ago gave this place a lease of life. It's the biggest employer in the area and the students bring millions into the local economy. Part of the attraction for students is the location. We're seen as a safe, quiet place to live and study. We have none of the hustle and bustle of Cambridge or the crime of some of the Essex towns. It's a huge draw for overseas students, who bring in massive amounts of foreign money — even if some of our more conservatively minded residents aren't too fond of them."

Nodding his understanding, Jones tried not to feel patronised by the unnecessary lecture and oblique reference to his status as a newcomer, opting to reply with a simple, "I see."

"So, DCI Jones, I want you to give this case top priority. I'll back you completely resource-wise. Pull everyone off what they are doing and get them to focus fully on solving this murder. We have some spare money in the Major Incident Budget, so feel free to offer overtime and buy in all the forensics you need. I'll sweet-talk Uniform into giving us some bodies for routine stuff. Let's nail this bastard."

Jones nodded, not trusting himself to say anything. He could see how it was going to be. This case was a big deal and a lot was resting on his shoulders. It was his first case as a DCI and it looked as though it was going to be sink or swim. He had the deeply uncomfortable feeling that the outcome of this case would set the tone for the rest of his time in Middlesbury. Suddenly, the banana he had eaten for breakfast seemed to be weighing heavily in his stomach. His palms felt damp and his collar too tight. As if a major incident such as this weren't enough for him to deal with, now he had to negotiate local politics as well. For the first time since his move, Warren allowed the ever-present whisper of doubt that lurked in the back of his mind to speak louder.

He'd known that becoming the DCI of such a small unit in a semi-rural town would probably be less glamorous and exciting than his previous job with West Midlands Police and that the shameful downfall of DCI Gavin Sheehy had left a lot of collateral damage that he might well have to deal with, but the simple fact was that there were already plenty of DCIs in the WMP and he'd risked getting stuck in a rut as a detective inspector. If he ever wanted to make it as a detective superintendent or even a chief superintendent, he needed the command experience. Consequently, when the vacancy in the Middlesbury CID unit had become available, Jones had been encouraged to apply.

Making his excuses and repressing the treacherous voice at the back of his mind again, Jones left the office and went into the main briefing room. A large conference room, it lacked the sophisticated wall-mounted plasma screens that were being installed as he left the West Midlands. Nevertheless, there were several oversized marker boards on wheels and plenty of chairs. As a concession to the twenty-first century, a ceiling-mounted projector allowed video and computer imagery to be displayed on the back wall.

Most importantly, a large urn bubbled away on a corner table, next to a wicker basket filled with packets of tea, coffee, sugar and powdered creamer. A stack of cardboard cups served those without a mug. The old coffee tin now doing double duty as an honesty jar was suspiciously empty, and Jones hid a smile. Human nature was human nature, and coppers were all too human. Before doing anything else, Jones made himself a strong black coffee. After a moment of indecision, he emptied three sachets of sugar into the cup. The resulting brew was far sweeter than he liked, but the caffeine and sugar hit would hopefully chase away the remaining cobwebs. As an afterthought he chucked a fifty-pence piece into the honesty jar — lead by example and all that…

It was now five to eight and the CID dayshift were starting to file into the room. After two weeks, Warren could put a name and a rank to most of the faces. Some acknowledged him with a nod, one or two with a cautious, "Good morning, sir." Warren was again reminded of the veiled scrutiny with which he was being viewed. Suspicion was probably too strong a word, but there was still a certain wariness. He was acutely aware that he was on probation with these people and that he had to prove himself to be up to the job.

By eight, he judged the room to be full, with a couple of dozen detectives of various ranks seated in rows. Grayson and Sutton stood at the back, watching. Calling for quiet, he wished all those assembled a good morning. Taking a deep breath, he launched in.

"As I am sure that most of you have heard, there has been a murder at the university in the Biology building up on Mills Road. At 22:19 hours last night a call was received from a member of the public and approximately ten minutes later two uniform colleagues on patrol confirmed the finding of the body of a middle-aged white male in a first-floor office within the main research wing. Paramedics confirmed that the victim was dead when they arrived. Preliminary identification is that of a Professor Alan Tunbridge, the occupant of the office. The PM will be held later today, but early indications are that the deceased was bludgeoned, possibly with a souvenir granite rock, before having his throat sliced open. Probable cause of death, exsanguination."

A low murmur rippled around the room. Looking around, Warren was relieved to see that he had everyone's attention. Or almost everyone — Grayson and Sutton had their heads together, quietly talking. Neither of them glanced his way. Forcing away any thoughts about what they might be discussing, Warren continued.

"The body was found by a Thomas Spencer, one of the professor's graduate students who happened to be working late that night also. Time of death has been tentatively put at no earlier than about 21:30 hours. Scenes of Crime officers made a preliminary investigation and will resume their work this morning."

A hand promptly went up: Detective Sergeant Hutchinson.

"Do we know who was in the building at that time and does Spencer have an alibi?"

"Unfortunately, we're waiting for the head of campus security to return from up north before we can review the CCTV footage and the building's swipe-card logs to see who came in and out. The two guards on duty last night were based in the main security building on the other side of the campus and don't have the know-how or the computer passwords to access that information."

A few grumbles went around the room and Jones heard at least one muttered utterance about "bloody rent-a-cops".

Ignoring the dissent, Warren continued.

"The building's fire-safety log claims that when we arrived there were only two people in the building, although we can't yet identify them. The system simply counts people in and people out. The two occupants were presumably Spencer and the deceased. None of the building's fire exits had been opened and all the windows were shut. A search by uniform found no other people in the building. Spencer claims that he was working alone in a small equipment room at the opposite end of the building for about an hour before he discovered the professor's body. There are no direct eyewitnesses but he says he bumped into two other students on the way over there who were just leaving for the pub. Apparently the room also has a swipe-card entry system to protect the expensive equipment inside. First thing we need to do when the head of Security arrives is check out Spencer's story."

A hand rose at the back. "Where is Spencer at the moment?"

"Back home. He's due to come in for another interview this afternoon. Forensics bagged him and tagged him at the scene last night and he accompanied us here for a full trace-evidence exam and to give a preliminary statement. So far he hasn't called for a lawyer and is co-operating fully, so we haven't yet arrested him." This last point was important. The moment that a suspect was arrested the clock started ticking and the police only had a short time to decide whether to release the suspect — on police bail if appropriate — or charge him and get him before a judge. By delaying arresting Spencer, Jones had successfully pushed back that deadline. However, it was a dangerous game and those questioning him would have to be very careful about making sure that he knew and understood his legal rights, lest they incur the wrath of any future defence counsel and scupper any prosecution before it even got off the ground.

Another hand went up. "What about Tunbridge's immediate family: wife, partner, kids?"

"Family Liaison broke the news to his wife last night. His kids live away and are on their way home. Early indications are that the wife was having a meal in a busy restaurant with a half-dozen friends at the time of the murder. We'll check out her alibi later today."

Looking around the room, Jones saw that nobody else had any questions. They seemed to be happy to let him get on at his own pace. Jones decided to paraphrase what the super had said to him before this meeting, figuring he couldn't really put a foot wrong if he quoted the boss.

"OK, people. This case is to be treated as our number one priority. I don't need to remind you that most murders are solved in the first twenty-four to forty-eight hours; the clock is already ticking. I will start assigning roles in a moment. Those of you that aren't given an immediate task should use the time to lock down any outstanding jobs so that we can turn all of our attention over to solving this case." Around the room there were a few quiet grumbles, no doubt from those worrying about the impact this temporary shutdown might have on their own caseload, but nobody dissented openly. They all knew the score without being told, Warren realised. Yet another example of the local instincts that he would need to develop if he was to succeed in this posting.

Warren consulted his notepad.

"Immediately after this briefing, DI Sutton and I will meet with the lab's experimental officer, Dr Mark Crawley, and the head of the Biology department, to see what we can find out about the deceased and have a look at what names come up. Head of Security should be on campus in an hour or so. I'll need somebody to meet him and have a quick look at any CCTV footage and the building's swipe-card access log.

"The neighbourhood around the building is mostly non-residential. However, there are a few houses up the north end of the road. DS Khan, I'd like you to organise a few bodies to go door knocking." A quick nod from the small man. "I'd also like you to go and see if the security guards working the warehouses on the opposite side of the road saw or heard anything. Check if any of their cameras point towards the university — it's a long shot but they may have picked up something."

He looked around the room, searching the assembled faces.

"DS Richardson, can you liaise with Traffic and see if any of their cameras have spotted anything? Remember, people, the time of death is likely to have been after 21:30 hours and Spencer's phone call was logged at 22:19 hours. Assuming that there was another person involved, they may have been in the area for several hours before the attack." A short squat forty-something clutching a bottle of mineral water nodded her agreement.

"DS Kent, I want you to set up an incident desk to collate incoming information. You'll be the shift co-ordinator — everybody should report their progress to you. Get HOLMES up and running and get Welwyn up to speed in case we need resources."

Kent nodded once and cracked his knuckles. A grey-haired man, well into his fifties, he was Middlesbury's resident expert on the Home Office's national serious crime database, HOLMES2. He had been one of the first people Jones had met after arriving at Middlesbury and his reputation for efficiency had preceded him. Even if he hadn't been on shift this morning, Jones would probably have telephoned him and offered him double time. For his part, Kent looked excited at the challenge. Middlesbury wasn't quite the back of beyond as far as policing was concerned; nevertheless, a big juicy murder, as this could well turn out to be, was a welcome diversion from the car thefts, drunken assaults and mid-level drug dealing that the station usually dealt with.

"The rest of you, get yourselves ready to move at a moment's notice. As we identify witnesses I want us to be able to pick them up for questioning before they get a chance to swap stories. Let's hit the ground running, folks." He paused, looking for questions. None, just impatient-looking faces, ready to get on with the task.

"Dismissed."

Immediately the assembled officers jumped to their feet, the experienced Detective Sergeants Khan and Richardson promptly corralling the detective constables into groups to assign them their tasks. Without so much as a glance in his direction, Sutton and Grayson headed out of the double doors in the direction of Grayson's office. Warren frowned, tempted to go after them, but he had more pressing concerns. Moving swiftly, he intercepted a young DC before she could be snagged by DS Khan.

"Karen Hardwick?" The young woman flushed slightly, no doubt a little taken aback to be identified by name by the new DCI.

"Yes, sir?"

Warren felt a twinge of sympathy for the poor girl. A probationer, she had only just finished her detective training, arriving at the station almost as recently as Jones. He vividly recalled his first few months as a trainee detective constable, desperately scared of screwing up or asking a stupid question in front of the boss. He'd hidden at the back of briefings, hoping to avoid catching the eye of anybody above the rank of sergeant.

"I've been reading your personnel file and I see that you were at university before you joined the force?"

Immediately, Warren cursed himself for his clumsy phrasing. It probably sounded to the poor woman that he'd pulled her file up especially, when in actual fact he'd been reading the files of everyone in the unit, trying to get to know his new team.

"Yes, sir. Bath, then Bristol." Karen looked puzzled. These days graduate recruitment was the norm, not the exception.

"I believe that you did some sort of biological sciences degree?"

"Yes, sir, I did a bachelor's degree in Biochemistry and then a masters by research in Molecular Biology."

"So I would assume that your degrees involved spending time in laboratories?"

"Yes, I did a twelve-month work placement in a pharmaceutical company during my first degree, then my master's degree involved three rotations in different laboratories within the Biology department." Karen now had an inkling where this might be leading.

"Well, Karen, my gut is telling me that the reasons for this murder might lie in that university department. I may need an interpreter, somebody who is familiar with the system and the language."

"I'll do whatever I can, sir."

"Good. Now let's go and round up DI Sutton. We've got some trees to shake and I get the impression that the DI is good at shaking."

Chapter 3

Jones, Sutton and DC Karen Hardwick were greeted in the lobby of the Department of Biological Sciences research building by a different young PC than the one who'd met them the previous night. After crossing them off his clipboard, he radioed ahead to let the crime scene technicians know that they had arrived. Apparently, Dr Mark Crawley, the laboratory's experimental officer, was already with them.

Following the same route as the night before — less than ten hours ago, Jones realised wearily — the three police officers headed towards the crime scene. This morning it was necessary to stop a few doors short of the office where the professor's body had been found, since the whole end of the corridor was now blocked off with blue and white crime scene tape.

Just past the barrier was a set of wooden double doors, with a large sign proclaiming "Tunbridge Group. Microbial Biology". Next to it were yellow warning stickers with the universal signs for biohazards and, Jones noticed with a touch of discomfort, radiation. A few metres further along the corridor the door to Tunbridge's office was open, white-suited technicians hard at work. A uniformed constable stood to attention next to the tape, his hands behind his back. Jones pretended not to see the copy of *The Sun* inexpertly concealed behind him. He had spent plenty of time as a uniformed officer guarding crime scenes and knew just how desperately dull it could be.

"DCI Jones. I was told that Dr Mark Crawley was up here?"

"He's in the laboratory, sir, with Crime Scene Manager Harrison, the lead forensics officer. I'll fetch him."

The constable stepped under the blue and white tape and slipped through the double doors into the laboratory. A few seconds later the doors opened again and a tall, middle-aged, rangy man stepped out. He was dressed in faded blue jeans with an open-necked checked shirt, a white forensic hairnet and white paper booties over his shoes. His eyes were red-rimmed behind small eye glasses and Jones noticed that he hadn't shaved. His right shirt pocket was overflowing with pens and pencils of different colours, one of which appeared to have leaked slightly. The left contained a second pair of glasses, with what appeared to be pink lenses. A lanyard with a photographic ID card and a couple of small keys completed the ensemble.

"Good morning, officers, I'm Mark Crawley, the Tunbridge Group's experimental officer." He extended a hand awkwardly. His accent retained traces of a Yorkshire upbringing, although many years in the south had clearly influenced his speech.

"I was familiarising your forensic team with the lab before they go searching for evidence. There's lots of chemicals and delicate equipment in there — we don't want any accidents."

"Good morning, Dr Crawley. I'm Detective Chief Inspector Warren Jones, this is Detective Inspector Tony Sutton and this is Detective Constable Karen Hardwick. First of all, let me extend our condolences on your loss."

Crawley acknowledged the sympathy with an incline of his head.

"We are here to find out about Professor Tunbridge and try to piece together what happened Friday night. Is there somewhere we can talk?"

"Of course, follow me. We have a tea and coffee area with seating."

Shucking the hairnet and booties and depositing them in a labelled bin, he led the three police officers back down the corridor past another two doors and ushered them into a small, crowded room. Jones looked around, quickly assessing the space. Metal bookcases crammed with journals and well-thumbed textbooks lined two of the walls. In the centre, a coffee table was surrounded by five soft chairs that reminded Jones somewhat uncomfortably of a dental surgery. Just like in a waiting room, the table was covered in magazines — or, rather more accurately, journals. A cursory glance at some of the headlines on the journals suggested that he would be unlikely to find any diets or salacious celebrity gossip between their pages. That being said, Jones did spot a copy of *Private Eye* sitting next to a pile of *New Scientist*.

On the wall to the left, a cork notice board was covered in paper, mostly to do with upcoming seminars or courses. The wall to the right had a similar notice board to which photographs of what Jones assumed were the rest of the lab, in a variety of staged and candid poses, were pinned haphazardly, some of them tagged with cryptic in-jokes. Jones recognised Tom Spencer and Mark Crawley in a few of them. To Jones' surprise, the only image that Tunbridge appeared in was a formal-looking group photo. He didn't seem to feature in any of the Christmas or other party pictures. A handwritten sheet of paper proclaimed itself as the sign-up sheet for a meal out at a local curry house next Friday. A dozen or so names were scrawled in different-coloured pens, some with '+1' next to them. Jones wondered if that would still take place — would the lab come together to raise a glass to the prof's memory?

A small window overlooked the car park below. Beneath it sat a small fridge, pulling double duty as a counter top. A mug tree jostled for space with four or five different jars of coffee, a jam jar of sugar and a box of PG Tips tea bags. The white plastic surface was ringed with brown stains from spilled drinks. Several dirty teaspoons were propped up in a coffee mug, itself in need of a good clean. Even by the standards of the CID tea room, the place was a health hazard. All three officers politely declined Crawley's offer of a hot drink.

Motioning them to sit on the over-stuffed dentist's chairs, Crawley flopped down himself. He looked physically exhausted, yet at the same time filled with nervous energy, Jones decided. Was it the weariness of grief? Worry about his job? Guilt? At this moment, Jones was keeping an open mind.

"First of all, Dr Crawley, could you tell us a little about yourself? I'm a bit mystified by the title 'Experimental Officer.'"

"Basically, I'm the person in charge of running the lab on a day-to-day basis. The lab manager, if you will, except that I also do my own research. Alan... Professor Tunbridge... does... or rather did a lot of travelling and so I was the person in charge of making sure the lab ran smoothly in his absence. I've been with Alan for about twelve years or so, I guess."

Jones nodded. "What can you tell me about Professor Tunbridge?"

Crawley sighed, took his glasses off and cleaned them, before placing them back again. The three police officers waited.

"Well, it'll all come out in the end, I suppose... Alan was

a brilliant researcher. His work was well-respected around the world, hence his constant travelling. He has dozens of high-impact papers in all the best journals and regularly referees the papers of others in the field before their acceptance into journals."

Jones sensed a "but".

"But on a personal level the guy was less than universally loved."

Jones' ears pricked up.

"Are you suggesting that the motive for his murder could be personal, rather than professional?"

"Look, all I'm saying is that, frankly, the bloke was a bit of an arsehole. He had a tendency to rub people up the wrong way, often for no good reason. He could really upset people and he just didn't give a shit, 'scuse my French. He got away with a hell of a lot because of who he was and senior management used to excuse him 'because he's a genius and they can be funny sometimes'. Try telling that to a master's student in tears because her dissertation has been sent back with 'crap — start again' scrawled across it in red pen." Crawley was clearly starting to unload years of pent-up frustration and Jones was willing to let him vent. Who knew what might come out…?

"The genius bit is bollocks. I've met a number of geniuses over the years and they were all nice blokes. Alan hadn't got his Nobel yet, but he still acted like a wanker. At least three graduate students made complaints against him and two technicians claimed constructive dismissal. But Alan's Teflon-coated. He usually got away with it."

Crawley's voice had started to rise and he broke off, breathing heavily.

"So why did you stay with him so long?" Jones asked.

Crawley sighed, the energy draining again.

"The sad fact is that despite all the nonsense, he was OK with me. I think he realised that he would be lucky to find someone else who'd put up with his behaviour. As for me, I've fallen with my bum in the butter. I can pursue my own research and I still get my name added to pretty much every paper that comes out of this lab.

"My problem is, I'm at the top of the research associate pay scale and my next career step is my own research group, but I've got a wife and three kids. The oldest will be off to uni next year, the youngest is still at primary school and has just been diagnosed with hyperactivity disorder and the family curse, dyslexia. My wife's parents will probably have to go into a home in the next twelve months. I don't have time to set up my own group, but I'm too expensive for anybody else to want me. Alan, for all his faults, was happy to keep on paying me. I guess we needed each other." He gave a humourless grin. "If we were having this conversation in five years' time, I'd say 'cuff me now', I've got every motive. I'd be ready to bump the old sod off and take over the group. But at the moment, it's the last bloody thing I need."

Jones nodded, not yet convinced. He moved on to another tack.

"Who else could have a motive for killing Tunbridge?"

"It'd be easier to ask who didn't. Frankly, he pissed off most people that he met. Plenty of collaborators over the years have complained that he was dictatorial and manipulative. He put plenty of noses out of joint by taking advantage of other people's research, but the simple fact is that there is one rule for us and one rule for people like him. But that was mostly professional jealousy. I can't see any of these guys killing him over who deserves to be first name on a paper in the *Journal of Bacteriology*."

"OK. Leaving aside professional rivalries, what about closer to home?"

"Well, he was a philandering bastard. He shagged at least one of his undergraduate students, not to mention a few colleagues that he used to meet at conferences. For somebody with such an unpleasant streak, he never seemed to have any problems getting laid."

"Can you give me any names?"

Crawley thought for a moment, his brow creased in concentration.

"I think one of them was called Claire or something. Rumour mill has it that she was one of the students on his Microbial Genetics course and he took a shine to her. There were the usual claims that he gave away good grades in exchange for sexual favours, but that's bullshit. I know for a fact that undergraduate essays are all marked independently and anonymously from the tutor that sets them to stop that sort of stuff happening. Anyhow, she moved on and we haven't heard from her since. This was some months ago."

Jones noted down the details, deciding to pursue the lead nevertheless.

"I guess the people with the biggest grudge against Alan would be his former grad students and postdocs. He treated some of them shockingly. I know, because I usually ended up picking up the pieces."

"Anyone in particular?"

"Well, I suppose Antonio Severino is the first name to spring to mind. He was one of Alan's postdocs until recently, then things went horribly sour."

"How? By the way, could you just clear up some terminology for me? What is a 'postdoc'?"

"Well, a postdoctoral research assistant or associate is a junior researcher at a university. Basically, you do your PhD, to become 'Doctor' and then do a couple of research positions of a couple of years apiece in other people's laboratories to gain experience. In some countries, such as Canada, you are still regarded as little more than a glorified student. Fortunately in the UK it's now a properly salaried position with all the usual benefits.

"Anyhow, Dr Antonio Severino joined us about two years ago. He's a smart guy and managed to solve a couple of really difficult problems that we were struggling with. Anyway, Alan being Alan felt a bit threatened by this as he realised that Antonio was inevitably going to share a lot of the limelight when the research was published and so he announced out of the blue that when Antonio's initial appointment expired in six weeks' time, he wasn't going to renew the post. Furthermore, he was going to hold off on the publication of several key papers until he had some more data. This really upset Antonio. You see, not only was he out of a job in six weeks, he is also not going to have any publications to show for the past two years. In this climate he'll be lucky if he gets a job cleaning glassware. The long and the short of it is that Alan absolutely shafted the poor bastard."

"How did Dr Severino take this?"

"How do you think? Not to be stereotypical, but Antonio is a full-blooded Italian. They had the mother of all shouting matches in the lab, which spilled out into the corridor. Half the building must have seen and heard it. Anyway, I finally persuaded Antonio to leave and go home for the day, promising I'd talk to Alan about the papers. Antonio did calm down enough to leave the building, but he went straight down to the pub.

"He's always been a drinker, but that day he excelled himself. According to a couple of Mick Robinson's group who were having lunch in there he got absolutely wasted. When they arrived he was already really pissed, drinking shots. They knew him and everyone sympathises with you when you're dissing the boss, so they sat with him for a bit. Eventually they figured he'd had enough and called him a cab.

"Apparently, he did get in the cab, but changed his mind halfway home and got the driver to drop him off outside here. I guess he was going to come back in and have it out with Alan again, but he got distracted by Alan's rather nice shiny BMW and used his penknife to slash all four tyres and his house keys to scratch some sort of Italian obscenity on the bonnet. Did about three grand worth of damage, I'm told, before one of the security guards stopped him."

Crawley's expression hinted that he might not have been entirely disapproving of his co-worker's actions. "Well, Alan was all up for doing him for criminal damage, but the University Disciplinary Committee decided that it wasn't going to do anybody's reputation any good if this got into the papers, so as usual I did my best to pour oil on troubled waters.

"In the end, I persuaded the university to let Antonio see out his last six weeks on gardening leave. Alan agreed to let me write him a decent job reference, which he signed and put 'papers pending' on the references list on his CV. Antonio consented to pay the excess on Alan's insurance claim. I tell you guys, some days I feel like the Secretary General of the United Nations in this place."

"How long ago was this?"

"About four or five weeks ago."

"And has Dr Severino had any luck in finding another job yet?"

"I had a request to pass on his references a couple of weeks ago to a lab at Leicester Uni. I haven't heard anything back from Antonio, so I'd guess he's probably been unsuccessful."

Jones nodded, taking note. Severino certainly had a big enough motive and if he had just been turned down for a job that could have been a trigger.

"Tell us about Dr Spencer."

"Tom? Oh, he's not 'Dr' yet. He's a final year PhD student."

Karen Hardwick half raised her hand almost as if she were at school. However, her voice was firm and betrayed none of the nervousness she was feeling at interrupting her superiors.

"What stage was his PhD at? Was he still working or writing up?"

A brief look of discomfort passed across Crawley's face.

"He was writing up, although he was still doing a few experiments to tidy things up."

"What stage was his thesis at? Was he still in his third year or was he in his write-up year?"

Jones listened carefully. He had no idea where Karen's line of questioning was going, but the vibes he was getting off Crawley suggested that he wasn't thrilled about the direction. That alone made the questions worth asking in Jones' book.

"He was in his write-up year. He'd submitted some draft chapters to Alan for editing."

"It's August now. Assuming he started in September, he must be pretty close to the end of his fourth year. Would that be correct? How was he funded and is it still current?"

"I'm not sure why this is relevant."

"Please, bear with me, Dr Crawley." DC Hardwick's eyes didn't leave the increasingly uncomfortable-looking scientist.

"Yes, he is within a couple of months or so of the end of his fourth year. He was funded by the Medical Research Council. The funding will have ended by now."

"How much of his thesis had Professor Tunbridge approved? Is Mr Spencer on course to finish within the four-year deadline?"

"I wouldn't know about that." The lie was weak, but Hardwick decided not to pursue it.

Sutton now picked up the gauntlet. "How would you characterise the relationship between Mr Spencer and Professor Tunbridge?"

"Well, Alan was a difficult man, as I think you are realising, and the relationship between students and supervisors is often tense, but I never saw them have a stand-up row like he did with Antonio Severino."

Jones looked at his colleagues; they seemed to be content for the time being. He looked forward to their thoughts. It was clear that Crawley wasn't telling the whole truth, but he was unsure how to proceed just yet.

"Well, thank you for your time, Dr Crawley. If you could give one of my colleagues your contact details that would be very helpful. I would also appreciate the names and contact details of other members of the research group. We may call you again in due course with some more questions. In the meantime, I believe that we have an appointment with the head of department, Professor Gordon Tompkinson."

Jones stood up, signalling the end of the interview. Crawley looked relieved.

"Let me take you to see Professor Tompkinson."

As they exited the small room, Jones spotted the young uniformed constable standing outside the taped-off entrance to Tunbridge's office. Beckoning him over, he instructed him to take down the details that he had requested from Crawley when he returned from taking them to see Prof Tompkinson. That should give him something to do besides read the newspaper, Jones thought.

Just then, another uniformed constable appeared.

"Sir, the head of Security has just arrived. He is ready to go through the CCTV and the building's access logs."

"Thank you, Constable." Jones turned to Sutton. "Tony, can you go and see what they've got? The sooner we can start corroborating some alibis, the better."

"Will do, guv." He turned smartly on his heel and strode off after the already departing constable.

* * *

"Dr Crawley, Mr Spencer claims to have been working in something called the 'PCR room' when the murder is believed to have taken place."

"He'll have meant Molecular Biology Suite One, on the ground floor. Do you want to go there?"

"Yes, please, if you wouldn't mind."

Motioning them to follow, Crawley headed back towards the front of the building. Taking them back down the stairwell that they had used earlier, he then doubled back on himself, so that they were heading back into the building again. To their left were more offices and Crawley motioned to a set of double doors.

"That's the main admin office where the head of department, Gordon Tompkinson works. I'll bring you back here after I've shown you the PCR room. I saw his car in the car park by the way, so he is in."

They continued down the corridor past yet more offices on the left. Through an open door, Jones caught a quick glimpse of another tea room, this one a little tidier, again overlooking the car park. The rooms on the right appeared to be service rooms rather than laboratories, with signs on their doors such as "Sterilisation Unit", "Media Kitchen" and "Central Stores". All the doors were shut but windows with old-fashioned wire-mesh safety glass afforded glimpses of darkened rooms beyond. The air was humid yet at the same time smelled musty. Jones made a note to ask Karen about it later, again reminded that in this environment he really was a fish out of water. Finally, they pulled up outside another set of double doors. Unlike the others in the corridor, there was no glass window to hint at what went on inside. The sign, 'Molecular Biology Suite One' meant nothing to Jones. These doors seemed sturdier and to the right of them was another swipe-card reader.

Crawley paused outside and motioned to the reader with the card that he wore on a lanyard around his neck. Jones thought for a moment — would entering the room compromise a crime scene? No, he decided, it was clearly a communal facility and besides which Spencer had been wearing latex gloves and other sterile clothing. It was unlikely that Forensics would get much in the way of useful trace evidence in there.

"Please, go ahead."

Crawley swiped the card and there was the quiet click of a magnetic lock. A green LED lit up on the card reader. Pushing the door open seemed to require some effort and Jones felt a blast of cold air.

"Positive air pressure," explained Crawley without being asked. "It helps stop dust and other contaminants getting in and damaging the equipment. There is also air conditioning to keep everything at a constant temperature and humidity. They look after the equipment better than they look after the staff," he quipped weakly.

Stepping in, Crawley reached and flicked on the lights. Jones and Hardwick followed him in. Jones was immediately glad of his suit jacket. The air temperature was a few degrees too cool for his comfort and a marked contrast to the warm August weather outside.

The room was like something out of a science-fiction movie, he decided. A reasonable size, it was nevertheless crammed with benches full of equipment. The three of them were able to fit into the room side by side, but to accommodate anybody else someone would need to shuffle along one of the other aisles. The doorway in which they stood was the only entrance and there were no windows. Over the rush of the air conditioning, Jones noticed a sound that reminded him of the Scalextric racing car set that he'd had as a child. A sudden, high-pitched whine, followed by silence, then repeated again, as if he were accelerating the tiny cars along the track, stopping them, then starting again.

"Welcome to Molecular Biology Suite One, the jewel in the crown of the Biology department." Crawley swept his hand in a wide arc. "There's the better part of two million quid's worth of equipment in here, or at least that's how much we paid for it when it was new. It's also the most secure room in the building, not including the animal house." He gestured upwards with a nod of his head, no doubt a reference to the unlabelled fourth floor that didn't exist on the building's public plans but which Jones had read up on when familiarising himself with potential terrorist targets.

It was certainly impressive. Pride of place was a large glass-fronted unit, the size of a commercial chest freezer, with "Affymetrix" emblazoned across it in blue. Jones hadn't got the faintest idea what the machine did, but it seemed to be filled with stacks of plastic trays. This, he realised, was the source of the noise. He watched fascinated as a robotic arm scooted, whining, across the length of the machine, delicately picked the top tray off a stack, before moving it to a different stack to its right. From above, a second arm appeared, this time bristling with dozens of metal prongs, which it inserted into some of the hundreds of tiny wells that Jones now saw made up the tray. Removing the prongs, the arm moved rapidly, but precisely, to the right, before lowering the prongs slowly onto what appeared to be a frosted-glass microscope slide.

Noticing Jones' interest, Crawley gestured towards the machine.

"It's a slide maker for gene expression studies — it's the reason for the security. It, and the equipment to read the slides, is worth hundreds of thousands. The university's insurers insisted that we put it behind locked doors in case it gets stolen. There is a growing black market for these things in the Biology departments of developing countries. It's also incredibly delicate, hence the air conditioning."

"Is this what Tom Spencer was using Friday night?"

"Oh, no. This is strictly the property of the gene expression laboratory. Tom was probably using the Tetrad PCR machine. It's not in the same league as the slide maker, but it'd still be worth nicking if you had a buyer for it."

Crawley led them down a side aisle to a squat black bench-top machine about the size of an old-style desktop computer sitting on its side. The equipment had four hinged lids, all closed, with electric-blue screws on top. A large keypad on the front was flanked by an LCD screen to the left and a stylised DNA molecule as a logo to the right. The machine seemed to be switched off. What appeared to be a booking sheet was covered in scribbled names. "Tom Spencer, Friday p.m." was scrawled under a column headed

"Block One". The other three blocks were empty at that time. Judging by the number of different names listed on the booking sheet, this seemed to be a popular machine. Even if Spencer wasn't wearing gloves when he used it, Jones doubted that they would find any useful trace evidence.

Motioning back toward the room's only entrance, Jones asked how to exit the room.

"There's another swipe card. Security keeps a log of everyone who enters or leaves the room."

"What if you prop the door open? How do you get out if your swipe card isn't working?"

"If you prop the door open, after about a minute an alarm sounds. Similarly, if for some reason you manage to swipe yourself in but can't get out, you can press that green fire-alarm-style button to release the lock. That also triggers an alarm. Either way, Security come running and you get a serious bollocking."

So it looked as though once you swiped in, you were in there until you swiped out again. With no more questions, Crawley led them back out into the warmth of the corridor. Jones removed his mobile phone from his suit jacket. Sutton answered within two rings.

"Tony, it's Jones. Have you had any luck with the head of Security yet?"

"Just getting there, guv. We're looking at the CCTV as we speak."

"Good. Can you also see if you can obtain a printout for the day's swipe-card access logs for the building's main entrance and for Molecular Biology Suite One?"

Jones heard his request being relayed in a muffled voice, followed by a short reply, too indistinct to understand. "Shouldn't be a problem, guv. I'll call as soon as we have anything, Sutton out."

Jones smiled slightly. Using mobile phones instead of radios was still a bit strange to older members of the force and so they had a tendency to resort to radio-speak when using them at work. Jones was no different. Susan had teased him for weeks after he had phoned her from the fish and chip shop one evening and ended the conversation with "over".

That reminded him, he'd better call Susan when he had a few minutes. She was fairly understanding about his work commitments, but insisted that she should at least be given a rough idea of when he would be home. Quite how understanding she would be today was another question. One of the reasons for her parents' visit was to celebrate Bernice's birthday. The plan was for Susan and Warren to take Bernice and Dennis into Cambridge for an early dinner, followed by a play at the Corn Exchange. Warren prayed that he didn't have to skip that, for then he would really be in the doghouse. As understanding as Susan was, an evening of frosty silence from her mother would not leave her in a good mood. Warren just hoped that the previous night's red wine had been good enough to temper Bernice's displeasure at his sudden departure.

With at least a couple of his questions answered, Jones suggested Crawley take them down to see the head of department. They were led back down the corridor in a thoughtful silence. Jones stared at the back of Crawley's head, his mind whirring. He'd started the day with only one potential suspect. Now it would seem that there may be dozens of people with motives. He glanced over at Hardwick. Her brow was furrowed and she was clearly thinking hard. Jones looked forward to her thoughts. One question in particular troubled Jones.

Why was the professor in his office at 10 p.m. on a Friday? And how had his killer known?

Chapter 4

The head of department's office was on the ground floor, close to the main reception area where the three officers had entered earlier. The entrance to the head's office was actually inside a larger office complex signed as "Department of Biology — Administration". A long, narrow room, it occupied almost an entire side of the building and was filled with a half-dozen workstations. Each desk had a comfortable-looking office chair, a desktop PC, a telephone and in and out trays, some empty, others stuffed with paper. A bank of cryptically labelled filing cabinets lined the wall underneath a row of windows overlooking the car park. A large photocopier and an industrial-sized paper shredder filled the remaining gaps along the wall. Two laser printers sat on top of the filing cabinets, along with a box of white A4 photocopy paper. The empty room smelt of stale coffee and ozone from the photocopier. The office seemed representative of the building as a whole, decided Jones. Sixties architecture, a couple of decades past its prime, struggling to do its job in a world that bore little resemblance to what the planners had envisioned.

The door to Professor Tompkinson's office was right at the back of the office. An effort had been made to create a sort of waiting area, with a couple of comfy chairs lined up beneath the window. On the opposing side of the room a workstation sat facing the visitors; a name plate on the table read 'Mrs C Gardner — PA to the HoD'.

Despite the shabbiness of the set-up, it reminded Jones a lot of the chief constable's office. The logic of the layout there was to keep the boss away from the day-to-day grind, shielding him from unwanted visitors and time-wasters. The HoD's PA was no doubt the guardian of the appointments calendar and probably a formidable obstacle. Jones himself tended to operate an open-door policy: if the door was open come straight in, no appointment necessary. If the door was closed ask Cathy, the secretary nearest to the office and Jones' unofficial PA, if it was worth knocking or if it would be better to leave a message. He found himself wondering if Professor Tompkinson was an open-door or closed-door kind of boss.

At the moment, the door was closed. As the two officers waited by the comfy chairs Crawley knocked once and entered the office. A few seconds later he emerged. "Professor Tompkinson is on the phone. He'll speak to you in a moment. I'd better get back to the lab and give those details to the constable."

He left quickly.

With the door still closed, Jones turned quietly to his colleague. "Impressions?"

Karen chewed her lip. She was clearly a little intimidated about being asked her opinion by someone as senior as Jones; nevertheless, she thought the question over carefully.

"Holding something back. He was definitely uncomfortable answering that last lot of questions. I reckon he knows more than he was letting on."

Jones nodded in concurrence.

"Karen, you asked some interesting questions there — what

was on your mind?" He was careful to phrase it as an invitation. Jones valued the instincts of his junior colleagues and encouraged their input more than some. The first DCI he had worked for had routinely told junior officers to remember that they had two ears and one gob, and to use them in that proportion. His aggressive attitude had made young constables nervous about voicing their opinions. Jones was convinced that more than one case could have been closed far faster if the crusty old detective had listened to his colleagues more. Fortunately, he had finally retired six months after Jones had joined CID and his replacement, Bob Windermere, had been the complete opposite. To this day, Jones still regarded him as something of a mentor and regularly sought his advice.

Karen Hardwick took the invitation.

"When I was back in uni, some of my friends were doing PhDs. More than one of them had a supervisor that they argued with. It could get pretty nasty. If this Professor Tunbridge was half as unpleasant and mean as Dr Crawley was saying, he could have given Tom Spencer a pretty good motive for his murder."

Jones nodded encouragingly. He'd had the same thoughts himself.

"What about the questions on funding you were asking about?"

"Well, typically a student funded by a body like the Medical Research Council is given three years' worth of funding for their project. That may be awarded directly to the student, but more typically it is part of a larger project grant that their PhD supervisor has successfully applied for. We'll probably find that Tunbridge's laboratory had a couple of large project grants running for several years and that his PhD students had studentships funded as part of the grant."

Jones made a note to follow that up, thankful to the gut instinct that had caused him to choose Karen Hardwick to accompany him and Sutton. Her insider knowledge of the mysterious workings of university departments was proving invaluable.

"Anyhow, full-time students normally have funding for three years and are expected to submit their completed PhD thesis — an eighty-thousand-word dissertation — within four years."

"What happens if they miss the deadline?" asked Sutton.

"In the worst-case scenario, I suppose they'd fail their degree."

"You seemed to think it important that Spencer was reaching the end of his four years. Could Tunbridge have been stopping him submitting? Crawley did mention that Tunbridge had been harsh to students in the past over their dissertations."

Hardwick shrugged. "I don't know. We should definitely ask though, sir. We should also ask about Tom Spencer's finances."

"Oh? Why?"

"If he was towards the end of his four years, he was probably pretty skint. The three-year project funding also extends to the student's living stipend. Students are usually told to save a bit of money during the three years so they can keep on paying the bills during their write-up period. Sometimes they can get some part-time teaching, but I knew PhD students who had to have bar jobs on top of their research just to make ends meet."

"Well, that's certainly a good enough motive," Jones mused. "If Tunbridge was stopping Spencer from graduating, he could have been in trouble financially. I think we've got a few more questions to ask Mr Spencer later."

Chapter 5

At first glance, Professor Tompkinson resembled a retired Geography teacher or librarian, Jones decided. Small and stooped, with generous ears and tiny spectacles perched on the end of his nose secured with a safety cord, he wore a grey woollen sweater, checked shirt and plain red tie. In addition, he was wearing a flat cap, as if he had just come in, although the empty coffee cups next to his phone suggested otherwise. Jones was unable to resist a surreptitious glance at the coat stand in the corner of the office and felt almost let down by the absence of a tweed jacket with leather elbow patches.

"Please, do come in. I'm very sorry about you having to wait. The chancellor of the university was on the phone; he's rather concerned about what happened last night."

After offering them coffee, which the two officers declined, Tompkinson sat down behind his desk. "First of all, please let me make it absolutely clear that you will have the full co-operation of myself and this department in solving this terrible crime. The vice chancellor and the chancellor have also expressed their willingness to assist in any way." He paused as if not quite sure how to proceed. "Ah, as you may be aware, Chief Inspector, the university will shortly be hosting a prestigious conference, with a number of high-profile guests." Warren nodded. "We are a little concerned as to the impact any investigation would have on the smooth running of the conference and the implications such a violent attack may have for the university's reputation. As such, we would appreciate it if you were able to keep us fully informed of the progress of your investigation." His piece said, he sat back in his chair.

As he did so Jones noticed that the man's hands shook slightly. Why? Was he nervous? It seemed unlikely — the professor was clearly a man used to moving in political circles. The presence of a police officer, even one investigating a murder, would be unlikely to unnerve him enough to give him the shakes. Jones made a mental note to check for an alibi. Perhaps he was just wired from too much caffeine.

"Of course, I fully understand, Professor. As soon as we have any information that we are ready to make public I will ensure that the university is informed."

Tompkinson's eyes narrowed slightly at Jones' careful wordplay, but he said nothing, merely nodding acceptance. Jones carefully maintained his poker face, but inside he was satisfied that he had discreetly but firmly laid out the ground rules — the investigation would be run on Jones' terms and his terms alone.

With the lines drawn and the rules of play established, Jones decided to start off with a little fishing to see what the professor volunteered, before getting down to specifics.

"Tell me, Professor, how well did you know Professor Tunbridge?"

"I suppose I've known Alan for about twenty-five years, to a greater or lesser extent. We were postdocs here back in the day, before we went our separate ways for a few years. Eventually, we both found our way back here and set up our own labs. We work in different fields, so we never collaborated. Nevertheless, this isn't a huge department, so we got to know each other as colleagues. As we became more senior and gained our chairs — professorships — we obviously spent time together on committees."

Jones nodded. "I see. And how would you say you were on a personal level?"

Tompkinson took his glasses off, and polished them on his tie, frowning. The two officers waited in silence.

Finally, Tompkinson replaced his glasses and let out a weary sigh.

"There's no point sugar-coating it, I suppose. Alan was a hard man to like. He had an abrasive personality and didn't suffer fools gladly. He was also arrogant, domineering and bullying, yet strangely petty at the same time. He was a genius, no question. But I can't really think of anyone that I would describe as a close friend of his."

Jones repressed a sigh. It seemed that the motives, and thus by extension the suspects, were stacking up.

"Alan and I had a lot of arguments, particularly when I became head of department. We butted heads frequently over all manner of policies. Pretty much any decision I made, Alan would question and because he was who he was, often the VC — the vice chancellor — would overrule my decisions and go with Alan's. Sometimes I wondered who the hell the head of department was, me or him."

"So do you think Tunbridge was after your job?" Was that a big enough motive, Jones mused, for murder?

Tompinkson let out a bark of laughter.

"Oh, dear God, no, you misunderstand completely. The last thing Alan would want is the hassle that goes with being the head of department, far too much pen-pushing and meetings. No, Alan was a research scientist through and through. He hated any type of 'admin bollocks' as he called it.

"No, Alan would far rather be the power behind the throne. He'd let me and others sweat out all of the details in meetings and just swan in at the last minute. The bugger probably only attended one departmental meeting in three and he was only one of a dozen or more faculty members, yet barely a major decision has been made in five years that Alan didn't have a hand in."

"Forgive me, Professor, but so far we haven't heard a good word about Professor Tunbridge. Some of the behaviours that he has been accused of sound suspiciously close to gross misconduct. Violent rows with postdocs, students reporting him for bullying, constructive dismissal claims and an alleged affair with an undergraduate student. Yet it seems that he hasn't been subject to any disciplinary action at all. Why is that, Professor?"

Tompkinson looked embarrassed. "You're right, of course, Chief Inspector. Much of what Alan did was unacceptable. Particularly the way he treated that poor undergraduate — getting her pregnant and then making her get rid of the baby left a bad taste in my mouth. You just can't act like that. But senior management decided that it would be in everyone's best interest if we hushed it up. After all, she was a consenting adult. It's not like any laws were broken."

Jones blinked; beside him he felt Hardwick stiffen. Tunbridge had got an undergraduate student pregnant? And then had it hushed up? Tompkinson had blithely admitted it, clearly assuming that if they knew about the affair, they must know about the pregnancy. Why hadn't Crawley mentioned it? If he was to be believed, he was Tunbridge's troubleshooter, stepping in after his boss to clear up the former's mess. Surely he had known about it. Was he trying to protect Tunbridge's memory? Unlikely, given the way he'd trashed the man's reputation for the past half an hour. What about the young woman's? Was he trying to protect her dignity? That seemed a little more likely, Jones decided. And what about his discomfort over questions about Tom Spencer's finances? Was he trying to protect him as well?

"Could you give me the young lady's name, please? I think we should speak to her."

Tompkinson looked a bit uncomfortable. "Is that really necessary, DCI Jones? She went through rather a lot. We decided that a fresh start was best for her. I'd rather we didn't open old wounds."

"I'm sorry, Professor, but I really must insist. Better that you give me the details discreetly, here and now, than I have to conduct enquiries."

Tompkinson sighed.

"The young lady's name was Clara Hemmingway. She's a current student, so student services will have all of her details. She was assigned to Alan, along with three other students, after choosing Microbial Genetics as one of her essay preferences. This would have been back in November. It's a long-standing tradition at the university, designed to bring undergraduate students into contact with the research side of the university. They get a tour of the lab and we even pay for them to go out to lunch with the lab members and encourage them to discuss their lab's work and findings.

"Sometimes students even manage to get summer jobs or internships with the lab later in their course. To the best of my knowledge, Miss Hemmingway has not had any work experience with the lab, but she certainly made an impression!" His laugh was bitter and his expression suggested that he found the situation far from amusing.

"Thank you, Professor. Now, back to the original question. Why was Professor Tunbridge allowed to behave in the way he did, seemingly with no consequences?"

Tompkinson leant back slightly, before sweeping his hand in an all-encompassing gesture. Again, that nervous tremor.

"Look around you, Officers. This is the University of Middle England, not Oxford or Cambridge." Seeing their uncomprehending gazes, he leant forward.

"How much do you know about university funding? Are you familiar with the Research Assessment Exercise?"

Seeing their shaking heads, Tompkinson adopted a professorial air — appropriately enough, thought Jones.

"Funding for UK universities comes from many different sources, but broadly it can be categorised in two ways. There is specific funding for a specific project. The university and individuals bid for grants from a wide range of different funding bodies. Some are governmental, such as the Medical Research Council or the Biotechnology and Biological Sciences Research Council, others might be charitable, such as the Wellcome Trust or Cancer Research UK. These grants may be a few thousand pounds to fund a series of particular experiments; a few hundred thousand pounds to run a research project and employ staff and students or tens of millions to build a new research centre."

He gestured around the office. "Then there is the more general funding that is used to pay for teaching, maintain our research facilities and run our administrative departments. This comes from central government. You may have heard about the proposed cuts in higher education funding?" Nods all round. "This is the budget that the government is slashing.

"The problem is the way the funding is allocated. Every five years or so, universities undergo a Research Assessment Exercise — an audit if you will. They grade us based upon the quality of our research. The key measure that they use is whether our research is 'world-leading'. Those departments that are judged to be 'world-leading' are rewarded by a bigger bite of the funding cherry than those that aren't."

Tompkinson leant forward, taking his glasses off again, his voice becoming heated.

"We produce some bloody good research, damn it. But we are a small university. The RAE is intrinsically biased against smaller institutions like us. Alan Tunbridge was our biggest name. His work is internationally recognised and he is one of the world's leading authorities on antibiotics. We simply can't, or rather couldn't, afford to lose him. Academia is a dog-eat-dog world and top-flight researchers are constantly being poached by other institutions. Oxford, Cambridge, UCL, Manchester, Warwick and Liverpool have all tried to woo him in the past few years that I know of. And that's just this country. Harvard, Johns Hopkins, The Pasteur Institute… they've all had a go as well. Gold-plated salaries, state-of-the-art laboratories, the promise of no teaching… they've offered him far more than we ever could. So we couldn't afford to piss him off in case one day he'd turn around and say, 'I've had enough, I'm off to Oxford.' So whatever Alan wanted, Alan got. And within reason, we let him get away with bloody murder. Sorry, poor choice of words."

Tompkinson now leant back, the passion leaving him.

"So why did Tunbridge stay? No offence, but the University of Middle England is hardly a household name. Surely working in Cambridge or Oxford would have been hard to resist. Why would Tunbridge stay here?"

Tompkinson shrugged. "A good question. Why does anybody stay in a place? I have thought about it over the years and I think it was for a number of different reasons."

He held up his hand, ticking the points off one at a time. Again, Jones noticed the man's hands shaking. His voice seemed calm and confident, however.

"First of all, the comfort factor. Alan's been here for years. Despite his travelling, I think he regards this part of the world as home. He and his wife bought a lovely house at exactly the right time, years ago. You'd never get anything close to it at today's prices in places like Oxford or London.

"Second, the hassle. Moving laboratories is a big deal. Even with professional movers and managers, it's a logistical nightmare. Even the best-planned laboratory moves can knock you back six months. And what about his staff? How many would go with him? Mark Crawley, his experimental officer, has a wife and kids — would he be likely to up sticks? Even moving to Cambridge might mean an unacceptable commute for some staff.

"Third, he likes being the big fish in the small pond. I've already told you about how much influence he has here. You can't paint the toilets here without Alan's say-so. No other institute is going to let him have that much power without the responsibility, least of all Oxbridge. And in terms of stature, he might have got a Nobel one day — but in Cambridge he'd be working alongside people who were invited to Sweden when Alan was still doing his university finals.

"Finally, Alan was almost certainly going to go commercial with his work within the next couple of years. You may have seen in the paper that the university just broke ground on a new incubator building. Brand-new state-of-the-art facilities and expertise designed to support new start-up companies. He'd have been first in line for one of those new labs and the university would have been happy to help him commercialise his work. He'd probably have kept his lab over here doing basic research — which would have been good for us in the RAE — whilst all his commercial work would have migrated to the incubator building."

Jones nodded; on the face of it, Tunbridge's reasons for staying seemed plausible.

"Forgive me, Professor, but it would seem that a number of people have motives for wishing Tunbridge was dead, not least yourself." Jones watched Tompkinson very carefully, gauging his reaction to the implied accusation.

Tompkinson smiled, almost in amusement.

"I am well aware that some might see me as having a motive for Alan's death. And I'm certainly honest enough to admit that my life would have been a lot easier over the past few years without him second-guessing me and breathing down my neck. But believe me, Chief Inspector, if I'd wanted to kill him it would have happened a long time ago. Besides which, it no longer matters. In two months I retire. I'm hanging up my lab coat. Frankly, I was looking forward to a quiet last few weeks wrapping up a few personal projects and making sure that my research group are ready to move on. The last thing I need is this."

Jones wasn't convinced.

"I can see your point, Professor. However, sometimes unexpected things happen; arguments flare up, old grudges simmer until they reach boiling point. In fact, if you don't mind me saying so, you look a little young to be retiring. Did Professor Tunbridge have any influence in that decision?"

Tompkinson laughed, a short bark.

"The man had influence, but he wasn't God! No, Alan Tunbridge had nothing to do with my retirement. If anything, he'd probably have liked me to stay in the job, since whoever replaces me will probably be less of a pushover. No, it's probably genetics and bad luck that is forcing me out."

Noting the police officers' blank looks, he held out his hands.

"I'm sure that trained observers such as yourself have noticed that my hands shake. I'm afraid that it isn't nervousness, too much coffee or the after-effects of a good night out. I've got Parkinson's disease."

He took off his hat, revealing an almost entirely hairless scalp, bisected by an angry-looking red scar.

"I was diagnosed a few years ago. The symptoms were kept in check for a while by drugs, but as I'm sure you know it's a progressive disease. A year or so ago I had deep-brain stimulation." He gestured at the scar. "Unfortunately it's had little effect. Maybe if this had happened a decade or so from now, I would have phoned a few old colleagues and seen if I could wangle a place on a clinical trial for stem cell therapy, but it's a little too early for that yet."

He sighed regretfully. "Since the beginning of the year it's been obvious that I am going downhill pretty fast. The shakes are getting worse. I daren't go near any of my students' work in case I have an accident and wipe out six months' research. Most days I slur my speech and nod my head constantly, but I've learnt how to regulate my medication, to 'overdose' on days that I need to speak more clearly or move more carefully. My GP doesn't recommend it, of course, since the pills have side effects, but a lot of patients do it. Anyway, I decided a few months ago that enough was enough. The university has been very understanding and I've managed to secure a fairly generous pension. My wife and I are going to move to the South of France to be near our daughter and enjoy the grandkids whilst I still can."

There was an uncomfortable silence for a few moments. The

man's story would need to be checked out, of course, and nothing he had said would make it impossible for him to be involved in Tunbridge's death, but Jones mentally moved him to the 'unlikely' list.

"I see. Well, leaving aside yourself, it would seem that there are still a fair number of people with a motive for killing Professor Tunbridge. I would like to ask you a bit about some of the members of his laboratory. First, Thomas Spencer."

"Ah, so those rumours are true. I heard that Mr Spencer had been arrested at the scene. Covered in blood, I heard." The Professor looked excited. Not an unusual reaction, noted Warren — the popularity of crime drama on TV and in bestselling fiction was a testimony to the fascination of the general public when it came to crime. And, of course, the more lurid and salacious, the better. It would seem that news was spreading fast, probably aided by the security guards present at the scene. The building's virtual lock-down wouldn't go unnoticed either, as the various Saturday workers were turned away at the door. Nevertheless, it was important to make sure that any information was accurate, particularly when the press turned up. Which would probably be any moment now, Jones realised.

"Mr Spencer found the body and is currently assisting in our enquiries. We would greatly appreciate your help in ensuring that any information that gets passed to the press is accurate and won't compromise the investigation."

Looking suitably chastened, the professor nodded.

"Of course. Well, in anticipation of your interest, I took the liberty of pulling Mr Spencer's file. I had only just started to read it when the chancellor phoned. But there is a slight problem. If, as you say, Mr Spencer is merely helping with your enquiries I am afraid that, under the Data Protection Act, I cannot let you look at his file without a warrant."

Shit. Bloody lawyers.

"I fully understand, Professor, and I will have no problem getting a warrant. Indeed, I will be getting one issued as a matter of course to assist in our investigation. However, it will take some time for a warrant to be signed. In the meantime, we could well have a killer on the loose."

The older man licked his lips nervously. Jones could see the conflict in his eyes. It was obvious that the man genuinely wanted to help the police and was almost as frustrated as Jones that bureaucracy was threatening to get in the way. Unfortunately, under the Police and Criminal Evidence Act, any information that Jones saw might well be inadmissible in a court of law unless he had that warrant.

Of course there was a compromise and Tompkinson was an intelligent enough man to see it.

"What if I were to allow you to take a peek at the information, informally of course, and then if you found anything of interest you could then read it officially after having shown me the warrant?"

Jones suppressed a smile. He didn't need to look at Hardwick to know that she too had been hoping for the offer. "Thank you, Professor, that will be most useful."

The file was rather thick, Jones noticed. As if reading his mind, Tompkinson gestured into the main office.

"You are welcome to photocopy the file once you have the warrant, to read it at your own leisure, but in the meantime what if you tell me what you are looking for?"

"Well, first of all, how well do you know the lad?"

"Not at all well, I'm afraid. In fact, although his name rang a bell,

I couldn't recall his appearance. I do recognise him though, now that I have seen his picture in his file. I have probably said a few words to him at the Christmas party or the summer barbecue, but his work is too different from my own and his lab too far away for me to have spoken to him much."

"Well, why don't you tell us a bit about his background?"

Slipping his glasses back on, Tompkinson flicked through the pages of the file.

"OK, I have his original application form. Thomas Michael Spencer. Born June twenty-sixth 1985. Parents' address is given as Stockport, although this file is four years old now and that address may not be current. You would need to speak to Student Services to find out the address he lives at when he studies. He's listed as unmarried, ethnicity white British, no disabilities, sexual orientation heterosexual." He looked up, slightly embarrassed. "Equality monitoring. World's gone bloody mad. Again, you will need to speak to Student Services to check if that's up to date. For the marital status that is, obviously his ethnicity hasn't changed or his sexual orientation… actually I suppose that could have changed and he could have had some sort of accident… sorry. Where was I?" He cleared his throat.

"Ah, yes, well, Mr Spencer joined us in October 2007, having got an upper-second-class degree from Sheffield University. He worked, as you know, in Alan Tunbridge's group and was directly supervised by Mark Crawley."

Tompkinson leafed through a few more pages.

"OK, so he passed his first year with distinction, with the recommendation that he be allowed to transfer onto the PhD course." Tompkinson paused and backtracked slightly. "It is common practice for students to be registered for a Master's in

Philosophy initially — an MPhil — and then transfer to a Doctor of Philosophy, PhD, after the production of a satisfactory first-year report, roughly equivalent to a master's dissertation. It's a safeguard that allows students who don't wish to continue their studies to graduate with something."

"And Spencer was passed with distinction? Who examines the dissertation?"

"The report is marked initially by the student's supervisor, in this case Tunbridge, and then passed on to two other members of faculty, who will also verbally examine the student to make certain that it is their own work etc. Alan signed off on it and then Professors Abdullah Omara and Jennifer Stokes marked it formally as a distinction."

"So he was a promising student?"

"It would seem so." Tompkinson leafed through a few more pages. "Here is his second-year report. This time it's the result of a verbal meeting between the student and the faculty advisor. Jenny Stokes reported that Spencer was progressing well in his research and was confident that he would be in a position to start writing up within the next twelve months. Alan Tunbridge again signed off on the report, saying that Spencer had made sufficient progress and that with hard work he would be in a position to write up within twelve months. Neither Jenny, Alan or Mr Spencer reported any concerns, either publicly or confidentially."

Tompkinson carried on reading.

"Oh. This is his mid-third-year report." He adjusted his glasses again and peered over them, a gesture that Jones was starting to recognise as his "teaching pose".

"Standard full-time PhD courses, such as the one that Spencer was enrolled on, are funded for three years by the funding council, in this case the MRC. The expectation is that students complete their research, write it up and submit at the end of those three years. Either way, they stop being funded and they are no longer paid. In reality, we have found that most students take about three and a half years to finish and write up. The funding councils get very antsy if they don't submit in four years and can penalise the university. So about halfway through the third year we start progression-to-submission meetings.

"Mr Spencer, at this point, was still working full-time on his research, but was confident that he would be completed within the next few months and written up by the beginning of his fourth year. That's fairly typical. Alan has signed the bottom to say he agrees. No further action required."

He turned the page.

"Three months from the three-year deadline. Spencer is still working full-time. Some experiments have had to be repeated. He will start writing up when they are completed. Signed by Alan."

Another page.

"Three-year deadline. Spencer is still repeating key experiments. He agrees to submit a first couple of chapters of his thesis to Alan for checking by the end of the month. Both sign the form."

Another sheet of A4.

"Hmm. This is three months later. Spencer has started another set of experiments. He has submitted his first two chapters, which Alan has signed off as satisfactory. However, he requested a confidential meeting with Jenny Stokes where he expressed concern that Alan was insisting that he complete more research and won't accept the conclusions of a paper that he has written for the *Journal of Bacteriology*. Jenny advises him to follow Alan's advice for the time being."

Jones sat up a little straighter. "So Spencer and Tunbridge had an argument."

Tompkinson waved a hand in a dismissive gesture.

"I wouldn't read too much into that, Inspector. Disagreements between PhD students and their supervisors aren't uncommon at this stage. In fact, there is an old saying that your PhD supervisor is the first person that you have a truly professional argument with. It's almost a rite of passage. Strange as it may seem, at this stage Mr Spencer will probably be the world's leading expert on that one tiny facet of his research. He will have lived and breathed his project for the past three years and so will be very possessive of his work."

Tompkinson's eyes misted over and he smiled slightly. "It's been thirty years but I remember the arguments with my PhD supervisor like they were yesterday. Of course, my prof was right and his decision to force me to delay publication of my first paper was absolutely correct. In the end it was published in a far more prestigious journal than it would have been otherwise. At the time though I thought the old bastard was past it and nearly walked out. I went to his eightieth birthday a couple of years ago and he still teased me about it."

Jones nodded silently, but filed the information away nevertheless. Crawley had suggested that Tunbridge had a reputation for being possessive about his lab's research. Could this have been enough to provoke Spencer to kill him? And why hadn't he mentioned this when they spoke to him earlier?

Tompkinson flipped over another couple of pages.

"Here is his three-and-a-half-year meeting. Spencer is still working in the lab and has not submitted any more chapters. The head of Graduate Studies, Professor Davidson, has put Spencer on his 'cause for concern list' and scheduled a meeting with Alan, Jenny and Mr Spencer."

He turned over the page.

"The outcome of the meeting is that Alan did not feel that Mr Spencer had fully proven his hypothesis and recommended a number of further studies to back up his claims. Spencer has agreed to do the studies and Jenny has agreed to meet regularly with him to ensure that he keeps on track. They also agreed upon a schedule to write up the less contentious parts of Mr Spencer's thesis." Tompkinson turned to two pieces of paper stapled to the current page. "Professor Davidson and Professor Stokes have both written private memoranda commenting on the tense atmosphere between Tunbridge and Spencer. Jenny has spoken to Mark Crawley and asked him to keep an eye on the situation."

"Is that sort of thing normal?"

Tompkinson looked a little embarrassed. "A complete breakdown in the relationship between a student and his supervisor is rare but not unprecedented, and of course Alan had a reputation for being a little… difficult, shall we say? Mark Crawley is Tom Spencer's immediate line manager and is used to Alan's ways."

"I see."

Tompkinson continued flicking through the folder.

"It seems that Spencer unsuccessfully applied for a hardship grant from the Student Welfare Office. They don't usually help students who are in their fourth year unless something exceptional has happened. However, they did promise to try and arrange some more teaching and demonstrating hours for him."

So, pissed off and broke? The motives were certainly stacking up against Spencer. Again, why hadn't Crawley mentioned this? Jones knew that at times like this a person's loyalties were torn. Crawley might well have been trying to protect Spencer, not because he felt that Spencer was guilty, but because he felt responsible for the lad and didn't want to cause him any trouble. On the flipside, he'd shown no such loyalty to the postdoc Severino. Why? Mark Crawley was worth a second visit, Jones decided.

"What is Spencer's current situation?"

Tompkinson flicked forward to the last page of the folder.

"He's coming up on four years. He needs to have submitted by October first at the latest. Apparently he submitted several more draft chapters, all of which Tunbridge accepted. However, there is still some disagreement over the final results."

"What happens if he misses the deadline?"

"Well, there are a couple of options." To emphasise his point, Tompkinson held out a hand, counting off the fingers. "First, he misses the deadline and has to apply to the Board of Graduate Studies for an extension. They have to consider the university's standing with the funding agencies as well as what is best for Mr Spencer.

"Second, they decide to simply ditch the disputed work and write up what he has completed for submission. That'll depend on how critical the work is to the thesis."

Another finger. Warren wondered if it was just his imagination — now that he was looking out for it — or was Tompkinson's hand trembling more?

"Third, he could well fail the PhD. In which case we would probably submit his earlier work and examine him for an MPhil."

"How big a blow would that be to him?"

"Catastrophic. The thing with PhDs is you only get a single bite of the cherry. He could very well end up in debt, with a four-year hole in his work history and bugger all to show for it. It would almost certainly hamper his career. He could massage his CV a bit, claim that he went for MPhil then stayed on and did more research, but it probably wouldn't stand up to scrutiny in a job interview."

So Spencer certainly had a motive. The question was, was it enough to make him snap? Warren was looking forward more and more to this afternoon's scheduled interview.

"Moving on, another name that has been mentioned this morning was that of Dr Antonio Severino. What can you tell us about him?"

Tompkinson sighed, taking his glasses off and rubbing them for a few moments before replacing them, something that Jones was starting to associate with the professor being forced to answer unpleasant questions.

"Another of Alan's diplomatic triumphs." The irony of the statement was clearly masking a genuine irritation and anger at his former colleague.

"Officially, Dr Severino is taking overdue holiday whilst he waits for the renewal or otherwise of his contract."

"And unofficially?"

"Alan got rid of him. He claims that Severino had completed the project for which he was originally employed and that his services were no longer required."

"What about the disagreement over the publication of Severino's findings?"

"Again, officially the papers are 'in preparation' with other members of the lab finishing their part of the project. Unofficially, Severino's contribution to the overall manuscript was so great that Tunbridge would struggle to justify his position as lead author. Alan was pretty tight-lipped about the results from this particular research, but the rumour mill has it that they had solved several significant problems in the field of antibiotic resistance. I suspect that Alan was going to use the interest garnered by the publication of the research to kickstart his search for funding to start his own company, with him as boss. The last thing he'd want is to share the limelight with someone else. Based on gossip in the tea room, Alan was probably going to split Severino's work into two separate manuscripts and dilute his influence by padding out the papers with other results from the lab. That way he could retain first authorship on both papers. In the meantime, Severino has practically nothing on his CV to account for the past two years of work, making him almost unemployable."

"Is that ethical?"

"Absolutely not. But try and prove it. Severino did lodge a formal complaint with the university — and was no doubt planning on writing to the editor of whatever journal Alan finally submitted to — but it would have been his word against Alan's and he wouldn't have stood much chance."

"How did Severino take this?" Jones had already heard Crawley's version of events; he was interested to see if Tompkinson agreed.

"Badly. Apparently they had it out in the corridor and he very nearly got himself escorted off the premises. From what I've heard he made a beeline straight for the pub, before returning rather the worse for wear a few hours later and vandalising Alan's car. Security prevented him from entering the building to find Alan."

"So what happened then?"

"Alan was livid and wanted him arrested for criminal damage. However, a few of his colleagues in the department calmed him down enough to agree not to press charges as it was in nobody's interest to see it splashed across the newspapers. Mark Crawley brokered a peace deal in the end and I believe that Severino agreed to work out his notice from home and pay for the damage. In return, I think Alan agreed to let Mark write any job references that came his way." Tompkinson shook his head. "I don't know how he does it. Mark's been with the bugger for over ten years. That man deserves a bloody medal."

So far at least, it seemed that Tompkinson's story matched Crawley's, although Jones still wanted to speak to Crawley again about the omissions he had made earlier.

"Do you know of anyone else who may have harboured a grudge against Professor Tunbridge? I hear that other lab members have also left on bad terms. What about other current members of his lab?"

Tompkinson chewed his lip thoughtfully. As he did so his head twitched forward and backward slightly and his hands, which were now resting in front of him, tapped out a rhythmless tune. Time for more medication? Warren wondered. As if noticing Jones' scrutiny, Tompkinson clasped his hands together tightly, arresting the tremors.

"You'd need to speak to them, I would imagine. Personnel can give you the details of all the current and former members of the lab. As to whether any still bear a grudge, that's hard to say. He did have two technicians speak to their unions about a constructive dismissal case concerning alleged bullying. However, they decided not to pursue the case after finding better-compensated work elsewhere in the department."

"You bought them off?"

Tompkinson's shrug was non-committal. "They found a better position and decided it wasn't worth their time and effort to pursue the case."

I'll bet the unions were annoyed about that, thought Jones, but said nothing.

"I believe that he also had run-ins with some of his other graduate students, although nothing serious enough to cross my desk."

Jones made a quick note to get onto Personnel and Student Services to find out their details. His list of potential suspects and people to interview was growing longer and longer.

Karen Hardwick had remained silent throughout most of the interview, but Jones could see that she had been paying close attention.

"What will happen to Professor Tunbridge's research group, now that he is gone?"

"A tricky question. This has never really happened before. A few years ago a young Principal Investigator was tragically killed on holiday. However, he only had a single PhD student and a research technician. The student moved into another lab, taking enough of the lab's funding to complete his project. The research technician was also redeployed and the research group was wound up. It was a bit messy for a few weeks, but it all sorted itself out.

"Alan's lab is another matter. For a start it's much larger and it has rather a lot of allocated funding. I suppose there will have to be a meeting of all of those concerned. In the interim at least, the lab will probably continue running under Mark Crawley. The students will be dealt with on a case-by-case basis — some may go and work in different laboratories with like-minded research groups, others may continue to work with Mark. As to the long-term, the funding agencies and the university will have to decide what happens."

So, it seemed as though Crawley might be the heir apparent to the research group after all. Would he want it, though, or would it be, as he'd claimed, a weight of responsibility he could do without? A point for future consideration, Jones decided.

"Well, thank you for your time, Professor. We may need to ask you a few more questions in the future. In the meantime, could you speak to your Personnel and Student Services department and let them know that we will be asking to see your records?"

"Of course. I suspect I'll be in here all day if you want to contact me. But I'm surprised that you are leaving so soon."

Jones blinked in surprise. "I'm not sure I see what you are getting at."

"Well, it would seem that you have missed the most obvious motive, Chief Inspector."

"Oh? What might that be, then?"

"Well, money, of course."

Jones blinked in surprise.

"Money? How would killing Professor Tunbridge make his killer rich? Was Professor Tunbridge particularly wealthy?"

"No, at least not that I know of. However, Alan's work was potentially very lucrative."

"So, tell me about Professor Tunbridge's research and why you think it provides a motive."

Tompkinson took off his glasses and polished them again, before replacing them and resuming his "teacher pose".

"Where to start? OK, to fully appreciate how big a motive this is, you need to understand some basic science. I'm sure that you've heard about the problems with bacteria becoming resistant to antibiotics? So-called 'hospital superbugs' such as MRSA, resistant to even the strongest of antibiotics?" Jones and Hardwick both nodded.

"Well, the problem cannot be overstated. There are strains of *Staphylococcus aureus*, the bacterium that MRSA stems from, that are resistant to all commonly used antibiotics, even the so-called 'last resort' drugs such as vancomycin. Let me be clear, here. If you develop an infection from this strain of bacteria, you *will* die. And it's not just hospital superbugs. Extreme Drug-Resistant Tuberculosis, or XDRTB, is now being seen in TB hotspots around the globe. The current vaccination against TB, the BCG, is woefully poor and it'll be years before the latest version comes online. TB is spread by coughing and sneezing. Regular TB still kills millions of people each year. Without antibiotics to kill off the infection, the death rate will soar. These days, a person with TB can pick it up on one side of the world and cough and sneeze his way across the globe in twenty-four hours, infecting everyone he comes into contact with. Can you imagine what it would be like if the strain that the person was carrying was XDRTB?"

Jones tried to imagine such a scenario and felt a cold chill sweep over him.

"Of course, drug companies are trying to develop new antibiotics as we speak, however the speed at which bacteria can become resistant to these drugs is frightening. Did you know that the first antibiotic, penicillin, was first used to treat patients in the 1940s yet within four years cases of resistant bacteria were reported? By the 1960s it was present in hospitals and by the end of the 1990s almost 40 per cent of *Staphylococcus* bacteria were resistant. Since penicillin's discovery, dozens of different antibiotics have been discovered — almost all of which are now resisted by bacteria. Some of those antibiotics were rendered all but useless within ten years. Because of that, there is actually *less* incentive for drugs companies to invest in new antibiotics."

"Huh? You've lost me, Professor. Surely with such a need for new antibiotics, whoever discovers a new one stands to make a fortune!"

Tompkinson smiled sadly. "Unfortunately, it doesn't work like that. It takes up to a billion US dollars and anything up to fifteen years to develop a new drug. The success rate from good idea to pharmacy counter is tiny. The vast majority of potential drugs are eliminated in the early stages of development because they don't work or have unacceptable side effects. Drug research is an incredible gamble, with the pay-off being massive exclusive sales in the years before the patent expires after which everyone and his uncle can use your research to make your drug at a fraction of the cost and undercut you. Because of that, pharmaceutical firms favour drugs that will recoup that investment. They like to play safe. So what's the point of spending a billion dollars developing a new antibiotic that 90 per cent of bugs are going to be resistant to before you've even made your investment back?"

The question hung in the air.

Scratching his head and trying to keep up, Jones asked the obvious.

"So where is the motive, then? Presumably anyone stealing his idea would still have to spend millions doing the safety trials. I don't know much about this sort of thing, but I seem to recall from an article in some Sunday supplement that the bulk of the cost of developing a drug lies with the safety testing. Who is going to murder the prof over something that won't make them any money?"

The professor nodded.

"You are quite right, of course. As regards the bacteria acquiring resistance, rumour has it Professor Tunbridge had solved that particular conundrum."

"He's developed a multi-pronged attack to delay the onset of antibiotic resistance, hasn't he?"

73

The question was blurted out from DC Hardwick.

Tompkinson nodded enthusiastically as if praising a favourite student.

"Very good. I see that you know something about this, Constable. Did you study at university before joining the police?"

She nodded, confidence buoyed somewhat by the praise.

"Yes, sir. I did a Molecular Biology degree and we learnt a lot about antibiotic resistance. You mentioned that Professor Tunbridge was planning on going commercial with his work — is this what you meant?"

"Yes, 'Trident Antibacterials' was the name he was considering. Alan was just starting to put out feelers for potential backers. It was all very hush-hush, of course. I believe that he was in the process of protecting the work with patents before he went public. The word on the grapevine is that he had successfully developed a drug system that attacked three unrelated drug targets simultaneously. The theory is that whilst the odds of one bacterium developing a chance mutation that renders the cell resistant to an antibiotic is fairly good when you consider the trillions of bacterial cells that will be treated over time, the likelihood of all three targets being thwarted simultaneously is infinitesimal. Even if a cell becomes resistant to one or even two of the methods of attack, the remaining drug target will still remain viable."

"So you are saying that Tunbridge's murder may have been, for want of a better word, industrial espionage?"

Tompkinson shrugged. "I would say it's a possibility."

"Who would benefit from his death, then, and how?"

"I suppose the most obvious candidate would be a rival pharmaceutical company. The idea of a multi-pronged attack isn't in itself brand new. I've no doubt that dozens of laboratories around the world are working on similar approaches. Stopping Tunbridge from launching Trident would buy them time."

"Murder seems a bit extreme. Why not just buy him out? If the stakes are as high as you say they are, surely somebody could just throw a few million quid his way to sell them his work, or even offer him a job in their company to finish it with them."

"That may well have happened. However, knowing Alan as I do, working for another company wouldn't appeal to his ego. For Alan, being the CEO of his own company that produced this miracle cure would be the ultimate goal. He was a huge self-publicist and he'd have relished the idea of a four-page spread in *New Scientist* or even the front cover of a major news magazine such as *Time*. In terms of money, if he wanted to sell his work, then he'd make much more if he was able to sell a fully working product. If it is as successful as he wanted it to be — and it is still a big if — he could float Trident on the stock exchange or even license it to the highest bidder. In this case we could be talking hundreds of millions, if not billions."

"What about the research that he has already published? Surely, the cat's out of the bag now. Isn't it just a question of time before somebody else follows his work? What about the other members of his lab? Surely, if they got together they could assemble the pieces and finish the work?"

"Perhaps one day, but you have to realise how controlling Alan was. He still performed some of his own research. That's rare — most professors of his standing haven't wielded a pipette in anger for years. I would imagine that the central piece of the jigsaw is all Alan's own work and he probably hasn't shared his data with anybody else. I fear that when Alan died, Trident died with him. And with him millions of people who could have been saved from a horrible death."

Chapter 6

As Jones and Hardwick left Professor Tompkinson's office they were met by a young PC. "Sir, DI Sutton has found something at the main campus security office he thinks you should see."

Motioning for the young man to lead on, Jones and Hardwick followed him out of the Biology building into the bright sunlight. "Main campus Security is just along here, sir, a few minutes' walk."

The temperature had picked up a little now, but the air was still fresh. In a couple of hours it would be too warm for his suit jacket, Warren judged. Impatient to see what Sutton had discovered, he walked as briskly as possible, arriving at the small building slightly out of breath, his calf muscles aching. His more youthful colleagues, he noticed with mild shame, seemed to have taken the rapid pace completely in their stride, so to speak.

You're getting old, Warren. Too much time behind a desk, not enough time on the beat, he admonished himself.

The campus security centre was a nondescript building, tucked away next to the library on a busy main road. Seeing them arrive, Sutton opened the door to let them in. In his hand he held a sheaf of printed sheets of A4 paper. He was clearly excited; even his customary smirk was absent. As quickly as was polite he introduced Jones to Terry Raworth, Head of Security. A solidly built man, his ramrod straight bearing and no-nonsense attitude suggested either ex-police or former military. Noting the tattoos on the backs of his wrists as they shook hands, Jones decided upon ex-military. Tattoos hadn't been encouraged in the police back when this man would have been serving and it seemed unlikely that a retired copper would suddenly develop an interest in body art.

Raworth led them through the back into the main control room. It was small and cramped, one whole wall given over to banks of black and white TV screens, with digital video recorders blinking below. An ancient desktop computer sat on a rickety desk, its fan wheezing loudly. The air was close, smelling of stale coffee and unwashed bodies. Sitting on an even more rickety-looking plastic chair in front of the monitors was another man, similar in age although without Raworth's military demeanour.

"What have we got, Inspector?"

"First things, first — it looks as though Spencer is off the hook. The security logs for the PCR room show him swiping in at 21:05 hours. He remained in there until 22:13, six minutes before he reported the murder. Coroner reckons the time of death was about 21:30 to 22:00 at the latest. Furthermore, if he'd done it, he'd have been covered with a lot more blood. I can't see how he could have killed the professor, changed out of his bloodstained clothes and got rid of them in six minutes."

"What if he had an accomplice?" Jones was unwilling to dismiss Spencer just yet.

"The logs for the main entrance show that building was completely empty by twenty past nine that night, except for Spencer and Tunbridge. The last half-dozen to leave included the two graduate students that Spencer claims he spoke to just before he went into the PCR room. We'll have to review the full CCTV footage to make sure that we didn't get anybody sneaking in on somebody else's coat tails earlier in the day, but it seems unlikely."

"So who the hell killed Tunbridge, then?"

Sutton smiled, clearly enjoying himself.

"Well, guv, I think we might just be able to answer that little question." With a flourish, he motioned towards the bank of video monitors. As if on cue, the video started playing.

"This is the front reception desk in the Biology building. It's the only entrance to the building and the only security camera inside the building." The image was black and white but clear, evidently shot from a camera positioned above the swipe-card doors, angled to take in as much of the reception area as possible.

Raworth took over the commentary, pointed a stubby finger at the screen. "During the day, whoever is manning the reception desk can control the cameras, panning around or zooming in and out if they want to. The rest of the time it can be controlled from here. At that time of the night it is left in standby mode, covering as much of the lobby as possible with a wide-angled lens, recording only when it detects movement. A rolling buffer means that the system also saves fifteen seconds either side of the trigger, to ensure that nothing is missed."

He pointed at the time stamp at the bottom of the screen. 21:35h. As he did so, a figure emerged from the right of the screen, outside the building, the automatic glass doors opening to admit it. The person — it looked like a man to Jones — walked beneath the camera. The footage was slightly jerky, but from what Jones could see the man appeared to be of average height, wearing a dark-coloured hoodie. Underneath the hoodie was a baseball cap, completely obscuring the mystery person's features. A crude, but effective, disguise. Both the hoodie and the baseball cap had what appeared to be small logos. Warren felt his heart skip a beat. He was certain that image analysis could identify them. Clearly visible in the mystery man's hand was a credit-card-sized white plastic rectangle. Without hesitation, or so much as a glance up towards the camera, he swiped the card through the machine and entered the building proper. A few more seconds elapsed before the footage stopped.

The time stamp at the bottom of the screen jumped forward to 22:10h. The mysterious form re-emerged from the bottom of the screen, coming through the door. This time he was clutching what appeared to be a bin bag in his left hand. Clearly in a rush, he half ran across the lobby and out of the front doors, heading right again towards where he had emerged thirty-five minutes earlier.

"That's the only person entering or leaving the building after 21:00 hours that night."

Jones turned to Raworth. "Can we follow him before or after he left the building?"

"I'm afraid not, Chief Inspector. He heads along the side of the building next to the car park. Unfortunately there's a blind spot all along that wall a couple of metres wide. As long as he kept close to the wall, there's no way we could spot him." He shrugged apologetically. "Budget cuts, I'm afraid. We had a spate of vandalism a few months ago in the car park. We didn't have the money for new cameras, so we repositioned the ones we already had to cover the car park rather than the side of the building." He shrugged again. "Not my idea, I must say, but as the old saying goes, 'who am I to question why...?'"

"It doesn't matter though, guv. We know who he is." Sutton held up the sheets of paper triumphantly. "The building's swipe-card log. And guess who swiped in at 21:35 and swiped back out again at 22:10?" He pointed to two highlighted entries on the list.

Dr Antonio Severino.

Chapter 7

Sutton and Jones walked up the front path of the small suburban house, barely a fifteen-minute walk from the Biology building. After reviewing the video footage, it hadn't taken long for them to find the address of Severino or to arrange an arrest warrant and a search warrant for his home. The house was a well-maintained two-up, two-down semi in a quiet cul-de-sac. Apparently, Severino had rented the house with his fiancée for the past two years. As Sutton and Jones approached the front of the house two more officers approached the rear, ready to stop any escape attempt via that route. Parked a discreet distance away, two police cars and a police van plus a half-dozen uniformed officers were waiting ready to assist. All of the officers wore stab vests — they'd seen what Severino was capable of and they had no desire to end up the same way as the late professor.

Jones paused at the door before pressing the doorbell. He heard its echoing ring in the hallway, muffled by the front door. Nothing. Not so much as a twitch from the drawn curtains. He paused a few more seconds, before ringing the bell again, this time holding it down for a couple of seconds. Still nothing. Jones contemplated shouting, "Police, open up!" through the letterbox, but he was reluctant to give up the advantage of surprise so soon. He decided to ring one last time, before radioing back to the forced-entry team on standby to bring over their solid-steel two-man battering ram, guaranteed to open pretty much any door.

Holding the bell push down for a full fifteen seconds, Jones was finally rewarded by sounds of movement behind the door and muttered cursing. The door opened and a wave of whiskey and stale cannabis fumes assaulted his nostrils. Standing in scruffy, striped boxer shorts and a stained grey T-shirt was a twenty-something man of average height. His skin had the slight olive cast to it common amongst those from Mediterranean countries, his unruly hair raven black. He blinked at Jones, clearly struggling to wake up fully.

"Dr Antonio Severino?"

The man nodded, puzzled. Jones held up his warrant card.

"You are under arrest for the…"

That was as far as Jones got. Severino's face promptly lost all of its colour, turning in an instant to a pasty white. Without a word, he turned on his heel and bolted back into the house.

"Shit! Don't let him get away!" yelled Sutton, somewhat unnecessarily since the two officers at the rear of the house were waiting by the back door with open arms. Much to Jones' surprise, however, rather than heading through the kitchen and towards the back door, Severino dived up the stairs.

Jones took off after him, Sutton a pace behind. Thundering up the stairs, the two officers struggled to catch up with the fleet-footed Italian. Where the hell was he going? To destroy evidence? Was there somebody else in the house? Maybe he was going to kill himself, throwing himself out of the bedroom window. Christ, it would really screw things up if he topped himself, Warren thought fearfully.

Reaching the top of the stairs, the fugitive carried on running, crashing into what was clearly the bathroom. Barely a second behind, Jones followed, expecting to see the man rummaging through the medicine cabinet for a weapon or a means to kill himself. Instead, he saw the man on all fours leaning over the toilet bowl being violently sick. The sour stench of whiskey and bile filled the room.

Catching his breath and trying to ignore the smell, Jones tried again. "Antonio Severino, I am arresting you on suspicion of the murder of Professor Alan Tunbridge."

Severino finished vomiting and turned around, opening his mouth as if to speak. He seemed to be having trouble focusing. After a pause of a few seconds, his eyes rolled back into his head and before Jones could catch him he fainted clean away, his head hitting the porcelain of the toilet bowl with a solid smack.

"Reckon you'll probably have to read him his rights again, guv," Sutton noted from the open doorway.

* * *

A cursory inspection by a paramedic pronounced Severino to be dead drunk but otherwise fit and so the semi-comatose Italian was loaded into the back of the waiting police van. Back at the station, he was roused enough to be read his rights before being stripped and put into a paper suit, his own clothes bagged and sent off to Forensics. Severino was clearly in no state to be interviewed and his lawyer would doubtless try and get anything he said declared inadmissible as evidence. Therefore, Jones decided to play it by the book. Dumping him in the drunk tank to sleep it off, he asked the desk sergeant to organise a solicitor and, as an afterthought, an Italian translator for when he awoke in a few hours. The last thing they wanted was any language problems slowing down the interview process.

In the meantime, Jones and the rest of his team finally had time to eat and an opportunity to compare notes. Unfortunately, the station's small canteen was closed for hot meals at the weekend, so the team had to make do with the rather sorry-looking sandwiches left over in the self-service fridge from the previous day. As a result they decided not to linger over lunch. All of them were keen to get on with their work, but Jones insisted that they take a short break.

Despite the rapid early progress of the investigation, Jones knew from experience that a murder investigation was a marathon not a sprint and he wanted his team to remain fresh. Furthermore, Jones firmly believed that a few minutes' break would allow each officer's subconscious to process what they had learnt so far, supplying new insights and new questions. Besides, Severino wouldn't be going anywhere for a while and Spencer wasn't due to return for further questioning for some time.

Whilst the others tucked into the stale sandwiches, Jones snagged Sergeant Kent and asked him to collate the latest reports from his incident desk. Glancing at his watch, Jones then decided he had time to ring Susan and headed into the corridor for some privacy. The phone connected on the third ring. "Hi, sweetheart, it's me."

"It's Bernice. Susan's busy preparing a salad for the picnic. And of course it's you — it says so on the screen."

Jones stifled a groan. He had hoped to have a private chat with Susan, explaining what was going on. But that clearly wouldn't be possible. Mustering all of his tact and injecting a false note of positivity into his voice, he addressed his mother-in-law.

"Hello, Bernice, Happy birthday."

A sniff at the other end of the line.

"I'm sorry I had to leave so suddenly last night. Unfortunately I got an emergency call."

"I see. And that kept you out all night? I suppose you are calling now to say that you won't be coming to Cambridge for the picnic today?"

Bloody woman, she wasn't making it any easier for him. Susan must be a bit annoyed as well. Normally she tried to wrestle the phone from her mother; today she was letting him stew as Bernice grilled him. Changing tactics, he decided to appeal to her baser instincts. Bernice loved to gossip and the idea that she had got the inside scoop on such a big story before any of her friends would appeal directly to her self-importance. Besides which, the press had already started sniffing around. It wasn't as if he was telling her any information that wouldn't be in the public domain within a couple of hours.

"I'm afraid so, Bernice. It's all a bit hush-hush, you understand, but last night a famous scientist was found murdered at the university." Warren could almost hear Bernice's interest pique. It wasn't exactly a lie, after all; in terms of celebrity, Tunbridge was famous in the field of antibiotic research, wasn't he?

"Really? Which college? It wasn't that lovely Professor Hawkings, was it? He was on television last week and I said to Dennis, 'It's such a shame, such a wonderful mind trapped inside that poor broken body.' Who could murder that lovely man when he's so helpless? I tell you, Warren, there are some truly wicked people out there! Why have they brought you in? Isn't Cambridge a bit out of your jurisdiction?"

Jones blinked as he tried to process the torrent of misunderstanding flooding down the phone. It was no wonder Dennis never said anything in public.

"Er, no, it wasn't Stephen Hawking, Bernice, it was a Biology professor and it was at our local university, the University of Middle England."

"Oh." A pause. "I didn't realise that Middlesbury had a university."

"Oh, yes, it's quite a good one." Warren suddenly felt an irrational need to defend the institution against the withering disdain of his mother-in-law.

"Anyway, the body was discovered late last night. We had to secure the crime scene and then this morning we started our enquiries."

"So will you be coming to the picnic?"

"No, I'm sorry, we have too much going on at the moment. But I promise that I'll make it tonight."

Bugger! Why did he just promise that? What if he couldn't make it?

Slightly mollified, Bernice offered to pass the phone over to Susan, who pointedly walked out into the garden so she could talk in private. Even so, she kept her voice low and Warren could imagine Bernice staring through the French windows, trying her best to lip-read Susan's half of the conversation.

"I'm sorry, darling, there was a murder up at the uni last night and I'm lead investigator."

"I thought Stephen Hawking worked at Cambridge University? Why are you investigating his death?"

Warren stifled a curse. "No, it's not Stephen Hawking. It's a local Biology professor at UME. Your mum just got the wrong end of the stick."

"So are you coming tonight?"

"I should be, yes. I'll ring you a bit later and we can decide where to meet. I'll probably come straight to the restaurant."

"Well, don't forget the table's booked for six-thirty and the show starts at eight. And I suggest that you bring some sort of peace offering." Whether it was for Susan or her mother wasn't clear. Warren decided he would play it safe and get something for both of them.

Hanging up, he turned to see Sutton grinning, clearly having heard at least part of the call.

"Mother-in-law's birthday," Jones offered weakly by way of an explanation.

Remarkably, Sutton's expression changed to one of sympathy.

Given the strained relationship between them, Jones decided to take advantage of this slight wind change and attempt to build some common ground.

"Do you have the pleasure of a mother-in-law, Tony?" It was a weak opener, nevertheless Sutton seemed willing to run with it.

"I have two."

"Two? How the hell does that work?" Jones grimaced. Maybe he should cut the man some slack, he thought — it must be a tough life with two of them.

Sutton let out a bark of laughter. "Badly!"

Jones said nothing, simply smiling in sympathy. Sutton accepted the implied invitation. "My current wife has a mother who is very much alive and kicking... mostly kicking. She's never really liked me and isn't very good at hiding it. Sometimes I think she watched a little too much Les Dawson and decided that's what mother-in-laws were supposed to be like."

Jones chuckled. "Now, take my mother-in-law. No, please, take my mother-in-law," he intoned in a fair interpretation of the comic's rich, northern baritone. Sutton smiled in acknowledgement of Jones' attempt at levity.

"Mother-in-law number one, Betty, is also still on the scene. She doesn't like me very much either."

Jones raised an eyebrow in surprise at the intricacies of Sutton's personal life.

Sutton shrugged. "Long story, short — Angela and I got married far too young. Everybody said it wouldn't work, but we were young, stubborn and in love." He smiled wistfully. "Anyway, we did our best for five, six years but it was hard work. I was a young copper on a constable's pay; Angela worked shifts at the local hospital. We rarely saw each other and when we did, we never had any money to enjoy ourselves. So we did what hundreds of foolish young couples have done before us and decided to have a baby to bring us together."

"And did it?"

Sutton snorted. "What do you think? At first it was great. Angela had a pretty good pregnancy and we were both thrilled when Josh was born. The excitement lasted a year or so, until Angela went back to work. Then it was as if the clock had turned back twelve months. We both still worked shifts, so we still hardly saw each other and when we did we could never have any time alone because Josh was there.

"Fortunately, Betty and her husband Doug lived nearby and loved Josh to bits, so they would babysit whilst we went out." Sutton's expression turned thoughtful. "You know, in many ways, although she didn't like me very much, I really think Betty wanted me and Angela to succeed. The problem was, we were both feeling hemmed in. Angela wanted to go back to college to study for her nursing degree. I wanted to go to night classes and do a degree before studying for my sergeant's exam, but that was no longer possible. So we carried on as we were for another year or two, before I fucked up. Big time."

"What happened?" Warren asked cautiously. Sutton's candour was unexpected and he didn't want to kill the moment.

"It was such a bloody cliché. I got absolutely hammered at the nick's Christmas party and woke up the next morning in bed with one of the civilian office workers. Needless to say, when I finally slunk home, Angela was furious. I didn't try to deny it. There was no point — it was bleeding obvious what had happened. I packed my bags, left the house and kipped on a mate's floor.

"That could have been the end of it. Angela kicked me out, fair play, and I'm sure Betty and Doug were happy to tell her 'I told you so', but there was still the issue of Josh. Angela never wanted to see me again, unsurprisingly, but amazingly Betty stood up for me. By now Angela was back with her parents and Betty basically said, 'My house, my rules. Josh needs his dad and I'm not letting him get off scot-free.' I think at first she was worried that I'd just piss off and leave them.

"As it happened, I was terrified that it would all have to go to court and I'd end up taking Josh to McDonald's once a month if I was lucky. Anyway, she turned up at the bedsit I was renting and said in no uncertain terms that I was a shit husband but a good father and that a boy needs his dad. So that was that." He shook his head slightly, as if he still couldn't quite believe his own memory.

"Josh stayed with his mum and Betty and Doug helped her look after him whilst she went back to college. I started night school and with a little help from my own mum and dad managed to afford the rent on a two-bedroom flat so Josh could stay over. I saw him most weekends, and when he got a bit older and started going to school, Betty used to insist that Angela and I co-ordinate our shifts so that when Angela was on nights he could stay with me and I'd take him to school.

"Anyway, he's seventeen now, starting to think about university. He's always got on well with my second wife, Marie, and he probably spends as much time at mine as his mum's. He has his own room in our house and he's only a ten-minute walk from Angela's so he often turns up in the evening to watch the footie with me on Sky. Angela and I still aren't the closest of friends, but we both go to parents' evening and any reports from school are sent around to me as well."

Sutton shook his head again, as if in wonderment or disbelief. "It's amazing. Betty still doesn't like me very much, yet without her I'd be like half the fathers in this nick, barely seeing their kids and constantly going to court over broken access orders."

Jones was at a loss for words. Sutton had just shared a clearly intimate part of his life with him. Maybe the two of them could work together.

"You make me feel guilty for all the wicked thoughts I've been having about my own mother-in-law, Tony. I'll make sure I get an extra big bunch of flowers when I see her tonight."

Sutton grinned, then turned sober. "Well, sir, may I suggest that we crack on, then? Sooner we're done, sooner you can find a garage with a cut-price deal on daffodils."

Chapter 8

As Sutton headed back to the canteen to round up the rest of the team, Warren unwrapped the cling film from his cheese and tomato sandwich. He carefully peeled back the top slice of bread and plucked the sorry-looking slices of tomato from on top of the micron-thin layer of Cheddar resting on a much thicker layer of margarine. The tomato's juice had soaked the top layer of bread, making it soggy. Carefully wrapping the tomato in the cling film, he deposited it in a nearby waste basket. Why couldn't a man just get a plain cheese sandwich? Biting into the sandwich, he grimaced. Where it wasn't soaked with tomato juice, the starchy white bread was dry, verging on stale, and the cheese was indistinguishable in flavour from the margarine. One bite was enough, he decided, and the remains joined the tomato and cling film in the bin.

Rejoining Hardwick and Sutton in the briefing room, he saw that a number of other detectives had also returned to the station. There was a low buzz of conversation. Kent, he saw, had started making use of the whiteboards, summarising the information flowing in from the investigators. Doing his best to ignore the faint, tantalising smell of somebody's microwaved ready meal — clearly somebody better prepared than he to work on a Saturday — Jones called the meeting to order.

By agreement, it was decided to leave Spencer and Severino

until last, to see if anything else came out of the mix before they narrowed the investigation prematurely. Starting with DS Kent, he asked the man to fill everybody in on what information had been acquired so far.

First of all, the house-to-house inquiries at the few residential properties nearby had resulted in no leads; no strange noises or suspicious strangers hanging around during the time of the murder or in the hours preceding it. Similarly, as expected, none of the local businesses had CCTV that overlooked the university building. The traffic cameras along the roads adjacent to the department were also useless, focused as they were on the roads and a nearby junction rather than the building itself. It looked as though between the university's CCTV blind spots and the patchy traffic camera coverage in the area, it would be quite possible to approach the building and enter it on foot undetected.

Turning to the call-centre logs that night, no reports had surfaced as yet of any crimes taking place within a mile or so of the Biology building. Overall it had been a fairly quiet Friday night with no more than the usual amount of closing-time fisticuffs, drunken vandalism and domestic violence.

Dr Crawley and the university's Personnel and Student Services departments had been helpful in supplying the names and details of the laboratory's various workers and students, including the undergraduate student, Clara Hemmingway, that Tunbridge had his alleged affair with. A list had been drawn up on one of the whiteboards, headed "Potential Suspects" with additional columns such as "Motive?" and "Alibi?". Jones had a feeling that before the day was out, a second board might be needed.

On a different whiteboard, a second list had been drawn up headed "Witnesses". The two students that Tom Spencer claimed to have spoken to immediately before locking himself in the PCR room were named. Officers were on their way to interview them to check that they corroborated his story. A third whiteboard was simply labelled "Forensics". This was blank at the moment.

Now it was Jones' turn. Quickly, he summarised the interviews with Crawley and Tompkinson, adding a few more names to the suspects board. With that done, he moved on to Spencer. With the swipe-card logs from the PCR room and main-building entrance and assuming that the two students corroborated his story, Sutton proposed that they interview him one last time then eliminate him.

Jones shook his head. "Let's not be too hasty. We don't know that Severino didn't have an accomplice and he was the only other person in the building at the time. Something doesn't feel right about him."

Sutton grunted non-committally. Ignoring him, Jones pressed on. "Spencer aside, number one suspect at the moment is Dr Antonio Severino, an Italian postdoctoral researcher in Tunbridge's group. It seems that Tunbridge shafted him big time a few weeks ago and by all accounts he left in a furious if not murderous mood. We're doing background checks on him now. CCTV has an unidentified male entering then exiting the building within the timeframe consistent with the murder. The building's swipe-card logs suggest that the suspect used Severino's access card. We arrested him an hour ago at his house. Unfortunately he seemed to have been having a one-man party last night and is busy sleeping it off in the drunk tank. We've a brief and a translator standing by for when he rejoins the land of the coherent. In the meantime, Forensics are searching his house and looking for trace evidence."

Jones looked around the room. "Anything else to add? Any more questions?"

"Have we confirmed the wife's alibi yet?"

Kent answered this. "We've tracked down a couple of her dinner companions and the duty manager from the restaurant last night claims to have remembered the party. Till receipts match her credit card number. We're waiting on CCTV from the restaurant, but it looks as if she's cast iron at the moment."

Another hand. "Have we got any more forensics yet? What about the post-mortem?"

"Full results from the PM are promised by tomorrow evening. Preliminary forensics are consistent with what we had this morning. We can expect a full report from the unit at Welwyn tomorrow. No word as yet from Severino's place. A computer forensics team from Welwyn will be looking at Tunbridge's laptop, to see if there are any clues there, particularly as to why he was working alone on a Friday night."

No more hands were raised, so Jones decided to assign roles to those present and close the meeting.

Calling Sutton over, he outlined his plans. Severino wouldn't be fit for interview for a few more hours, so they had time to re-interview Spencer, who had just arrived at Reception. Jones was also keen to speak to the late professor's one-time mistress, Clara Hemmingway. A couple of uniforms were dispatched to her student flat to bring her in for questioning.

* * *

Making their way down to the station's number one interview room, Jones arranged for the desk sergeant to fetch Spencer. Moments later, the young man shuffled in. Dressed in a clean T-shirt and neatly pressed chinos, he was a far cry from the paper-suited, bloodstained mess from the night before. Escorting him was a middle-aged black woman in a smart, pinstriped suit carrying a briefcase. She introduced herself as Denise Jawando, his solicitor. Although he wasn't under arrest, Spencer's parents had insisted on her presence as a precaution. Jones noted that her handshake was perfunctory, her expression unsmiling.

As soon as all were seated, the recorders running and the appropriate introductions made for the tape, Jawando launched in.

"May I remind you, Chief Inspector, that my client is here voluntarily as the witness to a crime in which he played no part and that he is not under arrest?"

Smiling tightly, Jones kept an even tone. "Thank you for your assistance. Mr Spencer, for the record, could you tell us again what happened last night?"

All eyes turned towards the young researcher. Fresh clothes notwithstanding, he looked dreadful; it had been barely twelve hours since he had found the body, yet he looked as if in that time he had lost a week's worth of sleep. He was of average height and build, his hair a dirty blond, its length midway between scruffy and fashionably long. A few days' stubble darkened his jowls.

"I was working late, trying to finish off some PCR reactions before going home. I went down to the PCR room on the ground floor about nine." The student had a broad Manchester accent, although his diction was precise and absent the urban drawl possessed by many native Mancunians.

"Can anyone confirm that?"

"Like I said last night, I said 'Hi' to a couple of Stanley Westlake's lab who work near there, Chloe and Steven. They were going to the Hogshead for a pint. I said I'd try to join them in an hour or so, but not to wait for me in case I was late.

"I was in the PCR room for an hour or so — you can check that, because it has a swipe-card lock — before going back up to the lab."

"What were you wearing?" interrupted Sutton.

"What you found me in: jeans, T-shirt and a lab coat, with latex gloves."

"When did you leave the PCR room?"

"About quarter past ten, I guess."

"Did anyone see you then?"

"No, I don't think anyone was left in the building by that time, but again the swipe machine should confirm my exit."

"Where did you go next?"

"Nowhere, I went straight back to the lab. I put the completed PCR reactions in the freezer. I'd seen Alan's office light was on when I came back up, so I decided to pop my head around and say 'Goodnight'. That's when I saw the body."

"You were still wearing latex gloves, a lab coat and a face mask when we arrived. Seems a little strange that you didn't take these off if you were going to say 'Hi' to the boss."

Spencer shrugged vaguely. "I dress like that all day, every day. I probably just forgot."

"Tell me what happened then, Tom."

Spencer's eyes became downcast. "The moment I came in, I saw the blood. He was spun in his chair staring towards the doorway. I could see from the state of his throat that he had to be dead, but I checked for a pulse anyway. Then I dialled 999."

Jones nodded in understanding. "May I ask why you didn't use your mobile phone to call us? You young people seem to have them turned on constantly these days. I wouldn't have thought many people your age could use a landline." Despite his almost light-hearted tone, the question was a serious one. For Spencer's generation, the mobile phone was like an extension of their body. Office phones and other semi-obsolete equipment were almost invisible to them. Spencer had an expensive smartphone in his pocket when he was arrested, indicating that he wasn't a total Luddite.

"I saw a picture of one on the Internet and used Wikipedia to tell me how to use it," responded Spencer with an almost straight face. Warren smiled briefly in response, before becoming sober once more.

"Tell me, Tom, how much did you hate Professor Tunbridge for stopping you passing your PhD?"

The question was deliberately brutal and out of the blue; Jones wanted to see what Spencer's response would be. He blinked a few times, as if trying to understand the question. "Alan and I had our differences, sure, but I'd never dream of killing him."

Jones and Sutton said nothing, waiting. The silence stretched uncomfortably. Eventually, Spencer broke it, as they knew he would. "Anyway, I have done pretty much everything I need. I'd be mad to kill Alan — I needed him to sign off on everything." Jones and Sutton said nothing, apparently ignoring the contradiction with everything that they'd found out that morning.

"I was just doing a few more experiments, before I wrote up the final conclusion."

Now it was Jawando who broke the silence. "I think we've heard enough, gentlemen. My client has a provable alibi. He was merely in the wrong place at the wrong time." At that moment, there came a knock at the door.

Sutton answered it, stepping into the corridor. After a few moments he returned and whispered into Jones' ear, who nodded, then addressed Spencer.

"We've just got confirmation from the two graduate students that you saw on your way to the PCR room. Along with the security logs showing swipe-card usage, it seems that your alibi stands up. I think that's enough for today. We may need to contact you again in the future, however, to answer further questions."

Spencer slumped back into his chair in obvious relief. Jones arranged to have his statement typed up and signed, before seeing him to the front door.

When Spencer was finally gone, Jones called into the custody suite to check on Severino. The Italian was snoring loudly on the small bed. A half-filled bucket next to him and the stains down the front of his paper suit justified the police surgeon's recommendation that they wait another hour or two before attempting to interview him.

In the meantime, Jones decided to see what the professor's former lover had to say for herself. Whilst they waited for Hemmingway to arrive, Jones polled Sutton for his thoughts. "Well, I think we can rule out Spencer and I reckon this Severino character is good for it. We need to tie up a few loose ends, but it looks pretty open and shut to me. The super will be pleased — twenty-four hours to solve a murder investigation is pretty good."

"Well, let's not count our chickens before they've hatched. I think there is still a lot more to this than meets the eye."

"In what way?"

"Well, first of all, even if Severino did do it, was he working alone?"

"We'll have to see what he says, I suppose, but, even if there are others involved, the evidence so far suggests that he committed the murder alone."

"But what evidence? That CCTV image is pretty non-conclusive and anyone could have swiped his access card through that lock. Furthermore, how did he know that Tunbridge would be working late that night? Was that usual for him? If not, who tipped Severino off? And what about Spencer? Something's not right there."

"Well, it looks like it's as his brief said — wrong place, wrong time."

"Possibly, but something smells strange about this set-up. It's too bloody convenient. He just happens to be in the PCR room when it all goes down and then he stumbles across the body. He checks the pulse of a blatantly dead man, conveniently covering himself in the victim's blood to wreck any forensics. Why did he check the carotids? Don't most people check the wrist for a pulse? And his demeanour wasn't right. He's just found a freshly murdered co-worker, whilst on his own in a large, deserted building late at night. Chances are the killer is still in the building somewhere, yet he calmly makes a phone call and waits at the murder-scene for us to arrive. I don't know about you Tony, but I've seen enough slasher movies in my time to know that you don't hang around and call the police from the victim's phone, you run like hell and find somewhere to hide before using your mobile."

Sutton shrugged, clearly not convinced.

"I think you're over-complicating things, guv. Shock makes people do strange things."

Seeing that he was unlikely to budge his colleague based on what they had so far, Jones decided to give up. In the meantime, the desk sergeant was signalling that Clara Hemmingway had arrived. Motioning to Sutton, they headed for Interview Room Two to avoid contaminating Hemmingway with any trace evidence from Spencer's interview in Interview One. More than one case had been scuppered because the police had transported two different suspects in the same car or interviewed them in the same room and found it impossible afterwards to disentangle their separate DNA profiles.

Gathering his thoughts, Warren prepared for his next interview of the day.

Chapter 9

A uniformed constable led Hemmingway into the interview room. She was a youngish-looking twenty-year-old in jeans and a crop top with a slim figure, generous cleavage and carefully styled short blonde hair; it was easy to see why a middle-aged university professor might have been tempted. Taking a seat opposite the two detectives, she placed her large black handbag on the floor next to her. Jones introduced himself and Sutton for the benefit of the recording, before explaining that she was not under arrest, nor had she been charged with any crime. She nodded, looking curious but not overly nervous. Jones glanced at the slim file in front of him. Two police cautions in her early teens for shoplifting and a suspended sentence, aged seventeen, for her part in a drunken brawl in Colchester town centre on a Saturday night. Miss Hemmingway had certainly been through this process before, he noted.

However, she'd clearly cleaned up her act sufficiently to pass her A levels and convince the admissions tutor that she was worthy of a place at university. The University of Middle England might not be Oxford or Cambridge, but with the current demand for places they could afford to pick and choose who they offered those places to. He'd have to remember that. This young lady was clearly a little more intelligent than the stereotypes might suggest.

Watching her carefully, Jones started, "Now, the reason we have asked you down here is to help us with our enquiries regarding the murder of Professor Alan Tunbridge last night. How well did you know the professor?"

Hemmingway's eyes widened slightly. "Murdered? Why? Where?"

"He was found in his office last night. He'd been stabbed." Jones decided not to give out too much information at this stage. "Again, how well did you know the deceased?"

Hemingway paused for a couple of seconds. "Well enough, I suppose. I did a bacterial genetics module with him last year."

The answer was terse, short and cautious. Jones and Hemmingway locked eyes. She wasn't stupid. She knew that the only logical reason that she was here was because the police were aware of at least some of her past history with the murder victim. Nevertheless, the wariness forged by years of playing so close to the thin blue line had conditioned her not to give away anything more than absolutely necessary.

Jones spoke softly. "Come on, Clara. We all know it was a bit more than that. You and the professor were extremely close."

Clara stared at him defiantly. "So what? We fooled around a bit. He was rich and successful and not all that bad-looking. All those professors are the same. They just want a little bit of fresher pussy." She paused as if to gauge the reaction to her profanity. Seeing nothing, she pressed on. "You know what the older students call the first week of uni? 'Fuck a Fresher Week'. Of course the profs can't get in on any of that — Freshers' week is just for students. But when classes start and you start having tutorials — it doesn't take much. A little extra help on an essay or perhaps an extension… well, it's easy to come to an arrangement. And for randy old bastards like

Tunbridge, who blatantly hate teaching, it's probably the only thing that makes tutoring undergrads worthwhile." Jones noticed that as she became more animated her Essex accent became harsher, betraying her council-estate upbringing.

"Was that all it was, Clara? Just a bit of fun? Maybe it was more than that — he had a wife. Rumour has it you weren't the only one. How did that make you feel?" Now it was Sutton, his brusque manner a contrast to Jones' more measured tones.

"Yeah, that's all it was, just a shag. Earned me an extra week to write an essay I was having trouble with — didn't affect the grade though. He didn't mark it. I got that A fair and square." This last bit was delivered with conviction, the flashing in her steely blue eyes daring anyone to contradict her.

"And before you ask, no, I wasn't jealous of his frigid wife or any other slappers he slept with and, no, I didn't kill him." If she spotted the irony, she didn't show it.

"OK, Clara, I can accept that. Tell me, what was his reaction when you found out that you were pregnant?" The question was brutal, deliberately out of the blue, designed to push her onto the back foot.

Clara's mouth opened in surprise; clearly she hadn't been expecting the question.

"Wha…? How did you know? Who told you?"

"It doesn't matter who told us. Please, just answer the question."

Clara slumped back in her chair; for the first time since she'd entered the room the defiant façade cracked slightly.

"He was angry at first. Blamed it on me. Said I should have been more careful." She snorted. "You'd think that a Biology professor would know that it takes two to tango." This last sentence was delivered with no trace of mirth. "In the end, he made me get rid of it. Said it was for the best. He gave me some cash and arranged for me to move tutor groups so we wouldn't see each other again."

Jones now, in a gentle voice.

"How did that make you feel, Clara?"

She sighed. "Cheap." She looked at the ceiling and it was as if she'd forgotten where she was.

"The thing is, he was right. I couldn't have had that baby. Even with the university's support, I can't see how I would have looked after it. And Alan made it clear that he wasn't going to help. Not that I'd want him to anyway. The worst thing would be going back home. All the fingers pointing, all the whispering: 'See, I told you so, stuck-up bitch, thinking she's better than us.'" She looked the two detectives squarely in the eye, one at a time. "You see, I'm not only the first person in my family to go to university, I'm the first on my whole estate. Of all the kids I grew up with, not one of them stayed on to do A levels. Most of them barely finished their GCSEs. I got six A*s. Then I got an A and two Bs at A level." She laughed harshly. "Shit, with my background, when I got to university I ticked so many boxes on the outreach programmes I'm amazed the government didn't stick me in their election manifesto. It's just a shame I'm not a black lesbian in a wheelchair, then I'd have completed the fucking set. Anyway, that's all in the past. I can't say I'll mourn the bastard, but I didn't kill him."

The statement hung in the air, the look of defiance back on Clara's face. Despite her protestations, Jones wasn't convinced. This was one angry young woman and she had a hell of a motive. But it was time to move on. It seemed that everyone who'd ever met the professor could conceivably have a motive. And motive was only part of the equation. Without opportunity, motive meant nothing.

"Now, Clara, we would like to ask you some routine questions about your whereabouts yesterday evening, between the hours of 9 p.m. and 10 p.m."

Shifting uncomfortably, Clara gazed into space for a second.

"Boring night in. I watched a DVD then went out to Tesco to get some munchies. Figured whilst I was there that I'd do me shopping as well."

"Can anyone vouch for you? Flatmates, boyfriend, friends?" Jones continued probing gently.

"No, I was on me own. Me flatmate was away for the weekend and I ain't seeing anyone at the moment."

Nodding as if satisfied for the moment, Jones continued conversationally.

"So what time did you go to Tesco?"

"Must have been about half nine or ten. Cupboards were bare so I did me big shop."

"Very strange time to walk half a mile to the supermarket, 10 p.m. on a Friday. Especially when you have a corner shop just around the corner from you," Sutton interjected.

"Yeah, well, like I said, I was having a quiet night in and I wanted some snacks. Figured I may as well do me big shop then — it's quiet that time of the night."

Nodding as if the explanation was perfectly reasonable, Jones took over.

"I don't suppose that you have any witnesses? Bump into anyone that knows you? Did you keep the till receipt?"

"I didn't see nobody I knew, but I think I might have the receipt."

Bending down, Clara started to root through her handbag. As she did so both officers were treated to a look down her impressive cleavage. A small tattoo of a rose adorned the top of her left breast.

You could take the girl out of Essex… Jones supposed that was what happened when you aimed for 50 per cent of school leavers going to university. He felt a sudden flash of shame, both at the eyeful he was getting and his sudden unbidden academic snobbery.

He glanced over at Sutton, who smirked back at him and winked, before restoring his poker face. Clearly no shame being felt there.

Finally, Clara sat up holding a large purse in triumph. Opening it, she removed a till receipt from Tesco — a very, very lengthy till receipt. With a flourish, she passed it over. A cursory glance and Jones felt his hopes fade. According to the time stamp on the receipt, Clara had been at the checkout at pretty much the same time that Tom Spencer was reporting the murder of Tunbridge. If the receipt was to be believed, Clara really had done her "big shop" that night; he was amazed she'd managed to carry it all home. Even on a quiet Friday night, he couldn't see how she could have travelled to Tesco from the crime scene, filled a trolley this big, then put it through the checkout in those few minutes. He'd get her story verified by somebody as soon as possible. But it looked as though she was in the clear.

With everything concluded, Jones asked a uniform to see her out. Alone in the room with Sutton, he looked at him questioningly.

"Thoughts?"

Sutton was uncharacteristically wary.

"I don't know, guv. She has one hell of a motive and she was definitely not telling us the whole truth — her dialect wobbled quite a bit, the inner-city Essex came through more strongly towards the end. That might be an indication that she was lying." He sighed. "But that till receipt looks pretty convincing,"

"I agree. She was definitely holding something back, but we did hit her pretty hard with the questions about her pregnancy. She's clearly still upset over the incident — that may have been enough to rattle her cage. But, unless she had an accomplice, I don't see how she could have done a shop like that in the time she would have had. I'll send someone down to Tesco to speak to the manager and see if any of the checkout staff remember her or if she pops up on the CCTV. However, I think we can probably rule out Ms Hemmingway's direct involvement."

Chapter 10

By the time they had finished interviewing Hemmingway it was getting on for 4 p.m. Jones' stomach was growling, the breakfast banana and single bite of cheese sandwich not nearly enough to placate it. Thirty minutes more, he decided, then they were waking up Severino regardless. If he was to have any chance of making the restaurant for six-thirty, they needed at least a preliminary statement from him within an hour or so.

In the meantime, Jones decided he had to try and get something to eat, or, if that failed, more coffee. Heading back to the canteen, he was dismayed to find that not only were there no more sandwiches, all of the fruit was gone too. To add insult to injury, the vending machine selling crisps and chocolate bars had a large handwritten "out of order" sign sticky-taped across the coin slots. Heading back into the briefing room, he saw that the coffee urn was still plugged in, so he settled for another dark black coffee loaded with sugar. His fifty-pence piece remained alone in the honesty jar.

"Ah, Warren. I hear that we've made quite some progress this morning."

Jones nearly choked on his coffee. Jesus, the man must be wearing padded socks! He turned around to see a beaming John Grayson standing behind him.

"It's looking promising, sir. We've got plenty of leads and several suspects. We've almost ruled out Tom Spencer and it looks as though another member of the lab may be the culprit. He's sleeping off a rather heavy night at the moment though. I thought we'd do it by the book and make sure he's fully fit before interviewing him; besides, it gives us a little extra time to finish searching his house."

Grayson nodded, clearly not overly interested in the minutiae of the investigation. "I've scheduled a press conference for tomorrow morning, 11 a.m. I want you by my side for it. Ideally, we'll have charged this chap and everything can get back to normal. In the meantime, I'm about to issue a statement to keep the press happy. Any thoughts about what should be in it? Press liaison thinks we should hint that we're going to throw them a large bone tomorrow morning, drum up some interest and make sure that we are seen to be moving fast and decisively."

Jones' heart sank; he detested this nonsense. The twenty-four-hour news channels were like a voracious animal, constantly demanding to be fed, day and night. Although very much a product of the modern news era himself, Jones nevertheless longed for the old days when the beast was only fed once a day, in time for the deadlines for the late-night news or the next morning's newspapers. Back then, Jones and his team would have had the luxury of all of Sunday to firm up their evidence before a late evening press conference to reveal what they knew.

It also meant there was no way he could attend mass that morning. The local church had two Sunday services, the 11 a.m. service that Susan and Warren usually attended and an earlier 9 a.m. service. Neither would be possible tomorrow — another black mark against his name in the mother-in-law's book. For a brief, insane moment, Jones considered asking for the press conference to be postponed long enough for him to go to church with Bernice, or maybe he could run out now to attend the Saturday evening service that busy Catholics were allowed to attend in lieu of a traditional Sunday service. He mentally shook his head at the foolishness of the notion, a product of too little sleep and too much caffeine.

Answering Grayson's question, Jones had to advise caution at this stage. "We shouldn't count our chickens before they've hatched, sir. We're still waiting to interview Severino. Forensics are still searching his house. We don't know if anyone else is involved yet. I'd play it safe and simply confirm the identity of the deceased and the time of death, admit that we have a couple of people helping with our enquiries and ask for anyone with information to step forward.

"Besides, if Severino doesn't play ball, we may not be ready to charge him before tomorrow's press conference. Then we'd look a bit silly."

Jones could see that Grayson sorely wanted to say more, to make the following morning's press conference seem more compelling. Perhaps that way the news outlets would send out some of their big-name reporters, rather than the second-raters stuck with the Sunday shift that nobody wanted.

Tough, thought Jones, he was damned if he was going to let the tail wag the dog.

Chapter 11

Detective Constable Gary Hastings pulled up outside the Tesco Extra that Clara Hemmingway had supposedly visited on the evening of Professor Tunbridge's murder. Locking the doors of the Peugeot police car he'd borrowed — you couldn't be too careful, he thought, and he'd never live it down if anything happened to the car when he was on a routine job — he strode in through the automatic doors. A couple of teenage girls smirked at him, but he ignored them, the job too important for distractions from the local jailbait. Although he wasn't privy to all the details, he knew that this was a key part of the investigation into the Tunbridge murder.

Ever since he'd joined the police, Hastings had wanted to join CID. Now, after a couple of years as a detective constable, he was starting to prepare for his sergeant's exam. Being given sole responsibility for checking out the alibi of one of the apparently many suspects in the case was small beer, but you never knew, he thought, if he got himself noticed it could only help when he applied for promotion.

Walking purposefully up to the customer service desk, he introduced himself to the woman operating the till and asked to speak to the duty manager.

"Sure thing, love. That'll be Mr Patel today." She motioned to the security guard loitering by the cigarette kiosk. "Oluseye, go fetch Ravvi out of the office, will you, please?"

Grumbling, the security guard slouched off to a set of double doors marked "Staff Only". As he waited Gary discreetly eyed the woman. Her name was Maureen and according to her name tag she was pleased to help. About five feet and early fifties, he judged, she was large-chested and squat, probably a few stone over her ideal weight. Her grey hair and ruddy complexion reminded him of those bustling ladies of a certain age that seemed a permanent installation in the church that he'd attended since childhood. Any minute now he expected her to ruffle his hair and say that she knew his mum — unlikely since his parents both lived over a hundred miles away.

"They say that you know you're getting older when the police start looking younger. You look about the same age as my Amy's son Neville."

DC Hastings, acutely aware of the fact that at twenty-four years old he could still pass for seventeen, even in his dress uniform, fought back the urge to scowl. Mentally he upgraded her age to late fifties and, perhaps a little uncharitably, revised his estimate of her build to "morbidly obese".

Fortunately, he was saved from further pleasantries by the arrival of the duty manager, a small middle-aged man. Introducing himself, Gary asked if there was somewhere quiet that they could talk in relation to an ongoing investigation. The manager, clearly relieved that Hastings wasn't there to ask questions about selling alcohol or tobacco to underage kids, led him through the staff-only doors to "backstage" as he called it. Hastings noticed that the staff side of the door had a large poster on it proclaiming "Smile! You're going on stage".

In contrast to the brightly painted walls of the shop floor, the walls here were drab plasterboard. Mr Patel led Hastings down a maze of corridors, the walls adorned with "employee of the month" pictures — mostly spotty teenagers, Gary noticed — large eye-catching posters reminding staff to be vigilant about unattended parcels and shoplifters, as well as the obligatory health and safety notices. They passed a series of small, cubicle-like offices with staff busy working on PCs. One office, sturdier than all of the others, had an open door. As they went past Gary noticed a Securicor driver in helmet and body armour standing next to an open safe. Two similarly attired Tesco employees scowled at him as he was led past. It was all Gary could do not to stop and stare — by the looks of that safe, the long-predicted demise of cash in favour of credit and debit cards was still some way off.

Finally, they reached the duty manager's office. A little larger than the others, it had a generous desk and comfortable-looking chair. As they entered Patel grabbed one of the metal-framed visitor's chairs from behind the door, pushing it shut behind them as he did so. Once they had sat down, Hastings took out his notepad and the plastic wallet containing the photocopy of Clara Hemmingway's till receipt.

"Without going into specific details about the case we're working on, I wonder if you could identify the checkout assistant who served this customer last night. We have some questions that we need to ask them."

"Of course, I'd be pleased to help. Let me see." Taking out a small pair of reading glasses, the manager stared intently at the till receipt.

"Let me just look up which colleague dealt with this customer." Turning to his PC, he clicked the mouse a few times before rapidly typing out a series of numbers onto the keypad.

"Aha. Kevin Peterfield. He was logged onto the till."

"Is Mr Peterfield working today?"

A few more clicks of the mouse and Patel nodded.

"Yes, he started his shift about three hours ago. Would you like him to come in?"

"Yes, if you wouldn't mind. Hopefully it shouldn't take too long."

Patel picked up his phone, asking for someone to find Peterfield.

The two men passed the next couple of minutes in silence. As he concentrated Hastings became aware of the low-level hum of background noise surrounding him. Through the walls he could hear the tannoy system announcing three-for-two offers. Strange that they hadn't put an announcement over the speakers for Peterfield, he mused. As if reading his mind, Patel motioned with his head towards the shop floor.

"There's no point putting out a tannoy announcement for Kevin. Unless he's nipped off to the bathroom he should be sitting right at till number seven. Quicker just to walk down and collect him."

Hastings nodded and the two men settled back into silence. In the background, Gary could hear the whine of an electric motor and muffled voices shouting instructions. Probably a forklift in the warehouse, he guessed.

A few moments later, there was a knock at the door.

"Come in!"

A nervous-looking youth entered the room. Seeing Hastings, his eyes widened in curiosity, then worry when Hastings was introduced. For his part, Gary forced a smile. According to the manager, the kid was under eighteen. Why then did he look as if he could pass for Hastings' much older and bigger brother? He had to be six feet three and the five o'clock shadow that coloured his jowls looked a lot thicker than Hastings' fine stubble. Hastings shaved daily but rather in hope than expectation; once a week would probably have been sufficient.

"Don't worry, Kevin, you're not in any trouble. Take a seat. I just have a few questions about a customer that you served."

"Sure, anything I can do to help, Officer."

Even his voice was deeper and older-sounding than Gary's.

"According to the till receipts, last night you served this woman. Do you remember her?"

Hastings slid a headshot of Clara Hemmingway across the desk. Peterfield looked at it for a few seconds.

"Yeah, definitely. I can't remember the time, but I definitely remember her."

Hastings nodded encouragingly.

"What can you remember about her? Anything unusual? You must see hundreds of customers each shift — why do you remember her?"

Peterfield shifted in his seat, looking a little embarrassed. He glanced at Patel, who smiled tolerantly. He could probably guess why the teenager remembered her.

"Well, I remember her because she was kind of pretty, you know. It's a long shift and all the faces blur together after a while, but a couple stick in the memory."

"Fair enough. Anything else that you can remember? Anything at all? You never know how useful the smallest detail might be."

Peterfield blushed a bit, mumbling, "Yeah, she was wearing a bit of a low-cut top. You could see loads. And she had a tattoo on her tit... sorry, breast." He looked at Hastings, who remained stony-faced. "It was a rose or something. Left one, I think."

Well, that confirmed the ID, thought Hastings. The photo he'd shown Peterfield had been a headshot.

115

"Thinking back, what can you remember about her? What else was she wearing? Was she with anybody else?"

"I can't remember what else she was wearing."

Hastings hid a smile; typical seventeen-year-old lad. No way was he going to remember what Hemmingway was wearing below the waist. There was only one thing that was going to stick in his mind after such an encounter.

Screwing up his eyes as if to remember, Peterfield leaned back slightly in his chair.

"She was on her own, I do remember that. Trolley not basket. I think she used carrier bags rather than bags for life. She used her card, Chip and PIN. Hang on… Her name on the card was Clare or something."

"That's great, Kevin. Can I take your details in case I need to speak to you again?"

The boy nodded, probably figuring that a chance to see her again in a line-up was better than nothing.

After Peterfield had left, Patel turned to Hastings. "Well, Officer, if there is anything else that we can help you with, please don't hesitate to let us know."

It was clearly meant as a dismissal; it was after all a busy time of the day.

Hastings thought briefly; should he ask Patel to canvass any other members of staff for any other witnesses? It was probably better not to. This was Hemmingway's local supermarket; she was likely to be a regular customer. People might well get confused about the time or day that they had seen her and muddy the waters. Of course, there was one thing that didn't get confused and that was CCTV. A quick look to check that she was alone and that the times matched and he was done, he decided.

116

"There is one more thing."

Patel barely repressed a sigh.

"Do you have CCTV for the night in question?"

"Yes. The store is covered in cameras. We will have many hours of footage."

Hastings decided to take pity on the man.

"I'll speak to my guv to see if we need to pull in everything. In the meantime, could we just have a quick look to see what time she arrived and left and if she was on her own?"

Patel had clearly decided that there was no point arguing and that the sooner he co-operated, the sooner he could get rid of Hastings.

Motioning Gary out of his office and back down the narrow corridors, Patel led the young PC to another large, darkened room. In it sat a security guard, his eyes glued to a bank of half a dozen monitors, each with four changing views of the shop floor, car park and "backstage" areas.

Finding footage of Clara leaving was easy. The time stamp on the receipt clearly showed the time that she completed her transaction and locating it took seconds on the digital security system. She certainly had done a big shop, Hastings noted as she struggled out of the door, laden down with multiple bulging carrier bags. Her skimpy top did nothing to hide her cleavage from the overhead cameras, much to the delight of the bored guard, he imagined. He noted the time: 22:34h. One minute later than the time on the till receipt. Seemed about right, he figured.

"We can follow her backwards all around the store as she does her shop, if you like, but it'll take some time to set up the different feeds," offered the security guard, clearly welcoming the distraction.

"I'll keep that in mind and see what the guv says — just don't erase the footage. For the time being I just want to see what time she entered."

"No sweat, sonny. Can you give us a clue? It'll be quicker than just running the tape backwards 'til we find her."

Hastings looked at Patel.

"How quick do you think she could fill a trolley like this?"

Patel pursed his lips thoughtfully, clearly caught up in the investigation despite himself.

"Realistically, I'd say a minimum of twenty minutes, plus about seven or eight minutes to put it through the till."

Without being bidden, the security guard keyed in the command. The view shifted immediately. Running it backwards at four-times speed, it seemed to take for ever before a familiar flash of blonde hair appeared, walking into the store. At this angle, Hastings saw that the woman's coat hid her cleavage from the cameras. Bad luck, boys, he thought to himself.

Carefully noting the time, 21:41h, and that she was alone, Hastings thanked the staff for their help. He looked at the two times in his notepad: fifty-three minutes. She certainly took her time over her shopping, he thought.

After driving back to the station, he parked the car in the garage and went looking for DCI Jones. According to the desk sergeant, Jones was unavailable. Sitting down at his workstation, Hastings wrote up a short report, noting the positive ID, the time that she entered and left the store and that she was alone. Stealing a Post-it note from his neighbour's desk, he started to write a reminder to pick up the footage from the superstore.

Suddenly, his radio crackled into life with his call sign. Toggling it, he responded.

"Are you free, DC Hastings? Reports of a break-in at the Costcutter's on Bailey Street. You've attended before."

Hastings sighed. He certainly had attended before; three times before, as a matter of fact. The small shop and off-licence was a magnet for thieves and vandals, and old man Singh who owned the place practically had him on speed dial. CID were involved because they suspected that the culprits, who they had yet to positively link to the break-ins, operated on the periphery of a much bigger gang involved in large-scale thefts. The kids involved in the Costcutter break-ins were just local chancers, stealing alcohol and cigarettes to sell down the pub. The plan however was to catch them and use the threat of a conviction as leverage to get them to give information on the larger gang.

DCI Jones had asked that they lock down any other work and make the murder of Tunbridge their priority. Hastings mulled over his options. He had done what Jones had asked him to do at Tesco and written up the report. Popping over to see Mr Singh and arranging Scenes of Crime to dust for fingerprints wouldn't take long; then he could just add it to the file and worry about it again when the Tunbridge matter was resolved. Gary doubted that DCI Jones had meant for the lock-down to scupper ongoing investigations, and he knew that every time the kids broke in somewhere they potentially left behind the clues that might lead to their arrest.

Decision made, he trotted back down to the garage. He'd pick up the CCTV footage from Tesco later.

Chapter 12

After taking the call from Forensics, Jones and Sutton held a hurried strategy conference. Jones had already tipped off the Crown Prosecution Service's lawyers, briefing them on the evidence that they had and their proposed interview strategy. Whilst they did so, the desk sergeant went to wake up Severino and round up his solicitor and interpreter for a client meeting. Eventually the two police officers entered the interview suite.

Severino didn't look like a murderer — but then they rarely did. A twenty-eight-year-old of average height and build, with darkly Mediterranean good looks, he resembled a frightened child as he sat perched on the edge of his chair in the small interview room. His eyes were ringed with dark shadows and his waxy, pale complexion contrasted strongly with several days' worth of stubble. His hair was slightly too long and it was obviously a couple of days since its last wash. His breath smelt sour, a mixture of whiskey and stale vomit. Sutton set up the recording, whilst Jones eyed their suspect.

"Why am I here? My lawyer says I have been arrested for murder. How can this be?" Severino's English, although accented, was precise. Nevertheless, Jones decided against dismissing the translator just yet. The last thing he wanted was Severino's lawyer to claim his testimony was inadmissible because he didn't fully understand a question or he misspoke and inadvertently claimed to be "guilty".

Severino's lawyer, a young, earnest man who looked to be in his twenties, by the name of Daniel Stock, leant forward. "For the record, my client is unwell and was not in the clearest frame of mind when he was arrested. It is my belief that he was unable to understand his rights when read them at the time of his arrest. Anything he has said is therefore inadmissible."

It was true that Severino had been drunk and incapable at the time of his arrest, but the desk sergeant had read him his rights a couple of hours ago and the prisoner had been sober enough to request that the police arrange a solicitor for him. But since he had done nothing more incriminating than burp, puke and fart since his arrest that morning, Jones decided there was nothing to be gained by arguing the point.

"Firstly, the police surgeon has proclaimed Dr Severino fit enough to be questioned. Do you feel well enough to be interviewed?"

Although the young man was clearly fighting a brutal hangover, his desire to end the ordeal and get home was greater and he nodded his assent. Good, thought Warren, pleased that they wouldn't lose any advantage that Severino's illness might give them.

"Of course, I am happy to read Dr Severino his rights again." Jones recited the lines slowly and precisely, so that there could be no confusion, then reiterated what Severino was being accused of.

With the formalities over, it was time to get on with the questioning.

"What were you doing last night, Dr Severino, between about 9 p.m. and 10.30 p.m.?"

The young Italian licked his lips nervously, stealing a glance at his lawyer.

"Um, no comment," he said uncomfortably.

So that's the way it was going to be, thought Warren wearily. Severino's lawyer had clearly decided that with no evidence yet disclosed, his best advice was for the accused to keep quiet, avoiding the risk of incriminating himself.

"OK. Perhaps then you could tell us what your relationship is with Professor Alan Tunbridge?"

Again the young man looked at his lawyer, before repeating his previous response, "No comment." This time he seemed even less sure of himself and Warren felt a flicker of satisfaction. Despite his lawyer's recommendations, Severino's instincts were clearly telling him to speak up and end the interview sooner. Good, they could work on that inner conflict.

Warren leaned forward, feigning exasperation. "Oh, for goodness' sake. We know that you worked for Professor Tunbridge as one of his postdoctoral research assistants. If you can't even acknowledge something as easy for us to verify as that, we're in for a very long, very uncomfortable few days. So please, stop being silly and answer the questions, so we can all go home."

The doubt in Severino's eyes grew stronger, and he looked at his lawyer again, his eyes imploring. The young solicitor studiously avoided his gaze for fear of being accused of leading his client.

Sutton leant forward. "Look, son, we know all about Tunbridge. He shafted you over your job and then wouldn't let you write up any of your own research. Guy's a serious bully from what we've heard. We know all about you vandalising his car, but that isn't our concern. Call it karma; what goes around comes around, I say, but we need to know what happened last night. Tell us what you were doing between 9.30 and 10.30 p.m. and we can all go home."

Severino shook his head again; this time his "No comment" was almost inaudible.

Warren took over again. "Answering our questions at this stage can only help you, Antonio. If you can tell us where you were we can end all of this right now."

It was too much for Severino; his already pasty face turned bone-white and he clutched his stomach. Jones and Sutton pushed their chairs back quickly. Severino's lawyer wasn't quite as fast. With a loud groan, Severino vomited across the metal table, before turning to his lawyer to apologise, and doing the same thing again, all over the man's lap.

That pretty much concluded the interview, decided Jones as he called for a cleaner and offered a tissue to the hapless solicitor. They had until the following morning to charge Severino or apply for an extension. The young man was clearly conflicted. Perhaps a night of lonely contemplation would loosen his tongue. Who knew, they might even get a confession in time for the superintendent's press conference.

As they left the interview room they met DS Kent coming the other way. "How did it go?"

"Spilled his guts," deadpanned Sutton.

Chapter 13

Warren sat back in his leather chair. A tide of exhaustion swept over him now that the adrenaline of the day's events had finally subsided. He'd filled in the essential paperwork in record time and the rest of the bureaucratic make-work could safely be left another twenty-four hours, he judged. Glancing at his watch, he saw that it was now past six o'clock. With a sinking feeling, Warren knew that there was no way he could get to Cambridge for six-thirty for the start of the meal. Resigned to his fate, he called Susan's mobile.

"Oh, it's you. Susan's driving."

Warren closed his eyes briefly in pain. Bernice again.

"Hello, Bernice, I'm probably going to be late for the meal. Go ahead and order without me. I'm really sorry, but I'll be there as soon as I can."

A stony silence.

"I'll let her know." The line went dead.

Warren glanced at his watch, doing some quick arithmetic. If he took the A10, he would be going against the flow of the traffic. Most people would be leaving Cambridge now after a Saturday afternoon of shopping. The road was wide and long and he could probably get away with putting his foot down. Factoring in the time necessary to nip into a garage for a bunch of flowers, Warren reckoned he could get there in time for the main course.

Grabbing his jacket, he headed out of his small office towards the stairs.

"Ah, Warren."

Again!

"I was just getting ready for tomorrow morning's press conference. DS Kent tells me that Severino has confessed everything."

Warren blinked in surprise.

"Er, no, sir. He was 'no commenting', right up until the end when he was violently sick over his lawyer. I decided to terminate the interview. I thought I'd have another crack tomorrow morning."

"Then why did DS Kent say that…? Oh, I see, 'spilled his guts'. I must say, Warren, that joking about such a thing is a little unprofessional and has led to all sorts of confusion. I'll have to rewrite my speech now. By the sounds of things, we're essentially going to be repeating the statement I just released to the press half an hour ago."

Warren was too tired to correct his superior and pin the blame on Sutton for the misunderstanding. Besides which, he could hear the loud ticking of the clock in the super's office. "Sorry, sir. Won't happen again."

Running down to the car park, Warren jumped into his car, praying that no one else wanted to chat with him. The car's dashboard clock showed 18:25. As he pulled out onto the main road he flicked the radio on: Radio 4. He doubted that the superintendent's statement would have made it onto the national news, at least not for the half-hourly bulletins. Steering with one hand, Warren clumsily played with the auto-tune, looking for a local radio station. A sudden deafening blast of Wham! made him question yet again why he had to turn the volume up to twenty to hear Radio 4 clearly, yet all the way down to ten or less to avoid rupturing his eardrums when listening to Heart.

Finally, he found the local BBC station and suffered a few moments of a dreadful cover of an Elton John classic before the news headlines. Unsurprisingly, the murder was the top story. Warren was pleased to hear that the super had resisted the urge to spice up the statement too much, simply stating the facts, expressing the force's condolences and urging anyone with any information to come forward. The announcer then revealed that two men, believed to be former colleagues, had been assisting the police with their inquiries. This was followed by a brief statement from the university, which spoke of the shock of the loss of such a highly respected colleague and that he would be greatly missed, thus contradicting pretty much everything that Warren had been led to believe that morning.

Glancing at the clock again, Warren saw that it was still only twenty to seven. With any luck, he should make it in time to enjoy a quick plate of something before the show started. Relaxing a little, he retuned the radio to Heart; a guilty pleasure, their playlist reminded him of happy drunken nights in the students' union so many years before. Drumming his fingers on the steering wheel, he couldn't help humming along to the theme music to *Fame*. As he did so the tension seemed to drain out of him. His stomach rumbled and he started to fantasise about what he might have to eat. The restaurant was an Italian, he recalled, so something quick like a bowl of pasta. Meatballs would certainly fill the aching void. With lots of grated Parmesan. He glanced at the speedometer: sixty-five miles per hour. A bit over the limit, but not enough to get picked up. He decided to chance his arm a bit, since the road was so quiet, and edged up to seventy.

Pretty soon, however, it was time to ease back as the road started to wind through the quaint-sounding villages of this part of south Cambridgeshire. Soon enough he entered the village of Foxton and slowed to thirty, then watched in disbelief as the warning lights of the railway crossing started their amber flashing. He was too far away. Even if he dropped the car to second gear and floored it, he would probably be caught on CCTV as he skirted under the lowering barriers. He could imagine the headlines now: 'Police Chief Inspector Caught Dodging Trains at Level Crossing'. Christ, that was all he needed.

As he eased to a halt the barriers finally clanked into place. Now other headlines filled his mind, 'Police Chief Inspector Found Frozen to Death by Mother-in-law's Disapproving Stare' being the most prominent. Warren shook his head. Mother-in-law jokes? He must be tired. Drumming his fingers impatiently on the steering wheel, Warren prayed for an express train. A minute passed.

Nothing.

With a sigh, he turned the engine off, deciding that he might as well save some fuel.

Two minutes passed. The barrier was automatic, triggered by a passing train a couple of miles up the track. Unfortunately, the barriers didn't differentiate between a fast-moving express train and a slow-moving freight train, the latter taking much longer to pass through than the express, of course. Finally, the train arrived. Two locomotives hauling trucks laden with coal. It couldn't have been travelling at more than twenty miles per hour. No wonder, thought Warren as almost two minutes later the fortieth and final truck passed by. Warren restarted his engine.

Two minutes later he turned it off again. The alternating red lights remained stubbornly on, the barriers locked down. Eventually, a passenger train clanked past the barriers and into the station. Despite the train stopping past the crossing, leaving it clear, the barriers remained firmly in place. By now Warren was fantasising about ramming the barriers. In his mind's eye he replayed scenes from 1980s' TV shows, many of which featured reckless drivers either jumping over or smashing through level crossings without even scratching their paint.

Finally, the passenger train started off again, crawling out of the station. Warren resisted the urge to start the engine again, a brief flash of superstition suddenly convincing him that to do so would simply result in the barriers remaining down for another train. Finally, with almost no warning, the barriers started to lift. Warren restarted his engine and shot over the crossing.

He glanced at the clock. To his dismay, it was now gone seven and he had yet to buy any flowers and he still had to negotiate the Cambridge traffic. Entering the outskirts of the city, he sailed past the Trumpington Park and Ride. Even if he had the time to park up and wait for the bus, Warren had learnt the hard way that the park and ride was not designed for much more than afternoon shopping. He and Susan had decided to use it one Saturday but had then made the mistake of staying out on a whim for a quick bite to eat and an early-evening film at the leisure park. After waiting for thirty minutes in the rain opposite the sixth-form college, it soon became clear that the park and ride stopped running ridiculously early. A quick look on the internet had revealed a rather unpalatable choice between catching a regular bus to within a half mile or so of the park and ride then walking the rest of the way in the rain, or forking out fifteen quid for a cab to the car park. They chose the latter. The cab driver agreed with them that it was a farce and a disgrace, but seemed cheerful enough when they handed over their money.

Warren kept his eyes peeled, looking for a garage. Finally, he spotted one and pulled into the forecourt. A plastic bucket by the front door held a single bunch of flowers. Warren didn't know enough about flowers to even attempt to name the species, but he did know enough to see why these were the last bunch. Oh, well, beggars couldn't be choosers. Entering the garage to pay for the flowers, Warren finally accepted that he had missed any chance of a meal at the restaurant. The small shop had a tiny refrigerator filled with cans and bottles of drink. He selected a bottle of Diet Coke for the caffeine, although he was tempted to go the whole hog and risk palpitations from one of the so-called "energy drinks". The top shelf also held a couple of sandwiches and rolls. Picking through them, he saw that the selection included everything from mixed salad to ham and tomato and even coronation chicken, but no cheese, or something he could pick the crap off. The shelf below had a couple of Ginsters pasties — Spicy Chicken and Peppered Steak. Not even a Cornish or a cheese and onion slice. Warren's stomach rumbled loudly. In desperation, he turned to the snacks aisle. Finally, he settled on a couple of bags of crisps and a chocolate bar. As an afterthought, he also grabbed some strong mints to hide the smell of the crisps on his breath. Susan nagged him about his diet a lot. Since he'd met her, his palate had widened considerably; however, Susan would eat pretty much anything and just couldn't understand, try as she might, Warren's faddy tastes.

Back in the car, Warren texted Susan, telling her that he was in Cambridge and would meet her at the Corn Exchange, before setting off again. Warren disliked driving in Cambridge. The roads were narrow and the one-way system had no apparent logic. Added to that the seemingly endless roadworks and Warren could see why the park and ride, despite its limited running times, was so popular. Warren decided to follow the signs for the Grand Arcade car park, since that was the closest to the theatre. As ever, Warren kept his eyes firmly glued to the road, watching out for foreign students looking the wrong way when crossing and suicidally arrogant cyclists meandering from lane to lane without signalling.

Somehow, Warren made it into the car park without any mishaps. He was exhausted. He tried to calculate how many hours he'd spent awake out of the past forty-eight, but his brain was too tired to process the calculation. He had a few minutes to spare and so devoured the crisps and chocolate bar. Temporarily sated, his stomach stopped rumbling for what seemed like the first time in hours. Unscrewing the bottle of Diet Coke, he chugged half of it before finally grabbing the flowers, locking the car and heading for the theatre.

Warren arrived at the Corn Exchange at a quarter to eight. Pulling out his phone, he saw that he had just missed a text from Susan.

'Inside. Your ticket's at the box office.'

No name or kisses. Damn, Susan must be pissed off, he realised. He'd hoped to at least make his apologies outside before going into the theatre, but never mind. Queuing impatiently, he finally retrieved his ticket.

Glancing at the stub to remind himself what they were seeing, he realised that the show's name meant nothing to him. He couldn't tell if it was a comedy, a play or even a musical. Declining the offer of an exorbitantly priced programme from the young girl at the door to the auditorium, Warren made his way into the dimmed theatre. Whatever the play was, it was clearly popular. Almost every seat was filled. Naturally, his seat was in the middle of the row. Apologising profusely, he squeezed his way between the narrow seating, almost standing on Dennis' foot, before finally reaching his seat. He was sandwiched between Susan and Bernice. At his arrival, he saw Susan relax. "Sorry," he mouthed before turning to Bernice. "Happy birthday, Bernice, sorry I missed the meal." He offered the flowers to her and pecked her proffered cheek.

His mother-in-law had decided to go with what Warren privately termed her "Onassis" look. A sharply tailored suit and bouffant hairdo, which accentuated her enviable figure. In all fairness to the woman, she was still elegantly attractive and could pass for ten years younger than her actual age. If Susan maintained her looks half as well as her mother had, Warren would count himself a lucky man. A faint whiff of Chanel No 5 completed the ensemble.

The subdued lighting glinted off a pair of large earrings. With sudden inspiration, Warren decided on a gamble. "Are those new earrings, Bernice? They go well with your new haircut."

Miracle of miracles, Bernice actually smiled. "Yes, dear, Dennis bought me them. I'm glad you could make it."

"I'm sorry I'm so late. I'll fill you in on everything when we get home. You'll get to hear it before I give my press conference," It was a shameless exaggeration, but it worked. Bernice looked impressed.

Suddenly, the lights dimmed and music erupted from the orchestra pit. Warren quickly sat down next to Susan. She held his arm and whispered into his ear, "Smooth operator, DCI Jones." Warren simply smiled and kissed her on the lips.

Susan frowned slightly. "Cheese and Onion or Prawn Cocktail?"

* * *

On his way out of the theatre, Warren looked frantically for somebody selling a souvenir programme. Within two minutes of the curtain going up, the day's stresses and strains had finally beaten him and he'd fallen sound asleep. He assumed that he hadn't snored, otherwise Susan would have woken him up. He had no idea if Bernice had noticed. Nevertheless, he was determined not to get caught out by a grilling on the content of the show when he got home.

No sellers were to be seen. Typical, he thought, they were practically forcing them on you on the way in. Warren made a mental note of the name of the play, deciding to do a quick Google search before driving home tonight. A basic familiarity with the plot and the parroting of a few reviews should let him bluff his way out of any awkwardness. Susan and Bernice were excitedly discussing what they had just seen, so, to play it safe, Warren tried to engage his father-in-law in conversation.

It was like trying to interrogate a Trappist monk, he soon decided. It was a ten-minute stroll to the car park, during which time Warren ascertained that, yes, the garden was growing well; no, the recent dry spell hadn't done the lawn any favours but the hosepipe was compensating, and no, Dennis didn't think the England cricket team's recent performance was a promise of the beginning of a new golden age for the English game.

Finally, they reached the car park. Bernice and Susan got into her car on the ground floor. "Why don't you go with Warren, dear? Susan and I have things to talk about."

Just great, thought Warren, no chance for a crafty Internet search to swot up on the play. Still, the look on Susan's face suggested that she wasn't looking forward to the drive home with her mother either. Warren had a feeling that the subject of grandchildren, or rather lack of, was probably on the agenda.

Susan's decisions to marry a police officer and become a Biology teacher — in a comprehensive school of all things — were perhaps less of a disappointment than her apparent unwillingness to produce a grandchild. Moments before the phone had rung the previous night, Bernice had been rummaging in her oversized handbag for the newest collection of photographs from her latest visit to Susan's remarkably fecund younger sister, Felicity. This had almost certainly been the prologue to an uncomfortable discussion in which Bernice would have reminded Susan that she wasn't getting any younger. Warren experienced a brief stab of guilt at the relief he felt that he had been spared that conversation.

As for Felicity, married barely three years, baby number three had arrived only a few weeks ago. There was no suggestion that Felicity had married beneath her station; her husband Jeff was an investment banker in London earning at least ten times Warren and Susan's salaries combined. So impressed was Bernice by this that the fact that the couple's first child was born considerably less than nine months after their wedding was never discussed.

No, he'd rather take his chances with Dennis, he decided.

After waving the women off, Dennis and Warren climbed another flight of stairs to Warren's car. Getting in, Warren decided he might as well do some fishing, to see if he could gain some idea as to what they'd just seen. "So what did you think of the play, Dennis?"

The older man grunted. "Not a bloody clue, lad. I slept right through it."

SUNDAY

Chapter 14

For a second morning, Warren swatted the alarm clock's off button at six-thirty. He groaned. He'd gone to bed relatively early the night before. After arriving home from the theatre, the four-some had enjoyed a leisurely nightcap, before retiring shortly before midnight. Bernice had been impressed when Warren had related the events of the previous twenty-four hours. Even Dennis had ventured an opinion, commenting on the speed with which they had tracked down Tunbridge's suspected killer. Warren had apologised in advance for missing church the following morning and warned that, depending on how the day's events played out, he might not be back until late. That her son-in-law would be giving a press conference the next morning was enough to appease Bernice, who he suspected would be phoning her friends as soon as it aired to get them to watch it. In reality, Warren doubted that he would be saying anything. John Grayson would be the one to take the limelight — he'd probably even wear his uniform. Besides which, if Severino didn't hurry up and confess, there wouldn't be too much limelight to go around. He'd deal with Bernice's disappointment at his small role when the time came.

Despite his weariness, however, Warren hadn't been able to sleep. As he had lain awake, listening to the snores from the guest room, his mind had buzzed with doubts.

Foremost was the nagging thought that it seemed too easy. True, most murders were uncomplicated affairs, but this one wasn't. Severino hadn't just stuck a knife in Tunbridge on a street corner or strangled him in a fit of jealous rage. He'd gone into the university late at night, snuck up behind his victim, bludgeoned him and slit his throat. It wasn't a crime of passion per se. And how had he known that Tunbridge would be in his office so late? Was that normal behaviour for the professor? And what about the evidence? At first glance, it looked pretty damning, but on the other hand Forensics had yet to find any of Tunbridge's blood on Severino, whilst the CCTV images were far from conclusive.

Assuming that Severino was the murderer, was he working alone? Tunbridge had been a pretty obnoxious individual — could this have been a team effort?

Other small questions also worried away at Warren's confidence. Mark Crawley had been cagey when interviewed and both Spencer and Hemmingway had struck Warren as not entirely forthcoming.

Ultimately, Warren knew that the charging of Severino would only be the first step. The case was messy and they had to clean up a dozen and one loose ends before the case came to trial. Unfortunately, no prosecution was perfect. Life just wasn't like that; there would always be a few unexplained facts. Warren's job now was to make sure that none of those facts would trip them up in court and lose them the conviction.

As he had finally drifted off to sleep, Warren had been haunted by one last image. The look of uncomprehending fear in Severino's eyes just before he threw up, ending the interview. Was it the look of a guilty man who had just been caught, or the look of an innocent man facing his worst nightmare?

After a shower and shave, Warren tiptoed quietly downstairs.

He'd put on his best suit and smartest tie. His dress uniform remained in the wardrobe in a plastic suit carrier. Unlike some officers, Warren believed that, now he was in CID, the uniform should remain for purely ceremonial occasions and a conference to update the press on the progress of a murder case hardly counted, he felt. His lesson learnt from the day before, Warren quickly made some sandwiches and grabbed several pieces of fruit. Despite Susan's nagging he'd never really been a breakfast person, but this morning he was ravenous, his paltry diet from the previous day having left its mark. Not willing to risk slopping milk down his suit and tie, Warren settled for toast and marmalade and a slug of orange juice, tucking a tea towel into his lapel to catch any crumbs.

Warren arrived at the station at the same time as Severino's solicitor. In the early morning sun, Stock looked even younger to Warren. He drove a battered, twelve-year-old Vauxhall Corsa and his trousers weren't an exact match for his suit jacket — the same suit jacket he had been wearing the day before when his client had vomited in his lap. The two men exchanged a cordial good morning, then separated as they entered the police station, Warren heading up to his office, the young solicitor to the reception desk to announce his presence and get a visitor's pass.

Warren's office was pretty much as he had left it the previous night, with the exception of a number of scribbled messages, including several different ones from the numerous divisions within Welwyn's forensic department that were assisting on the case. Warren decided to deal with them later in the morning after he and Sutton had their first go at cracking Severino. Besides which, it wasn't even eight on a Sunday morning, he could spend hours playing voicemail tennis before tracking down what he wanted — he might as well wait until a more civilised hour.

The final note confirmed that CCTV from Tesco corroborated Clara Hemmingway's alibi. Warren made a note to remove her from the suspects board.

At 8 a.m., Sutton poked his head around the door. "Morning, guv. Good night out with the in-laws?" Jones' grunt said all that needed to be said.

"How we going to play this, then?"

"I'm not in the mood for pissing about this morning. Let's just haul him in, give him a chance to confess if he wants to, then turn up the heat. The super wants to give a press conference at eleven. If Severino confesses first thing, we'll charge him and announce it at the conference. Otherwise, we'll just keep the press dangling. Regardless, I want him charged by this evening at the latest, and in front of the magistrate tomorrow morning."

Sutton nodded his approval. "Sounds like a plan, Chief. I'll ring downstairs and get them to bring him in."

Chapter 15

By eight-fifteen, the two detectives were ready to start again. The custody sergeant had led Severino and his lawyer back into the interview suite a few minutes earlier. Their client conference had finished and they were now waiting for the interview to recommence. Sutton and Jones stood outside the room sipping coffee. "No rush, Tony. Why don't we let Dr Severino soak up the ambience of the room?"

Sutton smiled. "Seems only fair considering his contribution to that ambience." Warren had already been in the room to check the PACE voice recorder was working correctly. The pungent smell of bleach almost, but not quite, masked the smell of stale vomit from the previous day's interview. He doubted it would help the accused's frame of mind. Good.

Finally, after crumpling his cup and tossing it in a nearby bin, Warren led the way into the room. "Sorry," he apologised insincerely. "Urgent business."

A more experienced solicitor would have recognised the officer's tardiness for what it was — a crude attempt to unnerve his client. Although unable to do anything about it, he would have at least shot a scowl in the officer's direction. Severino's lawyer simply looked slightly bemused. Underneath the harsh fluorescent lighting, the mismatch between the solicitor's jacket and trousers was even more obvious. Warren felt a slight twinge of sympathy for the young man, quickly suppressed. As a newly qualified solicitor he was probably earning little more than a probationary constable, with the added burden of thousands of pounds of student debt. The chances were he only had the one work suit. This could well be his first serious case.

Good, thought Warren, pushing the sympathy aside, that'd make their job easier.

After starting the tape recorder, enquiring after the accused's health and reminding him that he was still under caution, they started in again. As before, the interpreter sat mutely in the corner, her services not needed.

"Dr Severino, as we said yesterday, it would greatly help us if you could confirm your whereabouts between 9.30 and 10.30 p.m. on Friday the twelfth of August."

"No comment," answered the young man, this time more confidently. Clearly, his lawyer had explained to him that with no evidence disclosed he should continue to make no comment.

We'll soon rattle that cage, thought Warren.

Opening his briefcase, he pulled out a glossy A4 print and pushed it across the table to Severino and his lawyer.

"DCI Jones is showing the accused an image, taken from CCTV cameras in the lobby of the University of Middle England's Biological Sciences building. The image shows a figure in a grey hoodie entering the building at 21:35 hours on August twelfth — approximately the time that post-mortem analysis indicates Professor Tunbridge was murdered. A second image—" he slid it across the table "—shows the same figure leaving the building via the same door at 22:10 hours, this time carrying what appears to be a large black plastic bag. We have reason to believe that the person on these images is Dr Antonio Severino before and after he murdered Professor Tunbridge."

Severino blanched again, what little colour there was in his cheeks immediately disappearing, although to everyone's relief he showed no indication that he was feeling sick.

He looked at his lawyer, clearly unsure what to do. His lawyer was unable to request a break for a conference, that being the responsibility of the accused. Nevertheless, there were ways around that and, inexperienced as he was, he was practised in those basic tricks. "I would just like to remind my client that he is under no obligation to answer any questions and that he can ask for a break to speak to his legal representative at any time."

Picking up on the massive hint, Severino requested the break.

* * *

Standing down the corridor, away from curious ears, Sutton and Jones held a hurried meeting of their own.

"Bloke's clearly shitting himself," opined Sutton. "I reckon if we keep to the game plan we might even get a confession. As long as he can keep his breakfast down." He smiled wolfishly.

Warren couldn't help a small smile himself. "I hope for his poor lawyer's sake that he does — where the hell can you get dry-cleaning done on a Sunday?"

Sutton grinned. "Doesn't matter, guv. This time of year, all of the major supermarkets are flogging school uniforms. Probably be cheaper for him to buy new."

The two men were still chuckling when Severino's lawyer signalled they were ready to restart the interview.

* * *

The moment that they were all seated and the voice recorder restarted, Severino's lawyer went on the attack. "This is nonsense, officers. My client denies categorically that this picture is of him. In terms of physical appearance, that individual is right in the middle of the bell-curve. Half the men in Middlesbury could be in that photo, myself included. If that's the best you've got, I demand that my client be released without charge immediately."

Warren ignored the man's bluster. "Tell me, Antonio, how would you describe your relationship with Professor Tunbridge? We know that the two of you had a big argument recently and that there were issues surrounding you writing up your research for publication. What were your feelings towards him?"

Severino's lips clamped tight. "No comment," he managed.

Now it was Sutton's turn. "If that person shown entering the building isn't you, Antonio, perhaps you could help us all by telling us where you were that night?"

Severino shook his head.

Warren again. "I think you won't tell us where you were Friday night because you *can't* tell us where you were. I think that picture is of you." Severino continued to shake his head. "Tell me, Antonio, where did you do your first degree?"

The Italian blinked in surprise at the non sequitur, answering without thinking, "University Trieste, in Italy."

Warren nodded, sliding another picture across the table.

"This, I believe, is the logo of the University of Trieste, just here above the left breast on the hoody that you are wearing." The image enhancement was blurry but clear enough for a positive identification.

"It's a little clearer here on the baseball cap."

Severino's eyes bulged. "No, there must be some mistake."

"How many people in Middlesbury do you think own a University of Trieste hoodie and baseball cap, Dr Severino?"

"That's circumstantial at best, DCI Jones," interjected Stock before his client could answer.

Warren ignored the interruption. "Tell me, Dr Severino, if this person, who looks like you and is dressed in your old university's hoodie, is not you and is in fact somebody else — then why did they swipe into and out of the building using your swipe card?" He thrust the annotated printout from university Security at Severino and his lawyer.

Warren generously decided to interpret Severino's strangled squawk as a request for a break and client conference. For the first time since they had started the process, Warren saw doubt in Daniel Stock's eyes. *That's good news for us*, he thought with satisfaction. When even your own solicitor didn't believe you, maybe it was time to think about cutting a deal.

* * *

Unfortunately, it wasn't going to be as simple as cutting a deal. When Sutton and Jones re-entered the room, Stock again went on the attack.

"This evidence is purely circumstantial, detectives, and I again request that my client be allowed to go free. You are coming perilously close to the twenty-four-hour detention limit. Either charge him or release him."

"We've plenty of time, Mr Stock," answered Warren pleasantly. "Now, Dr Severino, we can easily clear all of this up. Where were you on Friday night?"

Severino was slumped in his chair. He looked exhausted. Friday night's excesses, followed by almost twenty-four hours in a police cell, had clearly taken their toll.

"I was at home, watching TV."

"I see, and can anyone confirm that, Dr Severino? Was anyone with you at the time?"

He shook his head. "No, I was alone."

Warren nodded in satisfaction.

Good, no alibi.

"So, you have no alibi and the building's entry log registered your swipe card being used around the time of the murder. Tell me how that could happen if that isn't you on the CCTV?"

"No. There must be some mistake. I have not been into the university for at least a month. I don't even know where my swipe card is."

At a silent signal from Jones, Sutton took over. "Ah, yes, tell us about that. Why haven't you been to work for a month?"

Severino looked discomfited. "I have been working from home, finishing up before my contract runs out and I start a new job."

"Really? Where is that new job? I heard that the University of Leicester had turned you down." It was a calculated risk, since Jones had only Crawley's impression to go on. Severino swallowed hard. "I have applied for a few different posts," he tried weakly.

Jones glanced again at Sutton, who took the cue and leant forward slightly. "Look, we know that's you on the footage — why did you decide to go into the university? Did you want to speak to Tunbridge? See if you could get your old job back? Or a better reference maybe? As I said before, we all know what a bastard Tunbridge was and we know how he held your career in his hands. I imagine you wanted to try and reason with him in private when you knew that nobody is listening."

Severino shook his head vigorously. "I did not go into university Friday night. I stayed at home, watched some TV, had a drink, a bit of puff then fell asleep. Next thing I remember, the doorbell is ringing and you are standing at my door."

The lawyer spoke up. "My client is innocent. The evidence that you have shown is circumstantial. Your case seems to rest on nothing more than an inability to provide an alibi, a motive that from what I hear is shared by half the university to a greater or lesser degree, and some poor quality CCTV images that show nothing of any value at all. As for the swipe-card evidence, my client has not been into the university for over a month. Who knows what has happened to his swipe card?

"By my watch, you have less than two hours to charge or release my client."

Warren shook his head, reaching inside his jacket pocket. "Not quite. Detective Superintendent Grayson has agreed to my request for a further twelve hours' detention. Don't go anywhere, Mr Stock — this isn't over yet."

Chapter 16

Leaving Severino to stew a bit, Jones jogged up to Grayson's office to discuss the upcoming press conference. As he'd predicted, Grayson had taken the opportunity to dig out his dress uniform. To be fair to the man, a small police unit such as Middlesbury didn't get to make these sorts of announcements very often, so Warren couldn't really blame him for milking his fifteen minutes of fame — fifteen seconds by the time it was edited.

Grayson had two different sheets of paper on his desk. He gestured at them. "Which one do I use, Warren? The one that describes how we have just charged Professor Tunbridge's murderer; or the one where I feed the gentlemen of the press the exact same thing we gave them yesterday evening?"

It was a loaded question and an unfair one. Grayson had insisted on scheduling a press conference before he knew if they were ready to charge or not; frankly, Warren had no sympathy for him. Nevertheless, Warren's desire for self-preservation kicked in and he bit his tongue. "Short and sweet, guv, I'm afraid. Maybe we'll have something later for tomorrow's papers."

Grayson's grunt spoke volumes.

* * *

The press conference was held at Hertfordshire's headquarters in Welwyn Garden City, a forty-minute drive normally. Of course, one of the advantages of being a detective superintendent was access to the pool of police drivers and their high-speed cars. Sergeant Kearns was only too pleased to take a break from stopping speeding motorists and do a little speeding of his own down the A1. Consequently, the journey took little more than twenty-five minutes. This was clearly something that Grayson was accustomed to. Warren was somewhat less sanguine about the drive and he hoped the marks where his fingernails had dug into his palms wouldn't be too obvious.

The room was set up by the book, with a table at the front covered in blue drop cloths. Behind the table tall poster boards featured the force's insignia, plus an array of telephone numbers and web addresses. Superintendent Grayson sat centre, flanked by Jones on his right and the force's press liaison officer on his left.

In front of the three officers a bank of bright lights had been set up for the TV cameras. Grayson was wearing make-up, Jones noticed with a jolt, before wondering if he should be also. Memories of a recent TV documentary showing Richard Nixon sweating heavily, with five o'clock shadow, opposite a seemingly cool and collected John F. Kennedy came to mind. Warren pushed away the uncomfortable comparison and looked out. Behind the lights sat several rows of chairs, about half occupied by reporters. Most were busy tapping away on their mobile phones, looking bored.

Eventually, the clock ticked around to eleven and Grayson started the conference. After thanking all those present for attending, he extended the force's condolences to the family and loved ones of Professor Tunbridge. It had been decided that an appearance by the grieving widow wasn't really necessary, since they had a suspect and plenty of leads.

He briefly introduced Warren, before outlining the facts of the case and that a twenty-eight-year-old man was helping them with their enquiries. In response to a question from a local journalist, Grayson confirmed that they had applied for an extension to interview him longer. Warren had to admire the man's panache; by giving Severino's age and confirming that he had had his detention extended, Grayson had implied, without saying as much, that they had a suspect and were probably going to charge him.

The press asked a few more questions, most of which were politely rebuffed, given that it was an ongoing investigation. Warren had attended many of these press conferences but this was the first time he had ever been involved in one as a participant — albeit a rather inactive one. He was struck as always by how much of the whole exercise was a well-rehearsed game. The police knew precisely what they were prepared to give out and the press, courtesy of the briefing sheet distributed to everyone in the room, knew exactly what the police wanted them to know. The questions from the floor, with the hastily scribbling journalists, were nothing more than a show for the cameras. The public expected their press to ask certain questions and so they obliged. Everyone was happy.

By twenty past eleven, everything was over. After another high-speed race up the motorway, Jones was deposited back at Middlesbury station and left to get on with his work for the day. Grayson, for his part, jumped straight into his own car, still wearing his dress uniform, and left in a cloud of dust, instructing Warren through the Mercedes' open window to keep him posted on any breakthroughs, adding, "Have a good weekend," as an afterthought.

And you too, Boss, Warren added silently in his head, before trudging back into the station to continue his working day. The security door had barely swung closed behind him, when DS Kent appeared, slightly out of breath.

"Chief, Forensics are on the line from Severino's house. We've got the bastard."

Chapter 17

Sutton and Jones fought to maintain their calm outward appearances as they recalled Severino to the interview suite. They had deliberately not said anything to his lawyer about what time they expected to recommence the interview and knew it was likely that he would be hungry and bad-tempered by now. After concluding their latest client conference, Severino had returned to his cell and his lawyer to the small waiting room reserved for family and solicitors. The room consisted of four badly plastered walls, one with a scenic view of the next-door hotel's recycling bins. The posters on the wall were the usual Home Office approved notices about preventing crime, dealing with alcohol and drug problems and reporting domestic abuse. Between them, the posters contained enough words to keep a moderately literate adult occupied for two minutes at most.

By happy coincidence, the room had a clear mobile phone signal, but no 3G signal. After about forty minutes the desk sergeant, who could keep an eye on the room from his post at the building's entrance, reported that Stock had apparently phoned or texted everyone that he knew, given up on trying to get a strong enough 3G signal to surf the web and was now sitting, staring into space, with a look of utter boredom on his face.

He'll learn, thought Warren with amusement. The job of a police representative was to wait around. More experienced solicitors never went anywhere without their briefcases, which always contained something to read and something to eat.

"Why did you murder Professor Tunbridge Friday night, Dr Severino?" started Jones, back in the increasingly claustrophobic interview room. As intended, the question jolted Severino, who flushed red. Before he could answer, his lawyer stepped in.

"Hold on, Chief Inspector. It has yet to be established that my client had anything to do with the murder on Friday night."

Jones inclined his head slightly as if conceding a point. "You've had some time to reflect upon your situation, Dr Severino, and I wonder if you have perhaps come to any decisions about confessing to Professor Tunbridge's murder?"

Severino shook his head emphatically and his lawyer looked relaxed. Warren hid a smile at the young man's inexperience.

"DCI Jones, my client maintains that he is an innocent man and that the evidence you present is poor at best. I again ask you to release my client without charge and stop this foolish charade." The young man was trying to out-bluster experienced CID officers. It wasn't going to happen.

"If you are innocent as you say, Dr Severino, could you please explain why we found these stuffed down a drain at the back of your house?" Warren pushed over the glossy A4 photographs and sat back in satisfaction. The look of horror and muttered, "Shit!" from Severino's lawyer, Daniel Stock, would probably be the highlight of his week, decided Warren.

* * *

The telephone call from Forensics had been better than Jones could have hoped for. Although the inside of the house had yielded little in the way of evidence, it confirmed that Severino had certainly partied hard the night before. The coffee table in the lounge had been covered with the empty trays from ready meals, several days' worth at least, and two near-empty bottles, one of vodka, one of whiskey. The overflowing ashtray was home to the nub ends of several joints. Small wonder he had looked so ill when they had arrested him, Jones thought with a small amount of satisfaction. The house's décor supported the story that Severino shared it with his fiancée. However, there was no sign of her and the neighbours claimed not to have seen her for a fortnight. To Warren's experienced eyes and those of the even longer-serving Crime Scene Manager, the state of the flat suggested Severino had been slumming it on his own for a couple of weeks. It was unlikely, albeit not impossible, that the house would be in such a state if he was sharing it with his fiancée.

However, it was when the investigators moved outside that they found what they were looking for. Stuffed down a drain, the manhole cover clearly moved recently, was a black plastic bin bag similar to that carried in the hand of the mystery person caught on CCTV leaving the Biology building immediately after Tunbridge's murder. Inside, the bag contained a heavily bloodstained white lab coat with "A Severino — Tunbridge Group" written on the collar in indelible ink; wrapped up inside this were a pair of similarly stained jeans and a hoodie, just like that worn by the person caught on camera. In the bottom of the bag were a pair of bloody latex gloves, some plastic overshoes and finally — the pièce de résistance — a blood-encrusted scalpel.

The bag had immediately been dispatched to Welwyn for

DNA typing and a more thorough forensic analysis, but high-resolution photographs had been sent directly to Middlesbury CID for their use. Jones had printed these out on glossy A4 paper before going down to meet Severino.

* * *

After dropping their bombshell on the young Italian and his even younger lawyer, Warren and Sutton left the briefing room as they requested yet another client conference.

Sutton was jubilant, clearly on an adrenaline high. "Did you see the look on that young kid's face?" he crowed, rubbing his hands together. "He's thinking that any dreams he may have had of making his name overturning some great big miscarriage of justice have just gone up in a puff of smoke. I bet he even believed Severino!"

Warren smiled slightly, finding his colleague's mood hard to resist. "Don't get too carried away, Tony. Plenty of slips between the cup and the lip. Even if he throws in the towel and admits his guilt now, we have a lot of work to do to make sure the case holds together."

Sutton barely seemed to hear him as he downed the last of his cold coffee, grimacing slightly. "How long do you reckon we've got to wait?"

"Not too long. Either he cops to it right away or he tries to brazen it out. Regardless, we've done our bit. Let's charge him and get him in front of Stevenage Magistrates first thing tomorrow morning."

In the end, it took little more than twenty minutes before Stock signalled that the client conference was over.

Warren made sure that the PACE recorder was working before settling back into his chair. He and Sutton stared silently at Severino, knowing that the accused would speak first.

"I know nothing of those items or why they were down my drain. I know nothing about the death of Alan Tunbridge."

"The evidence would suggest otherwise, Dr Severino. I am therefore formally charging you with the murder of Professor Alan Tunbridge on August the twelfth of this year. Do you understand what I have just said?"

The young man nodded, numbly, muttering an affirmative. With that, there was nothing else to be said. Jones and Sutton left the accused and his lawyer in the cold, little room as the custody sergeant entered, ready to return him to his cell. Leaving through the empty doorway, Jones glanced back. The young man was now weeping floods of silent tears, his shoulders shaking as he fought to keep his sobs inside. Next to him, his lawyer sat uncomfortably, clearly unsure exactly what to say. His tutors at university had doubtless drilled him in the legal procedures that he would now need to follow on behalf of his client, but Warren doubted that they had given him much in the way of training for how to deal with a young man, almost the same age, breaking down as he contemplated spending the next few decades behind bars. The custody sergeant remained impassive; he'd seen it all before and his sympathy was limited.

As he left the interview room Warren knew that he wouldn't feel any elation until after the court case was concluded. Even then, he knew that it would be tempered by the knowledge that one person was dead and a young man's life ruined, along with the family and friends of both men. Nevertheless, he was unprepared for the strange detachment that he felt as he looked back at the scene. Something didn't quite sit right, he decided.

Chapter 18

By early evening, Warren had finished the paperwork from charging Severino. The Italian was due in front of Stevenage Magistrates court, charged with murder, first thing in the morning. He stretched and yawned, taking a masochistic enjoyment from the cracking and crunching coming from his stretching vertebrae. Reaching for his phone to warn Susan he'd be home soon, he almost knocked it off the desk in surprise when it rang underneath his outstretched hand; glancing at the caller ID he saw it was an internal call from the desk sergeant. "Crime Scene Manager Andy Harrison from Welwyn's Forensic Unit is here to see you, sir."

Warren blinked in surprise. He hadn't expected a personal visit, least of all this late on a Sunday. "Send him up please, Sergeant."

A few moments later the forensics investigator was making himself comfortable in Warren's visitor chair. The man was a short, rotund middle-aged man with a shock of unruly greying hair. No longer in his paper suit, he was currently dressed more like a builder rather than a skilled, expert scientist, wearing faded denim jeans, battered trainers and a tightly fitting green T-shirt proclaiming that 'Nerds Rock'. Mentally, Warren chastised himself, remembering a debate with Susan about what a 'scientist' should look like and how young children, particularly girls, still thought of scientists as stuffy, white, middle-class men.

Stuffy was not a description that would immediately apply to Harrison, Warren soon decided. The man had a booming Yorkshire accent and a face that seemed constantly on the verge of breaking into a smile. His choice of verbal language was in stark contrast to the formal, medico-legal jargon that the reports he handed Jones were written in.

"I hope that our preliminary findings were useful to you," Harrison started after the two men exchanged pleasantries.

"Just what we needed," Warren assured him. "It was plenty enough to charge him and probably get him denied bail when he appears in court tomorrow. I assume that you've come to deliver the full story now?" Harrison nodded his agreement, fishing a pair of reading glasses out of his top pocket.

"No great surprises from the autopsy," he started. "I popped over to watch and it were largely as you thought. It seems his attacker walloped him from behind with that bloody great piece of rock. Hair and blood from the rock match the victim and a compressed fracture at the back of the skull matches the shape. Minuscule fragments of rock embedded in the poor bugger's skull match the rock type.

"Apparently the rock was a souvenir from the University of Boulder in Colorado, where the late professor spent a couple of years. Mark Crawley reckons it's sat on the shelf above the door as long as he's known him. It's certainly dusty enough.

"From the angle of the impact, we would suggest that he was originally sitting with his back to the door, leaning over his laptop. Either he didn't hear his attacker enter in time to turn around, or was expecting them so didn't look to see who had come in."

"So was that enough to kill him?"

"Not outright, obviously, or he wouldn't have been squirting

158

like a fire hose when his throat was cut. It would almost certainly have severely stunned him and there is evidence of some brain damage. He could easily have died at a later time from the blow."

"So what happened next?"

"Tunbridge was on a swivelling office chair. It was rotated anti-clockwise away from his laptop; about forty degrees or so, presumably so that the attacker, who we think was standing to his right having entered the office from that side, was now directly behind him."

Harrison jumped to his feet. "Could you sit in this chair, sir? It's easier to show than explain."

Feeling slightly self-conscious, Warren got up and sat down in his visitor's chair. Harrison moved behind him, plucking a pen from the desk tidy. It reminded Warren somewhat of Saturday morning trips to the barber with his father as a child.

"The weapon found at the scene was a scalpel. The blood matches, as does the shape of the cut. It was probably taken from an opened packet we found in the consumables cupboard in the lab."

Leaning over, he placed his left arm across Warren's shoulder and chest, gripping the top of the chair; the effect was like a seatbelt. Holding the pen in his right hand, he placed it along the left side of Warren's throat, pressing gently into the artery pulsing below the skin. Suddenly the happy memories of Saturday mornings listening to Motown music on Radio 2 and looking at ancient car magazines, whilst his father had his weekly crew cut, no longer seemed as cosy to Warren.

"Contrary to what you see in the movies, slitting a man's throat ain't easy. Stunning him probably made it easier than if he were kicking and screaming, but still it's not a task for the faint-hearted.

The placement of the cuts was very precise. They sliced the left carotid, then continued across the windpipe." He moved the pen accordingly. "Then dug in and found the right carotid. It was a single stroke, although not necessarily extremely fast."

Warren processed the thought for a moment. "I can see how that would work, but surely that would leave Tunbridge facing away from the door? And wouldn't he have sprayed blood away from his attacker?"

Harrison agreed. "Exactly. At some point after the cut and whilst he was still pumping blood heavily, Tunbridge's chair was turned clockwise to face the door, covering his attacker in blood."

"Why?"

Harrison shrugged. "A little beyond my remit, sir. It's possible that Tunbridge gave a few death kicks, or even that the attacker let go with his left arm mid-swipe — perhaps his nerve failed when the blood started pumping — and the swiping action turned the chair back around in the direction of the cut. He might just be a real sick puppy who wanted to look his victim in the face — some sort of messed-up dramatic shit he saw on late-night TV.

"Either way, it wouldn't have lasted long. Bleeding out from both carotids takes only a few seconds. You can see from the colour of his skin that there wasn't much left. No question it was the cause of death. The rest of the PM didn't throw up any surprises." He picked up a sheet of paper and started reciting the findings. "A moderately healthy man in his mid-fifties, about what we'd expect for a middle-aged desk worker. Preliminary blood tox shows nothing unusual; stomach contents are consistent with him having eaten a bowl of spaghetti bolognese about 6 p.m., no alcohol present."

Warren nodded. It certainly seemed to fit with his working

hypothesis so far. He motioned to the rest of the photographs that Harrison had brought with him. "What else do you have?"

Harrison spread the photos out. "Here are the footprints out of the lab. Everything is a bit difficult to interpret, perhaps deliberately so. Our best story is that the killer was wearing those plastic overshoes that you found. He's a clever bastard. It looks as though he wore two pairs. The inner pair had inserts, probably cardboard, to stop us getting a tread pattern or shoe size. The outer pair would have been covered in blood — this is almost certainly the pair found stuffed in the black bag. The footprints lead away from the office for several metres down the corridor, where they abruptly stop. There are some traces of blood on the wall. I reckon that the killer removed the outer pair of booties and put them in the black bag at this point. He probably leant against the wall as he did so, leaving those traces. It's reasonable to assume that he took off the lab coat and his outer gloves here and also stuffed them in the bag, along with the scalpel."

"Fingerprints?"

Harrison shook his head in frustration. "Nothing. Working hypothesis at the moment is that he also wore two or more pairs of latex gloves. It's easy enough to remove a pair of gloves without getting what's on the outside on your hands, but you should leave traces of DNA or even partial prints on the inside of the glove. We've found nothing. Assuming it was someone in the lab, these guys are all molecular biologists — they know how to avoid contaminating their work with foreign DNA. Put that together with a DVD boxset of *CSI* for Christmas and we're talking pretty forensically aware individuals."

"Can you make any inferences about height et cetera?"

"Only general. Almost certainly right-handed as the slitting of the throat was definitely right-handed and it requires a degree of skill; the angle of the cut is slightly upwards, suggesting that the attacker would likely have been of at least average height and would need to have been moderately strong.

"The gloves were standard university issue, medium size, but they're made of stretchy latex so I wouldn't want to speculate on hand size beyond suggesting the attacker wasn't a NBA basketball player; similarly the booties were medium size and with the cardboard inserts it's impossible to determine the shoe size of the person that wore them. A measurement of the distance between the footprints again suggest a person of average height and build, but the margin for error is so large I'd never sign off on it for court.

"Best I can say, is that the person was not very small or weak, and probably right-handed."

"Bugger," said Warren quietly. None of the evidence presented excluded Severino — however it also couldn't exclude half of the males in the country and a fair percentage of the women as well. Severino's lawyer was right when he'd said that Severino was in the middle of the bell-curve.

There were still some photographs next to Harrison's briefcase. "Anything else?"

"I'm afraid so, Chief. We've analysed the blood staining on the clothes that you gave us. It doesn't contradict your theory, but it does raise a few awkward questions."

Warren sighed. "Go on, then, kill the mood even more."

The analyst rummaged through the photographs, ordering them carefully. Taking the first photograph, he placed it on the table in front of Warren.

"As you can see, this is the hoodie that you gave us—" he placed another photograph next to it "—and this is the lab coat. What do you see?"

Warren carefully examined the two images. "The front of the lab coat is covered in blood, loads of it — he must have been bleeding right at the attacker. The hoodie also has blood on the front of it, but only a triangle on the front from the collar down. If I had to do an interpretation, I would say the patterns are roughly consistent with a powerful arterial bleed straight at the attacker. The lab coat blocked most of the blood, with some getting inside to stain the hoodie that he was wearing underneath. In fact, rather a lot of blood got in." Warren frowned.

Harrison picked up on Warren's bemusement. "You are right, sir, that's a hell of a lot of blood. In fact, the size of the patch on the hoodie is consistent with the top three buttons of this style of lab coat being undone and the flap loose. Why the hell would you go to the trouble of sticking your lab coat on, only to leave the bloody thing wide open? Severino wore this coat every day — it's not as if he doesn't know how to do the buttons up."

Warren grunted his agreement, his mind spinning. "Perhaps Tunbridge struggled and pulled the coat open?"

Harrison didn't look convinced. "It's possible, but doesn't really sit with everything else. Besides, there's more." He pulled out another photograph; this one appeared to be the back of the hoodie. Clearly visible on the back were large smears of blood. Placing it on the table, he also took one of the blown-up CCTV images.

Warren looked closely. "Shit," he cursed quietly, "where the hell are those blood stains on this image? How can they suddenly have appeared on the back of the hoodie *after* his attacker exited the building?"

Harrison nodded. "We wondered about that as well. You can't see the front of the hoodie, so we can't tell if it has blood on the front. We wondered if he'd done some sort of switch, you know, stuck a new jumper on after taking the bloodstained one off. After all, he wouldn't want to walk down the street with a massive blood stain on his chest—" his finger stabbed the image again "—but that doesn't really explain how the blood got on the rear of the hoodie. So we had the blood analysed and got one of the splatter experts to give it a good look, and she reckons the pattern is consistent with the hoodie being rolled up before being stuffed in the black bag. The wet blood on the front was transferred to the rear as the two pieces of material came into contact."

"OK." Warren wasn't quite sure where Harrison was going with this.

"But she is adamant that the blood was still soaking wet when it was transferred, at most a few minutes old when it was rolled up. It's a good fifteen-minute walk back to Severino's. She reckons that if he'd walked home with the hoodie on and then taken it off and rolled it up, the blood would have dried to a different consistency and the transfer would have been different."

Warren saw the peculiarity at once. "So the attacker kills Tunbridge, covering himself in blood in the process. He leaves the office and removes his lab coat, second pair of booties and latex gloves and bags them, but leaves on his bloodstained hoodie and jeans. Now he is no longer leaving bloody footprints or handprints. Somewhere further on, he discards the second pair of booties and their cardboard liner, probably in a random bin somewhere. He now exits the building, but then decides to get rid of the hoodie and bag that as well."

Harrison nodded. "It's a reasonable interpretation so far, sir."

"The question is, why didn't he take the hoodie off when he removed his lab coat? Why did he exit the building, running the risk of bumping into somebody whilst covered in blood and *then* take the hoodie off? What about his jeans?"

"Well, the jeans are black, so he probably figured he was safe — there wasn't that much blood on them. I guess he stood close enough behind Tunbridge that he took it full in the chest. As to the other question, I suppose he could have not realised the blood was on the front, or perhaps he was wearing something that would identify him underneath, like a T-shirt with his name on it?"

Warren wasn't convinced and he could tell that Harrison wasn't entirely satisfied with his answer either. This case, decided Warren, had just got a lot more interesting.

MONDAY

Chapter 19

After a brief respite late Sunday evening, it was time to start the week with the goal of securing Severino's prosecution and determining if anybody else had been involved in the murder.

By 10 p.m. Warren had been unable to put off work any longer and with apologies all around, had retired to the kitchen table to plan out his to-do list and get ready for Monday morning.

First and foremost, Warren had circled the phrase "Why?".

Why was Tunbridge in work so late? Was this normal behaviour for him? Second, was Severino working alone? If so, how did he know that Tunbridge was in the building and alone? To answer both of those questions, Warren had felt that he needed access to Tunbridge's diaries and personal correspondence — phone calls, emails, texts. A close look at his phone bills — private, work and mobile — might shed some clues, whilst his email accounts, work and personal, could be extremely useful. His appointments diary might also prove useful. Did he use a paper diary or something electronic? They already had Tunbridge's mobile phone — a BlackBerry smartphone found in his trousers pocket — and a meeting was scheduled with the university IT support team to look at Professor Tunbridge's work laptop. It had just had its screen cleaned of Tunbridge's blood but nobody had yet accessed the machine's hard drive or his university filespace.

Warren had made a note to seize his personal laptop as well if he owned one.

The evening had ended on a sour note, after a whispered argument with Susan about Bernice and Dennis' decision to stay for another week. Warren had completely misjudged the situation, assuming that Susan would be as dismayed at the prospect of her overbearing parents staying for another week as he was. On the contrary, Susan welcomed their decision, since she was feeling overwhelmed with single-handedly organising the new house, whilst trying to prepare for a new job at a new school in less than a month.

Whilst he was sitting at his desk early on Monday morning, memories of the argument rang in Warren's ears and his gut twisted with guilt. Susan was absolutely right, of course, and he had been very selfish over the past few months. In all the turmoil of his promotion and now this murder case, he had forgotten completely about Susan.

Confirmation of his promotion had come through towards the end of May, meaning that Susan had been forced to hand in her resignation at her current school immediately to meet the period of notice required for her to start a new job in September.

Her resignation, from a school she loved, had come out of the blue and her head teacher had been very unhappy at the need to find an experienced science teacher to replace her at such short notice.

Although Warren would be getting a generous pay rise on his promotion and the couple had always been sensible with money, Susan had nevertheless found it very stressful knowing that she would be unemployed from September. Eventually, she had found herself a new position at a local comprehensive school on the outskirts of Middlesbury. In retrospect it would probably be a good career move — she was now Head of Biology, wearing a second hat as the person in charge of boosting the school's less than stellar GCSE science pass-rate — but the preparation required was massive. With the need to tie up all the loose ends at her old job, then the stress of moving house, before preparing herself for her new role, she had been working flat out since May, Warren realised, with barely a weekend off. A proper holiday was out of the question unfortunately — a small unit like Middlesbury had to operate a strict policy regarding booking time off, especially for senior officers, and almost every week over the summer holidays had already been booked by staff with school-age children or spouses who worked in schools. Next year, Warren would join that group of staff and be given first refusal of those choice dates, but this year it was too late.

Nevertheless, Warren felt he had to try something and so he scrolled through the online holiday booking sheet. He had at least managed to snag the October half-term week, but Susan really needed to get away sooner, just to unwind. Suddenly he spotted it — the last weekend of the school holidays was available. Warren did some quick mental calculations. If he started work early on the Friday, he could probably leave a little after lunch, then perhaps arrange to start work later on the Monday, giving them three nights away. The timing couldn't be better: a couple of days away before school started — the calm before the storm, so to speak. Feeling pleased with himself, he booked them off immediately, deciding that he and Susan could spend a pleasant evening deciding where to go.

With that done, Warren turned to his to-do list. He had scheduled a briefing for eight-thirty again and was deciding who to assign to which duty. There were a lot of loose ends to this case and the sooner they got them tied up, the better. He and Sutton would also take a trip to Stevenage Magistrates court for Severino's hearing. By ten past eight, he had done as much preparation as he needed and he was struggling to concentrate.

Early in their relationship, Susan and Warren had vowed never to let arguments simmer for long periods of time. Warren had planned to announce the holiday booking that evening as a nice surprise, but memories of the previous night's argument still weighed heavily on his mind.

He glanced at the clock again. Eight-fifteen. When he'd left the house that morning, Susan had been awake and reading a book. She'd offered up her cheek for a perfunctory kiss, but had clearly still been brooding.

Sod it! Warren decided. A quick phone call would no doubt cheer her up and perhaps she'd be in a good mood when he arrived home. He keyed the speed dial on his mobile, ringing the house landline. It rang so long that Warren almost hung up. Finally it was picked up, the voice on the end heavy with sleep.

"Jones house."

Bloody hell, Bernice again! Warren suppressed a groan.

"Hi, Bernice, it's Warren. I hope I didn't wake you up. Is Susan about?"

Bernice ignored the first part of the question, but her tone of voice betrayed the answer. "I think Susan is in the bathroom. The shower stopped a moment ago. Can you not call back?"

Warren thought for a moment. Susan was already out of the shower and Bernice was now awake. The briefing started in less than fifteen minutes after which he wouldn't have time to make a personal phone call. The damage was already done; he'd be better off trying to fix it now rather than letting Susan simmer — no doubt with the aid of Bernice — for the next few hours.

Bernice gave a world-weary sigh, before calling up the stairs to Susan. A few seconds later, Susan picked up the bedroom extension. Warren waited for Bernice to replace the downstairs receiver before starting. First of all, he apologised for the previous night's argument; Susan sounded marginally less annoyed and grudgingly apologised for being over-sensitive. Glancing at the clock, Warren saw the time was eight-twenty. Outside his office door, he could hear the chatter of officers passing by on the way to the briefing room. Cutting to the chase, Warren announced proudly that he'd managed to secure a weekend away before term started again and Susan should choose wherever she wanted, cost be damned.

The reaction was not exactly what he was hoping for.

"Are you bloody mad? The weekend before school starts? I'm going to be working flat out! The school is reopening that weekend after the summer building work. It's the first chance I have to get into my new classroom. And on Tuesday's staff training day I'm supposed to be delivering a short address on how we are going to improve our GCSE pass-rates. I haven't even started planning that yet. And don't get me started on the A level Biology schemes of work — there aren't any. It's no wonder that some teachers have 100 per cent A to C and others, teaching the same sort of kids, have barely 50 per cent — every teacher is doing it differently. I need to sit down and work out a common teaching strategy, especially since it's rumoured that OFSTED will be in this term."

She paused for breath, but Warren was too stunned to do any more than mumble, "Sorry, I didn't realise."

"Don't you listen to anything I have to say? I can't believe you sometimes. That's the worst possible weekend to be away."

173

Warren sighed; the clock ticked over to eight twenty-five.

"I'm sorry, sweetheart. I didn't think. Look, I've got to go. My meeting starts in a moment. I'll phone you after lunch and we can see if there are any other weekends that we can do."

Silence, followed by the phone being hung up.

"Just like her bloody mother," Warren groaned quietly, letting his head thump lightly on the desk.

"Problems, guv?" Sutton leant against the doorway, barely covering a smile. Saturday's brief bonding session over the woes of mothers-in-law appeared an age ago and Warren didn't feel in the mood for small talk.

"Nothing a few months' holiday wouldn't solve."

"Thought your missus was a teacher. Isn't six weeks enough?"

"Don't even go there."

* * *

The rest of the morning passed smoothly; the whole of CID seemed energised by the rapid apprehension and charging of Severino. Assigning duties was a quick task and by mid-morning Sutton and Jones were ready for the short drive to Stevenage Magistrates Court. A quick phone call to the cells confirmed that Severino was ready to be moved to court and the prisoner transfer vehicle was despatched.

After an uneventful trip to the magistrates court, Jones was glad to see that Severino's docket had been moved forward to a quarter to twelve. Standing in the dock, Severino simply confirmed his name, date of birth and address. When prompted he pleaded "not guilty". No application for bail was made and that was it: Severino was led away to the cells to await trial. As he left the courtroom, his head bowed, tears coursed freely down his cheeks. His solicitor whispered urgently in his ear, glancing towards Jones as he did so. Warren couldn't help but feel that he was the subject of their frantic conversation.

Dismissing the thought, Warren left the courthouse, before turning thoughtfully to Sutton. "I have to tell you, Tony, the more I learn about Tunbridge, the more I see why someone bumped him off. I sincerely hope that when I die, I'll be mourned a little more than the late professor."

"You'll have to start working on your reputation, Boss, make sure we all love you when you go. Of course, I know a good way to start."

"Oh, how so?"

"You could get the first round in. I think we've earned it."

Chapter 20

Sutton and Jones' trip to the pub was a necessarily brief affair. It was, after all, the middle of a working day and the two men had a lot to do. Besides which they were both on duty and Warren was driving. In deference to the celebratory mood, both men had a half of bitter, before masking the beer with a ploughman's lunch.

After dropping Sutton back at the station, where he was to co-ordinate the interviewing of the last few members of Tunbridge's laboratory, Jones headed off to finally see Mrs Tunbridge. Popping a couple more mints into his mouth to hide any residual odour of the beer he'd supped at lunch, he punched the address into the car's sat nav.

Ten minutes later, Jones was walking up the short driveway to the smart detached house in the upmarket "Writers' Village" part of town. One of the wealthier Middlesbury suburbs, it gained its nickname from the literary nature of its street names. Centred around the almost obligatory "Shakespeare Avenue", a maze of small cul-de-sacs sported names such as "Coleridge Close", "Marlowe Drive" and "Sir Francis Bacon Grove". The Tunbridges lived on "Chaucer Avenue". A pleasant, leafy street composed primarily of detached houses with generous front gardens, it clearly wasn't as exclusive as some of the others. For a start, the Tunbridges would have no problem striking up a conversation with their neighbours either side or waving to the occupant of the house opposite, when walking down the drive. A couple of the streets that Warren had passed on his way to Chaucer Avenue had eight-foot-high fences between the houses to protect the occupants' privacy. A couple even had wrought-iron gates to block off their driveway from the local riff-raff.

In front of the Tunbridges' house sat a silver BMW roadster, next to it a brand-new Ford Focus. Clearly his and hers. Jones found himself wondering what Mrs Tunbridge would do with the Beamer now. Whatever damage Severino had done to the car's bonnet had been expertly repaired; no traces of the alleged profanities remained.

Stepping up to the front door, Jones took a deep breath before ringing the bell. He really hated this, dealing with the bereaved. At least he hadn't had to break the news. He'd done it plenty of times in his career and it never got any easier. Thankfully, it wasn't a kid, although a murder victim could be just as hard, even if it was as unsympathetic a character as Tunbridge.

The door finally opened, a young man standing on the threshold. His lip curled in a scowl. "I thought we made it clear, we have nothing to say to the press."

"My apologies, sir. Detective Chief Inspector Warren Jones — I phoned ahead."

The young man flushed slightly. "I'm sorry. Your visit completely slipped my mind. A couple of local journalists have been sniffing around. When I didn't see a uniform, I just assumed... Sorry, won't you come in?"

He stepped to one side, allowing Warren entry. The hallway was surprisingly cool, tastefully decorated, with dark wooden floors and light cream wallpaper. A large, bulging backpack with flight labels sat to one side. Jones remembered that Tunbridge's son was studying in the US. It looked as though he'd just got back. He confirmed Jones' deduction with a handshake. "Simon Tunbridge. Excuse my scruffiness — I just flew in an hour ago." Up close, Jones could see the resemblance to the photographs he had seen of Tunbridge before he died. The same strong jaw and unruly hair, although the younger man's hair remained a dark black. At the moment, his eyes were bloodshot and puffy; he'd clearly been crying recently. As Jones opened his mouth to express his condolences, the doorway to the kitchen opened and a middle-aged woman dressed in a formless woollen cardigan and black leggings came into view.

This was clearly Mrs Tunbridge, the late professor's wife. She stepped forward, offering her hand. "Annabel Tunbridge. You must be DCI Jones?"

"Yes, ma'am. First of all, may I express my condolences and apologise for not visiting you sooner?"

Mrs Tunbridge dismissed Jones' apology with a wave of her hand. "Your job is to catch the person who did this and I would like to thank you on behalf of my family for doing so, so quickly. Hopefully we can put this all behind us."

Up close, Jones could see that Mrs Tunbridge was a handsome woman with a slender figure. Her eyes, although somewhat puffy, had been expertly made up to conceal her distress. According to the family liaison officer, Mrs Tunbridge was forty-nine years old, somewhat younger than her fifty-five-year-old husband, yet she could pass for someone even more youthful. Knowing that the late professor's tastes seemed to run to younger women, Jones couldn't help but wonder if his wife's youthfulness was down to good luck and genetics or if she had worked to keep herself looking so young.

"Now, I believe you have some questions for me? I thought you had caught someone?" She turned and headed through an open archway into a spacious living room. Taking her gesturing hand as an invitation, Jones sat down on a comfortable leather sofa. Tunbridge and her son sat opposite on the sofa's twin, a low-slung coffee table between them.

"Yes, Mrs Tunbridge, in fact I've just come from court, where he was remanded in custody until his trial. However, to make the case against him secure we need to make certain that we have dotted all of the Is and crossed all of the Ts. I just have a few questions that I need to ask you." He decided not to mention his suspicion that Severino might not have worked alone.

"Of course, please. Anything to make sure that evil man gets what he deserves."

"On the night of the attack, your husband was working late in the office. According to the university's security logs, this was quite unusual. Professor Tunbridge rarely worked past 8 p.m. Pretty much everything he needed to do online could be accomplished from home. Do you have any idea why your husband was working so late in his office?"

Tunbridge shook her head. "I was out that night with some girlfriends. Alan didn't mention anything about going into the university."

"I see. Do you have any ideas about how he planned to spend his evening?"

"He hadn't mentioned anything. I assumed that he would stay in and watch TV, or maybe go and read a book in the garden since the weather has been so lovely."

"What did you think when you got home that evening to find he wasn't home?"

The older woman paused, before pulling out a handkerchief tucked up her sleeve. Dabbing at her eyes, she sniffed and apologised. Her son slipped his arm around her shoulder encouragingly.

"I did wonder where he was, but I assumed that he had walked around to the bowls club for a game or a pint. I was just starting to think about phoning him when your officers turned up on the doorstep."

Waiting a few moments for her to compose herself, Jones opened his notepad.

"Did your husband have many hobbies, Mrs Tunbridge?"

"Not really. He enjoyed reading when he could, and whenever he went somewhere interesting for a conference or a meeting he would try and take some photos. Other than that though, he just played bowls at the Middlesbury Sports Centre up the road. However, he always said that he didn't really have the time to play properly — he was just learning the rules so that he could hit the ground running when he retired." She tried a weak smile, which Jones returned.

"We have been unable to find your husband's diary, Mrs Tunbridge. I wonder if you have seen it? That might give us some clues as to why he was in the university so late at night."

Tunbridge shook her head; she hadn't seen the diary at all recently.

"We feel that knowing why the professor was up at the university so late is key to this investigation. We are currently searching his university laptop for any clues. However, I believe that staff at the university are able to log in from home. Did Professor Tunbridge have a computer, Mrs Tunbridge?"

"Yes, he had a laptop in his study. Alan often used to work in the evening."

"Do you mind if we check it out, Mrs Tunbridge?"

She looked uncertain. "I'm not sure. You don't need to take it away, do you?"

Warren looked apologetic. "Our forensic team at Welwyn would look at it at their site for analysis. It probably wouldn't take more than a couple of days to search for anything useful. The procedure is little more than a copying of the hard disk. They might not even have to open the case."

He could see that she wasn't convinced.

It was Simon who broke the impasse. "Mum, don't worry about it. I've got my laptop with me. You can use it to keep in contact just as easily as your own."

Somewhat reluctantly, Tunbridge agreed and,led the way upstairs. The top floor of the house was as tastefully decorated as the downstairs, Jones noted. The stairs and the landing followed the same colour scheme as the hallway, although with a thick, expensive-feeling carpet instead of polishcd wood. The house was generous in size and Warren counted six doors. Assuming that one was the master bathroom and another the study, that left at least three bedrooms, four if there was no airing cupboard. The study was the last room at the back of the house and had clearly been Professor Tunbridge's domain, rather than his wife's. The tall bookcase was filled with scientific texts and the large wooden desk was piled high with journals and technical documents. A small laser printer sat on top of a half-size filing cabinet. The room boasted a single, director-style chair. Sitting on the desk was a large laptop, its lid open. It was switched off.

Annabel Tunbridge paused at the threshold of the room, clearly reluctant to go into her late husband's workspace. Simon touched his mother's arm comfortingly. "It's OK, Mum. I'll handle this."

Looking relieved, she left wordlessly. Warren pulled out a pair of latex gloves and a large, clear, plastic evidence bag with reinforced handles. Seeing Simon's quizzical stare, he shrugged apologetically. "Forensics are always nagging us about trace evidence. It's easier just to do what they ask."

Simon nodded in sympathy. Unplugging the laptop from its power supply, Warren carefully slid it into the plastic bag, following it with the power cable. Sealing it, he noted the time, location and crime reference number on the bag with a permanent marker.

"I'm not sure what you'll find. Dad wasn't much of a computer guy. For such an intelligent man, he really was clueless when it came to PCs. He could drive Microsoft Office, through necessity I guess, but beyond that he struggled. Mum's the computer whizz. She's put together some amazing websites for local charities. She loves trying out new tricks. Middlesbury Rotary Club probably has the most sophisticated website in the whole organisation."

"We're not sure what we'll turn up. At the moment, our biggest question is why your dad was working late on Friday and how did his attacker know? He might have used an appointments calendar or there might be a clue in his email."

Simon clearly wasn't convinced. "I doubt it. Dad was definitely a pen and diary kind of guy. My sister and I bought him and Mum a BlackBerry smartphone each for Christmas, one of those family contracts from Orange. Figured we'd drag them into the twenty-first century. Mum loves it — she uses instant messaging and everything. I think Dad might have sent a text once." He smiled sadly at the memory, his eyes going misty.

"Christ, I can't believe what's happened. You hear about murders in the States all of the time, but you never think it'll happen to you. Especially here." He waved his arm in a vague, all-encompassing gesture. "When I was a kid, I hated Middlesbury. It's so boring, nothing ever happens. That's part of the reason I went to the States, to seek out a bit of excitement. But after a few months watching the local news, you find yourself longing for England and its gun laws…" He trailed off.

Warren cleared his throat slightly. "If, as you say, your father preferred to use pen and paper, he may have written something down. Do you mind if I have a bit of a look around?"

"Sure, be my guest."

Moving carefully, as much to show respect as to avoid disturbing anything, Warren started leafing through the piles of paper on the desk. Most of it was printouts or photocopies of journal articles. Any writing on the papers was cryptic and technical in nature. Nothing appeared to point towards why Professor Tunbridge would have been in work that night. Simon hovered in the background.

"You know, if he was meeting someone or expecting a phone call at work, he almost certainly would have jotted it down in his organiser. He rarely went anywhere without it. It's one of the reasons we bought him a BlackBerry smartphone, figured it would save him lugging the damn thing around with him. But when I came home for Easter he had his old organiser sitting here next to his laptop."

Warren turned in curiosity. "We didn't find any organiser in his office on Friday night. Would he have left it here?"

Simon shook his head. "I doubt it — he never left it anywhere. Before I leave the house I check I have my keys, my mobile and my wallet in that order. Dad would probably check he had his organiser, then his keys and wallet. Nine times out of ten, he'd probably forget his mobile."

"Can you describe it to me?"

"I can probably do better than that — he doesn't usually throw away his old ones and he buys the same one each year." Turning to the desk, he opened the bottom drawer, which Warren had yet to get to. Neatly stacked were a half dozen or so bulging, A5-sized black organisers. He pulled the pile out. All of them were identical in appearance except for the year, embossed on the spine in gold. They were piled in order, the top one being the previous year.

Opening one at random, Warren saw that it was a multi-purpose diary. The front page had the usual personal information, filled in by what he was beginning to recognise as the professor's neat script. After that, a few pages of information such as mini calendars and random trivia including international telephone dialling codes and time zones were followed by a standard day-to-a-page work diary. The final few dozen pages were given over to contact numbers and addresses. Leafing randomly through the pages, Warren saw that the days were mostly filled with to-do lists and appointments, some personal such as "Dentist 10 a.m.", most work-related. A few pages had scribbled technical notes and cryptic reminders.

As he looked at them, he was reminded of the scene that had greeted him Friday night. The laptop, screen glowing, splattered with blood. The curiously clean space next to the computer...

"Simon, I don't suppose you know if your dad used an external mouse on his laptop, do you?"

Simon shrugged. "Not that I saw at home. Although Dad wasn't much of a computer expert, he was competent enough at operating one. I think he just used the built-in trackpad. Of course, he may have used one at work, but I don't see why."

So, it was unlikely to be a space for a mouse-mat, then. Had

Tunbridge's organiser been next to the computer? Had his attacker taken it? And if so, what was in it that was so valuable?

"Do you mind if I take these diaries, just in case?"

Another shrug. "Help yourself, Chief Inspector." A sudden thought occurred to him. "If you are going to check his emails, you'll probably save yourself a lot of time if I give you his password."

Warren could barely conceal his surprise. Simon smiled, slightly embarrassed. "It's no big secret. I told you, Dad was a complete novice with computers. He used the same password for everything. Not only that, he was the world's slowest typist. Two-finger typing would have been an improvement. It's a good job they employed typists back when Dad did his PhD, otherwise he'd still be writing his thesis now."

Warren dug out his notepad and pen. "If you can give me his password that would be really helpful."

"Well, you won't need that, I shouldn't think. His password was just that."

"Just that? One word or two words?"

"No, you don't understand. It was just that — 'password'. If the computer demanded something more robust he just put the first letter as a capital and a number at the end. Like I said, Dad wasn't very good with computers."

Warren shook his head, not trusting himself to speak.

Chapter 21

After leaving the Tunbridge's house, Jones went straight to his appointment at the university's IT department. Unlike the ageing Biology department, the building was brand-new, twenty-first-century chic, all glass and chrome and air conditioning. Truth be told, Warren rather liked this type of design, although he was careful not to voice that opinion too loudly around some of Susan's more aesthetically minded friends. Warren regarded himself as a pragmatic man. On the one hand, he appreciated the great beauty inherent in Britain's old buildings. He even had a rotating computer background showcasing photographs of some of the most stunning architecture across the British Isles. On the other hand, when it came to places to live and work, give him everything that the modern age had to offer. Why waste good money on an antique, hand-carved solid oak desk — like the one that Susan's sister had just bought — when less than one hundred pounds could buy you a robust, self-assembly unit from IKEA with twice as many drawers, an easily accessible cupboard to hide the printer in and cable tidies? Not only that, Warren could slurp coffee to his heart's content and not worry about the cost of French-polishing. After a journey home full of robust debate after admiring Felicity's new desk, Warren and Susan had agreed to disagree.

Like many organisations, UME hid its IT support departments

in the basement, away from prying eyes. This, Warren learned from the interactive display that dominated the building's lobby, was as much to do with cost efficiency as keeping the geeks out of sight. The rows and rows of file-servers and processors that kept the university's IT infrastructure ticking over generated phenomenal amounts of heat. In order to avoid spending even more money on expensive air conditioning to keep everything cool, the building funnelled the heat up through the centre of the building. In winter it was enough to reduce the building's heating bill by half. In the summer, the unwanted hot air was used to generate electricity.

The display was on its third rotation before the receptionist finally announced that the university technician that had been working with the specialists from Welwyn's Forensic Computer Unit had been tracked down.

"Sorry, I was out on an urgent call on the other side of campus," he apologised as he shook Warren's hand. The crumbs in the young man's goatee beard suggested otherwise, but Warren let the white lie slide. Following the young man down the corridor, Warren mentally compared the young computer expert against his personal database of stereotypes and prejudices. Very young for such a senior role — check. Somewhat socially awkward — check. Badly dressed — a matter of opinion, Warren decided. He wasn't wearing a suit and tie, but his shirt was sober and ironed and he wore pressed trousers and leather shoes. Poor personal hygiene — crumbs aside, all Warren could smell was soap and a faint whiff of spicy cologne. All in all, another prejudice debunked, Warren decided.

After walking a lengthy distance along softly carpeted corridors past numerous offices, they eventually stopped at yet another unremarkable office door. Without knocking, his guide Jeremiah walked straight in. For the first time since entering the building Warren finally felt his expectations were being met. The atmosphere in the room was a mixture of stale coffee, warm electronics and even warmer bodies. The room was clearly some sort of repair room. Vertical racks of plastic boxes on runners stretched to the ceiling, full of equipment or components. Each container had a sticky label, some of which made sense to Warren, others could have been written in Sanskrit for all they meant to him.

In the centre of the room was a large workspace, and on it sat Tunbridge's laptop. It was recognisable as Tunbridge's because, despite being cleaned after its physical forensic examination, dark, bloody stains still marred the plastic body of the machine. The physical state of the machine was irrelevant, Warren saw, as the hard drive had been removed from the laptop and attached instead to another laptop, this one with the familiar Herts and Beds Major Crime Unit logo on its lid. Network and power cables snaked their way to wall-mounted sockets.

Hunched in front of the laptop was the tallest person Warren had ever seen. As he looked at the man Warren decided that if he were ever asked to describe this individual in one word, that word would have to be 'long'. From his impossibly lengthy legs, somehow folded under the desk, to his spindly fingers and oval face, it was as if the man had been stretched vertically.

Without standing up — he had no need to: his arms could easily reach Warren standing near the door — the man put out a huge hand. "Pete Robertson, Forensic IT," he announced, in a surprisingly high-pitched voice. Warren returned the courtesy, marvelling at how his hand was swallowed up by the giant sitting in front of him. Robertson was a civilian worker, Warren noted from his badge. That wasn't unusual — most of the force's computer specialists were recruited from outside the police. Nevertheless, Warren found himself wondering if the police still had height limits for new recruits. He strongly suspected that Robertson would not have been within those limits.

"What have you found then, Pete?"

"A couple of things, some of which I think you probably already know, others which I imagine will be a surprise." Robertson turned to face Warren, who had perched himself on the end of the table.

"First, Professor Tunbridge probably wasn't the most confident of computer users. It seems that he learnt exactly what he needed to complete a particular task. He could run basic Office programs fairly competently — you don't have much choice these days — and he used email and web browsers, but, with the exception of a couple of surprising skills, which he had clearly taken the trouble to work out, he was a generally unimaginative user."

Jeremiah nodded his agreement. Not for the first time, Warren felt a touch of paranoia when sitting in the presence of IT specialists. He regarded himself as a fairly practised computer user; nevertheless, he always imagined that the moment he left IT Support and the door closed behind him, all of the technicians fell about laughing at his incompetence.

Pushing the thoughts to one side, Warren gestured for them to continue. Jeremiah took up the story. "Professor Tunbridge used the university's standard email client, Microsoft Outlook, on his work laptop, but hadn't gone to the trouble of configuring his smartphone or his home laptop to pick up his email as well. If he wanted to check his email in the evening from home, he'd log into our remote client, then access it as if he was on campus. Bit of a faff if you ask me. Instructions and help are available for any staff or students who want to pick up their email without having to log on, but he never used them, it seems."

Warren raised a hand. "Back up a second. You mentioned remote access. Does this mean that he could get access to his computer files and email from home?"

Jeremiah nodded. "Of course. We have full remote access to our systems from home via a thin client server system. Staff and students simply follow a link on our website, download a piece of client software and then it's as if they are sitting at their desk in their office, or a public access terminal in the library."

That was an interesting wrinkle, thought Warren. If Tunbridge could work from home just as easily as he could from campus, then why was he sitting in his office at 10 p.m. on a Friday, when he could have been enjoying the comforts of his own living room? And had his killer had anything to do with that decision?

Jeremiah continued, "Going back to Tunbridge's usage of computers, a lot of our staff use electronic calendars. Everyone has smartphones these days and so they can use an electronic calendar, rather than a traditional paper diary. We even run a server application to let users share appointments and documents more easily. According to our records, Tunbridge has never even logged on to the system." He glanced at Robertson, who took over.

"When he was found, a smartphone was in his pocket. A look at its contents showed that, despite owning it over six months, he had only ever used it to make and receive calls and send the odd text message. He'd never even used the calendar function, let alone synchronised it with his work account. The only photo in the gallery is a blurry self-portrait, taken at arm's length on Christmas Day. If I had to guess, he came across the camera function when he was playing with his new toy and never used it again."

Warren felt slightly deflated. So it seemed that Tunbridge's laptop was unlikely to help shed a light on why he was working so late on a Friday night, nor was it likely to help explain how or why his killer targeted him that night. He said as much.

"Don't be so sure, DCI Jones." Robertson's grin was slightly disturbing, given his distorted features. He turned back to the laptop. "The interesting stuff is what's in his Internet browsing history — or, rather, not, in his case. His entire history was deleted some time in the twenty-four hours preceding his death."

Warren shot forward off his perch. "Say that again?"

"His entire Internet browsing history was deleted some time in the preceding twenty-four hours before he was found. Actually, twenty-two hours if we're being pedantic, as the whole history was there when his computer's profile was backed up automatically at midnight, the previous day."

"Who did it? And why?"

"As to the first, we can only speculate. Tunbridge may have done it himself, or his killer may have done it immediately after killing him — we can't be sure. If his killer did do it, it was sloppy and silly. There are loads of ways to find a person's browsing history, especially on a private network like the university. Deleting your Internet history just raises a bright red flag saying, 'Hi, look at me. I've been browsing where I shouldn't!'"

Robertson emphasised his point by waving his arms, almost taking Jeremiah's eye out in the process.

"As to the why, that's your call, Chief Inspector, but a look at the sites he's been visiting might be useful." Robertson's grin broadened. Warren could hardly blame him. He'd let him have his moment of glory, he decided magnanimously; poor bugger probably never got the recognition he deserved.

"Here we have a list of all of the sites that Tunbridge visited in the last three months, including the day he died. I'll email it to you, but here are the highlights." Robertson called up a lengthy list of website addresses. The site's specific address was highlighted in blue as a clickable link. Next to it a one-line sentence described the link. "Most of the stuff is crap and fairly innocuous. He generally started his day with a trawl of the BBC News website followed by a browse of some select journal articles — he received a daily email alert to help him do that. Most of the rest of the sites are ones that Jeremiah tells me are fairly run-of-the-mill sites of interest to the biological research community.

"However, there are two sites that may be of interest to you. First, his university email account wasn't his only account."

"He had a Hotmail account?" guessed Jones.

Robertson shook his head, smiling. "Better than that. He had his own domain name." Seeing Warren's uncomprehending expression, he expanded, "With the aid of a help tutorial from the online version of *What PC*, a couple of months ago he bought the domain name 'TridentAntibacterials.com' on his credit card. Bundled in with that came a couple of gigabytes of web storage and an email client. He could set up as many email addresses ending '@TridentAntibacterials.com' as he wished. He only set up one, 'CEO@ TridentAntibacterials.com', but it is active."

"Trident was the name that Professor Tompkinson mentioned in connection with Tunbridge's research," recalled Jones. "It sounds as if he was setting the groundwork for starting up his own company. Having his own email address sounds a lot more professional than using Hotmail or even his university account. Have you had a look at his emails yet?"

Robertson nodded. "Bloody easy to get in — would you

believe he uses the same password for his university and personal accounts?"

Warren smiled. "Let me guess — 'Password'?"

Robertson frowned, the wind briefly taken out of his sails. "Yes, well, anyway, I'll leave it to you to decide upon the importance of his correspondence, but almost all of the emails he exchanged were with a single address: 'JPriest@CaliforniaBioInvest.com'. The last email that he received was at 9 p.m. on the day he was killed."

Warren felt his face flush with excitement. It could all be a coincidence, he cautioned himself, but nevertheless his gut tightened. "Do we know who this person is?"

"Here's where it gets really interesting. I decided to look up this person." His long fingers moved rapidly across the keyboard and a new browser window opened. Typing rapidly, he entered the email address into the browser's search bar. Instantly, the familiar Google results page appeared, with a single entry 'California Biotechnology Investment Ltd'. Without being asked, he clicked on the blue link. Immediately, the page turned to the familiar white '404 not found' page.

"Shit," swore Warren.

"That's what I thought, but then I remembered — in cyberspace nothing is ever really deleted." Robertson clicked the back button on the browser, returning to the search results page. Moving the mouse pointer, he highlighted the results again.

"It may no longer be active, but it was up long enough for Google to cache it." Without being asked, he explained, "In order to speed up searches, search engines take a snapshot of webpages that they index. It allows them to extract keywords and whatever other information that they need. Google stores these in a cache and allows users to actually access the snapshot and see what the

193

page looked like at the time that it was indexed. It can be several days out of date, but that doesn't always matter if the page doesn't change very often."

Sure enough, a light blue link next to the entry read "cached". Warren remembered seeing that link plenty of times in the past as he'd conducted web searches, but couldn't ever remember clicking it. Robertson did so.

Immediately the page changed to a photograph of a shiny, metal and glass fronted building. Superimposed over the bottom left of the picture, an ethnically diverse group of lab-coated young people with impressively good teeth — some with clipboards, others holding what appeared to be laboratory equipment — stared earnestly at the camera. Across the top of the page "California Biotechnology Investment Ltd" was emblazoned.

To the right, the company mission statement proclaimed that CBI Ltd was a privately funded venture capitalist firm specialising in "funding today's ideas to solve tomorrow's problems".

At the bottom of the page a small disclaimer read "Enquiries by invitation only" with a mail icon next to it. Robertson hovered the mouse pointer over it revealing the mysterious contact's email address.

"Is that it? I don't see any other links."

"That's it. Either this is the holding page for a very selective venture capitalist firm — 'don't call us, we'll call you' — or it's a scam. Either way, it appears to have become unavailable some time during the past seventy-two hours since Google last indexed it."

Warren digested the implications for a few moments. It was too much to take in all at once; he needed time to think. "I think we're starting to build a picture here, but I'm not sure what of.

Pete, can you send me copies of all of the correspondence sent and received from this email account? Further, can we try and track down this company and maybe this J Priest?" Robertson nodded. "Oh, and can you keep a monitor on this account, in case we get another email? I think we need to get back to the station and try and piece this together."

Robertson agreed but held up a cautionary hand. "Just one more thing I think you might be interested in."

"Oh, what might that be?" Warren paused, wondering what was coming next.

"Jeremiah?" Robertson nodded to the young university staff member to take over.

"At 21:55 hours on Friday evening, somebody copied all of Professor Tunbridge's files onto a USB memory stick."

Chapter 22

Back at the station, Warren called for a meeting at 5 p.m., to pull together the day's findings. That gave him a half-hour or so to go through the email correspondence between Tunbridge and the mysterious J Priest.

The ten emails had been archived into a single document, in chronological order, and Warren was able to print them out and read them like a transcript of a conversation.

The first, sent by Priest to Tunbridge, hinted at the way the two had met.

From: J Priest <JPriest@CaliforniaBioInvest.com>   Sent: 25/07/2011 09:34:26
           Prof Alan Tunbridge
To: <CEO@TridentAntibacterials.com>
Subject: Meeting at Antibacteria Is 2011

Dear Prof Tunbridge,

Thanks a lot for taking the time out to chat about your work at yesterday's break-out session. Your work is fascinating and, as I said at the time, is something that CBI Ltd might be interested to know more about.

Unfortunately, I have to fly back to Los Angeles tonight and so can't take you up on your offer to tour your laboratory at the moment. Nevertheless, I will be speaking to colleagues about your work. To that end, I wonder if you would be kind enough to send me a copy of the PowerPoint presentation you gave.

Yours,
Dr J Priest,
Senior Investment Scout, California Biotechnology Investment Ltd.

Tunbridge's response had been quick and to the point.

	Prof Alan Tunbridge	
From:	<CEO@TridentAntibacterials.com>	Sent: 25/07/2011 09:52:12
To:	J Priest <JPriest@CaliforniaBioInvest.com>	
Subject:	Re: Meeting at Antibacterials 2011	
Attachment: Antibac2011.ppt		

Dear Dr Priest,

Thank you for your continuing interest in my research. I enjoyed our chat at the conference and would be delighted to send you a copy of my talk.

Yours,
Prof Alan Tunbridge
CEO Trident Antibacterials.

Leafing through the emails, Warren watched the relationship unfolding. Priest, whoever he was — he now signed his emails John — was smooth and subtly flattering. Within a couple of emails, he had Tunbridge sending additional data and was promising to present Tunbridge's work to the board of investors. With the benefit of twenty-twenty hindsight, it was obvious that Tunbridge was being played perfectly. The question was, who would know Tunbridge well enough to hoodwink him so thoroughly?

The correspondence continued over the course of several weeks, becoming increasingly technical in nature and difficult to follow. Warren was contemplating the need for another cup of coffee, when suddenly he sat bolt upright.

From: J Priest <JPriest@CaliforniaBioInvest.com>   Sent: 10/08/2011 17:53:09
            Prof Alan Tunbridge
To: <CEO@TridentAntibacterials.com>
Subject: Telephone Conference?

Alan,

Great news!

I spoke to the board and they were extremely interested. Our CEO has a long-standing interest in the field of anti-microbial compounds and has actually requested a telephone conference with you. You'll forgive me for the cloak and dagger approach, but all of our investors are very private individuals with significant business interests and influence worldwide. For them to express an interest in a technology, regardless of the depth of that interest, can result in changes in stock prices and ill-informed speculation. As responsible investors, we would try to avoid that. For that reason, we would prefer not to reveal the identity of any of our members, until we can speak directly. We would also ask that you refrain from mentioning this upcoming meeting.

He can give you an hour at 2pm on Friday 12th August, California Time. I apologise that the time difference would

make that 10 p.m., UK time, unfortunately that is the only
space in his diary.

In addition to the CEO, some of our scientific and legal
team will be part of the call. We would therefore ask that
you are prepared to answer any scientific or legal questions
that arise and are able to send or receive any electronic files
necessary.

Obviously we would be happy to sign any necessary con-
fidentiality agreements. Please feel free to send them to this
email address.
I look forward to doing business,

John.

Bravo! thought Warren, for a moment his admiration for the
skilful manipulation making him forget the ultimate outcome of
this exchange. Tunbridge's reply, agreeing to the conference call,
had ultimately sealed his fate. A final email on that fateful Friday
merely confirmed that he was precisely where his killer wanted
him, at the right time and with all of his data gathered in one place.

The question therefore remained: who was John Priest and
what was his relationship with Antonio Severino?

Chapter 23

After gulping down the remains of his coffee, Warren called everyone into the briefing room. He started by filling the team in on Severino's early morning court appearance and congratulating the team on their success, before reminding them that they still had to chase up any loose ends.

Next, he filled them in on his visit to Mrs Tunbridge, underlining the need to find Tunbridge's diary. His revelation that Tunbridge had been apparently conversing online with a fake venture capital firm created a buzz of excitement. Sutton was the most vocal, voicing the opinion that Severino would know exactly which buttons to press to get Tunbridge to believe him.

"Mark my words, this John Priest is nothing more than a figment of Antonio Severino's imagination. And furthermore, if we look hard enough we'll find that missing diary and a memory stick full of data and covered in Severino's prints."

Murmurs of agreement had rippled around the table.

"What have we got from the other members of the Tunbridge lab?" asked Jones.

"Not much in the way of other suspects, I'd say," said Sutton, who'd reviewed the interview transcripts taken by the rest of the CID team. "The only other two current members of the laboratory have alibis. A first-year PhD student by the name of Juan Morales has been visiting his parents in Spain for the past week. The local plods have kindly visited him directly to check him out. The laboratory's technician, Patrick Burnell, has been up in Leeds visiting his sick father in hospital since Wednesday. Apparently the old man is on his last legs and Burnell has been practically sleeping at the hospital, in full view of nursing staff and other visitors. In terms of opportunity, I can't see how he could have made the journey."

"What about former members of the lab? Tunbridge had a reputation for poor treatment of lots of staff and colleagues, not just Spencer and Severino."

Sutton shuffled his notes. "In terms of motive, there are three former staff that had a good reason, although it would seem as though they have moved on. Another PhD student that started at the same time as Tom Spencer, Refah Patel, had a miserable first year with Tunbridge. She was diagnosed with depression at the end of that year, with Tunbridge's behaviour a major contributing factor. However, unlike Spencer, she has a second supervisor, Professor Crawshaw, and in her second year was able to switch the focus of her research to effectively become Crawshaw's student and now works almost full-time in that lab. She only needs to meet the Tunbridge Group occasionally. That seems to have suited Tunbridge fine. He's always regarded graduate students as a pain in terms of administration.

"Moving to Crawshaw's lab was the 'best thing that ever happened to me' to quote Patel directly. Probably due in no small part to her meeting her current fiancé there. She has basically finished her thesis and is awaiting her viva — an oral exam on her work — before graduating. She's already got a job lined up."

"Sounds unlikely, I agree. What about an alibi?"

"She was out with her fiancé that night having a meal. We're sending someone out to check that as we speak. It's also worth noting that she's roughly four feet ten inches tall and weighs about as much as a packet of chocolate HobNobs, which if the forensics are to be believed pretty much rules her out."

A few titters ran around the table and Warren couldn't help smiling himself at Sutton's colourful choice of words. With Severino charged and awaiting trial in near record time, the team had every right to be in a good mood, Warren thought. However, they still had a duty to present a watertight case to the Crown Prosecution Service and so he continued the meeting.

"Who else have we got?"

"Two former technicians who brought a constructive dismissal case against Tunbridge. Again, they certainly had a motive at the time — about two and a half years ago — but they both claim to be very happy in their current positions. Alibi-wise, one was stuck with her husband and kids on the M6 travelling north for a family wedding, the other is a single parent and spent Friday in front of the TV with the kids upstairs in bed. We're checking her out at the moment."

"What was the constructive dismissal over?"

"Unreasonable working demands apparently. Both women had young families and worked a job share. Tunbridge decided upon a new set of experiments that the lab was going to perform that required the technician working that day to be in the lab by 8 a.m. or earlier. Something to do with the need to make up essential chemicals fresh that morning, rather than making them up the previous evening and leaving them overnight as is usual practice. Not only was this in violation of their contracted working hours, he would also give them very little notice that he was planning on running the experiments. It wreaked havoc with their childcare plans. When they finally said enough was enough and refused to set up the experiments without reasonable notice, he humiliated them in the weekly departmental meeting by blaming them for a lack of progress on the project."

"Nice guy," muttered Hastings quietly. A few heads nodded in agreement.

"Anyway, they took advice from their union rep and resigned, threatening constructive dismissal. The university finally stepped in and moved them from Tunbridge's lab into another research group and gave them a regrading to boot. Apparently they are both very happy in their jobs and claim to be doing well."

Warren nodded. "They all sound unlikely suspects. Let's just dot all the Is and cross all the Ts and move on."

At that moment, the door to the conference room opened, and one of the administrative assistants poked her head around the door.

"Sorry to interrupt, but there is a phone call for DCI Jones. It sounds urgent." Excusing himself, Warren headed back to his office. Picking up the call, he was surprised to hear the youthful voice of Antonio Severino's lawyer.

"What can I do for you, Mr Stock?"

"My client would like to have a talk with you."

"Really. Decided to confess, has he? He should save that for the trial, change his plea."

Severino's lawyer sounded frustrated. "Hardly. Antonio was in extreme shock when he was interviewed, not to mention severely hungover and not thinking straight. Now that he's had time to calm down, he has some information that you might find useful."

Warren fought down a sigh. "Let me guess, he has vital

information that he will only share with me and so I am expected to race down to The Mount Prison on his say-so to find out this incredible information he has locked up in his mind."

"Actually, quite the opposite. He's told me about it in great detail and I think it's extremely interesting information that you will find useful. Let me be candid, Chief Inspector. I'm doing this on legal aid, I'm underpaid and overworked. I assure you that if he was yanking your chain, I wouldn't be wasting your time or mine. I really think it is worth a trip down here to hear for yourself what he has to say."

Warren thought for a few moments. The solicitor's call had certainly got him intrigued. In his experience, despite their obviously different goals and divergent views on the merits of a particular case, most defence solicitors were actually hard-working, decent enough folk. The majority of them also acted as fairly effective bullshit filters, although they were ultimately bound to follow their clients' wishes.

For that reason, Warren decided to chance it. He agreed to meet the lawyer outside the prison the following morning, before going in to see Severino together. Hanging up, Warren drummed his fingers on the table as he thought about the unexpected request. Eventually, he decided that he was wasting his time speculating and so headed back to the briefing. Nevertheless, a nagging feeling in his gut told him that something significant was about to happen.

Chapter 24

Warren finally made it home at eight that evening. The atmosphere in the house was strained, with Susan clearly still smarting from their argument on the phone that morning. Susan and her parents had already eaten, so Warren ended up eating reheated lasagne alone at the kitchen table, whilst the rest of the house watched TV.

Normally Warren and Susan made an effort to follow the advice given by Warren's grandparents — married sixty-two years and counting — not to let the sun go down on an argument, but the presence of Susan's parents inhibited Warren from speaking out to clear the air. Remarkably, it was Dennis that initiated the conversation as Susan and her mother watched old *Inspector Morse* repeats on the TV; his father-in-law was fascinated by the day's events, completely ignoring the exploits of the famous TV detective as he quizzed Warren on how they had identified Severino as their suspect and his subsequent arrest and charging. He even expressed an interest in watching Severino's eventual trial. Warren promised to let him know when the trial started and agreed to try and get him a seat in the public gallery.

Bernice, for her part, merely sniffed and carried on knitting, finding Colin Dexter's intricate twists and plots in genteel Oxford to be far more interesting than the real-life grubbiness of Warren's day-to-day existence. Susan said nothing.

Finally, Bernice announced that she and Dennis were tired and wanted to go to bed. Dennis didn't seem particularly tired to Warren, but nevertheless he wished Warren and Susan goodnight, before dutifully following his wife up the stairs.

Susan remained on the couch, her eyes glued to the late-night news bulletin. Inwardly, Warren sighed. She clearly wasn't going to make it any easier for him. He knew that he was in the wrong and that it was up to him to apologise; nevertheless, he felt a little hurt that Susan didn't seem interested in meeting him halfway.

Getting up from his armchair, he crossed the room and sat down on the couch next to his wife. The leather was still warm from where Bernice had vacated it a few moments before. Reaching over, he kissed her lightly on the side of her head. She didn't flinch, which was something, but at the same time she didn't take her eyes off the TV.

"I'm sorry, sweetheart. I've been neglecting you. I've been too wrapped up in my work to even ask how your day has been."

Finally, Susan turned to look at him.

"Warren, what colour were the walls in the hall when you left for work this morning?"

Warren blinked in surprise at the apparent non sequitur, before groaning silently. He knew where this was going and there was nothing he could do about it. How could he not have even noticed the smell of fresh paint when he walked in the house? Resigned to his fate, he played along with the game.

"A pale cream colour."

"And now?"

Warren wracked his brain, but it was useless. He sighed. "I'm so sorry, I never even noticed."

"Pale blue. Mum chose it." Susan looked close to tears. "We were supposed to choose that paint, not Mum. This is our first proper house, Warren. We were going to decorate it together. When we finished, we were supposed to be able to say, 'This is Warren and Susan's house.' From the shade of the walls, to the colour of the carpets, it was supposed to be *our* house. The way *we* wanted it. This afternoon, Mum and I painted the hallway, whilst Dad fixed all of those shelves in the utility room.

"I wanted to wait until you weren't busy any more, but I couldn't hold out any longer. The holidays are nearly over; I'll be back at school in three weeks. I have to start my planning by next week. Mum and Dad insisted that they help out and I couldn't say no. I couldn't tell them to leave it alone because I wanted to do it with you. They've been married forty years. To them it was just a job that needed doing and if you weren't able to do it, they would."

Warren felt helpless. She was right. It seemed such a small thing, but she was absolutely right. They had been planning their first proper home together ever since they had become engaged. Long nights lying in bed in their rented flat in Birmingham they'd fantasised about what they'd do and how it would look when they finished. At the time it had always seemed to be a few years away, but then suddenly Warren had been invited to apply for the job at Middlesbury and days later Susan had found herself handing in her notice to leave her current school.

Even then, they had expected to rent a flat whilst they looked around for somewhere more permanent; yet even as they'd visited the letting agency for the first time on a day trip to Middlesbury the picture in the estate agent's window across the road had caught their eye. A chat with their bank manager had revealed that, much to their surprise, their savings were enough for a deposit and, with their combined salaries, the mortgage payments were not much different from what they had budgeted to spend on rent. Even better, the current owner was looking for a quick sale and Warren and Susan were first-time buyers.

The moment that they had walked into the house for a viewing, they had felt as if they had come home. Work needed to be done and the décor wasn't to their taste, yet looking beyond the surface they had found exactly what they were looking for. It was fate, they had both decided as they lay in bed that night, their flat in Birmingham already feeling alien and cold to them; no longer a home but a way station as they headed for better things.

Warren was at a loss. All he could do was put his arms around his wife and whisper his apologies into her ear as her tears finally came. Eventually it was over, Susan dabbing at her eyes with her long-sleeved T-shirt.

An hour later, Warren lay awake in bed, staring at his wife's sleeping form. He could see her outline clearly in the glow from the street light outside as it passed through the thin, inadequate bedroom curtains. Curtains that they were supposed to have been replacing together, he realised with a stab of shame.

As he looked at the back of Susan's head, he felt sadness at the way things had changed. When had he started taking Susan for granted? Only a few weeks ago he had lain in this same bed in their old flat marvelling at how lucky he was. As long as he had Susan to come home to, it didn't matter what else was happening in the world.

Some said that there was no such thing as love at first sight, just a chemical, lustful attraction that with time grew into love. All Warren knew was that the first time he had clapped eyes on Susan he was smitten. To this day, Warren realised just how lucky he had been. Ordinarily there would have been no reason for their paths to cross. Susan had been undergoing teacher training at Birmingham University; Warren had been a detective sergeant working largely in Edgbaston near to the university campus, but he had hardly been a frequent visitor to that area.

The night that they met, Warren had been enjoying a few beers after a long shift, in one of the local bars. He and his three friends were winding down after a tiring day, looking forward to a relaxing weekend. By about 10 p.m., it was all that Warren could do to keep his eyes open. Draining his pint, he decided to pay one last visit to the Gents, make his excuses, then leave.

Returning from the toilets, he saw that two of his friends had clearly had similar ideas and were nowhere to be seen, no doubt already trying to hail a cab outside. Suddenly, the fourth member of the party appeared at his elbow.

"You can't leave now, mate," he said urgently. The speaker was 'Griffo', Robert Griffiths, probably Warren's closest friend on the force.

Warren stifled a yawn. "Sorry, mate, I'm running on empty here. Three early shifts in a row, I'm knackered."

"Shit, I need you — you're my wingman." He jerked his head in the direction of a group of young people that Warren had seen him talking to earlier in the evening.

Warren shook his head. "I can't. I'm falling asleep here."

But Griffo wouldn't be dissuaded. "Come on, Jonesy, I'm on a winner here — the blonde bird with the big tits is well up for it. Get a Red Bull down your neck. They've invited us to a party around the corner in their halls of residence."

Warren sighed. The last thing he wanted was to spend the night with a group of pissed-up twenty-year-old students. It wasn't that he hadn't enjoyed his own time as a pissed-up twenty-year-old student — far from it, his university days were some of the best days of his life — however that time was years past now.

"Why don't you go ahead? I'm tired. I wouldn't want to cramp your style."

Griffo snorted. "Don't be such a wuss. Besides, I can't go on me own, I'll look like a complete 'Johnny No Mates.'" His tone of voice turned to wheedling. "Come on, you know you'll love it when you're there. A couple of cans of Red Bull and you'll be partying all night; then you've got the weekend to get over it."

Warren groaned inwardly. He knew that he wouldn't get any peace until he agreed. It would be far better to go to the party, wait until Griffo was otherwise engaged then sneak out. Assuming the party really was around the corner, he could be back home in bed within the hour.

Reluctantly agreeing, Warren followed Griffo over to meet the group. They were a little older than he'd first assumed, he realised — postgraduate students, rather than undergraduates. After making their introductions, the group decided to leave the pub immediately and head for a local off-licence that Griffo's new friend — Katy — insisted would serve them after hours. Warren wondered idly if Griffo had mentioned their day jobs or if their new friends assumed that they were also students.

Fifteen minutes later, Warren found himself squashed into the corner of a student common room, clutching the two bottles of beer that he'd bought from the small corner store on their way over. Griffo had immediately disappeared with the generously proportioned Katy, leaving Warren to fend for himself. *Now look who's Johnny No Mates*, he thought darkly.

It was then that Warren saw her. Standing in the corner, looking similarly awkward, she was the most beautiful girl in the room:

average height, with gentle curves, long, dark hair and a snub nose. Something clicked in his head when he saw her. He just had to go and introduce himself. Or at least that was how Warren would tell the story in years to come; truth be told, after a few pints of lager and not enough sleep he couldn't remember exactly how the two of them had ended up chatting. Neither could Susan. However, they had ended up shouting at each other over the music, until Warren had suggested they move somewhere a bit quieter.

Out in the corridor, Susan soon learnt that Warren was not a new postgraduate student enjoying a fresher-week bash, but rather a gatecrasher, albeit a reluctant one. As was often the case, Warren observed, the moment he mentioned he was a police officer to a pretty and intelligent woman the interest in her eyes waned. The old prejudice that police officers were under-educated thugs still reared its ugly head from time to time. Nevertheless, Warren was determined not to let that get in the way and contrived to mention his first-class joint-honours degree in English and History and that he was on the fast-track promotion scheme at work.

With his academic credentials firmly established, he found that Susan was a bit more responsive and pretty soon they were engaged in a friendly debate about the merits of different crime authors, with Warren ranking them in terms of both literary style — as befitted an English graduate — and their accuracy — as befitted a detective. Susan ranked them in terms of how many hours' sleep she was prepared to sacrifice trying to reach the end.

Finally, Warren mentioned that he had just finished reading Lee Child's latest thriller and found to his delight that Susan was also a fan of the gigantic, taciturn hero Jack "None" Reacher. Even better, she hadn't read the latest novel yet. Without even thinking,

Warren had found himself promising to lend her his copy of the book, if only she would meet him for coffee the next day. To his amazement she agreed.

A few days later when he recounted the tale to Griffo — whose luck had run out after the buxom Katy's boyfriend had appeared unexpectedly — his friend's response had been surprisingly negative.

"Never lend a bird a Lee Child novel until you've had at least three dates, otherwise you'll never see that book again. Or her, for that matter. And especially don't lend them a hardback — that's just asking for trouble." And that was all he had to say on the subject.

Remembering those early days made Warren long for simpler times. One thing was certain though, his priorities had to change. Time to remember the old adage, "Work to live; don't live to work".

With that thought echoing in his mind, he finally fell into a shallow, fitful sleep.

TUESDAY

Chapter 25

Warren arrived at The Mount Prison on the outskirts of Bovingdon village a little after eleven-fifteen the following morning. Daniel Stock, Severino's solicitor, was waiting in the car park for him. Warren apologised for his tardiness. "Sorry, I put the postcode into the sat nav and ended up at a bloody paintballing place down the road. Happens all the time apparently."

Stock smiled tightly. "I guess you must be new to the area. I'd have warned you if I'd known."

Leaving the car park, the two men walked in silence to the gatehouse. No matter how many times Warren visited prisons, he never got used to them. The Mount was a category C prison built in the late 1980s on the site of a former RAF base. Despite its red-brick façade, which at first glance could have housed anything from a factory to an office complex, close inspection soon revealed its true purpose. Even in the warm summer sun, Warren felt a chill. He glanced over at his young companion and saw a similar look of discomfort on his face. This place housed misery; despondency hung thickly in the air.

Inside its walls, seven hundred or more individuals wasted their lives, marking the passage of time in a frozen limbo whilst the world outside continued without them. Some might emerge better men, willing to seize the second — or third or fourth — chance that life had given them, but Warren knew the statistics as well as anyone. A hefty percentage would end up back here or in another, similar institution. Of those that remained outside, many would live unfulfilled lives, struggling to get a job and forever fighting against the demons that had led them down this path in the first place.

A few paces away a young mother with a hard face and blue tattoos up her skinny, bare arms dragged a scowling child in T-shirt and shorts behind her. The young boy's face was a mirror image of his mother's, a vicious crew cut adding to his thuggish look. Warren knew he shouldn't judge by appearances, but he couldn't help it. Deep in the recesses of his brain, in the part that harboured the thoughts that he could never express out loud, a little voice said, 'She'll be visiting him before long.' Turning away, he buried the petty little thought as they approached the entrance.

The procedures at The Mount were largely the same as at any other category C prison that Warren had visited. His warrant card cut little ice here and he underwent much the same process as any other visitor. In deference to his position, Warren was spared an intimate body search, but he nevertheless had to empty his pockets, surrendering his wallet, keys and mobile phone. Stock fared little better, although his legally protected status as Severino's lawyer meant that he was allowed to keep his briefcase and a small Dictaphone.

After the preliminaries were concluded, both men were led to a private interview room where Severino was seated, alone at a metal table. Because, in the jargon of the Home Office, he was a non-convicted prisoner, Severino wore his own clothes, albeit without any laces or a belt, lest he killed himself or someone else.

Severino looked even worse, if that was possible, than the last time Warren had seen him — in the dock as he was remanded in custody. His face was gaunt, his eyes red-rimmed and sunken. The thick stubble on his chin and jowls now covered the whole of his lower face. He slumped forward as if even his spine had been confiscated, staring at the table top listlessly. When Warren and Stock entered, though, he sat up straighter, making eye contact with both men.

He half rose as if to shake hands, before remembering where he was and instead remained in an awkward half-pose, gesturing to the two other chairs as if he were inviting dinner companions to make themselves comfortable.

"Thank you for coming, DCI Jones."

Warren said nothing, merely nodding his greeting. Stock placed the Dictaphone on the table between the three men, quietly checking the levels. Warren and Severino eyed each other warily. Severino had asked Jones to visit him, a move which at first glance seemed to award Severino a degree of control over him when one considered the rules of this primal setting. However, the prisoner's precarious position instead meant the invitation was in fact Warren's to turn down. Overall, Warren figured he had the upper hand. Ultimately, he had something that Severino had to respect — the power to decide if he would listen to his story, take it seriously and perhaps set the wheels in motion for his release. Warren was a long way from being convinced so far.

Daniel Stock cleared his throat, causing the two men to break eye contact finally.

"This is Daniel Stock representing Dr Antonio Severino. We have requested an interview with DCI Warren Jones at The Mount Prison, as we believe that Dr Severino may have new information pertinent to the current investigation, which we hope may lead to the release of Dr Severino on bail and ultimately, the dropping of charges."

Warren maintained his poker face, hiding his true feelings. In his experience, few of these visiting-hour meetings had ever yielded useful information. When a suspect had been remanded in custody, especially for a crime as serious as murder, his world came crashing down. All but the most hardened criminals would start wracking their brains for a means to clear their name, whether by truth or lies. Warren knew that the odds were good that this meeting would be no different.

"Why don't you explain to DCI Jones what you told me yesterday?" invited Stock.

Severino leant forward, licking his lips nervously. Nevertheless, his voice was clear and strong, and Warren got the impression that he had been planning what he wanted to say carefully. That in itself was not an indicator of guilt, Warren reminded himself. Severino might speak impeccable English, but it was still his second language. Furthermore, he had spent much of the past twenty-four hours waiting for this meeting. It was inevitable that he'd rehearse what he wanted to say.

"I may be able to explain where the bloodstained clothes that you found stuffed down my drain have come from—"

At this point his lawyer leant forward, interrupting. "It should be noted that it has not yet been determined that the clothes belonged to my client and he has not admitted to owning them or seeing them before."

Warren resisted the urge to roll his eyes; even Severino didn't seem impressed by the interruption. If the clothes weren't Severino's then who the hell else in Middlesbury was wandering around wearing jeans from the Italian equivalent of Marks and

Spencer and a hooded top from the University of Trieste with the name "Antonio" stitched on the left of its chest? Regardless, a positive ID would come back pretty soon from Forensics, Warren was certain.

"A few days ago, the Friday before Professor Tunbridge was murdered, I met a girl in a bar." The Italian looked uncomfortable.

"Go on."

"I had been drinking a lot and I was pretty drunk. Anyway, we got on very well and she came back to my house."

"Where was your fiancée at this time, Dr Severino?"

He looked guilty and ashamed.

"She is visiting her parents in Germany. Things have not been so good between us since I lose my job. She wanted to take a break. To 'clear her head' as you say." Warren made a note to get this checked out, as much to check on the safety of his fiancée as anything else. The man had after all been charged with murder. Severino couldn't remember her parents' address off the top of his head, but pointed Warren to the address book on his mobile phone, which the police had confiscated when he was arrested.

"So what happened next, Dr Severino?"

"We had some more to drink. A lot more—" he looked embarrassed "—and we went to bed. I woke up the next morning feeling sick, and she was gone. She could have stolen my clothes and my swipe card then."

"I see. Were they missing?"

Severino paused, then sighed, clearly not wanting to be caught out in a lie. "I don't know. I never notice. I tend to wear whatever is on top of the pile of clothes at the bottom of the wardrobe. I haven't seen my swipe card for long time. I assume it hanging on the back of the door with my coat, but it could have been gone for ages and I wouldn't have noticed."

"So, what was her name? Had you met her before?"

A slightly embarrassed shrug. "I'd never met her before that night, I'm pretty sure of that. Her name was Joanna, I think. She said to call her Jo."

"Can you describe her at all? Her appearance? How she sounded? Did she have an accent?"

Severino shook his head slowly. "I was so drunk. She was blonde and pretty — I remember that from the bar. I don't remember her being very tall or fat. She was… average, maybe in her twenties."

"How did she sound? Was she British or foreign?"

"I am not so good with accents, you know. But I think she was English. Normal like they have around here, not weird like Georgies or Broomies I think you call them."

Warren ignored the slight. A Coventry native, to the uneducated he sometimes sounded like his Brummie cousins twenty miles down the road in Birmingham.

"Are there any witnesses who can back up your story? Where did you go?"

"No, I am sorry. I was on my own until this girl came over. I was in a small pub in town, the White Bear I think it was called. It was quiet. After a few more drinks we went to a club, Mr G's in town, then we walked back to my house. I had wine and some weed."

Warren sighed. "You haven't given us a lot to go on, Dr Severino. You go out to a bar, get drunk and stoned then claim a mystery woman seduces you and steals your clothes whilst you sleep. You can't describe her, there are no witnesses and you don't have any evidence. Is that about right?" He was starting to get annoyed. Yet another bloody time-waster.

"I am sorry." Severino looked crestfallen and Warren almost felt sorry for the young man. Almost, but not quite.

"Tell DCI Jones about this Friday."

Severino perked up slightly. "I gave her my number in the pub, before we decided to go clubbing. She called me Tuesday night and asked if she could come over on Friday night."

Warren blinked. The girl, if she existed, could potentially supply Severino with an alibi. Why in God's name was he only just mentioning this now? He put the question to the young researcher. Severino looked embarrassed. "She never came. I went out and bought some drinks and sorted out some weed from a friend. She said that she be over about 8 p.m. When she didn't turn up I phoned her, but it wasn't answered. She didn't have any voicemail. I text her, but she didn't reply. I phone her a few more times but nothing. In the end I smoked the weed and I think I must have drunk all of the booze. I don't remember anything until you woke me up banging on the door."

Warren mulled this over silently. If Severino was telling the truth — and he was far from convinced yet — then this mysterious girl could have set him up. Seducing him in the pub, stealing his clothes and swipe card, then later making sure that he was home alone without an alibi whilst the murder was committed. It seemed almost too farfetched.

"And you have no idea who this girl was? Can you think of any other details about her? What she was wearing maybe?"

Severino screwed up his face in concentration. "I was so drunk... I think she might have been wearing jeans and a pink top. That's all I can remember."

Suddenly, Warren had a thought. "If she phoned you Tuesday and you texted her Friday, then you must have her number."

Severino looked excited, then dismayed. "I never saved the number." Then he perked up again, speaking at the same time as Warren and his lawyer. "The phone's call log!"

Forensics had seized Severino's mobile phone and laptop computer when his house was searched. Warren made a note to have Welwyn prioritise their analysis; he also noted down the need for a warrant to look at Severino's phone records.

With nothing else forthcoming from the prisoner, Warren stood up to leave. As he did so Severino leapt to his feet, his expression desperate. Ignoring his solicitor's repeated instructions to sit back down, he half lunged towards Warren, who backed up so fast he knocked his chair over.

"Mr Jones, you must believe me. I did not kill Professor Tunbridge. I am innocent." With Warren safely out of reach, he turned to his lawyer who still sat, his mouth open in surprise. He grabbed the young man's wrist, pulling him closer. "Please, Mr Stock, you must get me out of here. I am innocent." At the sound of raised voices, the guard, a large white man with a shaven head, entered the room, grabbing the thin Italian, pulling him backwards as he shouted for assistance. Stock tried to pull away, but Severino was stronger than he looked. Warren grabbed at the man's hands, trying to prise his fingers from the terrified lawyer's wrist. The door crashed open and two more guards raced in.

Barely pausing to assess the situation, the newcomers waded in. The first guard rapped Severino smartly on the forearm, breaking the man's grip, whilst the second struck him twice on the back of the knees, causing them to buckle. Finally the three of them wrestled the now barely coherent Severino to the hard, concrete floor. With practised moves, the guards pulled Severino's hands behind his back and secured them with plasticuffs. Face down now and breathing heavily, Severino had quietened to a whisper. "Please get me out, I didn't kill him," he repeated again and again.

Warren took the shaken solicitor by the shoulders and led him out of the room. Unable to resist one last glance back, he looked at the accused prisoner, lying face down on the floor, sobbing. Twisting his head, Severino managed to look towards the departing men, locking tear-filled eyes with Warren. "Please," he mouthed as the door clanged shut behind them.

Shaken more than he would have thought possible, Warren looked over to the solicitor. The young man was a ghastly shade of white, his breath coming in shallow gasps. He had clearly never experienced anything like that in his short career. Warren felt sorry for the poor lad.

"Puked on and attacked by the same client within three days. I hope you charge extra for that type of treatment."

The white-faced brief looked at Warren for a few long seconds, before managing the barest of smiles. "No chance. God, I hate fucking legal aid cases."

Chapter 26

After collecting his belongings and being let back out of the prison, Warren headed immediately back to the station. Ordinarily, Warren experienced a sensation of relief as he drove away from a prison visit. The feeling usually gained in intensity as he put more miles between himself and those places of misery.

Today was different somehow. Warren didn't feel his usual cynical annoyance. Naturally the prisoner had professed his innocence — rarely if ever did they call you in to confess — so that didn't bother him. Even the tears hadn't fazed him or the violent end to the meeting. He'd experienced them all before. It was the eyes, he thought. The raw terror and pleading had left him feeling more shaken than he'd been willing to show in front of Stock or the prison staff.

Stopping by Sutton's desk, he filled the detective inspector in on the interview. Sutton had been unimpressed the previous evening when Warren had received the phone call, describing the visit as a waste of time. Today, he went further, his rudeness bordering on the insubordinate.

"Of course he claims he didn't do it. And this mysterious bird who's supposed to have seduced him then stolen his clothes and his swipe card, who he conveniently can't describe, frankly I'm disappointed that's the best he was able to come up with after spending twenty-four hours cooling his heels at Her Majesty and the tax-payers' pleasure."

Warren briefly considered hauling Sutton into his office for a tongue-lashing about his attitude, but he decided to choose his battles. Nevertheless, he was unwilling to let Sutton have it all his own way.

"Well, whilst I'm out checking Severino's story, you can keep yourself busy tracking down his missing fiancée. He claims that she returned home to her parents in Germany a few weeks ago. See if you can speak to her. She's been here for several years, so she should speak English." He handed over the details that he had taken from Severino's lawyer. "I'd also like you to speak to the Italian police and see if they have had any previous contact with him. Check with International Liaison about what warrants might be needed and who is the best person to contact."

Sutton didn't even try to hide his groan. Trying to get information from one EU country was hassle enough. Dealing with two countries promised to be a nightmare. Warren successfully hid his smile until he had his back turned.

Before he wasted any time tracking down a mystery woman that might not even exist, Warren phoned Welwyn's IT department. As a matter of routine, they'd requested Severino's phone records when they had arrested him on Saturday. The delay caused by the weekend meant that they had yet to appear from the phone company. Warren had seen no point at the time in asking for a rush job, since they hadn't seemed important. Now he wished he had.

According to the helpful civilian worker at the end of the line, the phone provider had promised the records would be with Warren by late afternoon. Unwilling to wait that long, Warren asked to be reconnected to the evidence room.

After identifying himself to the officer in charge and giving the case number, he asked for Severino's mobile phone to be pulled out. His next request was met with some incredulity.

"You want me to do what?"

"I just need you to power it up, enter his recent calls list and tell me any numbers that he called Friday night."

"Are you taking the piss? Is this a wind-up? I'm fifty-three years old — I still miss using a bloody dial. I can barely send a text message."

Warren closed his eyes briefly. "No, Sergeant, I'm serious. I need those numbers and don't have time for the hour-long round trip down to Welwyn to pick up the phone and do it myself. Is there somebody…" He almost said 'younger' but bit his tongue at the last second. "Someone more used to mobile phones that could perhaps try for me?"

Warren chose to ignore the mumbled profanities and references to 'the Carphone Fucking Warehouse', as the grumpy, veteran police officer stamped off down the corridor in search of a member of the mobile generation.

A few moments later a flustered constable who sounded as if his voice had barely broken came on the line. Warren explained what he wanted him to do. Fortunately, the phone had enough battery-life left to fulfil this simple task — Warren could only imagine the response he'd have received if he'd asked them to track down a charger as well.

The phone's log confirmed an incoming call lasting less than three minutes from another mobile phone on Tuesday evening and then showed several outgoing calls to the same number on the Friday evening, none of which were answered. It seemed that Severino's story was at least partially true. With that accomplished, he next got the officer to look up Severino's fiancée's and parents' numbers and address for Sutton.

Finishing his call, Warren returned to the main office. Sutton was away from his desk, so Warren left the numbers and addresses on a Post-it note stuck to the screen of his computer.

Calling over Gary Hastings and Karen Hardwick, he filled the two young constables in on his morning. He handed over the number that Severino claimed belonged to his mysterious liaison.

"Have either of you ever requested telephone records before?"

Hardwick shook her head immediately. It wasn't that surprising given that she had only just joined CID. Hastings had assisted in drafting a warrant a couple of times. Warren reminded them how under the Regulation of Investigationary Powers Act, police had to fill in a special warrant for every phone, computer or similar device that they wanted information on. Each device was dealt with separately and a justification given each time. The amount of information they could request varied, from a simple enquiry about a phone's ownership, to a list of calls made and or received; a track of the phone's historic movements, using either GPS or cell tower triangulation; a track of its current whereabouts; or in the rarest of cases an interception of calls, text messages, instant messages, emails or anything else that could be thought of.

Warren asked Hastings to show Hardwick how to draft a request for the ownership details and the previous twelve months' usage records for the number found on Severino's phone. He had a feeling that RIPA was going to be an increasing part of a police officer's day-to-day governance and he wanted all of his officers trained in its use. When they had completed the request, he told them they were to show it to DS Kent, who was an expert at finessing such requests to get what information they needed.

Before leaving the office, Warren did a quick Internet search and located the pub and club that Severino claimed to have been drinking in. Both were in the town centre, within easy staggering distance of each other and Severino's house. Grabbing his car keys, he decided to target the White Bear first, before retracing the couple's steps to Mr G's nightclub.

Situated at the north end of the town centre, the pub had a large plastic polar bear sitting above the porch-style entrance. Surrounded by neon lights, it might look enticing and exciting in the dark, after a few beers and if small market towns in north Hertfordshire were your sole experience of big city night-life. At one forty-five on a Tuesday afternoon it just seemed seedy to Warren, who was used to the somewhat more glamorous drinking establishments on offer in Birmingham or London. The fact that the once-white polar bear was largely covered by the green mould that covered white plastic garden furniture if it was left outside too long further dispelled the illusion.

The sturdy front door was locked, but inside Warren could hear the sound of a vacuum cleaner. Peering through the window into the gloom beyond, he could make out someone behind the bar doing something with the till. Next to the door was a doorbell. Warren pressed it.

"Deliveries round the back!" a voice shouted over the din of the vacuum cleaner.

"I'm not delivering..." started Warren before being interrupted.

"Then come back in fifteen minutes. We ain't reopened yet."

"It's the police. Could you open the door please, Mr... Stribling?" Warren took a guess that the person most likely to be opening the till early afternoon on a weekday would be the landlord, whose name was listed on the licence above the door.

"Oh, bollocks. What now?" Warren watched through the window as the landlord made his way to the door. It took almost a minute for him to open it, turning three different keys and sliding across two different bolts. The man was short and portly with dirty-grey hair slicked down with gel. A scraggly moustache clung to his top lip, its colour a mixture of white, grey and nicotine yellow. He had one of those smoker's faces that could be anywhere between forty-five and sixty-five.

Holding up his warrant card, Warren introduced himself. Looking around, he noticed the faded décor and scratched tables. The source of the vacuuming came from the farthest corner where a plump young woman unenthusiastically ran the machine forward and backwards. With her back to the door and the white headphones of an iPod clearly adding their own din to that of the vacuum cleaner, Warren doubted she was even aware that an extra person was in the room.

A strong smell of cigarette smoke hung in the air, which the landlord dismissed quickly. "Must 'ave left the back door open when I 'ad me fag break." He casually tossed a bar towel over the burning cigarette in the half-filled ashtray on the bar top, clearly hoping that Warren hadn't noticed.

"What can I do fer you, Officer? If it's about them sixth-formers, they had fake ID, real good 'n all. 'Course, soon as I realised they was underage, like, I chucked them out."

Not before getting a few quid out of them first, I'll bet, thought Warren. He decided not to point out that detective chief inspectors didn't usually investigate reports of seventeen-year-old A-level students having a crafty pint.

Now the man looked really worried and Warren wondered what he was hiding. Nothing to do with his case, he thought, but it might come in useful as leverage. By the looks of things, Mr Stribling was your basic dodgy landlord who kept his head above water by skirting around the law and turning a blind eye to some of the more dubious deals run by his customers, perhaps taking a small cut of the action for his trouble.

"I'm sure you did your duty, Mr Stribling."

"Call me Larry, please. Every time you say Mr Stribling, I fink you're talking to me old man!" His laugh was cut short by a wheezing cough that suggested that the person most inconvenienced by the smoking ban in this pub was the landlord. Or perhaps not, thought Warren, eyeing the faint wisps of smoke still curling from under the bar towel. He made a mental note to check out any 999 calls to the fire brigade later on.

"I wonder if you recognise this man, drinking in here on the evening of Friday August fifth."

Stribling's eyes narrowed and he barely glanced at the mugshot of Severino. "Nope, never seen him."

"You seem very sure of that, Larry. Are you certain? Perhaps you could take a closer look at the photo. It's funny how when you take a closer look at something, you notice things that you didn't before." He glanced meaningfully at the smouldering ashtray. "Things that you realise that you need to do something about."

Stribling scowled, clearly uncomfortable about the idea of betraying one of his punters to the police and possibly by extension himself. Warren decided to make it easier on him. "Look, it hasn't got anything to do with you or this bar. We're simply trying to track the movements of this man and your pub came up as somewhere he might have stopped for a drink."

Stribling sighed, but pulled the photo over anyway. Plucking a pair of reading glasses from his shirt pocket, he squinted hard at the photo. "Eleven days is a long time ago, Chief Inspector, and Friday nights are our busiest night." He continued looking at the photo, a frown puckering his forehead. "I have to say that he does look a bit familiar. Last Friday, you say… yeah, definitely. He was here for a few hours. I remember 'cause he sat at the bar, getting in the way of people trying to get served. I was gonna tell him to move, but he was spending a fair bit, you know. Most of the punters were students here for my Friday night drinks promotion. By the time I've paid the duty and VAT and taxes, the profit on each pint is two-thirds of fuck-all. He was drinking good stuff, though — probably made more profit from him than ten of those bleedin' students."

Warren felt a surge of excitement. "Can you remember if he was here with anyone else?"

Stribling shook his head. "On his own at the bar, like I said. Looked bloody miserable, to be honest."

"Any idea why?"

Stribling looked at him incredulously. "Not a bloody clue. This isn't *Cheers*, you know, where everyone knows your name. None of my business what's upset him. I just serve the drinks."

Warren persisted. "And he didn't meet anyone here?"

Stribling shrugged helplessly. "I wasn't really paying attention, to be honest. I was mostly serving down the other end of the bar. Although, come to think of it, he did eventually move from the bar to one of the tables in the corner. He might have gone over with someone."

Warren struggled to hide his frustration; all he had so far was that Severino had gone to the pub a week before Tunbridge's murder. He tried to picture the bar that night. Heaving with students guzzling pints of cheap lager, whilst Severino sat alone on a bar stool getting steadily more drunk. Warren looked at the bar again. It was long and straight, closed at both ends to deter cheeky, DIY pint-pourers, but with hinged lids to allow staff easy access to and from the area behind the bar. Two modern tills with touchscreens meant that servers didn't have to turn their backs to the customers when they took their money. Two tills…

"Was there anybody else working that Friday?"

Stribling looked at him as if he was soft in the head. "Yeah, 'course. Can't run a bar on my own, can I? Friday night it's our Kel behind the bar and Dazza collecting glasses."

"May I speak to them, please?" asked Warren, deliberately keeping his tone polite.

Stribling shrugged, then called out to the young woman with the vacuum cleaner.

"Kel!"

Nothing.

"Kel!"

Still nothing.

Marching around the bar, Stribling reached out and tugged on one of the leads. The earphone popped out and she jumped in surprise.

"Bloody 'ell, Dad! What did you do that for?"

"'Cause you're always plugged into that sodding thing. Could be a bloody air raid and you'd never know anyfink about it."

Or a fire alarm, thought Warren, noticing that the abandoned cigarette still seemed to be doing its thing. He thought he'd read somewhere that modern cigarettes were supposed to go out if left unattended. He wondered how long that was supposed to take.

The young woman was about nineteen or twenty, Warren guessed, although it was a bit difficult to tell under all of the piercings and white and black face make-up. He supposed she was what kids these days called a Goth or was it an emo now? Warren remembered them from when he was her age, although he and his mates had just referred to them as miserable buggers.

He forced a smile and introduced himself, showing her Severino's photograph. As she spoke to him Stribling disappeared off to find "Dazza", the third member of this family enterprise.

Squinting at the picture with the one eye that wasn't obscured by her jet-black fringe, she nodded and smiled briefly.

"Yeah, I remember him.". She pointed at a bar stool in front of the till nearest the front door. "He sat there all night, drinking. Didn't say very much, just stared at his drink. One of those dark, moody Mediterranean types." Clearly the sort of man she found attractive, Warren thought, amused.

"Did he meet anyone here?"

She frowned, then brightened as she remembered, then frowned again as the memory clearly irritated her. Warren hoped for her sake that she never took up poker; hiding what she was thinking was not one of this girl's strong suits.

"Yeah, some blonde bimbo sat herself down next to him late in the evening. She clearly wasn't his type—" Warren discounted this observation as potentially biased "—but she wouldn't give up. Eventually they moved to the corner over there." She pointed to a small, circular wooden table flanked by short, cushioned stools. "They had a couple more drinks and then left." She sniffed her disapproval. "He was clearly pissed — she shouldn't have taken advantage like that."

Warren fought the urge to smile; he doubted that Severino had felt taken advantage of. And if he was, he doubted that he would care too much. Then his amusement disappeared like a puff of smoke as he considered that Severino might well have been taken advantage of in more ways than he could have imagined at the time.

"Did you know her at all?"

"No, but I know the type. Skinny, blonde, big tits." Everything Kel wasn't, thought Warren, feeling a twinge of sympathy for the girl.

"Can you remember any more details?"

Kel squeezed her eyes shut as she tried to remember one single customer from several days previously. "I think she was wearing a pink top and jeans."

"How old would you say she was? Was she tall?"

"Probably about twenty, average height." She shook her head. "That's all, sorry." Warren smiled encouragingly as he handed her his card. "Thank you. If you remember anything else at all, no matter how trivial, please call me."

As Kel returned to work Stribling reappeared, followed by a young lad of about seventeen, presumably "Dazza". The lad was pale and pimply, with a spectacular case of bed-head. The T-shirt he wore above the tracksuit bottoms had clearly been slept in and was somewhat vintage, judging by the smell. The logo proclaimed that the owner was experiencing the same shit but on a different day.

"This is my Darren. We call him 'Dazza' or 'Daz', like the washing powder. We was gonna call him Ariel but that's a girl's name." The pause for a laugh stretched uncomfortably.

"I suppose you could have named him Percival and called him Persil for short," suggested Warren, unable to help himself. Everyone looked at him blankly. Warren decided not to comment that it was a "Bold" choice of name for someone so unused to a washing machine.

Stribling continued, "He helps us out if it's busy — just collecting glasses, of course," he added hastily. Warren pushed the photo across.

"Oh, yeah, I remember him. Sat on his own all night before some bird suddenly appeared out of nowhere and before you know it they was off in the corner and getting all cosy." Dazza had clearly been impressed by Severino's quick work.

"Can you remember anything about the woman?"

Dazza didn't even pause. "Oh, yeah, she was well fit. I served her a couple of times." Warren pretended not to notice the lad's slip-up, although the glare from his father suggested that words would be had about what not to say in front of police officers. Unfortunately, he couldn't remember specifics, although he was fairly confident that he'd remember her if he saw her again. None of the bar staff knew her name or could remember seeing her before that night or since. The bar didn't have CCTV, although there were some council-owned cameras further up the street that might have caught an image.

Thanking them for their time, Warren headed for the front door, before pausing briefly.

"Oh, by the way. You might want to deal with that sooner rather than later." He pointed to the smoking bar towel covering the smouldering ashtray, which had now caught alight.

Chapter 27

The next stop for Warren was Mr G's nightclub. Warren had secured a good parking space near to the White Bear, so he decided to stretch his legs and walk to the club. At a brisk pace, he was there in just over five minutes. Even allowing for a slow, drunken stagger, it was obvious that the club was within reasonable walking distance from the pub.

Mr G's was set slightly back off a side street and took up two floors. The ground-floor bar was already open, although the half-dozen customers visible through the floor-to-ceiling windows were sitting at small, round metal tables drinking coffee rather than beer. The neon "Mr G's" sign above the door was turned off and, instead, wooden chalkboards advertising the soup-of-the-day and the lunch-time special flanked the entrance.

Stepping inside, Warren introduced himself to the young woman serving behind the bar and asked to see the manager. A few moments later, a youthful-looking man in a pair of light chino trousers and a pale-blue short-sleeved shirt came down the stairs. Walking briskly over to Warren without any hesitation, he stuck his hand out and introduced himself as Jack Baker. Responding to Warren's request for a private word, he led the way up the stairs to the main club.

There was something not quite right about an empty nightclub, with the lights on in the middle of the day, Warren reflected. It seemed empty and lifeless. It reminded him of the times he'd visited Susan's school after home-time or during the holidays. Without the crackle and fizzle of youthful energy, the building seemed almost lonely. Of course, more than one teacher had commented that the school ran a lot more efficiently without the pupils getting in the way and interrupting the paperwork.

The club was fairly straightforward and unpretentious. Most of the floor-space was given over to a large, square, empty dance floor, surrounded on three sides by a raised dais with tables and chairs. A boxed-in DJ booth faced the bar, now shuttered, that took up most of the fourth side. The room smelt faintly of stale beer and air-freshener. An elderly lady in an apron was mopping the floor by the DJ's box.

Flanking the bar were two doors. One with a toilet sign, the other with 'Staff Only'. Leading Warren through the second door, Baker turned right and entered an office. Much to Warren's surprise, the office was light and airy with large windows overlooking a generously sized pub garden. Two desks that wouldn't be out of place in a bank or a solicitor's office occupied most of the floor-space. In the farthest corner from the door a large, steel safe, the size of a king-size refrigerator, dominated the wall. To Warren's astonishment, the closed door of the safe was adorned with hand-painted children's pictures and the artist responsible for the masterpieces was sitting in the corner on several sheets of newspaper cheerfully splattering paint all over another sheet of A4.

Baker smiled at Warren's look of surprise. "Not quite what you were expecting, Detective Chief Inspector?"

Regaining his composure, Warren shook his head. "I have to say, Mr Baker, that I have been in the back offices of many pubs and clubs in my time and the word that usually springs to mind is 'dingy'. This is somewhat different."

Baker laughed good-naturedly. "I should hope so. I'm a businessman first and foremost, not a publican. I have a degree in business and law and spent most of the first ten years after university working for blue-chip companies in London. I've tried to bring some of that ethos with me to Mr G's."

"So how does a London businessman end up in the middle of Hertfordshire, running a nightclub?" asked Warren curiously.

Baker waved a hand vaguely in the air. "Sometimes life just leads you where you least expect it to. In London I had my own office and secretary and a view of the river, but I wasn't really enjoying myself. My Dad, George — that's where the 'Mr G' came from — ran this place for thirty years and it was just like you'd expect. Dingy. I never thought I'd ever have anything to do with it. Anyway, he dropped dead of a heart attack about five years ago and I inherited the place, just as I was starting to fall out of love with London. I was worried about Mum being all alone and I'd been rekindling an old friendship from my childhood, so I decided to jack the job in in London and come back here to run this place. I married the friend and decided I didn't want to move away from where I grew up.

"To be honest, for the first twelve months this place was a bloody millstone around my neck and I hated it. The books were a mess, the place was a dive with a real reputation as a Friday-night meat market. We had drug problems and frankly it was the sort of nightclub you'd have had to drag me kicking and screaming to on a night out normally.

"In the end, I decided enough was enough and I closed us down for two months. I sacked the door staff, who were responsible for half the drug-dealing anyway, and turned downstairs into a nice, decent bar suitable for a quiet drink or a coffee at lunchtime and a meeting place in the evening. Upstairs, I just decided to go back to basics, making the dance floor as big as possible and concentrating on giving people what they want: decent music to dance to on the weekend and live music and comedy to listen to during the week.

"As you can see, I run this place as I would any other business. The one thing I was missing about working in London was my office. So I gutted the old office, painted the walls white instead of black, got rid of the topless calendar on the back of the door and entered the twenty-first century." He nodded towards the toddler in the corner. "I even bring my daughter to work a couple of days a week to save on childcare. Marlene, who sits over there, was my dad's assistant for years and I kept her on. She treats Isla here like another grandkid." At the mention of her name, the little girl looked over and gave a big, gap-toothed smile, before resuming her painting. "I don't think anyone expected me to succeed, to be honest, even my mum. But last year we turned a profit for the first time in nearly a decade. By the end of this year, the club will have made enough to pay off the second mortgage Dad took out on his and Mum's house to keep this bloody place open."

Warren was impressed and said so, before getting down to business. The contrast with Larry Stribling couldn't have been greater. Without even being asked, Baker offered to call up the security footage of the night in question.

"One of the things I decided to change was the club's relationship with the police. I'm not saying my old man was a crook, but he skirted the law and regarded the police as something of a hindrance rather than a partner. As a club we have a proactive

239

approach: drug dealers are shopped immediately; under-age drinkers are photographed and banned and they can't come back until they have proof of age; and we keep our eyes and ears open for any dodgy booze and fags and report it to the police. We're also helping set up a zero-tolerance zone with other pubs and entertainment venues like the cinema — anybody banned from one place has their photo taken and it's immediately circulated around everywhere else. We've got about two dozen people who can't get served in any of the pubs in the scheme. Our goal is to extend the system across the town centre."

Watching the footage was just a question of accessing the digital video files held on the club's computer system. They kept footage for the previous month, before archiving it. As Baker pointed out, the cost of storing digital imagery was so low these days, they might as well. You never knew when it might be useful.

The club had a number of different cameras, including wide-angled cameras above both bars and the beer garden, the front door and the staff-only areas. The footage Warren was most interested in was that from the camera mounted over the main door.

Severino had been vague as to what time he and the mysterious young woman arrived at the club, but Warren doubted it could have been earlier than about 10 p.m. The digital video footage was surprisingly easy to manipulate and, after a few moments of tutorial, Baker left Warren to get on with watching the video. He soon got into the rhythm of fast-forwarding the video at eight-times normal speed, then hitting the slow button as customers came through the door to get a good look at them. After a few false starts, Warren finally got what he was looking for. According to the time stamp on the bottom of the screen, Severino appeared, mystery woman in tow, at 11.52 p.m. The camera showed a clear black and white image of Severino's darkly handsome features. Even on the slowed-down video feed it was clear that Severino was very drunk; it took him a couple of attempts to get his wallet out of his pocket and he swayed as he did so.

Unfortunately, the young woman was hanging off his arm, her face half turned towards him as he fumbled in his pocket for the entrance money. Warren slowed the video down again and replayed it, hissing in frustration. At no point did the young woman look at the camera directly. The best that Warren could make out was that she was of average size, wearing a light, probably pink top. Her hair was cut to a medium length and appeared blonde on the black and white image.

Seeing that Warren had hit a brick wall, Baker returned to his side.

"You are welcome to look at the footage from the other cameras and see if she looks towards the camera. If she got served, we probably have a good shot, but it was a busy night and you could spend a lot of time finding the image."

Warren nodded his agreement. It was frustrating, however; he was now convinced at least that Severino had met some mysterious woman in a bar. But it still left many unanswered questions: did this woman go back to Severino's and take his swipe card and clothes? And if that was the case, who was she?

Chapter 28

After taking a copy of the footage that Baker had given him from the nightclub's video feeds, Warren headed back to the station. He popped the USB memory stick containing the video footage into a Jiffy bag, addressed it to the Image Analysis department and slipped it into the internal mail. Then, to ensure that it didn't go missing, he logged the request into the computer system and emailed the department to be on the lookout for its arrival.

Warren spent the remainder of the afternoon shuffling paper, before deciding that, in view of the hours he'd already put in over the weekend, leaving work at a decent-ish hour wouldn't be unreasonable. It would certainly stand him in good stead with Susan and the in-laws. Nevertheless, before going home, Warren decided to try his luck with some more of Tunbridge's acquaintances.

Using the directions given by Annabel Tunbridge, Jones pulled into the car park at the Middlesbury Sports Centre. Getting out of the car, he locked up and looked around. Straight ahead of him was a wide-open cricket pitch. A half-dozen teenage boys dressed in shorts and T-shirts were playing catch with a cricket ball under the watchful eye of a middle-aged man. Two more sat on the ground tying on pads. The fresh scent of newly mown grass hung in the still air. To the right, a small pavilion with a canvas awning was home to a dozen or so folded plastic chairs and a handful of circular metal tables. Behind, a long, flat-roofed single-storey brick building bore the signs "Changing Rooms" and "Clubhouse". A large pair of padlocked double doors was flanked by a handful of metal beer barrels, presumably empty, awaiting pickup by the brewery.

To the left of the cricket pitch another clubhouse, this one wooden and in need of a lick of paint, sat looking over a large square of tightly mown grass. On the grass seven or eight older men were playing bowls. The green was slightly sunken, surrounded by a gravel ditch with lane markers planted in it. Making his way across the car park to the bowls club, Warren stepped onto the concrete verge surrounding the grass. To his right a robust man, anywhere between the ages of fifty-five and seventy-five, was watching a pair of bowlers intently.

"Excuse me, sir, I'm looking for the club captain."

Tearing his eyes away from the game, the man gave him a quick once-over.

"You're speaking to him. Graham Weatherby. I take it you're here about Alan Tunbridge." It was a statement, not a question.

Jones raised an eyebrow quizzically.

"You're hardly dressed to play a game and after thirty years on the force, I'd recognise CID a mile off. We've all heard about Alan, of course. Terrible business."

Jones found the man's upfront manner refreshing, "DCI Warren Jones. I wondered if I might have a word, sir."

"Of course, although I'm not sure about a detective chief inspector calling a lowly sergeant like me 'sir'". The man gave a grin and stuck out a dry, weathered paw for Jones to shake. He motioned towards a park bench next to the clubhouse.

"You'll be after background, I suppose. Tying up those annoying loose ends after that remarkably quick arrest?"

"Pretty much," admitted Jones. "We're still dotting the Is and crossing the Ts on the prosecution case. The suspect in custody isn't admitting anything, so we're doing all the legwork."

The former policeman snorted. "I've been there, lad. What would you like to know?"

"Well, first of all, how well did you know Professor Tunbridge? What sort of a man was he?"

Weatherby thought for a moment. "Alan started playing here six, seven years ago. Not a bad player. He'd join us for a roll-up most Tuesday nights and played a few matches for us on a Saturday."

Jones raised an eyebrow in surprise and Weatherby chuckled. "Bowling slang, a roll-up's what we call a practice session. He had the makings of a good player, although he was a busy man and couldn't really commit to all the fixtures. We try to get younger players in, but there's no getting round the fact that most of us are retired and can play pretty much whenever we're needed." As if to emphasise his point he gestured at the players, all of whom were free early on a weekday evening. "To be honest, we're more of a social club than anything. All the decent players go off to join the Avenue. We just enjoy ourselves."

"I see. How well did you know him?"

"Not as well as I know some of the blokes. He didn't come to many away fixtures, so we didn't spend a lot of time chatting on the bus. All I really knew was that he was some sort of scientist at the university. Had no idea he was a professor until I saw the paper yesterday. He was polite enough most of the time, followed the etiquette, like, and bought his opponent a drink, but as soon as he'd finished it he'd usually disappear off. Most of the lads here are working class, builders, brickies, a couple of ex-coppers. We didn't really have that much in common."

"Would you say he was well liked?"

Weatherby sighed, clearly unwilling to speak ill of the dead. "To be honest, not really. He didn't have much of a sense of humour and could be a bit rude on the green. I had to have words with him last season about his attitude. He didn't suffer fools gladly and was rather arrogant." He nodded in the direction of a stooped, elderly man with a walking stick talking to another player. "That's Ernie over there. The old boy's eighty-seven years old and, to be honest, his best days are well behind him. He's as deaf as a post and half blind. He struggles to get it up some evenings — that's more bowls terminology, before you ask, means he can't always get the bowl far enough up the rink — but he's been a member of this club for forty years. Until he had his hips done, he mowed the lawn twice a week and was always first in line to do any repairs to the clubhouse. Ever since his old lady passed away a couple of years ago, we've made sure we look after him. Drag him out of an evening to stop him getting lonely, that sort of thing.

"Anyway, unless it's an important match we select our teams by lottery and Alan was drawn with Ernie, Fred and Ronnie in the fours. They drew straws and Ernie ended up as Skip, which means he was always the last on the team to play each end. Anyhow, Alan was third to play and placed a lovely shot right on the jack. Unfortunately, Ernie came in a bit heavy and knocked Alan into the gutter and gifted three shots to their opponents. Well, the language he used just wasn't on. I was a copper for thirty years and I can swear with the best of them, but he shocked me. Poor old Ernie might not have heard all of it, but he got the bloody gist. Fred and Ronnie nearly threw in the towel, they were so disgusted. God only knows what our guests thought. I'm just glad that none of the ladies were in earshot."

So it seemed that Tunbridge was as belligerent in his private life as he was in his professional life, mused Warren.

"Based on what you know about Professor Tunbridge, could he have upset anyone enough to have made them want to kill him?"

Weatherby snorted. "Well, nobody here takes things that seriously — a handshake and a pint will usually smooth over most disagreements. But I'll tell you one thing — that man had a nasty streak to him. I can see him upsetting someone enough for them to have a pop at him. And he was a randy old bugger, made a right nuisance of himself in the clubhouse with the barmaids. Landlord had to have words with him. Makes you wonder if there are any jealous husbands out there."

He looked Jones up and down shrewdly.

"Of course, you already have your man in custody. Not having second thoughts, are you? Between you and me, I've seen a few convictions over the years that I've had my doubts about. None of them have ever succeeded on appeal and, on balance, I reckon we got the right man, but take a little bit of advice from someone who's been there. Follow your gut. If it's telling you something ain't quite right, it's probably worth checking. Don't take someone else's word for it — make certain in your own mind. It's you who has to sleep at night."

Jones nodded thoughtfully. The old copper spoke a lot of sense. In the meantime, he decided that there was nothing else to be gained by staying here any longer. Standing up, he stuck his hand out again.

"Good to speak to you, Sergeant."

"And you too, Detective Chief Inspector. Any time you fancy a roll-up, we're always on the lookout for young blood and I'd love to hear the full story when it's all wrapped up."

Warren smiled. He had to confess to being just a little tempted. The gentle clack of the bowls against each other seemed light years away from the pressures of work. And since moving to Middlesbury, he and Susan had yet to make many friends outside work. Who said he had to retire first?

Saying goodbye, he headed off towards his car.

"Oh, DCI Jones, just a quick question." It was Weatherby again. "I was wondering, do you think it would be appropriate for us to send flowers to Mrs Tunbridge, or do you think we'd be better off sending them to his kids?"

Jones blinked in surprise. "I don't see why not. Why wouldn't Mrs Tunbridge want them? It would be a very thoughtful gesture."

"Well, what with all the trouble they've been having, I didn't want to upset anybody."

Jones' mouth ran dry. "What trouble would that be?"

"Oh, I assumed you'd know — he was quite open about it. He'd just left her."

* * *

Arriving home that night, Warren found a somewhat warmer atmosphere than he had been greeted with the previous evening. Instead of reheated leftovers, he found that the others had waited for him to return and they all sat down to a pleasant meal of risotto, washed down by a couple of glasses of a light white wine.

This time, Susan had been to the hardware store during the day but had insisted on returning with nothing more than a dozen sampler paint tins. Whilst Bernice and Dennis sat in the living room, Warren and Susan daubed the different-coloured paints on the kitchen walls, before both deciding on a pale cream scheme that would contrast nicely with the darker wooden kitchen units due to be delivered later in the week.

The young couple had retired to bed early and Susan, always the first to fall asleep, had nodded off with a happy smile on her face. Warren for his part lay awake for a few minutes, enjoying the sound of his wife's relaxed, peaceful breathing.

Soon, however, his thoughts turned to the day's events. It had been a long busy day, with lots of twists and turns. Deep within his gut, Warren felt the doubts rolling around, almost like a stomach ache. The wise words of the retired detective sergeant that he'd met at Tunbridge's bowls club echoed in his mind: *"Follow your gut. If it's telling you something ain't quite right, it's probably worth checking. Don't take someone else's word for it — make certain in your own mind. It's you who has to sleep at night."*

His gut certainly was telling him something. What was the significance of the mystery woman who had seduced Severino the week before the murder? Who was the mysterious John Priest? And was Severino working alone or was he just one member of a conspiracy? These questions churned around in Warren's head, keeping his exhausted mind from closing down. Finally, some time after the digital display on the alarm clock changed to 3 a.m., he finally started that slow, delicious descent towards darkness.

As the world finally slipped away, though, the last conscious image that flitted through his mind was that of the desperate Antonio Severino, tears coursing down his cheeks as the prison guards restrained him.

WEDNESDAY

Chapter 29

Wednesday morning arrived all too soon, the alarm clock pulling Warren from a fitful sleep far too early. A muffled curse from Susan's direction reminded him that if it weren't for the presence of the in-laws he would probably have been banished to the spare room long ago. After all, it was the school holidays and no way was Susan getting up at the same time as she would during term-time.

Barely an hour later, Jones sat in his office planning his itinerary for the morning briefing, a steaming cup of coffee by his elbow. A sudden knock on the door startled him from his reverie. Sutton stood outside, his face red with excitement. "Sorry, guv, but we've just had a call from The Mount. Severino's tried to kill himself."

* * *

It took the better part of an hour for Warren to finally speak to The Mount's governor, who was clearly in damage-limitation mode and reluctant to give out any details that might get into the media and prejudice the inquiry now under way. Eventually, after Warren promised to keep everything off the record and away from the press, the harried official relented, and furnished Jones with the details that he had available.

After Jones' visit the previous day, Severino had been returned to his cell. He'd been looked over by the prison doctor and moved to the suicide wing as a precaution until he calmed down. After a restless night, he'd finally settled down and was believed to be asleep until early morning when the prisoner in the adjacent cell had alerted the guards to strange noises coming from his neighbour.

Guards had entered to find Severino unconscious, with a make-shift noose around his neck. After promptly administering CPR, they had transferred him by emergency ambulance to the nearby A and E, by which time he had regained consciousness. He was expected to remain overnight for observation, but should make a full recovery. The governor sounded relieved at that fact, but Warren could tell he was still worried — and understandably so. Prisoners should not be able to attempt suicide in a well-run prison, least of all prisoners on suicide watch. Reading between the lines, Warren surmised that if the prisoner next door hadn't raised the alarm Severino might well have succeeded in killing himself before the guards did their next check.

How did he manage it? he wondered. Prisoners weren't allowed belts or shoelaces, to prevent just this type of thing occurring. Furthermore, prison cells were designed so that prisoners couldn't hang themselves. There was nowhere high enough for them to loop the noose and drop. The governor was cagey at first, but after reas-surances again that nothing would be leaked to the media before the prison's official statement and the results of their inquiry he had admitted that Severino had wrapped his jeans around his neck, then around the frame of the bunk-bed — and simply fallen backwards.

Whether Severino had known that there was no way to achieve a hangman's drop in such a short distance and so throttling was the only way to cause death was not yet known: he wasn't ready to be interviewed just yet. Nevertheless, the technique appeared reasonably effective. The governor had a note of grudging admiration in his voice as he noted that very few people had the strength of will to throttle themselves to unconsciousness. Their survival instinct almost always kicked in and saved them. It appeared that Severino had managed to override this instinct until it was almost too late, although the prisoner who raised the alarm said that he was alerted by thrashing noises, so it seemed that he had saved himself in the end.

Nevertheless, it had been a close call. Thanking the governor and once again promising not to say anything to the media, Warren hung up. Staring at the wall, he thought back to the meeting the day before. A cold chill ran through his body, before settling in the pit of his stomach as he remembered his last look at Severino. Warren knew that the look of terror on the man's face would stay with him for a long time.

* * *

The unpleasantness of the conversation with the governor of The Mount weighed heavily on Warren's mind and he was therefore glad when Karen Hardwick knocked on his office door a few minutes after he hung up.

"Guv, I've just got back the information on the mobile phone that the mystery woman used to contact Severino, but it doesn't look as if it will be much use." Karen Hardwick tried to keep the disappointment out of her voice as she handed the email that she'd just printed over to Jones.

The document was short, just two pages in length. The first

confirmed that the phone number belonged to an unregistered, pre-paid, Pay-As-You-Go SIM card on the T-Mobile network. No customer name was available. No top-ups had been made as the card had been bought with two hundred minutes and one hundred texts, and paid for by cash, so there were no associated credit card details. First usage on the network had been on Saturday July thirtieth.

The second page listed all incoming and outgoing calls. Karen had already circled Severino's number, which had been called on Tuesday ninth August, presumably to arrange their planned meeting on the Friday of Tunbridge's murder. That Friday evening, there were a further half-dozen calls from Severino, none of which were picked up.

Interspersed between these calls were several different numbers. Looking carefully at them, Warren spotted that they came from three separate numbers. Looking quickly down the rest of the list, he saw that in the weeks since the SIM card had been activated, only those three numbers had been called. His gut told him that it wasn't a coincidence.

Sensing Karen's disappointment, Warren put on a smile for her. "This isn't completely unexpected. The likelihood that somebody planning a murder would use their own mobile phone number is pretty slim. Criminals have been using throw-away mobile phones for years. These days, the networks have made it even easier for them. They just have to buy a Pay-As-You-Go SIM card. That's much easier to dispose of than a whole phone, which if it is tracked back to you will probably be covered in your DNA and fingerprints."

Karen made a face. "Great. Sometimes I wonder if the phone companies do this sort of thing just to make our jobs more difficult."

Warren chuckled in agreement. "Having said that, Karen, don't be too harsh. The phone companies have done us a little bit of a favour. Criminals are increasingly using their own personal handsets now, just replacing the SIM. And if we can link the SIM card to the handset we can get all sorts of other useful information from their phone."

"But how do we link the two, unless we already have them in custody and have confiscated their phone?"

Warren pointed at the list of mobile-phone numbers. Beside all of the outgoing calls was a string of numbers. The same digits each time, Karen noted.

"This is the phone's IMEI code. Every mobile device has one and it is unique to that handset. Your telephone number is linked to your SIM card. Change the SIM card and you change the telephone number."

Karen nodded her understanding and Warren continued. "However, the handset also has its own code, which it transmits to the network. So, each time a call was made from this SIM card, the IMEI number was sent along with the telephone number. One of the purposes of this is to allow stolen phones to be blocked. If you get your phone nicked, then your phone's IMEI code can be blocked, making it useless."

"So can we look up the IMEI code of the handset and see who owns it?"

Warren sighed. "Sadly not. Registering your phone with the network is the owner's responsibility and most people don't bother — it's daft really as it protects your phone from being used by thieves. I guess people figure that as long as they get a replacement handset, it doesn't really matter what happens to their old one. If everybody who bought a phone was automatically registered, it would make our job a lot easier and make mobile-phone theft deeply unattractive immediately.

"If the owner of this handset was registered, it would say so on here. All we know is that the phone is a BlackBerry Curve smartphone."

"What about the SIM card — do they keep records?"

"I would imagine that the card was bought with cash. But it's a lead worth following. Why don't you get on it? You might get lucky and we may be able to get CCTV footage of the SIM card being bought. And in the meantime, do another request for the records from these three new numbers, high priority. If we can demonstrate that these telephones were all chatting to one another on the night Tunbridge was killed we might be able to bring them in on a conspiracy charge at least."

Chapter 30

Jones looked at the list of names on his notepad. The team had made a lot of progress over the last few days in tracking down and interviewing many acquaintances of the late professor. Pretty soon, it would be time to start re-interviewing some of those that the team were less happy about.

With Antonio Severino in custody, now was the time to make certain that the case that they had was watertight. The last twenty-four hours in particular had started Warren worrying that the case might not be as straightforward as it had first seemed. One thing seemed certain and that was that some of the interviewees had been holding back. Exactly what they were holding back and precisely how significant that might be, Warren didn't know, but it made him uncomfortable.

It was for this reason that at midday, Jones and Gary Hastings pulled into a quiet suburban street in the north of Middlesbury. Although not nearly as exclusive as the leafy avenue that the Tunbridges had called home, it was a pleasant enough collection of modest, paired semi-detached houses. This particular neighbour-hood of streets were named after flowering plants common in the area: Rose Drive, Peony Close and, in this case, Petunia Avenue. Warren wondered if in years to come there would be a Japanese Knotwood Close.

"Won't Dr Crawley be at work this time of the day, guv?" asked Hastings, puzzled.

"I certainly hope so. It's not him that we've come to see."

With that, he slowed to a halt a few doors down from number 128, the address listed as belonging to Crawley and his family. Before they got out of the car, Warren briefed Hastings quickly as to what his strategy was and what part he wanted Hastings to play.

Number 128 was paired with an identical mirror, number 126, and it was up this carefully maintained driveway the two police officers strode. The doorbell was answered almost instantly, presumably by the person who had watched them approach through the upstairs net curtains. This was a good sign, Warren hoped.

The door opened bare inches before being stopped by a flimsy chain. A mass of curly white hair, framing a carefully made-up right eye, behind thick glasses, peered curiously through the gap between the door and its frame.

"Yes, may I help you?" The voice was strong but clearly that of an older lady. Its tone was the mixture of annoyance and curiosity often expressed by private citizens unexpectedly disturbed by a knock to the front door in the middle of the day.

"Police, madam. My name is Detective Chief Inspector Warren Jones and this is Detective Constable Gary Hastings, Middlesbury CID." Both men held up their warrant cards.

"Oh, my." The woman's tone turned to one of concern mixed with excitement. "Has something happened?"

"Nothing for you to be concerned about, Mrs…?"

"Turnbull, Patricia Turnbull," she supplied reflexively, confirming the identity that Warren had found from his computer checks earlier.

"As I said, nothing for you to be worried about. We are simply conducting some routine enquiries. I wonder if we could come in?"

"Of course, officers." The door closed briefly as the chain was released, then reopened fully to admit the two officers. Mrs Turnbull was a sprightly-looking older woman that records showed to be seventy-nine years old. Dressed in a flowery summer dress, she exuded a faint smell of lavender as she stepped back to let the two officers into her home. Warren was pleased to note that even though the ground was dry as a bone and his shoes couldn't have been at all dirty, Hastings instinctively wiped his feet on the welcome mat as he entered. Small details like that mattered to some people and Warren immediately knew that they had just edged up a notch in the old lady's estimation.

She led the two men into her living room. Glancing around, Warren could see it was a classic example of what he privately called "generic middle-class elderly couple". It was furnished in lighter colours such as cream and beige, the predominant motif "flowery". Large bay windows with net curtains dominated the front wall, giving a huge panoramic view of a sizeable chunk of the street. A three-piece suite surrounded a large wooden coffee table covered with flowery coasters. Warren noted that the carpet surrounding the armchair nearest the window was depressed with additional indentations, as if the armchair was regularly moved from its current position. He smiled to himself as he mentally worked out the chair's new position — directly in front of the bay window.

The rest of the room was the well-dusted and eclectic mixture of photos, ornaments and knick-knacks that a couple of this age would be expected to accumulate. A heavy tread announced the arrival of the other half of the couple, preceded by a booming voice, "Was that the doorbell, Pat? It better not have been those bloody Jehovah's wotsits again. Men of God or not, I'll give them a piece of my bloody mind... Oh, hello..."

The owner of the voice stopped dead in his tracks, his face flushing red with embarrassment as he took in the sight of Warren and Gary, dressed in suits not dissimilar to travelling preachers, Warren now realised.

"Detective Chief Inspector Warren Jones and Detective Constable Gary Hastings, Middlesbury CID. We're just conducting some routine enquiries and wondered if you could help us," he introduced himself hastily, sparing the poor man's embarrassment.

"Oh, er, Donald Turnbull, pleased to meet you." A short stocky man with a small pot belly, dressed in brown corduroy trousers and a checked shirt open at the neck in deference to the warm summer weather, his handshake was strong. Warren could feel the roughness of calluses that spoke of a lifetime of working with his hands rather than sitting in front of a desk.

Mrs Turnbull smiled as if vindicated. "See, he never even heard you come in. Deaf as a post, he is, but he won't admit it." She turned to her husband as if looking for confirmation.

"Not so deaf I can't hear your bloody nagging, woman," he replied waspishly. Deciding to get them all back on track before he and Hastings became witnesses to a double homicide that had probably been brewing for fifty years, Warren cleared his throat loudly.

"Oh, sorry, officers, where are my manners? Please, take a seat."

By unspoken consent, Warren and Hastings each took an armchair. The Turnbulls sat next to each other on the sofa. The positioning of the furniture meant that questions could come from either side, a tactic that often worked for reluctant interviewees since if used skilfully it could disturb their equilibrium. Warren suspected that wouldn't be necessary in this case.

"So how can we help you? Is it about the murder up at the university? Our next-door neighbour worked with the poor man, I believe." Mrs Turnbull was practically salivating with excitement. No need for a lengthy explanation then, or good cop, bad cop with this one, decided Warren wryly.

"Yes, we're just conducting some routine enquiries."

"Why? I thought you'd caught your man? Italian chap, wasn't he? You don't suspect Mark Crawley, do you?" This from Mr Turnbull.

Warren raised a hand quickly to forestall his questioning. "Like I said, Mr and Mrs Turnbull, these are just routine enquiries." He was beginning to sound like a parrot, he realised, and he could see their scepticism at the over-used cliché. "Whenever there is a major investigation it's normal for the police to check out the background of every person connected to the victim to build up a fuller picture of them. We're just dotting the Is and crossing the Ts." Inwardly, Warren winced. He'd repeated that cliché so many times in the past few days he was in grave danger of coining a catchphrase.

"Oh. They only seem to focus on the suspects in *CSI*," said Mrs Turnbull, looking a little dubious.

"That's because they only have sixty minutes to tell the story, not including twenty minutes of bleeding adverts," interjected Mr Turnbull, rolling his eyes at his wife's apparent foolishness. Warren said nothing, neatly avoiding an awkward discussion.

"Well, anyway, first of all, how long have you lived here, Mr and Mrs Turnbull?" Warren started.

It was Mr Turnbull who answered, after a few seconds of

stroking his small, trim moustache. "Fifty-one years this October, I believe."

"Yes, that's right. We had our eldest, Charlie in 1959. He'll be fifty-two this year. We were living with my mum and dad at the time whilst we saved for a place of our own. Little Charlie arrived a bit sooner than expected. We'd hoped to be in our own place before we started having children. There wasn't really enough room to bring up a baby as well, especially since my two youngest sisters were still at home also. But we coped. And then Donald's grandmother — God bless her soul — passed away leaving him a small sum of money. With our savings, it was just enough to put a deposit down for this place. And here we still are." She looked at her husband.

For the first time since arriving, Warren caught a glimpse of the affection that, contrary to first appearances, still bound the couple together after more than half a century. He wondered if he and Susan would still have that after fifty years… bickering on the outside but in love more today than the first day they had met.

Warren mentally pinched himself. Where the hell had that come from? Not once in the days since he had asked Susan to marry him had Warren ever thought for one second that they would be anything but deeply in love until "Death do us part". Suppressing the disconcerting line of thinking, he forced himself to focus on the task in hand. Fortunately, it seemed that getting information out of these two would probably not be a great test of his interrogation skills.

"Is that Charlie on the mantelpiece?" Hastings had clearly interpreted Warren's pause as an invitation for him to step in and was pointing at a picture above the fireplace. It depicted a middle-aged man with his arm around a similarly aged woman, both sporting haircuts and clothing that were fashionable a decade or so ago. In front of them stood two teenagers, a boy and a girl. The backdrop behind them was that of Walt Disney World. The whole group were beaming ear to ear.

"Yes, that's him with his wife and their children, Maddie and Tim. That's a few years old now. Tim would probably be about your age now, Constable." Mrs Turnbull smiled fondly. "You know, Tim complained bitterly before they went that Disney World was just for little kids. Charlie reckons it was the best family holiday they ever had and Tim loved every second from the moment they arrived."

Hastings chuckled. "I remember thinking that when I went to Disneyland Paris. By the end of the visit, I didn't want to leave!"

"So you would remember when the Crawleys first moved in next door." Warren now took over again.

"Yes, now, let's see… their eldest is going to university next year and Lizzi — that's Mrs Crawley — got pregnant with him just after they moved in… It was the winter, I think…"

"They moved in just after Christmas 1992," proclaimed Mr Turnbull. "I remember because she told us she was expecting at that little barbecue we had in the spring to mark my retirement. Do you remember? She was drinking lemonade and I asked her why she wasn't drinking something stronger, since it wasn't like she had to drive home. And even if she did, Mark never drinks anyway — she could give him the keys."

"So would you say you knew the Crawleys well?"

"Fairly well, I suppose. They are a nice enough couple and the kids have never been any real bother. We chat over the fence and usually invite each other over if we are going to have a barbecue, you know, just neighbourly, really. In fact, they had us over for a few drinks last summer to thank us for putting up with all the mess and noise from when they had their new kitchen and patio extension built," started Mr Turnbull.

"I used to talk to Lizzi more years ago," continued Mrs Turnbull. "She didn't work for a few years off and on whilst she had the kids and I would chat to her as they played in the garden or she hung out the washing. I even kept an eye on them occasionally if she needed to pop to the corner shop.

"In recent years we've spoken a little less. The children are older and don't tend to play in the garden any more and, with her parents being so ill, she tends to spend a lot of time visiting them."

"What's the matter with them?" enquired Warren casually.

"Well, her father's been ill for a number of years. He had a stroke and he's very frail, but her mother was fit enough to look after him at home and he's still sharp mentally. But in the past couple of years, she's been getting a bit forgetful. They think it might be, you know, *Alzheimer's*." She whispered the last word as if uttering a curse word or profanity, which Warren supposed it could be seen as, especially as you reached old age yourself.

"Anyway, she is probably going to have to go into a home, but they are worried that he doesn't qualify for funding, so they may not be able to find them something together unless they sell their house. I know that they are very worried about it all."

"So how would you say the Crawleys were as a couple?"

For the first time there was a pause. Mrs Turnbull shifted uncomfortably. "Well, I'm not one for gossip, you understand."

Her husband snorted. "Then what's the use of all the eavesdropping you do?"

His wife shot him a poisonous glare, before continuing as if uninterrupted. "However, I do hear things now and again. And sometimes when I'm out watering the plants in the garden they come outside to talk on the mobile phone, privately, like."

"Never occurs to her to go back inside and grant them privacy," interrupted her husband again, earning an even more poisonous scowl. Warren was feeling the urge to shoot him a look as well. Who knew what she was about to tell them?

"Anyhow, it seems as though money is a big worry right now. They took out a second mortgage for the extension, hoping it would add value to the house. They want to move somewhere a bit bigger. Then of course this credit-crunch thing with the banks happened and they found themselves in negative equity or whatever it's called. They owe more on the house than it's worth. Then of course this thing with her parents happens and their lad wants to go to university next year, which will cost thousands now the government has raised tuition fees."

"And don't forget the little one," prompted Mr Turnbull, despite himself.

"Oh, yes, their youngest is just about to go to secondary school, but he's been diagnosed with that ADHD and dyslexia. He always was a little bit naughty and I told him off for climbing over the fence and standing in our flower beds once or twice, but I had no idea he had a *condition*."

"Runs in families sometimes, that dyslexia," interjected Mr Turnbull knowledgeably. "Gets it from his dad, they reckon. I asked him one day, when he was out on the porch reading the newspaper, why his reading glasses were pink. He said apparently the brain deals with colour images differently from black and white and, for some reason, wearing coloured spectacles or using coloured inks and paper can help him read more easily. I didn't really understand it, to be honest, but he thinks it works. But their little boy has it

265

worse apparently than his dad and they are worried that he won't get enough help at this new school, so they might have to fund a private tutor."

Warren bit his lip. Susan had taught plenty of students with special educational needs over the years and, like most teachers, had strong opinions about dyslexia and other learning disorders. However, this was hardly the time or the place for that debate.

Nevertheless, it seemed as though Crawley had been, if anything, downplaying his troubles at home, certainly in terms of finances. In fact, it sounded as if the man was in desperate need of some extra cash or the pay-rise that presumably would accompany his change in status to group leader. But was it a big enough motive to kill Tunbridge?

It looked as though they had got all of the information that the Turnbulls had to offer and Warren started to thank them for their time. As they shook hands with Mr Turnbull his wife looked at Warren indecisively, chewing her lip.

"Is there something else, Mrs Turnbull?"

"Well, I'm not sure if I should say anything really. It's just a hunch, you know."

"Well, you never know, Mrs Turnbull. Why don't you let us be the judge?" Warren tried his most disarming smile.

"I think that Mark Crawley might have been having an affair."

Chapter 31

Jones and Hastings walked down the Turnbulls' drive.

"Well done, Gary, you have good instincts. You kept the conversation flowing nicely with the chatter about Disney World. In interviews like that, you have to remember that they are undergoing a conflict internally. People such as Mrs Turnbull are natural gossips and their first impulse is to help the police, but they are understandably reluctant to get anyone that they know into trouble.

"The key is to relax them and get them to open up naturally, as if they are just having a conversation."

"I see, but why did you choose me, rather than DI Sutton or another DC like Karen Hardwick?"

Warren smiled. "A couple of reasons. First, I'm trying to work with as many different people as possible over the next few weeks, to get to know the team better; Second, I took a gamble and played the odds a bit, using some tricks my first DCI taught me.

"He said that if you are going into an interview like that and have the opportunity to do some basic research on your interviewees, do it as it might give you some ideas about how to conduct the interview. I looked up the nearest neighbours to Crawley's house on the electoral register and saw that his next-door neighbours were an elderly couple. I also saw that the area has an active

Neighbourhood Watch scheme. It's a bit of a dodgy stereotype to say the least, but I figured Mrs Turnbull could very well be a curtain twitcher — the local gossip that knows everything — so I decided we should pay a visit."

"Well, it might be a dodgy stereotype, but it seemed to work quite well. But that still doesn't explain me being there."

"Well, that's an even dodgier stereotype, Gary, and I hope you'll forgive me. Although there wasn't any information on the web, there's a good chance that a couple of that age have middle-aged kids. And that those kids may well have had their own kids. It's not unreasonable to guess that at least some of those grandkids are about your age — mid-twenties.

"Elderly women in particular tend to be very fond of their grandsons, so there was the possibility that you would remind her a little of him. If she didn't have a grandson, she might have a granddaughter, and you'd be the perfect sort of young man for any young lady to introduce to her gran."

Hastings stood with his mouth open next to Warren's car. "You brought me along for that? On the off chance that some old lady would take a shine to me and tell us more information? I don't know how to take that."

"Don't think about it too much," Warren advised. "It was little more than a stab in the dark and, to be honest, she was such a gossip I could have brought along DI Sutton in a tutu and she'd have still told us everything."

Hastings clambered into the car, still shaking his head. He looked over at Warren surreptitiously. *Either he's a genius or a madman*, he decided. *But which is it?*

* * *

Mark Crawley pulled into the end of his road. He'd left work early, recognising the early warning signs of a crippling migraine. Hardly surprising, he thought, given all of the events of the last few days. He had a handful of known triggers for his migraine; some were easily avoided, such as alcohol, others less so, such as stress. He was usually a pretty laid-back kind of person — you had to be to work with Alan Tunbridge — but recently his stress levels had been sky-high. It was a miracle he'd lasted this long without an attack. Now all he wanted to do was crawl into bed with the blinds down and take his pain medication. If he was lucky, he'd kill it there and then and be back to himself in a couple of hours. At the worst, he could be bed-ridden for the next thirty-six.

As he rounded the curve that led toward his house it was all he could do not to slam on the brakes in panic. Coming out of his next-door neighbour's drive was DCI Warren Jones and another young man that he didn't recognise. Forcing himself to slow his breathing, he fought the urge to turn the car around. There was only one reason that he could see for Jones to be visiting his neighbour and that was to ask questions about him.

He saw that Jones was carrying on an animated conversation with the young stranger and was not paying any attention to Crawley's car. Fighting every instinct in his body, Crawley kept on driving at a steady twenty-five miles per hour, past his driveway, past the Turnbulls' and past Jones' Mondeo. Neither man so much as glanced up. Carrying on, he drove to the far end of the road, one eye on the rear-view mirror. To his relief, he saw Jones pull away from the kerb and continue on to the end of the road, without doing a U-turn. Clearly he'd realised that the road was a wide curve, joined at both ends to the same main road.

Now, with the road clear, Crawley stopped and executed

a clumsy three-point turn. Pulling into his driveway a few seconds later, he raced into the house. Much to his surprise, the sudden adrenaline jolt seemed to have scared away the migraine. That happened occasionally and he decided to hold off taking his pain medication. The pills were strong and made him a bit dozy, so he didn't like to take them unnecessarily.

Slumping down onto the couch, he thought about what he had just seen. What did it mean? Why were the police investigating him? Was it just routine or did they have another reason? He picked up his mobile phone, checking for any messages. No texts, two emails to his personal account. He opened up his email app and saw that they were both junk mail, one from lastminute. com, another from Tesco. Closing the email, he automatically opened his NewsFeed app and flicked through the BBC headlines. Crawley was an unapologetic newshound and constantly read the news online. He'd not had time all morning and was craving his information fix. He flicked past the usual depressing stories about the economy and suicide bombings in Afghanistan until a local news headline made him stop, his mouth turning dry. He double-tapped the expand icon to bring up the full story. As it came up his stomach contracted painfully. The news article was brief, with few facts, but contained everything that Crawley needed to know. Guilt washed over him like a tide.

Feeling sick, he closed the browser and called up the phone's dialler. The call was answered on the second ring.

"It's me — we've got a problem. We need to meet."

Chapter 32

Hastings and Jones returned to the station just before 1 p.m. Jones headed off to his office and Hastings made a beeline for his desk. His stomach was rumbling and he fished in his desk drawer for his sandwiches and banana. Peeling the fruit, he glanced surreptitiously out of the corner of his eye in the direction of Karen Hardwick's desk.

The small band of detective constables stationed at Middlesbury were a fairly close-knit group, and they'd all heard about the rookie's visit to the university with DCI Jones on Saturday morning. One or two of the older constables had been a little jealous that she had been singled out so early in her career, but Hastings was fairly sanguine about it. He knew that she had experience with that sort of environment that others in the department lacked and it seemed sensible to him that Jones should use it.

Besides which, she was very pretty, he thought to himself. A few casual questions had ascertained that she was single and Hastings had to admit that things had been very quiet on the girlfriend front lately. Of course, if he were to explore that possibility any further, it would mean having to strike up a non-work-related conversation with her and that was where things fell down.

At the moment, she seemed to be concentrating on her mobile phone. Ignoring the sandwiches in front of her, she was quietly cursing the handset. Finally, she flipped it over and removed the battery.

With a jolt of excitement, Hastings realised he had been handed the perfect opportunity. Hastings wasn't an overly religious man, but if this wasn't a sign from heaven then what was?

Clearing his throat and discreetly checking his hair and tie were straight, he wound his way over to her desk.

"Problems with your phone?"

"Uh-huh." She barely looked up.

"It's a loose connection to the battery. When the phone gets warm it causes the wire to flex, which interrupts the power and the phone reboots itself."

Karen looked up in surprise. "How the hell do you know that?"

Hastings smiled shyly as he produced an identical model handset to Karen's from his pocket. "I had the same problem myself. What are the symptoms?"

"It just seems to randomly switch itself off. I'll be doing something, like browsing the web, reading an email or making a call and suddenly the screen fades and it switches off. It's completely unpredictable and it's getting worse. Sometimes I can turn it straight back on again, other times it won't restart. Last week, it switched itself off at night and so my alarm clock didn't work. Fortunately, it's been so muggy the last few weeks, I woke up naturally about half an hour later. I just made it into work on time." She laughed ruefully. "Much later and I'd have been sitting at my desk in my nightie."

Hastings tried not to think about Karen in her nightie.

He motioned to her dismantled phone. "Do you find that taking the battery out helps it restart?"

She nodded. "Yeah, sometimes. Hopefully it'll do that today."

"It sounds as if it's exactly the same problem I had. I guess removing the battery jiggles the loose connection again."

"Can I get it fixed? I'm guessing you've had yours repaired?"

"Yeah, you just need to take it back to the shop where you got it. They send it back to the manufacturer. I read on the web that the manufacturer knows all about the fault — there's a whole batch of them. But you need to back everything up to your computer as they don't repair it. They just send you a replacement one. You'll need to copy all of your files and apps over to the new one."

"Just great. How long will it take to sort out?"

"A couple of weeks, I'm afraid, and they use a really rubbish courier company; if you aren't prepared to wait in all day, you have to go to their depot in bloody Daventry."

"I can't really do without my phone that long."

"Well, you could always try and get a courtesy phone, although they wouldn't give me one. Failing that, if you can live without Internet access, I bought one of those really cheap ones that old people use. They can make calls and send texts and that's about it."

"Oh, lovely," groused Karen.

"Hey, don't knock it. The one I've got has extra big buttons for people with cataracts or arthritis."

Karen laughed.

Result! thought Hastings, smiling back.

* * *

Karen Hardwick had not been oblivious to Gary Hastings' interest, but decided that now was not the time to get involved with a co-worker. She stole a quick glance in his direction. He was a good-looking man in his own way, she supposed, with a rather cute smile, especially when he was feeling shy. He was considerably more experienced than her, coming up on three years in CID. Nevertheless, he was actually twelve months younger than her and, worse, looked at least five years her junior — she knew that she would be in for some serious teasing from her best friend Martha if she ever brought him around.

She blinked, hard, and shook her head slightly. How on earth did she ever find herself thinking about Gary Hastings in that way, cute smile or not? Unfortunately — or perhaps fortunately — her thoughts were interrupted by the chime of an incoming email. All thoughts of Gary Hastings were now forgotten as she opened the incoming message.

The telephone records for the three unknown callers formed a very small pile in the laser printer's out tray. One glance at the records, each only two sheets of paper, just like the records of the mysterious young woman who called Severino, confirmed what Karen already suspected — each of the three SIM cards was an anonymous, pre-paid, Pay-As-You-Go SIM card, bought recently and activated for the first time on Saturday July thirtieth.

As before the records recorded the IMEI number of the handset that it was used in, but again this was unregistered. Karen sighed in frustration. It was obvious that the records were a potential goldmine, if only they could be linked back to their owners. A cursory look showed that all of the calls made by the three SIM cards, plus the mystery woman's, were confined to those four numbers, the initial calls to Severino notwithstanding.

With only a few calls made per SIM card, compiling them into one table using a spreadsheet wasn't difficult.

First Karen assigned names to the different numbers, to make the records easier to follow. Since the SIM cards were also used exclusively with a single IMEI number, she also noted the number and the phone model next to the name.

Anonymous 1: Blackberry Curve

Anonymous 2: iPhone

Anonymous 3: Nokia

Anonymous 4: Blackberry

A Severino: Nokia

Next she listed the calls in order, noting who they were from; who they were to; the duration of the call or if it was a text. She included an extra column next to the labels in the hope that they would eventually identify the owner of each phone. Printing the spreadsheet out, she took it over to Jones' office.

Date	Time	From	Real Name?	To	Real Name?	Duration
Sat 30th Jul	18:30h	Anon 1		Anon 2		Txt
Sat 30th Jul	18:30h	Anon 1		Anon 3		Txt
Sat 30th Jul	18:30h	Anon 1		Anon 4		Txt
Sat 30th Jul	18:31h	Anon 2		Anon 3		Txt
Sat 30th Jul	18:31h	Anon 2		Anon 4		Txt
Sat 30th Jul	18:33h	Anon 3		Anon 4		Txt
Fri 5th Aug	21:03h	Anon 1		Anon 2		Txt
Sat 6th Aug	09:26h	Anon 1		Anon 2		Txt
Tue 9th Aug	19:30h	Anon 1		Severino	Severino	00:03:58
Fri 12th Aug	20:00h	Anon 2		Anon 1		00:03:02
Fri 12th Aug	20:03h	Anon 2		Anon 1		00:00:58
Fri 12th Aug	20:04h	Anon 2		Anon 1		00:00:45
Fri 12th Aug	21:00h	Anon 2		Anon 1		00:00:36
Fri 12th Aug	21:00h	Severino	Severino	Anon 1	Unanswered	
Fri 12th Aug	21:30h	Anon 2		Anon 1		00:00:32
Fri 12th Aug	21:35h	Severino	Severino	Anon 1	Unanswered	
Fri 12th Aug	21:41h	Anon 1		Anon 2		Txt
Fri 12th Aug	21:56h	Anon 1		Anon 2		Txt
Fri 12th Aug	22:01h	Severino	Severino	Anon 1	Txt	
Fri 12th Aug	22:07h	Anon 1		Anon 2		Txt
Fri 12th Aug	22:20h	Anon 1		Anon 3		00:02:56
Fri 12th Aug	22:30h	Anon 3		Anon 4		00:01:47
Fri 12th Aug	22:40h	Severino	Severino	Anon 1	Unanswered	
Fri 12th Aug	23:15h	Severino	Severino	Anon 1	Unanswered	
Fri 12th Aug	23:42h	Severino	Severino	Anon 1	Unanswered	
Sat 13th Aug	05:32h	Anon 2		Anon 1		00:04:56

Warren greeted Karen warmly and spread the sheet out across his desk and motioned for Karen to sit next to him. "This is good work, Karen. Already we can see a few patterns here."

He pointed to the first set of texts, all at roughly the same time on Saturday the thirtieth of July. "This quick flurry of texts between four brand-new SIM cards — it looks to me as if they were texting each other their numbers, rather than bothering to type them in."

Karen nodded her agreement, before pointing at the sheet herself. "Then the next block, all from Severino's mystery woman. That's why I grouped them. If she was working with somebody else to set him up, then one interpretation is that she texted her co-conspirator at nine o'clock on the Friday before the murder to say that she had made contact with Severino. She then texts the following morning to say she successfully lifted his clothes and swipe card.

"Finally, she phones Severino on the Tuesday, to arrange a date with him on the Friday."

Warren nodded his agreement. "I think you could be right, if we accept Severino's version of events." He moved his finger down the sheet.

"Friday, the night of the murder. Leaving aside Severino's repeated, unanswered calls to his mystery woman, almost all of the traffic is between her and this number here, Anonymous 2. There are five calls from Anonymous 2 to this woman between 8 p.m. and about 9.30 p.m., when they switch to texts and she starts contacting Anonymous 2. Nine-thirty is about the earliest time that Tunbridge could have been murdered." He flicked through another sheet on his desk. "It is also just before Severino's swipe card was used to enter the building."

"Well, we know from the IMEI numbers that it wasn't Severino's regular handset making all of those calls, although he could have been using a second handset and an anonymous SIM card to build an alibi," Karen pointed out, playing devil's advocate.

Jones mulled this over. "I suppose we shouldn't dismiss it out of hand.

"Looking at the remainder of those calls, the last text between these two is from Anonymous 1 to Anonymous 2 at 10.07 p.m. That's just a couple of minutes before Severino's swipe card was used to leave the building. There's nothing then between them until the following morning. In between those calls there were calls between Severino's woman and Anonymous 3, then between Anonymous 3 and Anonymous 4."

Warren drummed his fingers on the desk in irritation. "We really need to put some names to those damn SIM cards. I think we need a few more heads in here." The numbers were starting to swim in front of his eyes now and a headache was starting to build. He had a possible scenario in mind and he needed people with a fresh perspective to check it for holes.

Getting up, he stretched his back.

"Karen, can you go round up Tony Sutton and Gary Hastings and ask them to meet us in the briefing room in five minutes?"

Nodding her assent, Karen also stood up, but before she could take a step towards the door it burst open. It was Sutton again. One look at his face and Warren's heart sank; he could tell it wasn't good news.

"You'd better come and see this, guv. Severino's mum is live on the BBC."

Chapter 33

Sutton's announcement sent a surge of adrenaline through Jones. "Shit," he groaned as he leapt to his feet, following Sutton into the main briefing room. Projected on the far wall was the familiar backdrop of The Mount Prison. A local BBC anchorman holding a microphone was gesturing silently towards the prison's main building. A scrolling ticker across the bottom announced that a prisoner on remand had attempted suicide early that morning. The next banner read "Prisoner's mother blasts lax security". The camera panned away from the anchor to reveal an uncomfortable-looking Daniel Stock standing next to a middle-aged woman of Mediterranean appearance. Beside them stood a dark-skinned man in a black suit. The woman, Mrs Severino presumably, was talking forcefully into the microphone.

"Some sound would be good!" called out Sutton.

"Sorry, leads aren't connected. There we go." A sudden blast of Italian came from the speakers as the stressed-looking DC fiddling with the laptop finally plugged the jack into the correct socket. They must be streaming live off the BBC's website, Warren realised.

The woman stopped speaking and the man in the black suit took over, speaking in heavily accented English. Her translator, Warren realised.

"Mrs Severino demands that there is a full enquiry into how

her son, who strenuously denies all of the allegations against him, was able to attempt to kill himself when he should have been on suicide watch."

Another blast of Italian. "We would also want to take this opportunity to demand that the police continue to investigate the crime that Antonio Severino has been wrongly charged with. Her son has clearly been framed for this murder. Evidence found at his house is little more than circumstantial. Her son has given the police a description of a woman that he believes—" At this point Daniel Stock stepped forward, cutting off the translator mid-flow.

"About bloody time he did something," snapped Sutton, angrily.

"Um, obviously this is the subject of an ongoing investigation and it would be unwise for us to comment any further," the young solicitor stammered.

"Too bloody late," said Warren quietly. "I don't speak Italian, but it seemed pretty obvious to me that Mum said everything she wanted to." He ran his hand through his hair. "Christ, what a mess. The press are going to be all over this one." He shook his head in dismay. "I can't believe the BBC gave her air time. How damned irresponsible of them."

"Uhm, guv, I don't think they had much choice." The young DC who'd been setting up the laptop looked up from another computer. Warren stepped over.

"They were just keeping up with the Joneses... er, so to speak." The constable flicked quickly through a half-dozen tabs on the computer's web browser. Warren groaned inwardly as the front page of every major news outlet proclaimed the same breaking news, with varying degrees of breathlessness. The page that caused the coldest chill to run down his back was that of the most popular tabloid.

"Tomorrow — Exclusive. Free my innocent son before he kills himself for real!"

Below a picture of Mrs Severino, a bulleted list promised to reveal:

"The woman who set my son up"

"Anger and hatred in top scientist's lab leads to brutal murder"

"How under-pressure police grabbed the nearest suspect"

Warren rubbed his eyes with his thumb and his forefinger, hoping to ward off the burning sensation in his temples threatening to become a full-blown headache. "If anyone can think of a way that this day could get any worse, please don't hesitate to tell me."

As if on cue, Superintendent Grayson's voice rang out across the room. "DCI Jones. In my office, please."

Be careful what you wish for, thought Warren ruefully.

* * *

"Damn it, Warren, this is the last thing we need." Superintendent John Grayson slumped back in his chair, massaging his eyes in the same manner that Warren had been doing moments before. Warren wondered if it would be any more successful for his boss than it had been for him.

"I agree, sir. This is an ongoing investigation. These details should not be released to the press, for fear of prejudicing the case."

"Yes, quite, that as well. In the meantime, the suggestion that a killer is still running around Middlesbury on the eve of that huge conference could be disastrous. And the suggestion on top of it all that we arrested the wrong man means that this department will be a laughing stock. This needs sorting out and quickly, Warren."

Well, there it was, Warren thought. It was quite clear that the biggest concern that Grayson had was political. Warren doubted he had even thought as far ahead as to what effect the threatened revelations could have on the court case.

"Where the hell did this all come from, Warren?"

"As far as I can tell, it all seems to be coming from Severino's camp, sir." He went on to outline to Grayson his visit to The Mount Prison and his subsequent investigations into the mysterious young woman that had visited Severino the week before the murder.

Grayson tapped his pen against his teeth thoughtfully, before shaking his head. "I don't know, Warren, it all seems pretty tentative. Compared to the evidence that we have against Severino, this is pretty circumstantial."

"I agree, sir, but—"

At that point, Grayson's phone rang. He glanced at the caller ID and motioned for Warren to wait as he picked up the phone. "Grayson here."

He listened intently for a few moments. "I agree, we should be able to get an injunction blocking publication. I'm a bit surprised they even tried. They must have known we weren't going to let them prejudice the case." He listened again. Warren tried not to fidget; he always felt uncomfortable listening to one side of a telephone conversation. Couldn't he just put it on speakerphone?

"He's here now, sir."

Shit, thought Warren. There were only a few people that Grayson called "sir", none of whom Warren was comfortable about being discussed with. Grayson put his hand over the mouthpiece. "Warren, are you certain that you haven't spoken to the press? The governor of The Mount Prison is doing his nut. Apparently the papers have all of the details of the suicide attempt."

Warren shook his head emphatically, "No, sir. Not a word. If

I were to speculate, it probably came through Severino's lawyer, Daniel Stock. He's a bit inexperienced. Severino may have told him what happened on a visit and he hasn't got the good sense to advise his client not to speak to the press."

Grayson nodded in agreement and relayed Warren's message to the voice at the end of the line. "The Mount have already released a statement refusing to comment on an ongoing investigation. I'll draft one from us stating the same thing and reiterating that we are investigating all leads and reminding the press of their obligation not to prejudice any upcoming trial."

He listened for a few more seconds, before closing the conversation and turning to Warren. "We're going to try and manage this debacle as best we can. Warren, you need to wrap this investigation up asap. Make sure that conviction's sound — the last thing we need is Severino's lawyers tearing holes in our case. And I needn't remind you that we have to keep the press on side. We can't afford the bad publicity right now." He stood up and started shovelling sheets of paper into his briefcase.

Warren nodded. "About Severino, sir, I'm not sure—"

Grayson raised a hand, forestalling him. "Sorry, Warren, it will have to wait. I have to get over to Legal and start the ball rolling on this injunction and get those press releases drafted." He smiled tightly, showing a glimpse of humour. "I seem to spend all of my time dealing with lawyers these days. Makes me long for the days when I was chasing rapists and murderers — at least I got to associate with a better class of people."

* * *

Tony Sutton hung up the phone with a mangled, "Grazie," and sat back with a smug smile on his face. After a few seconds of silent self-congratulation, he got to his feet, winding his way across the room to Jones' office.

Knocking, he entered. "Got some good news, guv."

Leaning back in his chair, Warren eyed him. For some reason, he had a feeling that what Sutton regarded as good news might be a little different from what he regarded as good news. Nevertheless, he gestured for Sutton to continue. "Go on, Tony, good news is always welcome in this office."

"Well, the first bit of good news is that I tracked down Severino's fiancée. It was just as he said — she is visiting her parents in Bavaria. Before I spoke with her, I had a quick chat with a local police chief, who kindly visited her and confirmed her identity from her passport. I figured that if Severino had done something to his missus, it would be all too easy for him to give us the address of a friend who could pretend to be her."

Warren nodded his approval. "Good thinking, Tony."

"Anyway, once he'd done that I spoke at length on the phone to her. Apparently, they have been together for several years now and engaged for the past six months. She claims not to have heard anything about his arrest, although the murder had made the news."

"So why didn't she contact Severino — his boss had just been murdered. Wasn't she even curious?"

"She says that she wasn't sure if she wanted to speak to him. Apparently, things have been rocky between them ever since he lost his job. She said that he was drinking too much, and implied he was smoking a bit too much weed also. They had a couple of really violent arguments — she insists verbal, not physical — and she eventually decided it would be better for both of them if she went home to her parents for a few months. Apparently, she's finishing writing up her own PhD thesis and could just as easily work in Germany as she could in the UK. It sounds as if she was going to call off the engagement."

"Well, that certainly matches what Severino told me. It would also explain why he is so depressed. His fiancée has left him and now he's accused of murder."

"Well, don't waste too much sympathy on the bastard. I've just got off the phone with an Italian prosecutor. It seems that our boy Severino has form."

Warren raised an eyebrow at Sutton's apparent glee, but said nothing.

"He's been arrested, but never successfully convicted, several times since his late teens. Apparently, he has a bit of a temper. His first arrest was for a fight at college, allegedly over a girl. It was claimed that he broke the nose of his rival and gave him a mild concussion."

"What happened? I can't believe that he would be accepted onto a British university course if he was expelled from college for fighting."

Sutton's mouth twisted as if he'd tasted something unpleasant. "The lad he hit dropped the assault charges. There is nothing in the file about the college's response. However, a background note attached to the file observes that his family are among the wealthiest people in that region of Italy. They are one of the biggest distributors of Italian wine in the world and are well-known philanthropists with political connections. I think you can draw your own conclusions from that."

"OK, but a bit of fisticuffs in college hardly sets him up for murder, does it?"

"Well, that was just the first of several, similar incidents. Each time his victim dropped the charges. Each time the alleged violence was more extreme. The worst case was four years ago. He got into a fight on the way back from a football match. It was claimed that he hit a rival supporter around the head with a metal pole, sticking him in a coma for two weeks. Guy still has blackouts, apparently, and can't work. Four witnesses initially came forward and Severino was arrested. Three days later the witnesses all withdrew their statements. Even better, the metal pole with Severino's fingerprints on it somehow went missing from a locked evidence cabinet. His victim is apparently living a lifestyle that would appear inconsistent with somebody unemployed and living off sickness benefits.

"It seems that without any evidence the case was on rocky ground and it was decided to spare the police department's blushes and drop the case. The original notes on all of these cases are all a matter of public record, of course, but in reality they aren't ever going to cause him any problems.

"I'm telling you, guv, this bloke is dirty and quite capable of murder." Sutton's expression was a mixture of outrage at the way in which Severino had played the system and vindication for his belief in the man's guilt. "We shouldn't be looking to do the defence's job for them. We need to put this bastard behind bars for a long time."

Chapter 34

Jones called a team meeting in one of the small briefing rooms. Pulling over a clean whiteboard, he summarised what the team had so far.

"What we know for definite was that Alan Tunbridge was murdered in his office Friday night. Saturday morning we found CCTV evidence that a person matching the description of Antonio Severino, a postdoc in Tunbridge's lab with a grudge against Tunbridge and a history of violence, was in the building at about the time of the murder. Records from the building's security system confirm that the person on the CCTV used Severino's swipe card.

"After his arrest, articles of clothing stained with Tunbridge's blood and the murder weapon were found, concealed at Severino's property. He's been charged, but denies the murder. Our job so far has been to tie up any loose ends and piece together exactly what happened that night."

Jones picked up a marker pen and wrote "Outstanding Issues" at the top of the board.

"First question — how did the killer know that Tunbridge would be working alone in his office late on Friday night?"

Sutton answered the question. "He was set up. An apparently fake investment company contacted him with a view to commercialising his work. They planted a fake website — now taken down — and arranged via email to telephone him at the university at 10 p.m. UK time on Friday."

Jones drew a line down the middle of the whiteboard and summarised Sutton's response on the left-hand side. At the top of the right-hand side he drew a large question mark.

Gary Hastings took over. "Who put the website up?"

Jones wrote "Website Author", before answering the question. "It was hosted by a cheap, offshore web provider. We're trying to track down who paid for it.

"Next question — did Severino act alone? What other people had a motive to kill him?"

Sutton sighed. "If we're going down that route, who didn't have a motive? It seems as though there wasn't anybody who didn't dislike the man for one reason or another."

"Well, let's just keep it simple for the time being. Who do we know about?"

Sutton started ticking them off on his fingers. "The main suspects would have to be Tom Spencer, Clara Hemmingway, Mark Crawley and Professor Tompkinson."

Karen Hardwick spoke up first. "I think we can rule out Professor Tompkinson. He's ill with Parkinson's disease and has an alibi for the Friday night. He's due to retire and it just wouldn't make sense for him to get involved with something like this. He's looking forward to spending his last few healthy years with the grandkids on a decent pension."

There were general nods of agreement around the table; it seemed too farfetched. Jones put a cross next to the man's name.

"Mark Crawley?"

Gary Hastings replied this time. "He's a complicated one. He has certainly got the motive, despite what he says. He needs the money that he'd get with any pay rise that would come if the university promoted him to group leader. He is also the best-placed person to benefit from any research coming out of the group — if the lab has made any breakthroughs then he could take them through to commercialisation. From what we've heard, others in the field wouldn't necessarily be suspicious if he announced a major discovery in the next couple of years."

Hardwick disagreed. "All of that is true but he has a pretty solid alibi for that night. He was looking after a group of kids at a birthday party. There's no way he could have got from the ten-pin-bowling alley to the university and back without his absence being noticed."

Sutton shook his head. "All that means is he didn't do the deed. It's quite possible that he and Severino worked together on this. Crawley could be the brains behind it and Severino the hit man. We know that they were fairly tight. Crawley smoothed over the incident with Tunbridge's car and negotiated paid leave for Severino whilst he looked for a new job. I could definitely see them working together. And if Crawley does become head of the research group, then what's to stop him rehiring his old friend Severino?"

There were mutters of agreement around the table. Warren put a large question mark next to Crawley's name. "Tom Spencer."

Karen Hardwick offered her opinion first. "He certainly has motive. Tunbridge has all but destroyed his future career. He's been treated as badly as Severino, but again he has a good alibi. He was working in the PCR room whilst the murder took place. If he was involved as an accomplice, why would he be in the building at the same time? If I was him I wouldn't want to be seen anywhere near the murder scene. Ideally I'd get myself a nice alibi. Even if he was waiting outside for Severino, I can't see him deliberately getting himself noticed by getting logged into the building and then finding Tunbridge."

"Maybe he wanted to find the body? He was covered in Tunbridge's blood and the forensics do show some inconsistencies with the blood patterns and his claims that he found Tunbridge dead and for some reason checked his pulse in his throat," Hastings suggested tentatively.

Sutton was dismissive. "The inconsistencies are weak and circumstantial. And what benefit was there in finding the body? The time between him leaving the PCR room and calling 999 isn't enough for him to substantially alter the scene. Severino would be better off doing that." He turned expectantly to Jones at the whiteboard, who was deep in thought.

"If he was involved, then his motive would have to be more than revenge." He pointed back to Crawley's name with the question mark beside it. "If he was in a three-person conspiracy with Severino and Crawley then his motive could have been for Crawley to sign off on his PhD. If Crawley takes over Tunbridge's group, then presumably he would also take over his responsibilities. From what Professor Tompkinson was saying, it was really only Tunbridge who was standing in the way of him submitting his PhD.

"Crawley might be in a position to rehire Severino and ensure that Spencer gets his degree." Warren thought a few seconds more. "No, I think that Spencer has to remain a possible." And with that he drew a question mark next to the man's name. Sutton grunted and crossed his arms, his scowl lending a silent voice to his disagreement.

Ignoring him, Warren moved on. "That leaves Hemmingway."

"She's got a solid alibi," said Hastings.

"That's true," allowed Jones, "but that doesn't mean she couldn't be involved. She certainly has a motive. Tunbridge treated her like trash — it could just be revenge, pure and simple. The question, though, is who was she working with? Severino? And what would her role be?"

Karen shook her head, dubiously. "I don't see it, sir. She had her affair with him back in November through until about March. Why would she suddenly, out of the blue, decide to murder him? And what does she gain? By all accounts, she is moving on with her life."

Warren nodded in agreement. "I see what you are saying, Karen. I don't know what her motive would be, beyond revenge. And again, who would she be working with? Severino again? Why and how did they hook up? She only visited the lab a few times back in November when she was writing her essay. Her affair with Tunbridge lasted until March but they kept it under the radar. I doubt that she was turning up at the lab to share her sandwiches with him at lunchtime. Why would she suddenly hook up with Severino seven or eight months later to plot his murder?"

Taking a deep breath, Warren put a question mark beside her name.

Hastings raised a hand. "Um, guv, shouldn't that be a cross?"

"Maybe, maybe not. What if we are going about this the wrong way? What if Severino is right and he was set up?"

"What?" The explosion predictably came from Sutton, his face reddening.

Warren raised a calming hand. "Listen to me. What do we have on Severino?"

Sutton answered immediately. "CCTV images, swipe-card logs, his clothes covered in Tunbridge's blood, latex gloves, plastic overshoes and the blood-encrusted murder weapon stuffed down his drain. Not to mention, no alibi, a massive fucking motive and previous form." He shook his head. "What else would you like? A confession signed in blood?"

"Well, that would be nice," snapped Warren, "but we aren't going to get one of those." He took a couple of calming breaths before continuing. He counted the points off on his fingers.

"First, the CCTV images. None of them have a clear shot of the suspect's face. We can match the clothes to Severino's and the calculated height and build cannot exclude Severino but, it's like his lawyer said, he's right in the middle of the bell-curve. It would never stand up in court as a positive ID.

"Second, the swipe-card logs only show that his card was used — it doesn't prove that he used it. Third, we've established that they are his clothes, so the presence of his DNA is not unexpected. However, neither his DNA or fingerprints have been found on the gloves, the overshoes or the murder weapon. Furthermore, no traces of Tunbridge's blood were found on his body."

Sutton interjected forcefully, "All that means is he watches *CSI*. The guy worked with DNA for a living — I'm sure he could figure out how to take off a pair of latex gloves without leaving his own trace evidence. He probably wore two pairs. And I'm sure he thought to shower after he got home."

Warren struggled to maintain his composure. "You know as well as I do how hard it is to remove traces of blood. And there was nothing in the plugholes of his sink or his bathtub. Besides which, you saw him when we arrested him. Did he look like he'd showered in the past forty-eight hours, let alone twelve?"

Sutton was unwilling to concede the point. "That's all conjecture. No jury would believe that."

Warren batted the point right back. "You forget, it's not up to him to prove he didn't do it, it's up to us to prove that he did! Beyond reasonable doubt. And everything we have got can be explained away as circumstantial. And all the stuff about his previous form is inadmissible. The charges were dropped. It's hearsay and nothing more. Plus, as you said yourself, everybody who ever met this bugger had a motive to kill him."

Sutton's face didn't change, Warren could see that he still had a long way to go to convince him. He decided to pull rank.

"Regardless, Inspector, let's look at some of the other problems. First of all, where does this mystery woman fit in? Who is she and did she steal Severino's clothes and swipe card to help set him up?"

Sutton snorted dismissively, but wisely decided to hold his peace. Jones ignored him and continued, "We know at least that this woman exists. Eyewitness accounts, plus CCTV, show that he was with a young blonde woman on the Friday night before Tunbridge's murder. The question is, did she set him up?"

The question lay heavy in the air. Nobody could think of a way to answer it.

"Assuming that Severino was telling the truth, then we have her mobile phone number. Karen, why don't you bring everyone up to speed on what you found out?"

Karen cleared her throat, glancing nervously at Sutton. The detective inspector's brooding presence clearly bothered her, "The mobile-phone number that we believe belongs to this young woman is linked to an anonymous Pay-As-You-Go SIM card that we have yet to trace. We have the telephone handset's unique IMEI code, but it is unregistered and we can't link it to anyone."

Sutton rolled his eyes, but said nothing. Rather than being intimidated by this, Karen instead flushed slightly pink and shot a glare at him, her voice becoming stronger. "What we do know is that this SIM card only contacted Severino and three other anonymous SIM cards, all of which were activated at the same time. Furthermore, these anonymous SIM cards — sorry, unknown users — only phoned each other. On the night of Tunbridge's murder, there was a lot of traffic between these phones, before and after the time of death."

Despite himself, Sutton started to look interested. "So where does Severino fit in?" he asked.

"He doesn't. Not unless he has a second phone with one of these anonymous SIM cards in it. His phone repeatedly called the young woman's phone on the night of Tunbridge's murder, the night that he claims she was supposed to be visiting him. She never picked up. If he did murder Tunbridge, then he kept on ringing this girl throughout the murder."

"Or somebody else used his phone to provide him with an alibi," Sutton suggested, still unwilling to drop Severino.

"A pretty weak alibi," commented Hastings, earning a poisonous look from Sutton.

"Either way," interjected Jones, "it would seem that whoever this mysterious woman is, these phone records suggest that she is tied into a conspiracy with at least three other people. This little network of four people activated their SIM cards on the same date, and on the night of Tunbridge's murder spoke exclusively to one another, before going silent again. That is far too big a coincidence for me. We need to identify who these four people are. We may be able to charge them with conspiracy to murder at least."

Silence around the table again. Hastings finally spoke up. "I know it sounds daft, but the only blonde girl that answers the description of the mystery woman is Clara Hemmingway." He pulled over one of the still images taken from Mr G's nightclub security camera. The image was too blurry, however, to be any use. The picture could easily have been Hemmingway or one of a hundred other girls in Middlesbury town centre that night.

"There's no way to tell from that image, without it being enhanced—" Jones sighed "—but I can't see how it would be possible. Hemmingway was taken on a guided tour of Tunbridge's laboratory as part of the preparation for her essay, way back in November. Apparently it's a big tradition at the university — the whole lab even goes out for lunch together. I don't see how Severino couldn't have recognised her when she turned up in the bar that night."

Silence fell again.

"So where does that leave us, sir?" Sutton looked directly at Jones, the look in his eyes almost daring Jones to say what he knew was coming next. Jones locked eyes with him, briefly, before standing straight and addressing the whole table. His voice was steady.

"We reopen the investigation and start over again. If Antonio Severino did commit this murder, he didn't do so alone."

"I knew it," snapped Tony Sutton.

"Inspector…" warned Jones.

"The moment his bloody mum came on TV complaining that her son couldn't possibly have done it and that he's so scared of prison he'd rather commit suicide…" Sutton stood up, unwilling or unable to finish his thought.

"Sit back down, Inspector," Jones ordered.

Sutton ignored him. "Of course he tried to commit suicide. For once in his privileged life, he's actually going to face the consequences of his actions. He fucked up. This isn't Italy, where his

294

family can just buy off whoever they need to. It's England, where nobody gives a shit how much wine his family flogs. He's going down and he knows it."

Jones turned to Hardwick and Hastings. "I think this meeting is over. DI Sutton and I need a private chat." The two detective constables left the room as fast as possible, without so much as a backward glance.

The door swung closed behind them. "Are you quite finished, *Inspector*?" demanded Jones, for the first time letting his anger show.

Sutton ignored the warning signs. "No. We have a perfectly good suspect in custody, with the means, the motive and the opportunity. He has no alibi and the murder weapon was found in his possession. Why do you want to scupper that? We solved a high-profile murder in barely twenty-four hours and had the suspect charged, in front of a judge and remanded in custody in little more than forty-eight. Now, you want to tell everyone, 'oops, maybe we were a bit hasty. Maybe we were wrong. He's all upset and says he didn't do it and his mum says he's a good boy really'. We'll be a fucking laughing stock!"

Enough was enough, Warren decided. "If you have such a big problem with this case, then there's the door. You can leave right now and I'll get you reassigned to something else."

He stepped closer, deliberately invading Sutton's personal space. "And another thing. Don't you ever question my orders in such an insubordinate tone in front of junior officers again. I will have you put on report for the next six months if you ever behave like that again. You can consider this your first verbal warning. Do I make myself clear?"

Sutton smouldered silently. Warren stared at him expectantly.

After a few seconds, the older man looked down. "Yes, sir. Perfectly clear."

"Dismissed."

Sutton turned on his heel and marched out of the room. The moment the door slammed shut behind him, Warren sat down and let out a deep shuddering breath. His hands were shaking. What the hell had just happened? It was the first time in Warren's career that he had ever had a stand-up row with a junior officer. He'd had plenty of disagreements; in fact, he positively encouraged dissenting viewpoints. But Sutton was downright insubordinate.

He thought back over the last hour, before casting his mind back even further. That Sutton had been less than enthused at his arrival at Middlesbury was no great secret, but so what? This was his first real command experience. Had he misinterpreted the signs? Should he have dealt with Sutton sooner? Did his habit of letting colleagues debate with him translate into a lack of respect?

He was reminded of the battles Susan had fought with some of her classes when she first became a teacher. Like most teachers she had learnt the hard way that it was better to start the term too hard and then relax, than try to do it the other way around. He smiled humourlessly; maybe he should make Tony Sutton write lines in his lunch hour: "I shall not question the boss in front of junior officers".

The smile slipped. Just what was he going to do with Sutton? The fact was that he had to work with the man. Middlesbury CID was too small for him to simply kick him off the case and replace him with another detective inspector or detective sergeant. And what signal did it send out to those watching, both above and below him in the chain of command? It suggested that he couldn't deal with junior officers effectively. What should be a punishment for Sutton's insubordination would rebound on Warren as an indictment of his management skills.

Sighing, Warren rubbed his eyes and straightened his tie, before walking out of the briefing room and into the main office. The room was buzzing quietly. The clicking of keys on keyboards, the murmur of voices on telephones and the quiet mutter of conversations mingled together in a familiar noise. Yet where the noise was normally comforting, today it felt strained. Walking steadily to his own office, Warren felt as if every pair of eyes in the room was surreptitiously watching him. Judging him. Was it just his imagination? He glanced over at Hastings and Hardwick, who studiously avoided his glance. Sutton was nowhere to be seen. Probably cooling off outside, Warren hoped. Closing the door behind him, he slumped into his chair, all of the energy drained from him.

He closed his eyes briefly, marshalling the strength necessary to follow his own order and start over again. The phone rang. Caller ID showed it to be an internal call. Warren groaned; ignoring it wasn't an option.

"DCI Jones, my office, now."

Superintendent Grayson. Perfect.

Chapter 35

Warren had known that he would need to convince his superior officer of the need to reopen the case, but he had hoped for a few minutes' respite after his bruising encounter with Sutton. It soon became apparent that Sutton had needed no such pause. It transpired that he had walked straight out of the meeting with Jones and into Grayson's office. Warren felt a flash of anger with the realisation that when he'd thought Sutton was outside cooling his heels, he was in actual fact in Grayson's office bad-mouthing his DCI.

Grayson still wore his suit jacket, clearly having been button-holed by Sutton the moment he'd returned from his various meetings with the force's lawyers and press liaison officers. He sat back in his chair, his face a mask. His voice was cold and detached, probably not a good sign, thought Warren.

"Warren, a couple of hours ago, we had a discussion in which I underlined the need for this investigation to be completed in a timely fashion and for us to make sure that we made our case against Severino watertight.

"I now find out, without any warning, that you have decided to reopen the investigation, essentially starting again from scratch. What next, Warren? Would you like us to release Antonio Severino, drop all charges and issue a public apology as well?" The sarcasm had a dangerous undercurrent that matched the glint in his eye. A small, compact man with greying hair, the superintendent nevertheless seemed to fill the office. Warren felt his temperature rise. He was stepping into politics now, he realised, an arena in which he had never felt entirely at home.

"I think that new evidence suggests that Severino may not be our man, or at the very least was not working alone," Warren suggested, his voice firm and confident, belying his discomfort.

"Well, let's see what we have on Severino. CCTV images, logs from the university swipe-card system, a bag containing his clothes covered in Tunbridge's blood, plus latex gloves, plastic overshoes and the murder weapon, also covered in his blood, stuffed down his drain. On top of that he has a huge motive, no alibi and it would seem previous charges, if not convictions, demonstrating a violent personality and an apparent belief that his family will come swooping in to clean up his mess. What the hell else do you need — a confession signed in blood?" Grayson's voice dripped with sarcasm and Warren could see that he thought that Warren was wasting his time. His use of the last phrase convinced Warren beyond a doubt that Sutton had been in here poisoning the superintendent against him.

Warren took a deep breath; he would deal with Sutton later. For the time being, he had to deal with Grayson. With as much patience as he could muster, he repeated everything that the team had just discussed, deconstructing the evidence against Severino point by-point. By the time he had finished, Grayson's expression had changed from sceptical to thoughtful.

The silence grew as the superintendent contemplated what Warren had told him.

"I'm still not convinced that Severino is innocent, but you are right that there is more to this case than meets the eye. The official line of this department is that Antonio Severino killed Professor Alan Tunbridge as revenge for his poor treatment. We are now simply tying up loose ends. You can have a small team to do just that: a senior officer and a couple of detective constables to do the legwork.

"Either this case is closed by Monday morning or you are standing in front of me justifying how you've fucked up and explaining why this town's university's reputation as a safe place to live and work is suddenly in the shitter. Do I make myself clear?"

Warren fought back a half-dozen comments. He couldn't believe the superintendent was turning this whole thing around and laying it on him. Nevertheless, he had a job to do. Not trusting himself to say any more, he merely nodded. "Yes, sir."

Turning, he headed for the door, before Grayson stopped him. "Oh, one more thing, Warren. This team of yours, make sure it includes DI Sutton. I don't approve of my officers going behind each other's backs. Nor do I expect to see them engaged in a pissing contest in front of junior officers. Sort it out."

"Yes, sir."

Chapter 36

Jones stalked into the squad room, heading directly for Sutton's desk. Enough was enough, he'd decided. He'd let it linger long enough and if he and Sutton were going to work effectively as a team the air needed clearing. A few detectives glanced up at Jones' purposeful stride, then, seeing the look on the boss' face, quickly averted their gaze.

Sutton was on the phone, listening intently. As he looked up his expression turned briefly to one of guilt and apprehension, before his poker face slid back into place. Clearing his throat, he cut off his caller with a mumbled apology and a promise to call them back. Turning his chair, he looked expectantly at Jones.

"Get your coat, Tony, we're going for a pint." Without waiting for a reply, Jones turned on his heel and walked straight back out of the room. Looking neither left nor right, he was nevertheless aware of the covert stares from the working detectives. Behind him, he heard Sutton scrabbling for his jacket and grabbing his keys. Not in the mood to share the lift with him, Warren jogged quickly down the stairs to the main reception. Half a turn behind him, he could hear Sutton struggling to catch up.

Good! thought Warren. For too long, he'd felt on the back foot at Middlesbury and it was about time he took control of the situation.

Sutton finally pulled alongside him as they crossed the car park; he had his car keys in his hand.

"Put them away, Tony. You won't be driving tonight."

If Sutton had other plans for the evening, he wisely decided not to share them. Warren kept up the brisk pace down the high street; his longer legs meant that Sutton had no choice but to push himself hard to avoid breaking into an undignified trot and his breathing became slightly laboured.

Finally, Warren spied what he was looking for: The Bricklayer's Arms, a traditional-style English pub. Inside, it was exactly what Warren was after. Dark, slightly dingy with a long bar and, most importantly, tucked in the far corner, a few faded velour bench seats with tables and wooden dividers, giving at least the impression of privacy. At 4 p.m. on a weekday, the bar was quiet, the only customers two elderly men with rheumy eyes and flat caps sitting in silence behind halves of mild. A rolled-up newspaper, a single pack of Golden Virginia rolling tobacco, some cigarette papers and a battered box of matches sat between them like a barrier. Both glanced up at the newcomers, but made no comment, returning to their contemplative silence.

Without asking, Warren ordered two pints of Theakston Bitter. He'd have preferred something a little lighter, but he remembered from Monday that it was Sutton's pint of choice. No change was forthcoming from his five-pound note and so he directed them to the corner booth. Sutton still hadn't said anything beyond mumbled thanks for the pint.

Warren took a long swig of the strong, aromatic beer, wiping the foam off his top lip. Sutton did the same, politely nodding his appreciation. Time to start.

"What's the problem, Tony?"

"Don't know what you mean, guv." His eyes flickered slightly, betraying the lie.

"Bollocks." Warren's voice was quiet and measured, but forceful. "Since when does a DI go to a superintendent to discuss a case behind his DCI's back?"

"Don't know what you mean — just being polite, is all. The super wanted a heads up on the case, you were busy, so I filled him in."

"Really, and so it's just a coincidence that when Grayson had me in his office he parroted, pretty much word for word, everything you said to me earlier?"

Sutton shrugged. "I'm not the only person who thinks you've got it wrong, sir."

He took another sip of his pint.

Warren mirrored him, letting the silence sit between them.

"You don't like me very much, do you, Tony?"

Sutton's eyes narrowed as he looked for the trap. "You're my DCI. You're in charge, doesn't matter if I like you or not."

"Damned right it doesn't matter. I'm your DCI and I'm in charge. If you've got a problem with the way I'm handling the case, you speak to me about it and my word is final. You don't go over my head to the boss unless you think I'm incompetent or breaking the law. Do you think I'm incompetent?"

Sutton contemplated him for several heartbeats. "Not that I've seen."

Warren nodded. "Good. We'll leave it at that."

The silence grew again, Sutton's expression sullen. The air still felt tense. It wasn't enough, Warren realised. All he'd done was mark a line in the sand and dare Sutton to cross it. Whether he did or he didn't was merely a matter of degree. Warren still hadn't tackled the core of the problem.

Fortifying himself with another swig of his pint — he was down to the last third, he realised — he started again. "You resent me being here, don't you, Tony?"

Sutton said nothing, continuing to stare moodily into the dregs of his own pint. Warren motioned to the barman for two refills.

"From what I hear, you were expected to take Sheehy's place when he retired next year." Sutton's eyes flashed at the mention of his former DCI's name, but he remained silent. "Unfortunately, that didn't work out, did it? Sheehy went down last year and, after months of scrutiny, you were passed over. Bet it really pissed you off when some fucking Brummie turned up out of the blue and took over your job." Warren's tone was deliberately provocative.

Sutton scowled and shook his head. "You aren't even in the ballpark. Sir."

"Really? So tell me how it is, then, Tony. And forget the 'Sir' bullshit. We're in the pub."

Sutton took a big mouthful of his fresh pint. The barman had replenished it quietly, taking his payment without comment, experience telling him that he would be better off not interrupting the two men.

"You're wrong about almost everything. I've heard the rumours too; that I was Sheehy's golden boy, his heir apparent, next in line for the throne. But it's bullshit. I've never wanted to be a DCI and Gavin knew that. I'm a beat copper, always have been, always will be."

Warren shook his head. "No, you aren't, Tony, you're a detective and from what I hear a good one. You are no longer a bobby on the beat. By definition, when you joined CID you joined a team and you need to be a team player."

Sutton interrupted. "No, you are wrong." He shook his head vehemently. "This isn't West Midlands Police, or the Met or even Devon and fucking Cornwall. This is Middlesbury. We are unique." He waved his hand in the air, suddenly reminding Jones of Professor Tompkinson as he described his university.

"We are *all* beat coppers in Middlesbury. They won't have told you any of this stuff when they posted you down here, because they wanted an outsider. Somebody to break up the status quo."

Warren was starting to wonder if Sutton was paranoid or delusional. He sounded like a conspiracy theorist; Warren wondered who the hell "they" were.

Seeing Jones' sceptical look, Sutton calmed down slightly. "Let me explain what I mean. I come from a long line of coppers. My old man was a sergeant and his old man before him a constable. When he did his National Service he enlisted as an MP, following his own father's footsteps, who did stints as an MP and as a civilian police officer in the interwar years. Two of his brothers also joined the force. The family history gets a bit hazy before the First World War, but my dad swears blind that there is an unbroken chain of us going right back to Robert Peel's 'Bobbies' and the start of the Met.

"None of my ancestors ever made it past sergeant. None of them wanted it. And none of them were detectives. All of them were bobbies on the beat. My granddad got the George Medal after talking down an armed robber in the fifties. All he had was a wooden truncheon and handcuffs. Could have been promoted on the spot, but he turned it down. He didn't want to leave his patch."

For the first time since arriving at the pub, Sutton's features took on something less than a scowl. "When I announced I was taking the detectives' course, my old man nearly disowned me. That was until he came and saw where I worked and met Gavin and the team.

"Middlesbury has always been a small place, even with the

outlying villages. Beat coppers really do know their beats and their beats know them. It's about as close to *Dixon of Dock Green* as you'll ever get in modern policing. Well, CID isn't much different. We all know our patches, who our grasses are, who is dodgy and who can be trusted. The fact is, it works. By any measure, we punch above our weight when it comes to solving crimes, you know that."

Warren nodded; it was true. Middlesbury had an impressive clear-up rate, putting it amongst the top-performing CID units within the country. He admitted as much.

"Yeah, well, tell that to the penny pinchers. A few years ago, Herts and Beds decided to pool resources and move all CID units to Welwyn Garden City. Gavin was devastated. You see, to Gavin's way of thinking, Welwyn is too far away for that sort of community policing. We'd almost be better off joining up with Cambridgeshire. In the end he made his case strongly enough that it was decided to make Middlesbury CID a local first-response unit, responsible for Middlesbury and the surrounding towns. We come in, assess the situation, use our local contacts where appropriate and request back up from Welwyn as and when we need it. But we are constantly under scrutiny. We've set ourselves a high benchmark in terms of our performance figures and any deviation from that could spell the end for the arrangement."

"OK, I'd figured that something along those lines must have happened — I still don't see what your problem is though." Warren had the feeling that he was being told something significant here, something that would impact upon his entire stay at Middlesbury, but he couldn't see what.

Sutton took another gulp of his pint. "Gavin Sheehy was a good man." He raised a hand as if to still any protest. "I know, what he did was absolutely wrong and he deserves everything he gets. Still doesn't change the fact that fundamentally he was a good man who fought for what he believed in. The battle to keep Middlesbury CID was messy and bloody and more than one promotion was earned based on the savings achieved from the merger. But Gavin wouldn't give up and he fought his way up the food chain, arguing his case. Eventually he won his battle. But it cost him. He never went higher than DCI. He pissed off too many people and burnt too many bridges."

Warren tried to hide his incredulity. Stick tens of thousands of human beings together and ask them to get on with a job as complex and important as policing and factions would inevitably emerge, but this seemed too farfetched.

Seeing that he still had some way to go in convincing his superior, Sutton took a deep breath and tried again.

"When Gavin was caught, it was seen by many as proof that we'd be better off under the direct control of Welwyn." He made a bitter face. "That way they can keep a closer eye on us and spot rogue officers like Sheehy before they do too much damage. Gavin's greed and stupidity might just scupper his whole dream. Our whole dream."

With that, Sutton slumped into a moody silence.

It's personal, Warren realised. Sheehy convinced Sutton and goodness knows how many others to go along with him and then turned around and betrayed them with his corruption.

Warren already had his suspicions what the answer would be but he asked anyway.

"I'm still not seeing why you have a problem with me or how I am dealing with this case."

"Isn't it obvious? With Gavin out of the picture, they've appointed you to do their dirty work."

Despite himself, Warren bristled. "I'm not here to do anybody's dirty work. I'm here to solve crime and do my duty."

Sutton raised a hand in a half-hearted gesture of placation.

"I'm not saying that you have anything but the best of intentions. There's no way you would be briefed in on this, but you are the perfect man for the job."

Warren listened in growing anger; he couldn't work out if he was being accused of naiveté or dirty tricks. "And what job would that be, Inspector?" His voice was now icy cold as he forced a lid onto his temper.

"To close down Middlesbury CID and see it merged with the rest of Herts and Beds Serious Crime."

Warren was aware that his mouth was open in surprise.

"Why on earth would anyone think that? Let me assure you, I have not been given any other job, other than to lead this unit to the best of my ability, and I am offended that anyone could think otherwise."

Sutton repeated his calming hand gesture.

"Don't get me wrong, sir, nobody thinks otherwise."

He took another sip of his pint.

"Before you came here, I did a bit of digging about you and it turned up a couple things. That you are a good copper, well-regarded and that you are ambitious."

"OK," drawled Warren, unsure where this was leading.

"As to the ambition, it's figured that you are tapped for greater things, that Middlesbury is just a stepping stone before you move on to senior officer positions. Give it a couple of years and there will be a few vacancies in Welwyn that you can pursue." Warren said nothing; Sutton wasn't completely off the mark. But ambition wasn't a crime, was it? He said as much.

Sutton agreed. "Far from it. But ambition can be used by others. If Middlesbury CID closes, we'll all be transferred to Welwyn, closer to the rest of the force. Some might say, 'closer to the action'. Some might suggest that such a move would be advantageous to those with ambition…"

Sutton took a long sip of his pint, eyeing Warren shrewdly over the rim of the glass, watching for his reaction. Warren's head spun at the implication.

"What about Grayson? His opinion will carry far more weight than mine."

Sutton all but snorted. He paused, then, clearly emboldened by drink, leant forward. "Between you and me, guv, Grayson's just marking his time card. He's got a few more years before he can retire and everyone reckons he's just after one more promotion to boost his pension. It doesn't matter to him if the promotion is here or at Welwyn."

Warren was slightly shocked at the man's candour, but decided to let it slide. "So why are you so keen to cosy up to him?"

"You're right that Grayson's opinion carries more weight than yours, but he's a follower, not a leader. If you make it clear that Middlesbury is the place to be, then he'll probably take your advice. But failing that we've got to make it attractive for him to stay here and an easy collar like Severino makes the likelihood that he'll be promoted in post more likely."

Warren sat back, his head reeling and not just from the effect of two pints of bitter on an empty stomach. What the hell had he landed in? He'd come to Middlesbury expecting to further his career and his education in an environment that would allow him to experiment and stretch himself, away from the pressure cooker of big-city policing. Instead he had stumbled across a rat's nest of intrigue, politics and back-biting. Listening to Sutton talk, Warren felt himself wondering if he was witnessing the start of a mutiny. He said as much.

"Look, we're fighting for our survival here. Shutting us down as soon as Gavin was arrested would have been too obvious — he acted alone and you can't punish a whole CID unit for the actions of one man. However, rumour has it that we will be subject to a review in a few months' time and they'll probably claim that we just aren't cost-effective enough to justify maintaining.

"That's why solving this case so quickly is so damned important. We've also earned the gratitude and admiration of the university, local politicians and saved a major conference from being moved out of the region. All of these are vital for the survival of our CID.

"Yet now, you want to turn this whole thing around. Tell everyone we've got the wrong person. You want to announce that out there a killer is still loose and we've got an innocent man in prison?" Sutton's voice was starting to rise, his cheeks flushing.

"With all due respect, sir, are you fucking mad?" he carried on before Warren could interrupt. "We've got a man with a prior conviction for assault, with a huge motive, no credible alibi and to top it all the murder weapon, his blood-splattered clothes and CCTV footage and computer logs placing him at the scene of the crime. Jesus wept, sir, what the hell else do we need? Are you really going to scupper this entire prosecution and with it the future of this police unit on the basis of a fucking hunch?

"Christ, sir, you know how a murder investigation works. There is almost never a single piece of irrefutable damning evidence. Every piece of the jigsaw can be removed and discarded if needs be, every bit of evidence can be argued to be circumstantial with enough imagination — it's what it all adds up to that counts. And this adds up to a clear conviction. It might not be as polished as we'd like, but who gives a shit? We've done our job. Now we let the lawyers and the courts do theirs."

Sutton leant back in his chair again, breathing heavily, his face flushed. Warren said nothing, letting the man cool down as he got his own thoughts in order. When he judged enough time had passed, he started again.

"Now you listen to me, Tony, let's be absolutely clear on one thing. I am not here to do anybody's dirty work and I have no intention of getting involved in this political dispute. As far as I am concerned, I am a detective chief inspector assigned to this unit to run major operations under the command of Detective Superintendent Grayson. When it comes to the future of this particular CID unit and its place within the larger police force, I neither have nor want any influence. If asked my opinion, I will state it clearly based on the evidence I have seen and I will not be swayed either way. Do I make myself clear?"

Sutton grunted non-committally.

"Second, as Officer in Charge of the Tunbridge murder, it is my duty to uncover the truth, no matter what that may be. I don't give a shit how that plays in terms of your personal agenda, DI Sutton. Let me make one thing absolutely crystal — try and circumvent me again by going behind my back and I will kick you off my team and put you in charge of domestic violence. Believe me, I can play as dirty as anyone when I need to."

Sutton said nothing, but was unable to conceal a wince at the threat of reassignment. Domestic violence was an important and vital part of modern policing, but the cases were messy, frustrating and often unsatisfying. It took a special kind of person to do the job and Warren had read Sutton like a book — both of them knew that he wasn't that kind of person.

"Finally, you told me that you are a copper's copper. Well, if that is the case put aside the political bullshit and look at this case as a bloody professional. You worry that if we reopen this case and admit we arrested the wrong person we'll look like fools. Well, think what we'll look like if it gets to court and it's shown that we had the wrong man! You don't have to believe that Severino's innocent, but you have to admit that there is mounting evidence that at the very least he had an accomplice."

Sutton shrugged, still seemingly unswayed.

"Look at it this way, even if he is the killer and acted alone, the case against him as it stands is flawed. If I can see the holes, then so can his defence team. If Severino walks because we put forward a weak case then Middlesbury CID will be closed overnight — and you know what? I'll be the one closing it."

His piece said, Warren drained the last of his beer and sat back. Sutton stared moodily into space. After a moment's thought, Warren gestured to the barman again. Sutton said nothing as another foaming pint was placed in front of him. Warren glanced at his wallet. He had no more cash — if Sutton didn't start contributing soon, Warren would have to find a cashpoint.

"I'm off for a piss," growled Sutton, lurching to his feet. Warren noticed that he wobbled slightly as he headed toward the gents' toilets. Glancing at his watch, Warren saw that it was almost five-thirty; soon the pub would start filling up with office workers. He'd also better phone Susan; he had a feeling that he had a lot more work to do with Sutton. Dialling her number, he refrained from opening the conversation with his customary, "Hello, darling," in case Beatrice answered again.

By the end of the conversation, he almost wished that his mother-in-law had answered. Susan had been extremely displeased when he explained that he was working late, not least because he slurred his speech slightly and was forced to admit that he was working in the pub. That ended the conversation rather abruptly.

Sutton still hadn't returned from the toilet, so Warren decided to make use of the cashpoint he'd spied next to the bar. Drawing out fifty pounds, he was not impressed to be charged a further two pounds for the privilege of accessing his own money. A further couple of pounds were exchanged for a random selection of bar snacks, the closest thing Warren had had approaching a meal since breakfast. Retaking his seat, he knocked the table with his knee, slopping beer over the dark wooden surface. Steady on, he admonished himself, time to start slowing down. If he drank much more, he would risk his professional standing.

Finally, Sutton reappeared.

"OK, I still think Severino did it, but let's see if he had an accomplice," he started without preamble. "Who could it have been and did they commit the murder with him, or were they just accessories?"

Good, thought Warren. If not a victory, then at least some progress.

"Let's look at the second question first and go back to motives." Warren held his hand out and started ticking things off on his fingers.

"First, Spencer. Tunbridge treated him like shit and may well have screwed his career — he has as good a motive as Severino, I would say."

"But his alibi is tight. He was locked in that PRC room or whatever the damn thing's called."

"I agree. He looks safe for now. If he was involved it was just during the planning — he may have told Severino when Tunbridge was alone and vulnerable. We could do with a look at his phone, but we'd need a warrant and we haven't got probable cause. OK, let's stick him on the possible list. Actually, have you got any paper?"

Sutton pulled out his notebook. "No, that's too small. Have you got any A4 paper?"

Sutton looked at him incredulously. "Do I look like a branch of bloody WHSmiths?" He started patting his pockets. "Hang on a minute, I'm sure I had a ream of photocopy paper here somewhere."

Despite himself, Warren started to laugh. Sutton's scowl turned into a grin. "Maybe the barman has some." He scrambled to his feet and wound his way to the bar. Gaining the man's attention, he asked for a few sheets of A4 paper and a couple of coloured pens. The barman's response was much the same as Sutton's had been to Warren a few moments before. Reaching into his wallet, Sutton pulled out his warrant card. "Detective Inspector Sutton, Middlesbury CID." He made a show of sniffing the air, before looking at the two old men with their tobacco and rolling papers. "Smells a bit smoky in here. You wouldn't be letting punters smoke in here, would you? That's against the law now, you know — hefty fine."

The barman rolled his eyes in disbelief. "Oh, for fuck's sake… wait here." He disappeared through the kitchen doors, presumably heading towards an office. A few moments later he returned with a dozen sheets of laser-printer paper and some black and red ballpoint pens.

As Sutton returned to his seat Warren smirked, pleased to

see that he wasn't the only one to use that little trick to ensure co-operation. "Community policing at its finest, DI Sutton."

For his part Sutton shrugged. "I think we'll have to move on for the next one — we may have overstayed our welcome."

Returning to the matter in hand, Warren spread the paper out on the table, careful to avoid the spilt beer. He jotted down their notes about Spencer.

"Moving on, who's next? What about the wife?"

Sutton nodded. "She's just found out that he wants a divorce and she knows that he stands to make a load of money if his company takes off. But what does she gain by killing him now?"

"He has life insurance and she'll be entitled to his pension. We should check and see how much that's worth. However, we know that she was at a restaurant that night, so she might be an accessory but wasn't the killer."

"In which case, what could she offer Severino? Half the life insurance money — a cut of the pension?"

"Hmm, when you put it like that, it doesn't seem worth it for either of them — stick her on the unlikely list, I reckon. Same would go for his kids."

Warren ticked off another finger. "Crawley. Again, his alibi's sound. The question is, what does he have to gain? He told us that he isn't in a position to take over the lab and that he's too expensive to find other employment. On the face of it, he's the last person who would want to kill Tunbridge at the moment."

"Strike him off, then." Sutton reached for the pen but Warren shook his head. "So far, we only have his word for it that he wouldn't want to run the lab, but we know that he is financially under pressure. And if Tunbridge's research has been stolen, there can't be many who would be in a better position to exploit it."

"It would be a bit suspicious, though, don't you think? Tunbridge is murdered and two years later his former experimental officer is making millions out of his research."

Warren shrugged. "I don't know. I have no idea if that would be suspicious or not. Tompkinson implied that it was a hot topic of research — surely that means that there must be others capable of one day catching up? In that case, it might not be a surprise at all if he's the one to do so. Leave him on the maybe list and make a note to do some more digging around his private life. I'll have a word with Tompkinson about what will happen to Tunbridge's research group and research, now he's gone."

"Speaking of Tompkinson…"

Warren shook his head. "I don't see it. He has some motive, I grant you, but if what he says is true he isn't in any state to benefit from Tunbridge's death. We need to confirm everything he says about his health and double-check his alibi, but it's a hell of a stretch.

"Next up, Hemmingway."

"Now, of all of the suspects so far, I could see her being one. She's a hard-nosed bitch, mark my words."

Warren blinked in surprise. "I didn't have her down as particularly likely."

Sutton leant forward, his former reluctance apparently gone now as he became involved in the intellectual challenge.

"Well, think about it. She has a hell of a motive — Tunbridge was an absolute bastard to her. Trust me, people have killed for less."

"Maybe so, but she didn't kill him. She has a strong alibi for the night in question, so she could only have been an accessory. In which case we're back to who else benefits? And how likely is it that she and Severino decided to team up and get revenge on the man that ruined their lives? I can see them both being happy that he's gone, but I can't see any prior link. Did they really get to know each other so well during her handful of visits to the lab to discuss her essay that they would later get together to kill him? And I can't see any possible financial motive."

Sutton looked thoughtful. "Well, if Severino is to be believed, a young woman who could certainly match Hemmingway's description set him up by stealing his swipe card and some of his clothes."

Warren shook his head in frustration. "But that wouldn't make any sense. Surely Severino wouldn't have brought up Hemmingway if they were in partnership — or if he was confessing and seeking to spread the blame, he would have named her outright. However, if he is telling the truth and this mysterious blonde woman did seduce him in the bar, then wouldn't he have recognised her? They had sex. This isn't Hollywood — she can't have disguised herself that effectively."

Sutton looked dissatisfied, clearly unwilling to dismiss her entirely. "We should probe a bit more. Something smells about that girl and I ain't talking about her cheap perfume."

Warren shrugged. "Fine, keep her on the further investigation list. We should at least put her photo around, see if anybody recognises her and have her back in for a follow-up interview.

"Now we get into the realms of the unknown. Who is this mysterious John Priest that has been contacting Tunbridge and why did his website disappear so suddenly?"

"That's a weird one, I grant you. And it could explain how the killer knew that Tunbridge would be in his office that night. The question again is, who did the killing?"

"IT support are trying to track down the owner of the website and who this person is. It would help if we had access to Tunbridge's diary. I bet he's recorded details of any conversations that he's had with this person. And who downloaded his data the night he was killed? Presumably that was his killer — why? I guess they intend to use it, but how?"

"You know, it does add a whole different complexion to this case," Sutton suggested thoughtfully. "Severino could have been a hired gun. He could have been employed by some commercial rival to bump off Tunbridge and steal his data."

"If that was the case, it was pretty bloody amateurish. Surely, the last thing they'd want is for him to be caught so easily — there's no guarantee he won't talk and lead us right back to them."

"True."

The two men lapsed into thoughtful silence.

"Of course, this all assumes that Severino did the killing and was he alone?"

Sutton sighed. "Look, guv, realistically who else could it have been? Severino was present — who else could he have met up with? Spencer was locked in that little room and the only other person in the building was Tunbridge. The only thing that makes sense is that Severino comes in, does Tunbridge, then legs it before Spencer returns."

"But how did he time it so well? How did he know that Tunbridge would be in his office so late at night?"

"Well, the obvious answer is that Severino is this John Priest and he lured Tunbridge in that night."

Jones frowned, unconvinced. "I'm not sure about the timing on that. Did Severino lose his job before or after Tunbridge met this J Priest? And besides, those emails implied that they had met — which surely rules out Severino?"

Sutton thought hard before shrugging. "I can't remember how the dates match up — we'll need to look it up. Stick him on the list to re-interview. He's not going anywhere."

Another thought occurred to Warren. "On top of that, how did he know that Tunbridge would be alone? Or that Spencer would be the only other person in the building but conveniently in that little room?"

Sutton frowned. "Well, I would imagine that he could be fairly sure that the building would be empty at ten on a Friday night, especially on a nice summer evening when everyone who isn't away is sitting in a beer garden somewhere. Maybe he just took a gamble? That would fit with the amateurish nature of the murder."

Jones leant back, drumming his fingers on the table top as he thought this through. "That's something else that bothers me. Assuming the two things are connected, setting up that website took serious premeditation and organisation, whereas the way Tunbridge was killed and Severino was tracked down so quickly implies something amateur and spur of the moment. Damn it, we really need to know who set that website up, so we can either pursue them or rule them out."

The two men sat in silence, staring at their now empty pints.

"Something else also bothers me," started Warren again after several long moments. "Spencer being locked in that little room. It's just too bloody convenient. We are taking his alibi at face value. I'm going back to have another look tomorrow, I think."

"Whilst you're at it, see if there is any other way in and out of that building. We'll look like right bloody chumps if it turns out that the killer walked through a fire door with a dodgy lock."

Warren nodded. "Well, all this is well and good, but our glasses are empty and by my reckoning it's your bloody round."

Sutton grinned, before looking around at the rest of the bar, which was now starting to fill up with office workers. The barman scowled when he made eye contact. "Well, I reckon we've burnt our bridges here. If I'm buying, then let's go somewhere a bit quieter that serves a decent pint."

Chapter 37

Stifling a yawn, Karen Hardwick let herself into the tiny bedsit she was trying her best to call home. It had been four months since Owen had finished their three-year relationship and two months since she had finally found a place cheap enough for her to rent on her own. The apartment was still only just affordable and in Middlesbury, as in most places within one hundred miles of London, to say that you got what you paid for would be an exaggeration. It comprised three rooms, including a bedroom-cum-sitting-room, a tiny bathroom and an even smaller kitchen, and Karen figured her days of hosting lavish dinner parties were on hold for the foreseeable future. The most people that she'd ever had in her sitting room at any one time was three — when her parents had stopped for a tea break whilst helping her move in.

After she had split up with Owen her mother had wanted her to come back home and live with them again. It was a kind offer and in fact, unlike many of her friends, Karen had never had a problem living with her parents, having spent various stints off and on between university courses and jobs staying in her old bedroom. But those days were gone now and, besides, her parents lived well north of Cambridge, making the daily commute impractical. Moving police forces was *not* an option, she had told her parents emphatically. She was just starting to find her feet and equally importantly she had just been accepted onto the detectives' course.

Nevertheless, she thought, as she hung up her coat in what the letting agency laughingly called the "hallway", a bit of company in the evening would be nice. Not a boyfriend — not yet; the relationship with Owen was definitely over, but her heart still missed him — but a bit of companionship. Perhaps she should have gone for a shared apartment with a flatmate? No, she decided, she'd had her share of flatmates at university. A mixed bunch to say the least: two of them she remained in close contact with, a third she had deliberately rejected all friend requests on Facebook from — in the same way that she had rejected all of his "more than friends requests" when they shared a flat together.

Opening her tiny fridge, she remembered that she still had some leftover pasta sauce from the night before. Sniffing it reflexively — another habit she'd acquired in her university days, when the age and or provenance of anything in the communal fridge couldn't always be guaranteed — she placed it into the microwave. She still had half a packet of fresh tortellini and so she filled the kettle. As she waited for the water to boil her mind wandered back to the case. Unlike DI Sutton and some others, she felt that DCI Jones might be right to be sceptical about the guilt of Severino. At the very least, she felt that something wasn't quite right about the whole thing. Nevertheless, she had no intention of raising her head above the parapet just yet. She'd been in the office that afternoon when Jones had stormed in and hauled Tony Sutton out. Rumour had it that Sutton had gone behind Jones' back to Superintendent Grayson to try and get Jones to leave the Severino charges alone. Karen wasn't entirely sure why Sutton was so set against probing any deeper into the case, but she was the new kid and had no intention of taking sides and offending anybody this early in her career.

The kettle started dancing around and belching steam. Its automatic cut-off was a bit dodgy and so Karen flicked it off at the mains and poured the water into a small saucepan. Turning the electric hob on, she brought the water back to the boil, before pouring in the pasta and dripping what she estimated to be a tea-spoon of olive oil over the top. At the same time, she started the microwave off. She could also use the timer on the microwave to time the pasta. "Jamie Oliver, eat your heart out," she said out loud.

Opening the fridge again, she took out a packet of fresh, grated parmesan. As she did so she noticed the half-drunk bottle of rosé wine. Looking at it longingly, she eventually decided against it. Drinking alone, even a glass or so, was only one step away from owning a cat. She did not want to wake up on the morning of her thirtieth birthday single, with an empty bottle of wine beside her and a cat yowling at the door. That, frankly, was a stereotype too far. She settled instead for some of the sparkling grape juice that she had recently developed a taste for.

The ping of the microwave informed her that dinner was ready. Turning off the hob, Karen strained the pasta through a colander. As usual she noted, despite what it claimed on the packet, adding a teaspoon of olive oil to the pasta as it cooked had not stopped it from sticking together. Oh, well, she rationalised, it all went down the same way, and with that she dumped it into a china bowl. Covering it with the reheated tomato sauce and a liberal sprinkling of parmesan cheese, she grabbed a spoon and her grape juice, put everything on a lap tray and walked the three paces to her sofa.

Flicking on the TV, Karen noted that she was still just inside the seven until 9 p.m. "dead zone", when the television offered up nothing more stimulating than endless, mind-numbing soap operas, crap game shows and insultingly contrived "reality shows". With nothing worth watching being broadcast live, Karen flicked over to the catch-up TV service. There were usually a couple of good comedy panel shows that she always seemed to miss each week. To her delight an episode of *Mock the Week* was available. Selecting it, she settled back on the sofa, spooning up a large dollop of pasta shells and tomato sauce. The familiar error message informing her that her cable company was "experiencing a high level of demand" from her area and to try back later almost made her throw her bowl at the TV.

Turning off the TV, she sat back, thinking dark thoughts about the large sums of money she was paying for this so-called service. After a few moments, however, her mind turned back to the case. Something about it didn't feel right. There were loose ends to be tied up, for sure, but that wasn't it. She had a feeling that there was something in front of her that didn't add up. Something that they had accepted at face value without questioning. She mulled it over as she finished her pasta and drained her grape juice. The chilled drink was a welcome relief. The last few days had been intolerably hot and Karen's apartment had direct sunlight. She kept her curtains closed during the day to minimise the heat from the sun. However, she had spent too long as a beat constable to feel comfortable leaving her windows open when she was out at work to circulate air through the apartment, even if she was on the top floor of a six-storey building.

But now she was in, she had no such reservations, opening the big window to the evening air. The building was old and, unlike modern apartments with their double-glazed uPVC windows, this one had an old-fashioned sash window that could be opened all the way. Unfortunately, the evening air wasn't much cooler than the air in her apartment. The complete lack of a breeze and the fact that she had no other windows meant that the stuffy air wouldn't circulate. Karen resigned herself to another night of poor sleep. At least she had Karin Slaughter's latest novel to keep her occupied. She'd picked it up from Tesco when she was doing her shop at the weekend. Now that she thought of it, she'd also seen a special offer on desk fans. Was it worth it? She knew that fans alone didn't cool air — they just circulated the hot air — you needed an air conditioner for that. She fantasised briefly about the air-conditioning units that American hotels attached to guests' windows. She'd experienced them firsthand when she had visited the US one summer. The temperature outside had been somewhere north of forty degrees Celsius, yet when she'd returned to her room she'd had to turn the unit off and put a sweater on to stop her teeth chattering. Sod her carbon footprint — she'd take the bus a bit more and turn down the thermostat in winter to compensate.

Suddenly it came to her in a flash of inspiration. She knew what didn't feel right. The air conditioning. Even as she thought about it, she felt yet another idea coming on. She paced around her room, all thoughts of her lousy cable TV signal or the stuffiness of her apartment vanishing. Taking a few deep breaths, she forced herself to calm down. She grabbed a piece of paper, and quickly scribbled down her thoughts, terrified that they would disappear if she didn't record them.

Next, she picked up her laptop. She hadn't used it in over a week and it seemed to take an age to boot up. "No, I don't want to install bloody updates for Java," she yelled at the machine in frustration. Finally, Windows stopped loading all of the unnecessary programs and patches it felt it needed and let Karen access what she wanted.

Navigating to her Documents folder, she pulled up her master's dissertation. The twenty-thousand-word document, stuffed full of pictures and hyperlinks to bibliography software, took an age to load. Scrolling through the document, Karen was transported back in time several years. To a time when the appearance or otherwise of a single white band on a black and white instant photograph was either a cause for celebration or the depressing realisation that two days' work had been for nothing and that she would need to cancel her weekend plans to repeat everything all over again. Despite the urgency of her situation, she found herself smiling at the memories. In the past few years, Karen had chased suspected robbers, grappled with drunken youths and even had a knife brandished at her, not to mention the heart-stopping terror of an eighty-miles-per-hour-plus car chase through a residential area late at night. She'd had more nightmares about that episode than having the knife pulled on her. She still trusted Kevlar more than some of her colleagues' driving skills, advanced driving qualifications be damned.

Nevertheless, despite all of that adrenaline-pumping action, she would have been hard-pressed to remember a more exciting time than when she'd finally seen that little white band appear and proven her supervisor's hypothesis to be true. The thrill was matched a few months later, when the same photograph was published in *The Journal of Cell Biology* with her name listed as second author.

Shaking herself out of her reverie, she carried on scrolling through the document, before finally finding what she wanted in the "Materials and Methods" section. Jotting down some notes, she quickly scribbled down some back-of-envelope calculations. The results were encouraging, but she knew to be cautious. Science moved on at a breakneck pace and what was state-of-the-art now was old news in just a few short years. She would need evidence to prove her idea — and that would have to wait until tomorrow.

Standing up, she felt the stuffiness of the room again. To hell with it, she suddenly decided, in a celebratory mood. She might not be able to afford an air-conditioning unit — and wasn't sure where she would get one anyway at nine on a Wednesday evening — but Tesco had twenty-four-hour opening and she could afford to splash out on a fan. Not only that, she'd been looking forward to starting that book all week and that rosé wine needed to be drunk. But she drew the line at getting a cat.

THURSDAY

Chapter 38

At 8 a.m. the following day, DC Karen Hardwick took several deep breaths and tried to stop her hands shaking. The scribbled notes that she had written the night before were damp from perspiration that had nothing to do with the heat. She could see that DCI Jones' office door was ajar, a sign that he was in and could be disturbed. But was he the right person to talk to? He was the boss. There were two more ranks between her, a lowly detective constable, and Jones, a detective chief inspector. Ordinarily, Karen would have spoken first to a detective sergeant or perhaps Detective Inspector Sutton. However, she had seen the faces around the table yesterday and realised that what she was about to suggest might not be popular.

Sod it, she decided. Time to bite the bullet. Jones seemed a sympathetic boss and he had actively sought her opinions a few times since asking her to accompany him Saturday morning. Screwing up her courage, she walked as confidently as she could to the office door. The administrative assistant nearest the door glanced up but said nothing, which Karen interpreted as "go ahead"; if Jones was busy or on the phone she would doubtless have said something.

With as much confidence as she could muster, Karen knocked twice.

"Come in." The voice was confident but sounded a little scratchy, Karen noticed.

Opening the door, Karen stepped in. She had deliberately dressed in her most businesslike clothes this morning. A modest grey skirt that came to just above the knees, a white, short-sleeved silk blouse and a pair of smart black, flat shoes. Her hair had been teased into a bun and she wore just the barest hint of make-up. If Jones noticed, he didn't give any indication and it was clear that he hadn't given quite as much attention to his appearance that morning.

His face was sallow, with pronounced circles underneath his eyes. Although he was clean-shaven, Karen noticed that he appeared to have missed a few patches around the bottom of his throat. He wore what appeared to be a freshly starched light blue shirt, rather than the white one that he'd been wearing the day before, but the tie appeared to be the same and the dark jacket on the back of his chair looked a little creased. As Karen approached the desk she noted that his aftershave appeared to be a little stronger than normal.

Perhaps he was coming down with a summer cold, she thought. Then she remembered the appearance of DI Tony Sutton this morning, who had also looked decidedly dishevelled. Jones had grabbed Sutton and hauled him out of the office mid-afternoon the day before, saying something about going to the pub. Interesting...

"Yes, Karen, what can I do for you?" asked Jones, stifling a yawn.

Taking a few deep breaths, Karen plunged straight in. "I've been doing some thinking and a few things just don't add up, sir. I think there may be more to what happened Friday night than we thought."

Warren contemplated her for a second, before gesturing at the visitor chair in front of the desk. "OK, what's on your mind?"

Karen sat down and spread her notes in front of her. "It's Tom

Spencer and his account of what happened on Friday night. I've been thinking about his trip to the PCR room and something doesn't make sense."

Warren motioned for her to continue.

"First of all, what was the weather like Friday night?"

Warren shrugged. "Hot and sticky, just like it has been for the past week."

"And would you say that it was like that in the laboratories and offices in the Biology building?"

"I would imagine so. I don't think that they have any air conditioning except in places like the PCR room."

"What was Tom Spencer wearing when he found the professor's body?"

"Jeans and a T-shirt, with a lab coat on. Why do you ask?"

"Well, do you remember how cold it was in the PCR room when Dr Crawley showed us around?"

Warren nodded, remembering how he'd been glad of his jacket. "I remember Crawley joked that the university looked after the equipment better than the staff."

"Well, according to the computer log, Spencer was in the room for sixty-eight minutes. If I was in that room for so long, I'd probably have brought along a sweater or jacket to keep warm, especially if I'd been working in stuffy conditions all day. The contrast would have been uncomfortable to say the least."

Warren frowned. "I can see where you are coming from, Karen, but maybe he forgot. Hell, it's been like this for at least a week — he probably didn't remember to bring a sweater to work. I guess he just had to grin and bear it. The room was cool, but I doubt he was in any danger of hypothermia."

"Well, that's the thing, you see — he didn't have to grin and bear it. He could have left at any time."

"I don't follow you."

"Spencer stated that he was doing a PCR reaction and that he used the Tetrad PCR machine. Well, the thing with PCR reactions is that you just set them up and then leave them to go. The whole process is automated. Spencer will have made up the solutions in his laboratory, placed his tubes in an ice bucket, then carried them down to the PCR room — witnesses did say that he was carrying an ice bucket. All he needs to do then is place the tubes in the machine, select the correct program, press start, then return when the run has finished. There is no reason to stay in a cold room for so long."

Warren looked into space for a moment, his mind buzzing furiously.

"OK, playing devil's advocate, maybe he did something else in there. Perhaps he was just on the skive, reading a magazine or something."

"Sir, it was nine o'clock on a Friday night. The building was empty. It would be pretty unlikely that he would be found out if he was reading a magazine. And I'm sure he could have found somewhere else more comfortable to read. Besides which, there's more."

Warren raised an eyebrow. "Go on."

"You said that he was wearing a face mask?"

"Yes, one of those sterile surgical masks. There was a box of them in the lab."

"I don't know why he would be wearing a mask. The chemicals used in PCR are harmless, certainly at that dose, so he wouldn't have needed protecting."

"Maybe it was to stop contamination of his samples — you know that Scenes of Crime Officers always wear them."

"Possibly, but the thing is that, from what I understand, Tunbridge's lab worked exclusively on bacteria. Any human DNA getting in the mix wouldn't interfere with the reaction as it wouldn't be recognised. Besides which, a few stray human cells with their DNA molecules locked away in the nucleus would be swamped by the pure bacterial DNA that he was probably using in his experiments. I rarely saw anybody wear masks when setting up standard PCR reactions. Some folks didn't even wear gloves, although that's frowned upon unless you have a latex allergy."

Warren contemplated her for a long moment. "It's an interesting thought, Karen, but it's all very circumstantial. Maybe he was already wearing it because of something else he had been doing earlier. He already admitted that he had simply forgotten to remove his gloves."

Karen nodded; she wasn't a fool. "Well, I can only speak from personal experience, but I know that I hate wearing those face masks and can't wait to take them off when I no longer need them. And they always told us in training that nothing is insignificant and that it's your job to decide what's important. Besides which, it's not just those things. The timing doesn't really add up. I don't think he was in there long enough."

"First you say he was in there too long, now you say not long enough. You can't have it both ways."

Karen flushed slightly. "That wasn't what I meant, sir. I mean that if he was just popping in to set up his PCR reaction before leaving, he was in there far too long. But if he decided for whatever reason to see his program through to the end, he probably wasn't in there long enough."

"How long is long enough?"

Karen looked a little uncomfortable. "It's hard to say, but I used to do a lot of PCR when I was a graduate student. The length of time needed varies a lot depending on what you are trying to achieve. And I have to point out that I did my master's degree a few years ago, and technology may have changed since then. But if my sums are reasonable, he was definitely in there too short a time."

"OK, well, talk me through your reasoning."

"First of all, sir, what do you know about PCR and DNA?"

"Probably a lot less than I should. I've heard the terms but, I'll be honest, I don't really understand them beyond how useful they have become to forensics. My wife is the biologist in the family, not me. Play it safe and assume I know nothing."

"OK, let's start with DNA." Karen drew two parallel lines on the back of her notes. "As I'm sure you already know, the DNA molecule is composed of two strands, coiled around each other in a helix." Warren nodded.

"Well, forgetting about the helix for a moment as it isn't relevant, you can imagine DNA as like a ladder. Two vertical bits with rungs. Now imagine if you took your ladder and cut down the middle of each rung, leaving the half rungs sticking out of the vertical bit, a bit like a comb."

Warren nodded again; Karen's diagram made it clear.

"Unlike a ladder, however, each of those half-rungs is one of four different types of chemical called a base, referred to by their first letters, A, T, G and C. These four bases are like the letters of an alphabet and just like the way that the order of the twenty-six letters of the Roman alphabet can be arranged to provide an infinite number of different sentences, so can the four letters of

DNA. The cell translates this code into the proteins that it needs to perform all of its jobs, in the same way that you translate the letters of the alphabet into a meaningful sentence."

"With you so far. I remember this from a training course."

"Well, remember that I said it was like a ladder, cut down the middle? Each of those rungs is made up of two bases joined together. However, they can only join up in a particular way: A must always be joined to T and G must always be bound to C. So if you have a sequence of ATCG on one side of the ladder, then the opposite side of the ladder must be TAGC."

To illustrate her point, Karen drew out the letters on the piece of paper

A T C G

T A G C

"We call each of these pairs a 'base pair'. Humans have about three billion base pairs of DNA."

"OK, I've got you. Now what is this PCR thing? I know it's important in forensics, but I don't see why Spencer would be using it — he works on bacteria."

"Well, sir, first of all you have to remember that DNA is DNA. It doesn't matter if it comes from humans, plants, bacteria, viruses or whatever, so PCR can be used on anything. But basically, the Polymerase Chain Reaction, or PCR, is a way of increasing the amount of DNA that you have to make more. What's more it can be very specific, so that you only amplify the bit of DNA you are interested in and ignore the rest."

"You'll have to elaborate a bit more here, I'm afraid."

"I'm sure you've seen shows like *CSI* where they take a single hair follicle and from that they are able to extract the DNA and perform loads of different tests?"

Warren snorted. The so-called "CSI effect" had raised the public's — and for that also raised juries' — expectations to unrealistic levels. The public expected results in hours rather than weeks and seemed to think that every crime scene, regardless of its triviality, should be subjected to thousands of pounds' worth of DNA analysis.

He gestured for her to continue.

"Well, the fact is that in most samples the amount of DNA is minuscule; far too little for scientists to do anything meaningful with. So they need to make more of the DNA; millions of times as much. At the same time, they can make sure that they only make more of the DNA that they are interested in. In the human being, for example, scientists might only want to look at a thousand base pairs, so they only amplify that DNA, ignoring the remainder of the three billion base pairs."

"OK, I can see why PCR is so important, but how long does it take?"

"That varies a lot, but I can do some estimates."

Karen turned over another sheet of paper.

"The process has a number of steps. First you prepare all of the chemicals back in your lab and dispense it into tiny plastic tubes, which you can then carry down to the PCR machine in an ice bucket. Next you place the tubes in the PCR machine — more properly known as a thermo-cycler, because its job is to change temperature very rapidly. If you want to know how long Tom Spencer should have spent in the PCR room, this is when the clock starts.

"Then you need to heat the DNA to ninety-five degrees Celsius for about five minutes. This is enough to split the DNA ladder down the middle of the base pairs, leaving unpaired DNA bases sticking out like teeth in a comb.

"Now, you are only interested in a small piece of the DNA. To identify this piece of DNA you need to add two short pieces of artificially made DNA — maybe twenty or thirty base pairs in length — called primers that will match the DNA sequences either side of the bit you are interested in. It's a bit like putting brackets around the word you are interested in in a sentence. To do this you cool the solution down to between forty-five degrees Celsius and sixty-five degrees Celsius for about forty-five seconds, which allows this primer DNA to join the matching sequences of the original template DNA.

"Now comes the clever bit. If you raise the temperature to about seventy-two degrees Celsius, an enzyme called a polymerase builds up the missing half of the ladder using raw chemicals that you added to the solution at the start. Depending on what type of polymerase enzyme you use, a good rule of thumb is that it takes about one minute to make a thousand base pairs of DNA. The result is that where you started off with a single very long ladder of DNA, most of which you don't want, you now have two short DNA ladders, only containing the DNA sequence you are interested in.

"But it doesn't stop there. If you repeat the cycle, you will use the new ladders as a template also, so those two molecules become four. Repeat again and the four become eight. Then sixteen, thirty-two, sixty-four, one hundred and twenty-eight…"

Warren whistled. "The power of powers, eh? So after all that, give me a figure, Karen. How long do you think this PCR reaction would have taken, assuming that he completed it?"

Karen looked uncomfortable, nervously shuffling her notes. "There is a lot of guesswork here and I'm using figures from my own reactions, which might be completely different from anything he is using, but if we assume that he does thirty cycles, with an extension time of one minute — assuming he is amplifying one thousand base pairs — then by the time he's added on another four minutes at the end to finish off any uncompleted reactions, I'm calculating eighty-four minutes, not including the time taken to actually set up the machine and retrieve his samples at the end of the run."

Warren looked at her figures thoughtfully for a few long moments, before scribbling a few numbers of his own. Karen forced herself to breathe normally.

"You realise that if he did an extension time of only half a minute, he would only need about seventy minutes. Same thing if he kept it at one minute but only did twenty-five cycles. That's getting pretty close to the sixty-eight minutes."

"I know. There is a lot of guesswork involved. I need to get a look at the program he used ideally."

Warren raised an eyebrow. "Is that possible?"

"I think so, sir. It should be stored in the memory of the PCR machine."

"All of this is pretty circumstantial, you realise? It's interesting, but not conclusive."

Karen nodded, unable to say anything.

"Good, just so you understand." He stood up. "Nice thinking, Karen. After my conversation with DI Sutton last night, it was decided that another look at that PCR room is on the cards — you've just bumped that up to our number one priority."

Chapter 39

Much to Karen's surprise, Jones' first act was to call in DI Tony Sutton. Her first impression of him that morning had been correct: he looked decidedly dishevelled. Jones filled in Sutton with an abridged version of what Karen had just told him. Sutton thought for a few moments, before nodding his head slowly. "Still doesn't let Severino off the hook, but it's definitely food for thought." He turned to Karen. "Nice thinking, Detective. That insider knowledge is something that a couple of old plods like DCI Jones and me lack. You get any more good ideas, you make sure that you share them with us."

Karen nodded, unable to speak. To her chagrin, she could feel her cheeks turning pink. Neither man seemed to notice, however, as they bantered in a way that she hadn't witnessed before. "I don't mind being called a plod, Tony, but a little less of the old, please."

* * *

After a few quick phone calls to arrange for someone at the university to meet them and for a forensics team from Welwyn to provide support, the three officers clambered into Jones' dark blue Ford Mondeo. As they pulled out of the car park Karen noticed that Sutton also appeared to be wearing rather a lot of cologne.

Sitting behind him, she got a full dose blown over her by the car's air conditioning. Karen could also smell what seemed like the faintest whiff of stale beer mingling slightly with the cologne. It didn't take a fully trained detective to work out what had happened the previous day. Although two senior officers getting drunk whilst in the middle of an ongoing case seemed a bit unprofessional to Karen, after work or not, she couldn't deny that it seemed to have cleared the air somewhat. The atmosphere between the two men had been almost toxic the day before, yet now seemed far more comfortable. Well, as long as it got the job done, she decided.

Pulling into the increasingly familiar car park to the Biology department, Karen noticed that there were far more cars present.

"The building reopened yesterday," Jones explained. "The end of the corridor with Tunbridge's lab is still taped off as a crime scene although it'll have to reopen soon. Forensics are pretty much done so we can't justify keeping it closed much longer."

Sutton scowled slightly. "Let's hope that we haven't lost any evidence in the past twenty-four hours."

Sitting in the back seat, Karen felt a slight stab of shame. She'd visited the PCR room Saturday morning, but it had taken her until last night to notice any potential discrepancies in Spencer's account. Sutton was right — who knew what evidence had been destroyed in the meantime?

Exiting the car, the three police officers headed in through the entrance. Jones showed his badge to the receptionist, who had been told to expect them. By the time the three officers had signed the visitors' log and each been given a badge on a lanyard, a soft-spoken young woman had arrived to greet them. When she introduced herself as Candice Gardner, Warren was slightly disappointed to learn that she was Professor Tompkinson's personal assistant. For some reason, when seeing her name plate on her desk on Saturday he had pictured Mrs Gardner as a late-middle aged woman, dressed in a voluminous flowery dress, peering over half-moon spectacles disdainfully at anyone wishing to disturb the revered professor. Warren had lost count of the number of stereotypes he'd had shattered over the past few days.

As they walked through the main administration office it was obvious that the department was operating at full capacity again. When Warren commented upon this, Gardner smiled tightly. "We've been closed for three days. It was the last thing we needed the week that the A-level results came out and clearing for university places started." Her tone almost made Warren want to apologise on behalf of Tunbridge and his murderer for the inconvenience. He exchanged a glance with Sutton, who raised an eyebrow, clearly thinking something similar.

The three officers entered Tompkinson's office, Warren introducing Tony Sutton, who had not yet met the professor. He remained seated, his hands shaking slightly. He looked exhausted, Warren noted.

"Forgive my manners. I'm having a bit of a flare-up today." As he said so his head bobbed backward and forward like a hen pecking for grubs. His voice was reedy and Jones noted a faint slur to the "S" at the end of "manners".

"Not at all, Professor. I hope not to keep you too long, I realise that this is a busy time of the year for you."

Tompkinson waved vaguely at a large pile of paper on the edge of the desk. "I've been trying to work out what to do with Alan's research group over the next few weeks. The funeral is next Monday, I believe, and we hope to be up and running again by the middle of next week — assuming that you have finished your investigation now?"

"Well, as you know, we have charged somebody with the crime. Now it's just a case of clearing up a few loose ends," Warren said carefully. Instinctively, he was unwilling to suggest that the investigation was still open, feeling it best to keep his cards close to his chest.

Apparently satisfied with the vagueness of the answer, Tompkinson gestured to Warren to go ahead with his request.

"We'd like another quick look at the PCR room, if you don't mind."

"Of course. I must admit I don't really spend much time there myself and wouldn't really know how to drive most of the equipment in there even if I did, but I can probably show you around. It's a shame that Mark Crawley isn't here today. He helped design and equip the room a few years ago." He chuckled slightly. "Alan was not impressed. Maggie Gwyer was supposed to be designing the room, but she broke her leg in a skiing accident and Mark had to take over. He spent rather more time on the project than Alan felt appropriate — probably glad of the opportunity to work away from the boss for a change."

"Where is Dr Crawley today?" Warren asked smoothly.

"He's at home with a migraine, poor man. It came on yesterday. He suddenly went as white as a sheet and had to be excused from our meeting." Tompkinson's gaze became sympathetic. "To be honest I'm amazed it took this long. The stress must have been intolerable for the poor man."

Warren clucked his tongue sympathetically, before suggesting that they move on.

"So what is it you are looking for?" asked Tompkinson as he led them down the corridor to the small room. His walk was slow, almost shuffling, Warren observed. Assuming that the man wasn't a great actor, Warren felt confident that their initial feeling that he couldn't have been the killer was correct. It didn't mean he couldn't be involved in other ways, of course, Jones cautioned himself.

"Like I said, just a few loose ends we need to tie up. Dot the Is, cross the Ts," Warren replied nonchalantly, repeating the cliché again.

Stopping at the door, Warren saw that the sticky blue and white striped crime-scene tape was still across the door. Slitting it easily with his keys, he stepped to one side whilst Tompkinson swiped his card through the lock. With a metallic click, the door unlocked and the familiar blast of icy cold air rushed out. The three officers exchanged quick glances, all of them thinking the same thing: that stepping into this room on a hot August evening wearing nothing but a T-shirt and thin lab coat would be uncomfortable to say the least. Spending over an hour in the room would be downright unpleasant.

The room, of course, was just how they had left it and so Karen went straight to the black PCR machine. Double-checking the sign-up sheet, she confirmed that it was indeed this machine that Spencer had booked to use Friday night.

Tompkinson moved next to her. "What are you looking for?" he enquired.

"I want to see what the last program run on this machine was."

Tompkinson looked at her curiously. "Why do you need to know?"

"Just dotting those Is and crossing those Ts," interjected Jones. "Would you be able to retrieve that information?"

"Sorry, Detective, I wouldn't have the faintest idea. By the time these PCR machines were all the rage, most of the bench-work in my laboratory was being done by my grad students and postdocs.

I understand the theory, of course, but I couldn't operate one of these things."

"Oh, hang on, this might help." Karen plucked an A4 folder off the shelf above the machine. "If in doubt, read the instruction manual, as my dad is so fond of saying. This'll tell us if the machine saves the last program used." She started leafing through the manual quickly. "Here it is. May I?" The question was aimed at Warren, who simply handed her some latex gloves.

"Are you sure you know what you are doing? That's a very expensive piece of equipment," asked Tompkinson, looking rather uncomfortable.

"No problem. I ran loads of PCR reactions when I was at university on a machine very similar to this."

Warren hid his smile; the young detective was quite feisty when she got going. Her personnel file had claimed that she was tenacious and not easily dissuaded when she felt she was on the right track. He had a feeling that she would go far in CID.

At his nod, the young detective started pressing buttons. Immediately the front panel and several LEDs lit up and a fan started whirring loudly. The small screen proclaimed it was running a diagnostic.

At a glance from Warren, Tony spoke up for the first time since entering the room. "This is a pretty impressive room, Professor Tompkinson. I have to admit that science wasn't my strong suit at school. I don't have a clue what any of this stuff does."

Turning to the burly detective, Tompkinson smiled. "Of course, I forgot that you didn't come in here on Saturday."

As Sutton continued to pepper Tompkinson with questions Warren focused his attention on the PCR machine. The start-up procedure was clearly finished and Karen pressed a few more keys. The screen switched to a list of cryptic names next to what appeared to be dates. The title at the top of the screen read 'User Log file'. Directly below that 'TOM1 Started 2107 8/12/11 Completed'.

"If I'm reading this right, the program TOM1 was run Friday night a few minutes after Spencer swiped into the room," said Karen, quietly.

"Can you see how long this program TOM1 would have run for?"

Pressing a few more keys, Karen called up the stored program list. The screen was arranged rather like a simple PC's file manager with folders on the left and programs contained within those folders on the right. Selecting a folder labelled TOM revealed a half-dozen programs, numbered sequentially. Karen selected "TOM1" and "view". The screen immediately filled with what looked like a basic computer program. Even to Warren's untrained eye, he could see each step of the program clearly. Karen pulled out her notepad and started jotting down numbers.

300s activate
45s melt
45s anneal
120s extension
30 cycles
300s final extension.
Shutdown

Even without doing the maths, Warren could see that the program would run for considerably longer than the sixty-eight minutes that Spencer was in the room.

"This is weird," whispered Karen. "The last command told

the machine to shut down, rather than hold the samples at four degrees Celsius until he fetched them. DNA is fairly robust, but it's good practice to keep your samples cool or even freeze them until you need them." She lifted each of the four hinged lids, revealing empty slots.

"And if the program did run to completion, why aren't his tubes in the machine still? He can't have come back down here to remove them after the run as it would probably still have been going whilst he was being interviewed."

"Not to mention that no one has entered this room since then." Warren stroked his chin thoughtfully. "So if Tom Spencer wasn't in here to perform PCR, what was he doing in here?"

* * *

With Karen's hunch looking promising, Jones decided to tackle the second question that bothered him about that evening.

Borrowing Tompkinson's swipe card, Warren leant close to the swipe-card lock. The keypad was clearly well used, with a multitude of tiny scratches now marring the narrow slot that the card was run through. After a few seconds, Warren concluded that even if the lock had been tampered with, he'd never know; he simply didn't know what to look for.

Giving up on the sophistication of the swipe-card mechanism, Warren turned his attention to the wooden door itself, looking for any evidence that it might have been forced. The door was a double affair; solid wood with a magnetic lock in the middle. Propping the door open, he looked carefully along the edges of both doors. Nothing. No scratches, no dents and certainly no evidence that it had been forced open.

Warren squinted carefully at the lock mechanism. It was easy enough to see how it worked. The lock was a sturdy metal bolt, recessed into the edge of the right-hand door, as you looked into the room. Either side of the central bolt were two metal contacts. On the opposite door was a metal plate with a hole in the centre for the bolt to slide into, again framed by metal contacts.

Closing the door, Warren heard a quiet clunk as the bolt sprang across. Swiping the card a second time, he heard the bolt spring back with an identical noise. It was clear how the mechanism worked. When the card was swiped, the bolt was drawn back; opening the door would break the electrical circuit formed between the contacts on the right-hand door and the metal strip on the left door. This presumably told the building security system that the door was open, triggering an alarm if the door was open too long.

An idea was forming in his mind. Looking very carefully at the edge of the door around the lock plate, Warren finally saw what he was looking for. The faintest smudge of dust, contrasting with the clean, laminated wood that covered the rest of the door.

Warren beckoned his two colleagues to join him. After showing them what he had found, he fished his mobile phone out of his pocket.

"DCI Warren Jones, Middlesbury CID. I need a full forensic team to the University of Middlesbury School of Biological Sciences, right now."

Chapter 40

Returning to the station later that day, Warren set Hardwick and Hastings off to look into the life of the newly interesting Tom Spencer. The morning's investigations had potentially blown a wide hole in his alibi and Warren needed to know more about the man before they pulled him in for questioning again.

The forensic team had arrived at the university within an hour. In that time, Warren and Sutton had used their authority to close off the main part of the building again. Shutting the busy department so soon after it had just reopened had not been at all popular with the staff, many of whom were still trying to recover from the weekend's unexpected close-down. One or two disgruntled academics had been of a mood to put up a bit of a fight; however, the arrival of a few polite but burly PCs soon quashed any rebellion. Nevertheless, Warren expected to be called into his superior's office to justify himself and his actions.

Not a problem, thought Warren with some satisfaction. His hunches had proven correct. The PCR machine, with its contradictory log, was now in evidence lock-up. The forensic team had spent just a few moments looking at the door lock, before praising Warren's keen eyes. Just as Warren suspected, it had been tampered with. A slight, sticky residue around the lock — revealed by the presence of dirt adhering to it — supported

Warren's hypothesis that a thin strip of metal had been stuck across the contacts. This effectively fooled the door lock into thinking it was closed, by completing the electrical circuit. The spring-loaded door bolt had then tried to spring back but had been stopped by the metal strip. The result was a door that thought it was locked but could nevertheless be opened easily.

It was unlikely that they would ever find the metal strip, Warren concluded, and needless to say, there were no fingerprints; however, the lab had taken swabs of the sticky residue in the hope of identifying the tape or glue that had been used. The forensic technician had also suggested that the perpetrator would have needed to practise it a few times until they were sure it would work. Warren made a note to search the door log again over the previous few weeks, looking for anybody swiping in and out of the room in quick succession, probably late in the evening.

After leaving the technicians to finish up their work in the PCR room, Warren had moved to the ground floor, where DI Sutton was supervising the search for alternative exits to the building. With the help of campus security, he had soon ruled out any tampering with the emergency exits. The locks on these were far more sophisticated than on the PCR room and covered by CCTV.

It hadn't taken more than half an hour, however, before a DC had interrupted his call updating John Grayson, to tell him that they'd found what they were looking for.

He'd been led to a small tea room, not unlike the one that Warren had interviewed Crawley in on Saturday morning. This one was on the ground floor, overlooking the car park. The room had a large, uPVC double-glazed window, which Warren saw was open.

Sutton was quietly triumphant. "Got it, guv."

The detective inspector pointed to the window, which opened to a distance of about twelve inches, before being stopped by a folding metal arm. It was a pretty standard set-up, Warren noted. The arm was supposed to stop people opening the window too far and falling out. It took only a few seconds for Warren to spot what was wrong.

"The arm isn't attached to the frame."

The screw that would ordinarily have fixed it to the window frame was missing. A firm push would open the window all of the way, making a gap easily wide enough for a person to climb through.

And then Warren saw what had really got Sutton excited. On the bottom edge of the window frame was the slightest smudge of dark red. Blood.

Warren turned to Sutton in excitement. "Care to take a bet that blood belongs to the late professor?"

"No chance, I never bet against a sure thing."

Warren turned wistful. "It'd be too much to hope that the killer cut himself clambering through the window; that would be just the evidence we need to tie him to the crime."

Sutton smiled wolfishly. "We might not need the killer's blood. We may just have the next best thing. Take a look at the lock, guv."

Warren leaned over, careful not to touch the frame, following Sutton's direction. On the bottom of the frame was a brass plate with a tapering groove that the bolt from the window would slot into. Caught around this and fluttering slightly in the breeze from the open window was a single strand of fibre.

Chapter 41

Returning to his office, Warren saw that he had a number of messages waiting for him. First was from Pete Robertson in IT. As Warren had suspected, all attempts to track down the venture capital firm that had apparently lured Tunbridge to his death, California Biotechnology Investment Ltd, had come to nothing. No records existed for any such firm either in the UK or the US. The note came with the caveat that the company might simply not be registered under that name, but it was looking increasingly as though the company was completely fictional.

The second message was equally frustrating and was from the company that the apparently fake venture capital firm had used to host their webpage on, Hosting4U.com. The person paying for the web space hadn't used a credit card, instead using the anonymous payment service PayPal. Warren was familiar with the system, having used it when purchasing goods off eBay and other websites. Unfortunately, the only information that Hosting4U.com could give Warren was the name of the PayPal customer that bought the service; the mysterious JPriest.

With a sigh, Warren drafted another warrant, this time requesting the payment details for JPriest from PayPal. He signed it as urgent and sent it off to DS Kent to get it signed by a magistrate and filed appropriately.

Leaning back in his chair, Warren closed his eyes. The morning's hangover had largely disappeared, but the best part of a week of early mornings and late nights was starting to take its toll. Two minutes, he promised himself, before he moved on to the next item on his list. Two minutes wasn't a lot to ask, was it? Just two minutes…

The knocking at the door woke him in a panic, adrenaline coursing through his veins. Shit! How long had he been asleep? He looked at the clock and felt his panic subside. He'd taken more than his allocated two minutes, but, depending on what time he'd actually dozed off, he hadn't been gone for more than ten or fifteen. He prayed he hadn't snored.

Grabbing a pen in an instinctive effort to look as if he had been busy, he bid his caller to enter. It was Karen Hardwick again, with Gary Hastings in tow. Karen seemed a lot more confident than when she had knocked on his door that morning, as well she might, Warren thought. Her late-night hunch might well have helped break the case.

"Ah, Karen and Gary. Any more ideas?"

"Just a thought about who to interview, concerning Spencer's character." Hardwick had deferred to her more senior partner but he was too polite to take credit for Karen's idea and said so.

"His university file didn't have much about his extra-curricular interests unfortunately, but did mention that he had represented his previous university in both karate and jiu-jitsu. So I decided to get on the web and see if he had a Facebook profile. He did and his privacy settings aren't set very high. It listed him as a fan of UME Shotokan Karate Club. The club has its own fan page, which lists the contact details and training times of the club, plus a mobile phone number.

"Even better, unlike a lot of university sports clubs, it isn't closed over the summer and isn't exclusive to students. The chief instructor is a school PE teacher, Mike Gibson, who lives locally and the club takes part in summer play schemes. We thought that a little visit to the club might be a good idea, sir. Perhaps have a chat with the instructor, see if he can tell us a bit about Spencer?"

Warren nodded approvingly. "Good thinking. When is the next session?"

Karen glanced at her watch. "The current session of the imaginatively titled Middlesbury Karate Kids Klub will finish in about forty-five minutes."

"Then it sounds as if you and DC Hastings have just enough time for a quick cup of coffee before you go."

Chapter 42

Karen's bright red Ford Fiesta wheezed to a stop outside the primary school hall that served as a temporary *dojo* for the Middlesbury Karate Kids Klub. A hand-painted sign stood outside welcoming children ages six to fourteen and promising four hours of fun, fitness and self-defence daily, run by qualified karate and sports instructors, all with clean criminal record checks. Something wasn't quite right about the sign, Karen noticed. The four words making up the club's name looked as if they had been painted by different people at different times.

The playground outside the sports hall was slowly filling up with parents. It was five minutes before the session was due to end and a large, well-built man, wearing a white-cotton training suit held closed with a well-worn black belt, was chatting to an indignant-looking parent. As the two police officers drew closer Karen overheard the mother, a rather well-spoken woman in a designer dress not entirely suited to the weather, as she argued with the instructor.

"Mr Gibson, I really must take Benjamin with me now. I need to go and do the weekly shop at Waitrose before I take him to cello practice. The lesson is clearly over and I am sure that your helpers are paid more than enough to put away a few pieces of equipment."

The instructor had clearly heard this before and remained in good cheer.

"Well, of course, Ms Linton, you are welcome to take Benjamin now, but I really wouldn't advise it." He gestured behind him to where two dozen or so children of different ages wrestled crash mats onto two wheeled trolleys. Most of the kids wore T-shirts and tracksuit bottoms and seemed enthusiastic but clueless, whilst a liberal sprinkling of children wearing cotton training suits and a rainbow of different belt colours helped organise the others. "The philosophy behind the Middlesbury Karate Kids Klub is that we all use the equipment, so we all help put it away. Kids have a strong sense of fair play at this age and they don't like to see other students not pulling their weight. Plus, all of the karate instructors here are volunteers from the local club. Nobody gets paid for giving up their time — the subscription fee only covers use of the school hall and insurance."

The immaculately coiffured Ms Linton looked for the briefest of moments as if she might cause a scene, before finally bowing to the inevitability of it and stalking back to her huge BMW SUV that was taking up the better part of two parking spaces. Karen and Gary resisted the urge to applaud.

Instead, not wishing to cause a scene in front of the gossiping parents, Hastings stepped up to the instructor and discreetly showed his warrant card. "Nothing to be concerned about, sir, but I wonder if my partner and I could have a few words when you are free?"

The instructor nodded, his face puzzled. "Of course. By the looks of things, just about every parent is here. We'll be empty in no more than ten minutes."

Nodding, Hastings decided to return to the car with Karen to wait. Despite their discretion, he noticed that a couple of the parents were openly staring, one or two clearly discussing the two formally dressed strangers. He wondered what rumours would be circulating amongst the chattering classes the following day. At least they hadn't borrowed a police car, he thought, and Karen's old banger didn't look as if it was the sort of vehicle you would be conducting official police business in. He mentally pinched himself for being rude about his colleague's car; after all, she didn't have to offer to drive.

As they sat watching the car park empty Gary tried to start up a conversation. "You know, I've been looking at that sign." He pointed towards the Middlesbury Karate Kids Klub sign, with its strangely painted lettering. "Imagine if the sign originally said Karate Kids." Karen nodded, unsure where he was going. "Then imagine that somebody, possibly from the council, decides that it needs to be a bit more explicit and so helpfully adds Klub at the end — spelled with a 'K' to keep the spelling 'cool' and consistent."

He paused for a few seconds to let her process the thought. "Then you might just see why somebody hastily added Middlesbury at the beginning."

Karen laughed out loud. "I can see why the Karate Kids Klub might not look good on council literature." She continued giggling. "Imagine what they'd find if they googled KKK."

Hastings smiled as the two of them leant back in companionable silence; he looked at her out of the corner of his eye. She really was very pretty, he thought. And she had a lovely laugh. He noticed that she was staring hard at the door as the last few students exited. The last student to leave was a gangly teenage boy with a brown belt, who decided to take a swing at his instructor as he left. Gibson barely seemed to move, but before the punch could connect the boy was effortlessly upended with a leg-sweep.

He landed flat on his back with a loud crack. Karen started in fear, before hearing the mingled laughter of the two martial artists.

"I nearly had you, *Sensei*," shouted the teen gleefully.

The older man snorted. "Nearly isn't good enough, James. Good break-fall though. You slapped the floor just right."

Karen sat back. "I thought he'd really hurt himself, with that big bang."

"No, they're trained to do it. You slap the floor really hard to dissipate the force of the fall and stop it from rattling your bones too much," replied Hastings absently. He noticed that Karen's eyes had flicked back to the burly instructor, whose white cotton *gi* had come partly open, revealing a rather well-developed torso.

Hastings cleared his throat and opened the car door. "Let's see what *Sensei* Gibson has to say about Mr Spencer." He noticed that Karen positively sprang out of the car.

After formally introducing themselves, the two officers quickly got down to business.

"Mr Gibson," started Hastings, "we're making some routine enquiries about a member of this club, a Mr Tom Spencer?"

"Oh, yeah, I know Tom. What do you want to know?" The karate teacher was busy filling a large canvas holdall with padded mitts and shin-pads. His cotton *gi* had opened even more and Hastings noticed that Karen seemed to be studiously ignoring anything below the man's hairline.

"How long have you known him for?" asked Karen, her tone crisp and businesslike.

Gibson paused to stroke his chin, "I guess it must be about four years now. He came to us as a new postgraduate student. He already had a first-dan black belt in karate from his previous university and was also close to gaining his black belt in jiu-jitsu."

"How well would you say that you knew him, Mr Gibson?"

Gibson waggled his hand in a so-so gesture. "I spoke to him a bit, but I can't say that I knew him terribly well. As you may know, although I run the university club, I'm no longer a student at the university. I did a degree in sport science followed by teacher training at UME. I took over running the club in my second year. When I finished uni I got a job in a local secondary school and so kept running the club. I merged it with a local non-university club that was struggling for numbers, which is why I'm now involved with the local school kids.

"The club has a big social event once a term, which I go to, but other than that I don't tend to go out too much with the students." He smiled ruefully. "I'm a little long in the tooth for pound-a-pint night down the Students' Union. And I doubt either my wife or my head teacher would be too thrilled if I went out boozing to the early hours on a week night."

Hastings found himself feeling strangely pleased that the man had mentioned his wife; he noticed that Hardwick's smile was slightly less bright.

"What sort of a person would you say that Mr Spencer was, Mr Gibson?"

The teacher frowned slightly.

"He was a very good martial artist, that was for sure, and a pretty good instructor as well. The club has four black belts at the moment and I encourage all of them to teach parts of the lesson. Tom would also take extra, advanced sessions on a Saturday morning where he'd teach us new stuff. Shotokan-style karate is a great martial art, but its repertoire of techniques can be a little limited — it's mostly punches, kicks and blocks. Tom used to teach us some different skills that he learnt from his jiu-jitsu, such as arm-locks, grappling techniques, basic throws, weapons work, that sort of thing. I learned a lot from him."

The two young police officers shared a look.

"What sort of weapons work do you mean, Mr Gibson?" asked Hastings, trying to sound casual.

"Oh, nothing too exciting!" the instructor said hastily. "We didn't use live blades and we'd never let the kids have a go." He'd clearly misinterpreted the officer's interest. "Tom had a collection of plastic training knives that he used to teach us with. He had proper blades of course, but he wasn't comfortable using those outside his jiu-jitsu lessons. You know, health and safety and insurance and that."

Hastings nodded understandingly. "Don't worry, we're not here about what practice toys you keep in your kit bag. On a different note, I can't help but notice that this entire conversation has been in the past tense, Mr Gibson. Is Mr Spencer no longer a member of the club?"

Gibson hesitated, looking uncomfortable. "I haven't seen him for about six months."

"Why is that?" asked Hastings.

The teacher sighed. "He left after a couple of unpleasant incidents."

Hastings raised an eyebrow. "What do you mean?"

Gibson had clearly decided that there was no point holding back any information and leaned back against the trolley of crash mats.

"He was becoming a bit too aggressive. I had to warn him about his control, or rather lack of it, several times and a few students complained that he was going in too hard during sparring sessions. The straw that broke the camel's back was when he nearly put another black belt in hospital after losing his temper in a routine match."

Hardwick spoke up. "I'm not sure what you mean by control. Do you mean like his temper?"

"Sort of. I had concerns about his temper, but when I said control I meant pulling his punches. Our style of karate is semi-contact — you aren't supposed to hurt your opponent. Here, let me show you. Put your hand up." He took Karen's hand, placing it vertically so that the fingers pointed upwards, her thumb just in front of her nose. "Don't move," he instructed.

Suddenly, with no warning his right foot whipped upwards in a roundhouse kick. His leg moved so fast all that Karen saw was a blur of white cotton. Yet the touch of his foot on the palm of her hand was as soft as a caress. Barely had the echo of his cry reached her ears than his foot was back on the floor, but it wasn't over yet; his foot snapped out again, this time his hips rotated in the opposite direction and it was the sole of his foot that tapped the back of her hand.

Karen's breath caught in her throat.

"That's what we mean by semi-contact and control. Clearly, if I had wanted to I could have hit your hand — or your head — hard enough to do some real damage. But instead I pulled the kick. In semi-contact, a point is awarded for the technique, not the damage you inflict on your opponent."

"Thank you for the demonstration," Karen managed. "So you wouldn't normally hit each other when training?" she asked.

"I'm not saying that we don't make contact with each other. After a good session, you usually have a few small bruises and tender spots, just like you would after a good aggressive game of football or rugby, but it's nothing a hot shower wouldn't normally put right. And of course, accidents happen. But Tom was regularly leaving his sparring partners with bruised ribs and even the odd black eye.

"It was starting to piss people off. You see, it's not just the fact that a punch in the ribs hurts, it's the lack of respect. Martial arts are about etiquette and respect as much as fighting. It's why we bow to each other before we start and when we finish. There are strict rules about how to enter a *dojo* and how to conduct yourself when you are in there.

"I teach kids PE all day and I find it really offensive when they spit on the floor because they've seen some dirty Premiership footballer do it. They think it's normal or even necessary. Yet when I teach karate we'll exercise for two hours flat out, the sweat will be pouring off us, but no one will ever even think about spitting on the floor. And if they did, I'd make them clean it up with a mop and bucket."

Hastings nodded in understanding.

"Tell us about the incident with the black belt."

"The kid he was fighting is a bit of a loud-mouth, to be fair to Tom. Going back to the etiquette thing, we are very polite in karate when we are fighting. In boxing and wrestling, opponents will often goad each other. That is frowned upon in martial arts. Well, anyhow, Hitesh is a bit of a cockney smart-arse, to be honest, and he just doesn't know when to keep his gob shut. I don't know exactly what happened, since I was sparring myself at the other end of the room, but Hitesh said something or other and before I knew it Tom was on him.

"Tom was probably the best fighter in the club at the time and he just went for it. Kicks, punches, even elbow strikes and he wasn't pulling any of them. Quite how Hitesh blocked them all

I'll never know. Anyway, me and three other higher grades dived in and managed to pull Tom off Hitesh, who had gone down on the floor after an elbow to the head. I got a split lip for my trouble and Tina, one of the other black belts, took a really hard punch in the solar plexus.

"I wrestled him out of the *dojo* and sent him to the changing rooms to cool off, whilst one of the other black belts finished up the lesson. Hitesh was bloody lucky he didn't end up with a concussion and Tina had a couple of bruises, but that was it. That was the last time I saw Tom. I emailed him and asked him to come and see me, but he never replied. He's no longer welcome at this club," said Gibson, firmly.

"Why do you think he was so aggressive?" asked Karen after a few seconds' pause.

Gibson sighed and shook his head.

"At first I thought it was just stress. I remember him saying how he was having a hard time with his PhD supervisor. He was working a lot of hours and not getting enough sleep. I encouraged him to do more exercise to help relieve the stress and relax himself, you know, and he did. Starting about eighteen months ago, he decided to go for his second-dan black belt and became fixated on the idea of winning the national student championships. He also started hitting the gym a lot more." Gibson paused as if unsure whether to go on. "I also think he started using steroids."

"What makes you say that?" asked Hastings.

"It's a number of things, really. First, he started to put on a lot of muscle-mass. We all shower together after training and, like I said, I did my degree in sport science. I had a fair idea how much training he was doing and I know that with the number of hours he was putting in, it would take more than a few protein shakes to bulk up like that. I noticed that he also seemed to be having a few problems with acne across his shoulders and back." Gibson blushed slightly. "Sorry, that sounds a bit dodgy. But we trained together three or four times a week for three years. The guy was in his twenties and had a clear complexion when I first met him. It's a bit unusual to develop acne at that age, unless there is a skin or hormonal problem."

Karen nodded her understanding.

"Then there were the mood changes and the aggressiveness, the change in personality. Like I said, I didn't know the guy that well, but we'd sometimes go for a quick pint after training and I sat next to him at the club's Christmas meal a few years ago. He was a fairly pleasant bloke to be around, you know. A good sense of humour and pretty laid-back."

Gibson looked down at his feet. "I was contemplating saying something to him. I guess I should have done." He looked up again. "I've no idea why you're interested in him, but I'm not a fool. You aren't here because he's run up too many library fines. Has he done something really bad?"

"I'm sorry, Mr Gibson, all I can tell you is that we are involved in an ongoing enquiry and we are looking into the backgrounds of a number of individuals."

Gibson nodded, looking morose.

With no more questions to ask, the two officers walked back to the car, leaving Gibson to lock up the school hall.

"You seemed to know a bit about martial arts before we went in. Have you done any karate?" asked Karen.

"Not karate, no." Gary shook his head. "But I have a black belt in jiu-jitsu and I try to train a couple of times a week."

Karen looked at him with renewed interest. "Really? The other martial art that Spencer does? You don't look the type."

Gary tried to keep the hurt out of his voice. "Well, we don't all look like PE teachers."

Karen smiled. "Sorry, I guess not. Mr Miyagi and Jackie Chan don't look much like Mr Gibson either."

Gary smiled, despite himself. "Have you ever done any martial arts?"

Karen shook her head. "No, not really. I did a few women's self-defence courses at uni and of course I did the basic training when I joined the force, but nothing else."

"You should give it a try some time. Why don't you come along to my club some time and have a go? It's a great way to keep fit and a lot of fun."

Karen put the car into gear. "Yeah, maybe I will. I'm getting bored of aerobics down the leisure centre."

Gary smiled to himself. Brilliant. Perhaps he could get her to go for a drink after training.

"Besides which," she continued, sounding excited, "it's all women at aerobics. Maybe I could meet an unmarried Mr Gibson lookalike."

Chapter 43

Warren arrived home at a decent hour for the first time all week. As a peace offering, he'd stopped off at the local Chinese restaurant and bought Susan's favourite dish. He'd also picked up some flowers.

In an act of sensitivity that Warren wouldn't normally associate with Bernice, his mother-in-law had dragged Dennis out of the house for a meal and a film at the local cinema. The movie wasn't scheduled to finish until about 11 p.m. That gave Warren about five hours to apologise for his behaviour that week. He hoped it was long enough.

The reception was decidedly frosty when Susan opened the door. She took the flowers, giving them a perfunctory sniff before taking the Chinese food off his hands. "I would have thought you'd had enough takeaway this week," was her only comment.

Warren smiled weakly. "To be honest, more of last night's kebab ended up on the pavement and down my shirt than in my stomach."

Her frosty glare reminded Warren who her mother was.

The two of them sat down at the dining-room table as Warren spread out the foil containers. Susan had already fetched plates and cutlery from the kitchen and proceeded to spoon out the rice as if she were trying to kill it. The silence stretched uncomfortably between them.

"Susan, I am so sorry about last night. In fact, I am sorry about the last week."

"Do you have a good explanation why I sat up waiting for you until midnight, before finally going to bed, then being woken up by you at half past one, stinking of beer and bloody donner kebab? And then, to add insult to injury, I come downstairs in my nightdress at seven this morning to find a total bloody stranger snoring on the couch?" Susan's voice was cold and calm. That, he knew from experience, was when she was at her most dangerous.

Warren knew that the only acceptable course of action in this situation was to tell the truth and take it on the chin like a man.

"Yesterday afternoon, Tony Sutton and I had a huge row over my decision to reopen the Tunbridge murder case. Immediately afterwards he went in to see Superintendent Grayson in the hope that he would cut me off at the knees and stop me revisiting the case."

"Let me see if I understand this," interrupted Susan incredulously. "One of your subordinates openly argues with you, then goes behind your back to try and get you into trouble and your response is to get pissed with him and bring him back here to sleep on the couch?"

Warren winced. "When you put it that way..."

"And what if my mother had been the one to find him? Can you imagine the scene?"

Warren could imagine the scene and for the briefest of moments found himself torn between maintaining a suitably chastened expression and bursting out laughing at the image. He maintained his expression. It was the correct decision.

"And just one more thing — what do you mean, 'reopen the Tunbridge case'? You've arrested and charged someone, haven't you?"

Warren sighed. "Let me explain from the beginning."

It took the best part of fifteen minutes to explain the events that had led up to him changing his mind. Despite herself, Susan soon became caught up in the case and was particularly impressed by Karen Hardwick's inspiration about the inconsistencies in Spencer's alibi.

"I can see why you have your doubts and, from what you've found out today, it sounds as though you were right. But I still don't understand why Tony Sutton was so against you reopening the case. And even more, why you went out on the piss with him last night and he ended up sleeping in our living room."

Warren recounted what Sutton had told him the night before. By the time he had finished, the two of them had cleared their plates and Susan was shaking her head in disbelief.

"When we moved down here, I worried that you would be bored in such a small unit after working for so long in the WMP. But it seems as if there's more going on inside the police station than outside."

Warren nodded his agreement. "Yeah, well, give me murderers and rapists any day, but please spare me the political bullshit."

Susan reached across the table and took his hand; it was the most affectionate gesture the two of them had shared all week, he realised.

"Sweetheart, when you went for the promotion, we knew that you would have to become more political. It comes with the territory."

Warren nodded, morosely.

"But the most important thing is that you must talk to me. Let me know what is going on at work. I had no idea that things had got so bad between you and Tony Sutton."

Warren squeezed her hand tightly and nodded. "You're right. No more secrets. And the same goes for you — I keep on forgetting that this is a big change for you as well."

Susan nodded in return, before standing up. Stepping around the table, she settled herself down on Warren's lap, her arms around his neck, kissing him on the forehead.

"What time is that film due to end?" asked Warren.

"About eleven, I think," she murmured into his ear.

"Then that gives us until about ten to eleven before we have to worry about tidying up the dishes before your mum and dad get home."

Susan's giggles were music to Warren's ears. When had they last shared a joke? Grabbing her hand, he raced for the stairs, Susan laughing all the way. Suddenly it was as if the years had melted away. It didn't matter that it was their own house and they were a married couple; it was like their first Christmas together. Warren had stayed over at Bernice and Dennis' with Susan. They had only been dating a few months and Bernice had prepared the guest room for Warren. The two young lovers were far too embarrassed to admit that they had been sleeping together for a while by that point and so had endured three frustrating nights and days before, finally, Bernice and Dennis had gone out for an afternoon stroll in the crisp December air.

As they hurried into the bedroom, it was as if they had been transported back in time to that magical afternoon. Tearing at each other as if starved, they had been like wild animals at a feast; desperate to fulfil their hunger, yet not daring to let their guard down in case predators attacked. The sound of a car door that day had almost sent Warren flying off the bed in panic, before he realised that it was the next-door neighbours.

Susan leant back on the bed as Warren stood and removed his shoes. As he took his tie off and unbuttoned his shirt, his gaze swept across his wife.

Susan had spent the day decorating the kitchen; her hair was tousled, with flecks of white emulsion. Her T-shirt was an old, baggy affair that she reserved for messy work. Her tracksuit bottoms were similarly shapeless, having been washed on too hot a cycle too many times. She wore no make-up and her fingernails were chipped and covered in paint. She was the most beautiful person in the world.

Warren finally finished undressing and joined Susan on the bed. Her kiss was tender, a tenderness he tried to match with his hands as he gently caressed her body, rediscovering her curves, the soft places that distinguished men from women. It had been too long, Warren decided, vowing there and then never to allow something as trivial as work to come between them. He closed his eyes, giving himself over to Susan's tender embrace.

The loud ringing of Warren's mobile phone shattered the mood as effectively as a football shattered a greenhouse window. The two of them stopped and lay there, completely still, holding their breath, as if by doing so the phone would magically stop ringing.

It didn't.

Warren thought about leaving it. "Answer it, it could be important," whispered Susan, the disappointment in her voice plain.

Giving in to the inevitable, Warren clambered off the bed, fumbling in his trouser pocket as the phone continued to trill. He glanced at the screen. Tony Sutton. With a sigh, he pressed the connect-call button.

"Sorry, guv, hope I didn't disturb anything. I wouldn't have rung, but it's urgent."

Warren mustered a smile. "Not at all, Tony, it's nothing that can't wait." He looked over at Susan apologetically. "At least tell me you've rung with some good news."

Sutton's voice was leaden. "It's not good news for Mark Crawley. He's topped himself."

Chapter 44

Warren and Sutton both pulled up outside Crawley's house at the same time. The number of vehicles in the road meant that Warren ended up parking several doors down the street, in almost the same spot he'd parked with Gary Hastings. Sutton squeaked to a halt just behind him.

Two police patrol cars and a police van with Scenes of Crime Unit stencilled on the side were parked either side of the Crawleys' drive. For the second time in a week, Warren noted an ambulance, lights and engine off with its back doors open, waiting for a passenger that wouldn't need all of the hustle and bustle of an emergency transfer to the local hospital. Warren wondered idly if it was the same crew that had picked up Tunbridge the previous Friday.

Across the street a few of the neighbours had gathered in a huddle. A couple of uniformed police constables had their notebooks out and were questioning the local residents. Warren and Sutton flashed their warrant cards and introduced themselves to the constable logging arrivals and departures.

A tall, willowy woman in the uniform of an inspector broke off from the conversation she was having with a sergeant. Hand extended, she introduced herself to Jones as Inspector Alison Carmichael. Sutton, she already knew.

"We thought it was just another suicide at first, but when we saw the note and realised who he was I figured we'd better get you guys down here, asap."

"So take us through what's happened, Inspector."

"The wife arrived home with the couple's kids about two hours ago. Found him hanging from a rope he'd rigged around the bannister at the top of the stairs. Looks like he did the sums; clean break, probably killed him instantly. Living room has an empty litre bottle of vodka and an empty pot of strong, prescription painkillers, made out in his name. He also left a suicide note on his laptop — looks like he confessed to being involved with killing that professor of yours."

"What state is the scene in?"

"Not too bad. His wife tried to lift him up, but she's no fool — she could see he was dead, probably a few hours. Obviously the paramedics saw it was a potentially suspicious death and as soon as they pronounced him they left the scene untouched. When we got here, and saw the suicide note on the laptop, we declared it a crime scene and called in you guys and Scenes of Crime."

Warren nodded in approval; until it was confirmed as a suicide he was treating the death as suspicious and unexplained. A suicide was just too coincidental at this time.

Sutton interjected, "Why did he leave his suicide note on his laptop? I reckon if I was about to kill myself, the last thing I'd do is wait for Microsoft bloody Office to load."

"Apparently he was extremely dyslexic," Warren volunteered. "He has special pink spectacles to help him read but I don't know if that'd help him write better as well. He probably used the computer's spell-checker to help him."

"That makes a lot of sense when you see some of the strange spelling mistakes he's made," agreed Carmichael.

"What state is his wife in?" asked Warren, anxious to speak to her.

"Holding up surprisingly well. She actually had the sense of mind to get her eldest to stop the two youngest kids from coming through the front door and seeing their dad like that." Carmichael shook her head in admiration. "It's amazing what a mum will do to protect her kids, even under those circumstances." Her expression became more sober. "It's just a shame the eldest lad walked in beside her and saw everything."

"Do you think she's up to talking?"

"She was when we last checked. She and her kids are next door with the neighbours and Family Liaison. We're tracking down friends as we speak. Before you go in, though, I think you should see the suicide note."

"Has she seen it yet?"

"No, and we've not mentioned it. You'll see why when you read it."

She pulled out a smartphone; on the screen was a series of photographs. "We didn't want to risk screwing anything up before the IT whizzes checked it out, so I just scrolled down the screen and photographed it."

"Good thinking, Allie. Ever thought of joining CID?" suggested Sutton.

"Not if I'd have to see your ugly mug every day, Tony. One evening a month was enough, frankly." Both officers grinned at each other, then sobered slightly. "Been a while, we must start playing again." Sutton nodded, his expression neutral.

"Tony used to play my husband and me at bridge, so I saw

more of him than I wanted to," Carmichael explained to Warren, who nodded politely, more interested in the contents of Crawley's suicide note than his inspector's social life.

The phone screen was small, but high resolution and Crawley had clearly used a fairly large font size. The suicide note was across three photographs and Warren had to swipe through to read it all. He did so twice, with Sutton looking over his shoulder. It was clear why Carmichael had been unwilling to let Crawley's wife see the note.

Deer Lizzy,

I am typing this because I can't bare to look in your eyes when I tell you the truth. I am so sorry for what I did. It was a wicked thing that we planned, I can only hope that by confessing to my crime one day you and the boys will forgive me. Please now that I only did it for us. Money is so tight and with your mum and dad so ill its only going to get worse. I couldn't bare the fought that you an the boys would be made homeless.

I am sure that you will learn all of the details from the press but I need to confess it here to you. Antonio and I plotted to steal the labs research and set up our won company. But we realised that we couldn't do it without getting rid of Alan first. Together we planned his killing.

I have decided to kill myself because if I have realised one thing in the past few days, it is that I love you and the boys more than life itself. I cannot bear the thought that my boys' father will be in prison for murder and I do not think that I could survive. I hope that by confessing my crimes I can also

gain your forgiveness. This will be the last time that we are
together, us and the boys.

    I love you all so much,

Mark

Warren and Sutton looked at each other.

"Well, that was unexpected," opined Sutton eventually.

"You aren't bloody kidding. Now I really want to speak to his wife." Warren turned to Carmichael. "And could you find out who the crime scene manager is and let them know we want a tour as soon as we've finished interviewing Mrs Crawley?"

He turned to Sutton. "Either you've been right all along, Tony, and I've been wasting our time, or this thing just got a whole lot more complicated."

Chapter 45

For the second time in two days, Warren found himself walking up the Turnbulls' driveway. A uniformed constable stood guarding the doorway to the couple's house, making sure that nobody intruded on the family's grief. Except for the local neighbourhood gossip, Warren realised, who had taken them into her home. He found himself hoping that the private grieving of a widow and her children didn't become fodder at the next WI meeting. He wondered if he should have a word with the family liaison officers to warn them against this possibility.

Immediately he decided against the idea and felt a flush of shame for suspecting the woman's motives. All too often in the past, after a hard day investigating the terrible crimes that people had perpetrated on others — often their neighbours — he had lamented that a bit more neighbourliness would go a long way towards solving much of society's ills. Yet the moment he witnessed an example in action he viewed it with suspicion. The cynicism left a sour taste in his mouth.

The Turnbulls' living room felt crowded. On the couch, surrounded by her three boys, was a tearful Lizzi Crawley. The two youngest boys were clutching each other and crying in the cathartic, shameless way that only children could. The eldest sat with his arm around his mother. Red swollen eyes and dried stains on his cheeks evidenced earlier crying, but now he was stony-faced. The hand that wasn't protectively draped around his mother held a tissue, which he was repeatedly screwing up and releasing as he balled his fist then relaxed it, again and again in a nervous tic.

Warren recognised the symptoms. The initial surge of grief and shock had been replaced and the boy — no, he was suddenly a young man now — was feeling a confusing mix of emotions. Grief at their loss; anger at his father for doing this to them; helplessness and perhaps guilt that he didn't see it coming; all topped off with the growing realisation that he was now head of the family.

Appearance-wise, the three boys were almost a perfect blend of both their parents, Warren realised. All of them had an appealing lankiness that Warren suspected would probably turn into the tall ranginess of their father, rather than the short plumpness of their mother. Their mother's influence was clear in the dark hair and eyes, whilst their pale skin and light freckling were probably an inheritance from both parents.

Sitting in the armchairs, unwittingly mirroring the positions of Warren and Gary Hastings the previous day, were the family liaison officers. A man and a woman, they were dressed smartly but were not in uniform. On the coffee table sat several cups of tea. Only the police officers' drinks had been touched; those in front of the Crawleys had acquired the glassy look that tea took on when it had cooled to room temperature.

Warren nodded a greeting to the two officers. What a horrible job, he thought every time he met them. All police officers had to deliver bad news at some point in their career — it went with the territory — and Warren knew that he had a reasonably sensitive manner when doing so. But he hated doing it and, when he'd done what was necessary, he couldn't leave the scene fast enough. Not these guys. Not only did they break more than their fair share of bad news, they stuck around to deal with the aftermath — sometimes for days, or weeks or months. Warren couldn't imagine what that was like.

Warren and Sutton introduced themselves to a tearful, but apparently rational, Lizzi Crawley. Warren could see that Mrs Crawley was unwilling to leave her children to speak to them alone and so he and Sutton decided to keep the interview as short as possible, extracting only the most important details. A more detailed interview, which might or might not reveal details upsetting to younger ears, could wait until they could interview her in a more private setting.

After expressing his condolences on their loss, Warren asked her to describe the past twenty-four hours or so, focusing particularly on her husband's state of mind.

In a surprisingly steady voice, Lizzi Crawley described how her husband had come home early from work the previous day because he thought he was about to come down with a migraine. This confirmed what Tompkinson had said that morning.

"I got home from town with the kids at about five o'clock. Mark said that he'd returned home at about 11 a.m. but by the time he'd got in, the symptoms were fading. It does that occasionally — he gets a sort of false alarm. I guess it was triggered by all of the stress at work and when he got home the stress had gone…" Her voice trailed off as she realised that the stress clearly hadn't gone, otherwise he wouldn't have committed suicide. Not wanting her to dwell too deeply on this, Warren quickly prompted her to continue.

"Well, he seemed slightly hyper. He gets like that sometimes when he has had what he calls one of his near misses. He insisted that we all go out as a family for pizza, the kids' favourite meal, and ten-pin bowling, the kids' favourite game. It was weird, because they had only been out the week before for Ben's birthday and done exactly the same. The night Alan was killed, as a matter of fact. I reminded him of this and he said that he just wanted a fun night out with the kids. The boys were thrilled, of course, to have their favourite treat a second time, and to be honest Mark's been so down lately I wanted to have a fun night out with him."

"How long had this mood lasted and what do you think caused it?" Warren asked gently.

"For the past couple of months, really. Since well before the school holidays, certainly. He just wasn't himself. He was brooding and sometimes a bit snappy. He also didn't sleep very well." She motioned her head towards her sons. "As you can imagine, these three have quite a bit of energy to burn off and Mark was really good at that normally. He'd take them down the rec ground with a football or a frisbee. In the summer evenings particularly, he and a few of the local dads would get together and organise rounders or cricket matches. But over the last few weeks, he claimed to be busy or said he had a headache. The boys would usually still get a game, of course, with the other kids, but I know that one or two of the dads complained that he wasn't pulling his weight."

"It wasn't as much fun without Daddy playing," interrupted the youngest of the three boys suddenly, his voice small and heartbroken.

"I know, sweetheart, I know," crooned his mother, gently kissing the boy's tousled head as new tears started to silently track down his cheeks.

Warren swallowed hard several times trying to remove the

lump in his throat. Out of the corner of his eye, Warren saw Tony Sutton cover his mouth and cough theatrically, patting his chest as if he had something caught in it. Whatever it was, it appeared to be making his eyes water slightly. He sneaked a look at the family liaison officers, who sat dry-eyed yet somehow conveyed the exact amount of sympathy required without seeming patronising. Warren wondered briefly if they practised in a mirror.

"So what happened yesterday evening?"

"Well, he was back to his old self. Last week, he seemed a bit on edge. He kept on checking his mobile phone and was distracted. Last night he was full of life and affection, probably a bit too much affection, since he kept on telling the boys how special they are and how much he loved them. You know how teenage boys can be about things like that." Marcus, the eldest, looked away, the pain on his face visible, his lower lip trembling.

Warren wondered if he was blaming himself — had he told his father to stop embarrassing him in public and now was worrying that by spurning him he had caused his suicide? Or was he just remembering the feel of his father's arms that last time and wishing he could go back and experience it just once more? He tried to catch the boy's eye and reassure him that it wasn't his fault. That he wasn't to blame, and that he knew how he felt. But the young man resolutely stared the other way.

"Well, anyway, it was a great evening and he insisted on letting the youngest boys stay up past their bedtimes — it is the school holidays after all, he said — and telling them silly jokes.

"When they finally went to bed, I was exhausted. But Mark was very, you know… *affectionate*." She glanced self-consciously at her three children, blushing slightly. "We were up very late."

"What about this morning? How was he then?" Warren couldn't

bring himself to call him "Mark", it seemed too intimate, yet "Dr" or "Mr Crawley" was far too formal.

"It was a complete change, as if he couldn't bear to look at me."

Warren could see the pain written across her face and mirrored in her children's. "He claimed that he could feel another migraine coming on and he worried it would be a big one. He asked if I would take all the kids over to see Mum and Dad, since he needed peace and quiet. Mum and Dad live a few miles away in Shepreth and they are both getting on a bit. I go over a few times a week to be with them. We left about ten o'clock, I guess."

She started to sob, quietly. "I shouldn't have left him alone. I knew that something wasn't right. All of that over-the-top jollity the night before — I thought he was trying to make up for the previous few weeks, but he wasn't, was he? He was trying to leave us with some good memories." She looked up at Warren and Sutton, "The reason he couldn't look at me or the boys this morning was because he knew that if he did, he wouldn't be able to kill himself."

She locked eyes with Warren, fixing him with a stare that seemed to reach inside him and grab his very heart.

"Please, DCI Jones, I need to know why my husband killed himself. Please let us know."

Warren nodded, unable to say anything. His knowledge of the contents of Crawley's suicide note burned in his mind. At that moment, if he could have he would have destroyed that note, and never revealed its contents to the woman and children in front of him. They'd been through enough and, despite their remarkable fortitude so far, he feared that the letter might just be enough to destroy them.

Chapter 46

Jones and Sutton emerged from the Turnbulls' house and walked down the driveway. As if by mutual consent, the two men paused before turning and walking the five paces to the left and entering the Crawleys' driveway.

"Shit."

It wasn't the most poetic of summations, Warren decided, but in this case Sutton had expressed both of their feelings perfectly.

"I agree entirely, Tony." He glanced back at the house that they had just left. "We need to get to the bottom of this, not just for the sake of the case, but for that woman and those kids in there."

Nodding grimly, Tony resumed his pace and the two men walked into the Crawleys' drive. Most of the gawkers from across the street had gone now and the area seemed eerily quiet. Only the Scenes of Crime van and the ambulance remained. Two police constables and Alison Carmichael were the only remaining uniforms in the area, the former standing guard at the bottom of the driveway and the front door.

Carmichael was busy on her BlackBerry smartphone; seeing the arrival of the two CID officers, she stopped and called in through the front door, "Andy, can you give that tour now?"

A few seconds later CSM Andy Harrison emerged, dressed from head to toe again in a white paper forensics suit. As usual, he didn't offer to shake hands.

"Hello again, DCI Jones, we must stop meeting like this." The man's cheerful demeanour again seemed slightly out of place, but Warren was nevertheless glad to see a familiar face. He'd been pleased with the speedy and professional response that he'd received earlier in the week from Harrison and his team.

"Are you the only Scenes of Crime duty officer that Herts and Beds employ?" asked Warren, only half joking. Harrison gave a short laugh. "No, but I get a lot of Middlesbury jobs because I live up here. I was on call tonight."

"What can you tell us about what happened?"

The three men entered the front door, Warren and Sutton slipping on latex gloves and plastic overshoes before they crossed the threshold.

The two CID officers stopped dead in their tracks. Both men had seen death in their career. Both men had seen violent and graphic death — most recently, of course, the previous Friday — but this was nevertheless a deeply disturbing sight.

Crawley's eyes were wide open and staring at them. His skin was a grey waxy colour and traces of vomit had dried in sticky trails down his chin, soaking into his smart white shirt. Around his neck he wore an expensive-looking blue silk tie that fitted well with the neatly creased trousers and shiny shoes. What went less well with the ensemble was a hangman's noose made out of multicoloured nylon rope, the sort used to climb mountains or as a tow rope. Warren made a mental note to work out which it was, the two being very different. As a friend of his had found out recently to her cost, a climbing rope is a hell of a lot more expensive than a tow rope — and if you used it for the latter it was no longer suitable for the former.

It looked as if Alison Carmichael had been correct. He had either done the sums correctly or chanced upon the correct length of rope from the bannister. From the unnatural angle of his neck, Warren could clearly see that the drop had been just sufficient to snap his spinal cord, causing instant death, rather than the slow death by suffocation that had so nearly been Antonio Severino's fate.

"Well, first of all, I'm going to go out on a limb and suggest unofficially and before the results of the PM or any tests that this wasn't a suicide — or at least an unassisted suicide."

Warren and Sutton looked up sharply. "What makes you say that?"

Harrison gestured towards the living room, a mirror image of the room that they had been sitting in a few minutes before, albeit with more modern furniture and a big-screen TV with a games console underneath. On the coffee table sat an empty bottle of Smirnoff Vodka and several empty blister-packs of the type used for pills.

"I believe that the scenario we are supposed to accept is that Mr Crawley set up his hangman's noose, then consumed a mixture of alcohol and heavy sedatives to numb the pain, before hanging himself."

Warren nodded. "It looks that way at first glance. What makes you think different?"

"First, do you know if Mr Crawley was a heavy drinker?"

Warren shook his head. "Quite the opposite, I believe. I think Mr and Mrs Turnbull said that he doesn't drink."

"Hmm, that just strengthens my theory. We'll have to confirm this by looking for signs of past alcohol abuse by looking for a history in his hair or by the state of his liver. But the fact is that it looks as though the late doctor drank pretty much this entire bottle of vodka this morning. Everybody's tolerance of alcohol is different, of course, but frankly George Best would have been struggling to stand up after this amount of alcohol and we all know that he wasn't a teetotaller. Add to that some of these migraine pills — we'll have to look at his stomach contents to determine how much vodka and pills he consumed exactly — and we are looking at a potentially lethal state of intoxication, especially for someone who isn't used to alcohol."

"What are you saying? That Crawley didn't die from a hanging?"

"No, not at all. I think that the PM will probably reveal exactly that — instantaneous death from a hangman's drop. What I'm suggesting, however, is that if he had been left to his own devices he would probably have expired a few minutes later anyway from acute alcohol poisoning and or an overdose of painkillers. What's more, he would have been so obliterated, I doubt he would even have been conscious, let alone able to get up from the couch, climb the stairs, place his neck in a noose and then clamber over the bannisters before dropping.

"Somebody did this to him."

* * *

There was a stunned silence after Harrison delivered his prediction.

"This is all preliminary, of course. But I would be willing to bet good money that the post-mortem will show marks on his body consistent with signs of a struggle and restraint."

"I think that your money is probably safe," whispered Warren.

"And another thing, although I am probably straying well beyond my professional remit here, that suicide note is decidedly fishy. The wording isn't right."

"Crawley had dyslexia."

"Oh, I could see that clear enough. It's the bits that aren't dyslexic that stand out to me. I would have somebody from Documents Analysis take a look at it, and have IT go over the laptop to see if they can find any other versions of the letter."

Warren nodded absently, his mind now frantically trying to rearrange the pieces of a jigsaw that he thought he had already mostly solved.

"One thing's for sure," remarked Tony Sutton ruefully. "I think we can be certain that Antonio Severino didn't kill him."

Chapter 47

The two men sat in a bar just around the corner from Crawley's house. It was past 10 p.m. and Warren knew better than to risk the wrath of Susan by turning up late again, smelling of beer. Their interrupted reconciliation notwithstanding, he was well aware of the fact that he was still in the doghouse. Besides which, he was driving.

Nevertheless, the two men needed something to clear their heads, to wash away the memory of what they'd seen and dull the rawness of the emotions that they had witnessed. Warren nursed the gin and tonic in front of him, making a mental note to crunch a few mints on the way home.

Sutton stared into his pint of lager, saying nothing, deep in thought. Eventually he looked up.

"I'm going to request a transfer to Welwyn."

Warren nearly choked on a mouthful of gin. This was the last thing he had expected. After the previous night's argument about how much Middlesbury CID meant to him, asking to leave the unit didn't make any sense. Warren said so.

"You were right last night. It's become an obsession. I was so desperate to preserve this romantic notion of Middlesbury CID that I had built up in my head, that I refused to accept the facts as they were presented to me." He took another swig of his drink. "I'm a detective, damn it. I'm supposed to follow the clues, wherever they lead, and leave my own ideas and prejudices at home."

Warren wasn't sure what to say.

"I'm amazed that I'm not suspended after the way I spoke to you yesterday. I was so far out of line, I'm surprised you didn't punch me."

Warren half smiled. "The thought did occur..."

"Anyway, I think I need to get away from here. Move to Welwyn, where I can work crimes all over the county. I need to be a detective again, digging out clues and following leads, without constantly worrying that if I don't work fast enough or hard enough, the whole unit could be closed down. I need some distance from Middlesbury CID and the ghost of DCI fucking Sheehy."

And that was it, Warren realised. That was what it was all about. Sheehy. The corrupt, former detective chief inspector, who'd made hard-working, honest men like Tony Sutton believe that they were doing something more than just their jobs. It was the sign of an inspirational leader, Warren knew. Making those who followed you view their job as more than just a way to pay the mortgage and put food on the table. But that had made his betrayal all that harder.

Warren looked carefully at the man in front of him. He saw the bags under his eyes, the lines on his forehead. He noted the way that he tore the beer mat into tiny little pieces, his powerful hands shredding the thick cardboard. His nails were ragged, bitten to the quick, Warren spotted now.

"Tony, tell me about Gavin Sheehy. Everything."

Sutton stared into his pint silently. The pause was so long that Warren didn't think he was going to speak. Finally speaking slowly and without looking up, Sutton started.

"I don't have much to tell. I didn't see it coming. The first

I heard of it was when I was pulled into the superintendent's office at 8 a.m. by three suits from Professional Standards and told that Sheehy had been arrested that morning on suspicion of corruption. They didn't say any more as I was part of the investigation. I was removed from active duty pending an inquiry, told to get myself a lawyer and instructed not to speak to anyone about the case.

"It was the most humiliating day of my life."

He took another mouthful of his beer. "Well, they investigated me every which way from Sunday and found nothing. Apparently Gavin claimed that I knew nothing and that he had acted alone. I suppose I should thank him. But I can't. Whatever he's done, I hope they throw the book at him."

"The papers have been quiet and there is remarkably little on the grapevine. What exactly is he alleged to have done?"

Sutton shrugged, but his eyes betrayed the nonchalance of the gesture. "I still don't know what the full story is. He doesn't come to trial until next year, when I guess it'll all come out."

"Rumour has it, he's admitted everything."

Sutton nodded. "I've heard that too. I don't know what to believe."

He stared thoughtfully at the small pile of shredded cardboard that he'd made. "That doesn't seem quite right to me. One thing about Gavin is he's a fighter. I can't see him giving in and pleading guilty without a fight. He'd rather stand toe to toe and defend his corner, even if in the long run he loses the opportunity to do a deal. He hated lawyers. I can't imagine his legal team are having much fun with him." His face twisted in a half-smile.

"And what about you, Tony?"

"Like I said, I was fully cleared of all involvement."

"That's not what I meant," said Warren quietly.

Again, Sutton took his time, destroying yet another beer mat. They'd have to ask the barman for more if he kept this up, thought Warren.

"After my divorce, I had a long hard look at my life. I realised that I had to grow up and do the right thing. I suppose that part of it was to do with my mother-in-law, Betty. She clearly hated me for what I had done to her daughter, but she put that to one side for the sake of her grandchild." He snorted humourlessly. "Never thought I'd ever see Betty as a model of Christian forgiveness, but there you go.

"Anyway, I started to get my life together, studying, doing what I could for Josh, trying to make myself a better man. I started going to church again, and that helped a lot." He looked at Warren, amused. "Don't worry, guv, I'm not some born-again nutter determined to shove my version of God down the throat of everyone I meet. I can't even remember the words to 'Kum Ba Yah'. I'm purely a Sunday morning believer.

"Anyway, that's when I met Gavin Sheehy. He was a DI, I was a newly minted sergeant assigned as part of a large team tasked with bringing down a drugs gang that we believed were using the big warehouses up on the Fowler Estate to redistribute cocaine.

"We raided the warehouse at three in the morning — only to find it empty. The white Transit van that they were using was nowhere to be found. As we were searching the area for clues, I spotted the guard at the next-door warehouse and went over for a chat. He hadn't seen anything, but he said that one of their security cameras overlapped the edge of the road that the two warehouses shared. I went in and had a look at it and, sure enough, we had the white van leaving the premises at half past eleven that night. A white Ford Transit, identical to about fifty thousand others throughout the country, too far away and at the wrong angle to see the licence plates.

"I called over Gavin Sheehy, who praised my quick thinking, but reckoned it was probably useless. But then as we replayed the tape again I saw one of the passengers. A white bloke, that was all we could make out, no use at all for an ID — but I spotted that he was on a mobile phone. They were easier to spot then of course, bit of a brick.

"I figured, it's half eleven in a lonely industrial estate in the back of beyond — just how many people were making a phone call that time of night? Sheehy liked my idea and so first thing the next morning we got a warrant for the phone companies and traced the only phone making a call using that cell tower at that time to a Darryl Wentworth. Already known as a small-time dealer, trying to climb a few rungs up the ladder, he earned himself a twelve-year stretch at Her Majesty's pleasure."

Sutton smiled at the memory. "Anyway, Sheehy was impressed with the way I'd pieced together the clues and my creativity and so he encouraged me to apply to do the detectives' course. When I graduated, he had made DCI and requested that I join his team."

"But he became more than a boss to you, didn't he?"

Sutton nodded. "First he became my mentor, then we became friends. We used to attend the same church." Sutton swirled the remains of his pint. "I haven't been back since his arrest. I don't know if he still goes to the same service. I'm not supposed to have any contact, so I steer clear.

"You know, I thought he was the most honest man I'd ever met. Not once in all the years that I knew him did I ever see him break the rules or even stretch them. And he wouldn't tolerate anyone else doing that either. Outside of work he raised a fortune for charity and he was always the first to visit officers who were injured or taken ill.

"We even used to play bridge — that's why I haven't seen Allie Carmichael for so long. Gavin was my partner. He taught me to play years ago when we did a stakeout together. Said that Judith, his wife, could just about manage snap, and he needed someone to play with." Sutton spoke quietly, and Warren knew that he wasn't referring to his card-playing abilities. "We were a bloody good team."

After a few seconds' pause, Sutton started again. "You know, I thought he was having an affair."

Warren blinked at the apparent non sequitur.

"I thought he was cheating on Judith. I didn't say anything, because how could I? He knew all about my stupid mistake. I didn't like it. I've always been fond of Judith and thought he was better than that, but I didn't know what their home life was like and I didn't feel I could pass judgement.

"It seemed so obvious — he was late middle-aged, probably going through a mid-life crisis. Safer to be bonking some bird than killing himself on a motorbike, I figured. So I said nothing. The times he disappeared out of the office unexpectedly, the furtive phone calls. It all seemed to point to an affair."

Sutton lapsed back into silence.

Warren chose his words carefully. "It's your decision, Tony, but I don't want you to leave Middlesbury. If you really decide that you want a fresh start, then I'll back your transfer request. But from what I've seen, you're a bloody good copper, Tony, and I want you on my team. Think about it."

Sutton nodded, his face still troubled. Warren looked at his watch; it was nearly closing time.

"Right, I've had enough for tonight. Any more and I'll have to catch a cab again. Are you coming?"

Sutton nodded. "Yeah, probably better make tracks. The missus wasn't impressed when I didn't come home last night."

Warren snorted. "Your missus wasn't impressed? How do you think mine reacted when she saw what I'd brought home?"

FRIDAY

Chapter 48

The following morning started even more early than usual, with the whole team at their desks by 7 a.m. The air crackled with energy; everyone felt that today would be the day. Jones briefed his team, plus a number of additional officers, on the previous night's events and outlined his plans for the upcoming day. At 8 a.m. the preliminary autopsy results for Crawley came through and Jones and Sutton attacked them hungrily. Attached to the report was a Post-it note, signed with Andy Harrison's scrawl, "*This is the second all-nighter we've pulled for you in a week, DCI Jones — we'd better be top of your Christmas card list!*"

Despite the grimness of the report it was attached to, Warren couldn't help but smile and made a mental note to find out what tipple Harrison enjoyed. He pushed it towards Tony Sutton, who snorted. "Top bloke, Andy Harrison. Most of the folks who work over there are bloody weird in one way or another — something about working with stiffs all day, I guess. They're all nice enough, but Andy's the only one I'd be seen in public with."

From the report, which was repeatedly annotated with comments in red pen that stressed conclusions were preliminary or simply stated "Pending Lab Results", it looked as if Crawley's death was definitely murder, not suicide. Furthermore, there was no sign of forced entry, suggesting that Crawley had known his attacker or attackers.

Based on the temperature of the body, the degree of rigor mortis and the state of his stomach contents the coroner suggested a time of death of about midday, plus or minus about two hours. Which fitted in with his wife and children leaving the house about 10 a.m.

A further look at the stomach contents had revealed the presence of most of the litre bottle of vodka as well as a large number of semi-digested painkillers. The blood toxicology analysis was still pending, and would be for some time, but it looked as if Harrison's initial belief that Crawley would have been too intoxicated to have successfully hung himself was correct.

Adding weight to his theory that Crawley had been an unwilling imbiber, the coroner had found pressure marks around the hinge of his jaw consistent with Crawley being forced to drink the vodka and swallow the pills. Curiously, there were no obvious bruises that suggested he had been restrained. However, a tiny nick in the skin close to his carotid artery was enough for Harrison to speculate that a very sharp implement — possibly another scalpel blade — had been pressed against his neck.

Warren shuddered. He'd seen firsthand what a skilfully wielded scalpel could do to a human throat. Add in a bit of coercion — perhaps a threat against his wife and kids — and Warren could see how Crawley could be forced to drink vodka and swallow pills. However, he doubted that they'd ever really know exactly what went on in that suburban living room.

The PM had also revealed some small bruises under the armpits consistent with an unconscious man the size of Crawley being manhandled up the stairs before having the noose placed around his neck and his being tipped over the bannister. The cause of death was as expected — severed spinal cord from hanging.

The rope used was a climbing rope that belonged to Crawley. He had been a keen member of a local club, along with his eldest son, and the cupboard under the stairs offered a selection of different ropes suitable for the purpose. Warren felt a flash of disappointment — another dead end.

Attached to the post-mortem findings were other reports from the scene. The vodka was a basic litre bottle of Smirnoff vodka, available in thousands of off-licences and supermarkets all over the country. Lizzi Crawley was adamant that it hadn't come from their house, since her husband never drank and she preferred wine. Their seventeen-year-old son had sworn blind that he knew nothing about it. A batch number had been taken off the bottle in an attempt to trace where it was sold from, but it wasn't expected to yield much in the way of useful information.

The bottle had been dusted for fingerprints and other trace evidence. The only fingerprints found were a single set belonging to Crawley, around the middle of the bottle in a classic drinker's hold. There were no other sets. This observation had been underlined twice in red pen. A handwritten annotation, prefaced with "Speculation" in large block capitals, questioned why there was only one set of prints — suggesting it unlikely, albeit not impossible, that Crawley had only touched the bottle once with bare hands between acquiring the bottle and his unscrewing the cap and swigging a litre of the fiery spirit. Even if that was the case, what about the fingerprints from the sales assistant from where it was bought or the person who placed it on the shop's shelf? The suggested conclusion was that the bottle had been carefully wiped clear of prints before being pressed into the hand of an already comatose Crawley. Given that Crawley was a known teetotaller, the killer would have needed to bring the bottle to the scene and it would have been difficult to justify buying a bottle of vodka in the middle of a heatwave whilst wearing gloves.

The pills were revealed to be a legitimate prescription for Crawley's migraines. His condition was openly acknowledged amongst his friends and co-workers, so it wasn't surprising that the killer knew of the pills. Combined with the vodka they would have formed a lethal cocktail that would have killed Crawley just as effectively as the hanging. And maybe they would have succeeded in passing it off as a suicide, Warren thought. It was just possible that the murderer's quite literal overkill might be their undoing.

More fingerprints had been taken from the cardboard box and the plastic blister-pack that had contained the pills. This time the box was covered with Crawley's fingerprints, plus a few smudged prints from his wife, consistent with her perhaps moving the box of pills around whilst looking for something else in the crowded medicine cabinet that they shared. Another handwritten note suggested that the thumbprints on the blister-pack where the pills had been pushed through the tin-foil might have been added after the pill was popped from the pack, but it had been annotated as "Highly Speculative" and so Warren disregarded it for the time being.

The next report was the preliminary findings from the Document Analysis Team on the suicide note. Since it had been typed on a Word Processor with an inbuilt spell-checker and left on screen, the amount of information that could be gleaned from the document was much less than would have been available from a handwritten note on paper. Nevertheless, the report made Warren sit up straight.

The note was largely consistent with a letter written by an intelligent person with dyslexia. Although it appeared the inbuilt spell checker had corrected any obvious spelling errors, it had been unable to fix the incorrect usage of homonyms; that is words that sound the same, but are spelt differently and have different meanings. Examples from within the suicide note included the opening "Deer", instead of "Dear"; "bare" instead of "bear" and "now" instead of "know". Other examples included transposed letters, such as "won" instead of "own". Incorrect apostrophe usage and other punctuation errors were also common throughout the letter, although the report noted that that was not necessarily a hallmark of dyslexia.

However, some parts of the letter deviated from this, with sections containing almost none of these errors. The analyst had noted of a repetition of the sentiment "I can't bear" and had highlighted it in the text. The first two instances incorrectly used the spelling "bare", whilst the third used the correct spelling. This third usage also correctly used "thought" rather than "fought". The analyst also noted a rare example of correct apostrophe usage in the word "boys" further on in the same sentence. The analyst underlined the examples.

Deer Lizzy,

I am typing this because I can't bare to look in your eyes when I tell you the truth. I am so sorry for what I did. It was a wicked thing that we planned, I can only hope that by confessing to my crime one day you and the boys will forgive me. Please now that I only did it for us. Money is so tight and with your mum and dad so ill its only going to get

*worse. I couldn't bare the fought that you an the boys would
be made homeless.*

*I am sure that you will learn all of the details from the
press but I need to confess it here to you. Antonio and I plotted
to steal the labs research and set up our won company. But
we realised that we couldn't do it without getting rid of Alan
first. Together we planned his killing.*

*I have decided to kill myself because if I have realised
one thing in the past few days, it is that I love you and the
boys more than life itself. I cannot bear the thought that
my boys' father will be in prison for murder and I do not think
that I could survive. I hope that by confessing my crimes I can
also gain your forgiveness. This will be the last time that we
are together, us and the boys.*

I love you all so much, -

Mark

The analysis team suggested that the note had in fact been written by two separate authors. One with dyslexia, one without.
A proposal was that an original note by Crawley had been edited
to change its meaning. The third sentence was almost certainly
added or edited and had been highlighted.

Other sentences might also have been added and it was impossible to know what, if anything, had been deleted. The analyst
suggested that an original version of the letter might be on the
laptop and the IT specialists were looking for evidence of the
original file on its hard drive.

Warren sat back and waited until Sutton had finished reading
all of the reports and looking at the attached photographs.

"Thoughts?"

"Murder, no question in my mind. And two people at least."

Warren nodded in agreement. "Taken individually, it's all circumstantial, but put it together and it's good enough for me."

"We really need that original note — I wonder why they didn't print the damn thing out? Leaving it on the computer screen like that was just asking us to look at the laptop. And I'll bet good money that even if they deleted it, it'll be somewhere on that computer's hard drive. IT will find it, no question."

Warren shrugged. "Could be as simple as them not knowing where his printer was or how it worked. I can't believe they turned up expecting to find he'd written a note to his wife on his laptop. More likely they saw it as an opportunity and took it."

"Speaking of which, what do you reckon is on that original version?"

"Well, I think it's a given that he is confessing to his role in Tunbridge's murder. Quite what the role was I have no idea. I would bet that he also names other people involved, probably the same people that killed him. Clearly, Severino can't have murdered him, which really only leaves Spencer and Hemmingway."

"What about this mysterious woman that Mrs Turnbull claims to have overheard him talking to? Where does she fit in?"

"Assuming that she does fit in. It could be a coincidence; he could have been filling his boots somewhere else. In fact, we're not even sure he was having an affair — all she knows is that he was making private calls in the garden and that he said he could come over because 'he's away'. It could mean anything."

"I don't know, boss, I don't like coincidences. My money is on him having a bit of quality time with Hemmingway. After all, we know that she's shagged Tunbridge and almost certainly Spencer. Why not complete the set? The girl seems to be the campus bike."

"It's possible," Warren conceded, a little surprised at Sutton's judgemental attitude, "but I think we may need to wait for that document to be found. Or for the results to come back on any trace found at the scene."

Sutton nodded, dropping it for the time being. "The question I would like to know is why kill him now? How could they have known that he was going to confess?"

"He went home early on Wednesday and was acting strange that evening. It sounds to me as if he had decided to make a clean breast of it that day. He was then killed some time on Thursday. Somehow his killers found out about his planned confession and decided to silence him. It will have taken some preparation. Unless they were intimately familiar with Crawley's house they will probably have needed to search for his climbing ropes, then figure out how to rig up the hangman's noose."

"Well, they wouldn't have wanted to do that with Crawley awake, surely," interjected Sutton.

"Good point," Warren agreed. "That means they probably subdued him and force-fed him the vodka and pills first. Or one of them could have searched the house whilst the other dealt with Crawley. I wonder how long it would have taken for him to pass out from the pills? And how much longer it would have taken for him to die — because that's the window they had to actually rig him up. Remember it was the hanging that actually killed him."

"And don't forget they had to fake the note as well. That would have taken some time."

"So what do we think, an hour in the house?"

Sutton nodded. "Reasonable, I reckon. They won't have wanted to stick around too long. So when did they do it? The coroner said he died at midday, plus or minus two hours, so he was hung between 10 a.m. and 2 p.m. If they killed him immediately then set up the fake suicide and doctored the note, they will probably have been out of the house by 3 p.m. at the latest."

Flicking through the various witness statements taken at the scene, Warren saw that the ever watchful Mrs Turnbull had spotted Mrs Crawley and children leaving for the day at about 10 a.m. The two driveways were only separated by a low wall, and the Turnbulls' living-room bay windows afforded a full view of the Crawleys' drive. She admitted that she could normally hear their doorbell ringing or even the front door opening and closing if it was quiet.

Unfortunately, she and her husband had left the house themselves at about ten forty-five to attend their weekly over-sixties club and didn't return home until after 4 p.m. Assuming that the killer or killers would have been spotted by the eagle-eyed neighbour — who Warren suspected was probably even more fascinated by her nearest neighbours after his visit the previous day — Warren decided that this meant that they couldn't have been at the house any earlier than just before eleven.

"Let's assume that the Turnbulls would have heard anyone coming to the house before they left and after they returned. So playing it safe, that leaves a window of opportunity between about 10.45 a.m. and 4 p.m."

Just then, Jones' phone rang; he ignored it. A few seconds later it stopped ringing in his office and immediately restarted outside as the call was diverted. He heard Janice, one of the support workers, pick it up. Cupping her hand over the mouthpiece, she called out, "Chief, it's Welwyn Forensics again."

Warren snatched up the phone, mouthing his thanks. Sutton sat opposite him clearly trying to look as if he wasn't deliberately trying to overhear the call. Taking pity on the man, Warren switched to speakerphone.

"DCI Jones? It's the trace lab from Welwyn. We've got a match on that bloodspot and the fibre you found yesterday on the window frame of the common room. The blood matches Professor Alan Tunbridge and the fibre matches the blue denim jeans worn by the witness Thomas Spencer on the night of the murder."

Warren looked at Sutton, his blood starting to sing again. "I think we've entered the end-game, Tony. Time to bring him in."

Chapter 49

Jones stood around the corner from Tom Spencer's student flat. He raised the radio to his lips. "How are things your end, Tony?"

Sutton's voice, coming from the rear of the house, was quiet but clear. "We're all set, guv. The curtains are still closed, no sign of life."

"We're good to go at 10 a.m. on the dot. Don't let him get near a phone — we don't want him letting any accomplices know what's going down."

Sutton acknowledged, then fell silent. The second hand on Warren's watch crawled around the clock face, achingly slowly. At thirty seconds to go, he glanced around at the team with him; Gary Hastings would be at his shoulder, whilst two detective sergeants on loan from Welwyn were with Sutton around the back and a specialist forced-entry team were hidden around the corner. Everyone wore stab vests.

Finally, the hand ticked around to 10 a.m. Immediately, Warren and Hastings burst forth from behind the white van that they had used for cover. Three long strides and the two men cleared the short garden path and were up the steps in front of the doorway.

Spencer's flat was a typical shared student house, according to the records held by the university's housing association. Four rooms, all leased to postgraduate students, with a shared kitchen and lounge. Spencer and his housemates had rented it for three years. The house had a single front door and a rear kitchen door, opening onto a concrete yard just big enough for recycle bins and a rusty barbecue. Spencer had the rear ground-floor bedroom, hence the need for additional officers around the back of the house, in case he bolted.

Jones and Hastings paid only lip-service to the rules of entry, hammering on the front door and ringing the doorbell only once. "Police! Open Up!" Jones hollered through the letter box. Silence.

Jones paused for as long as it took the forced-entry team to make their way up the garden path, before shouting again, "Police, stand aside from the front door." This was punctuated by a loud crunch as the two-man battering ram wielded by the forced-entry team made short work of the flimsy wooden door and cheap, student-landlord supplied locks.

Warren jumped quickly over the threshold, heading down the narrow hallway; behind him he heard the other members of the team starting to pound their way up the stairs to check out the upstairs bedrooms and communal bathroom. Everybody shouted the same thing over and over again: "This is the police. Stay where you are!"

The kitchen was untidy but empty and the open door to the lounge showed it to be similarly unoccupied, allowing Warren to keep on heading towards his goal, Spencer's back bedroom. The door was closed. A cheap laminate affair with a thick coating of cream emulsion, it had a cheap-looking handle with a simple Yale lock. Warren banged once on the door, shouting again "Police, open up."

No response.

No need for the battering-ram this time, Warren judged, and simply put his shoulder to the door. It gave way almost too easily, and Warren had to grab the doorframe to stop himself falling through.

The room was empty.

* * *

Tony Sutton came down the steps at the front of the house. His tread was heavy and Warren didn't need to turn around to see that the energy that had filled him barely twenty minutes ago was gone. Warren closed his phone and glanced at Sutton.

"Flat's completely empty. It looks as though Spencer is the only person living here — the rest of the rooms have been cleaned out. I guess it's the end of term and the new tenants haven't moved in yet."

"We'll see what we can find and return to the station."

"Understood, guv…" A pause. "You know it's not your fault, right? We didn't have enough to charge him with last night. Crawley's death was officially still a suicide and Spencer's alibi was still, in theory, watertight. All the evidence against it was circumstantial until that fibre matched. Arresting him would have been a waste of time."

Warren sighed. "Let's just hope the powers that be see it your way, Tony, because if we don't catch him soon, they're going to be looking for a scapegoat."

* * *

Lunch back at the station was a subdued affair. It looked as if Spencer had gone on the run. Unfortunately, there were no witnesses to Tom Spencer's comings and goings for the previous couple of days. However, a search of the house had proved inter-esting and useful. The absence of any sort of bag or rucksack in his room, coupled with a lack of any toiletries in the bathroom, suggested he had packed and left. Rather more worryingly, a search of all the drawers in his room had failed to unearth a passport. A recent photo pinned to his noticeboard of him standing next to a poster at a San Diego conference suggested that he did own one. Warren put out a ports and airports alert for him, in case he decided to skip overseas.

The contents of the top shelf in his wardrobe proved to be more illuminating. The large tubs of protein powders confirmed Spencer's obsessive interest in building muscle-mass. A number of unlabelled pills had been sent off for pharmacological analysis; Warren fully expected them to be identified as anabolic steroids.

With a nationwide manhunt approved, Warren was able to call upon a lot more resources, including those who specialised in such searches. And he soon realised that he would need them. Spencer didn't own a car, so number-plate recognition was out of the question. Assuming that he had escaped the immediate area, that left the trains, buses or, in the worst-case-scenario, a lift from a friend.

A trawl of the CCTV at the nearest local railway stations had proved fruitless, as had direct questioning of the rail staff. Unfortunately, Middlesbury was part of a well-connected public transport network. An hour-long bus journey could get him to any one of a dozen small, local railway stations and from there the national rail network. Scanning the CCTV footage at each station was technically possible, but would take too long to do much more than retrace his steps. Unfortunately, chasing down a domestic murderer, who was unlikely to pose a significant threat to the public, was well down the priority list when compared to the need to keep tabs on any would-be jihadists on MI5's watch list.

The decision was instead made to focus on his past life. Would he flee to somewhere that he felt safe, or would he be wise enough to keep away from known associates and try to remain anonymous? Hoping that he sought the familiar, rather than the unknown, the team sifted through what information they had on the fugitive's past. Local police forces were put on alert in Greater Manchester and Sheffield in case Spencer returned home or decided to seek refuge at his former university.

Now, it just became a waiting game.

* * *

Warren sat in his office, brooding. It seemed almost certain that Spencer had committed the murder and now he was missing. There was little Warren and the team could do but wait and hope to hear from the teams searching for him. Nevertheless, there were still things that didn't add up.

The web of mobile phone messages had clearly hinted at a conspiracy involving at least four people. Buried in a drawer full of random junk in his room was the box that Spencer's iPhone had come in, which contained a piece of paper with the phone's IMEI number written on it. This confirmed Spencer as Anonymous Phone User Number Two. With Crawley's Nokia confirmed as Phone Number Three, that left only phones numbers one and four to link to individuals. Who was the mysterious young woman, the apparent owner of Phone Number One, who it seemed had seduced Severino and stolen his swipe card and clothes? And what about the owner of Phone Number Four? What was their role in the sordid affair?

As Warren mulled over the unanswered questions, hoping to come up with a new approach, his phone rang. Glancing at the caller ID, he was glad to see that it wasn't from Superintendent Grayson; he wasn't looking forward to that particular conversation.

"Callum Foster, Image Analysis here. I've got some preliminary news on the nightclub footage you sent us from the Tunbridge case."

Warren grabbed a pen quickly, "That's great, Callum, thanks for the quick turn-around." Seventy-two hours was a frustratingly long time to wait in a fast-moving case, but a surprisingly quick response from the overworked and undermanned Image Analysis department. Besides which, Warren had been taught long ago that making the effort to be polite and sounding grateful for any assistance given to you by the people whose services you relied on was rarely effort wasted. You never knew when you might need to ask them for a favour.

"Well, don't thank me just yet. We've barely started looking at the feeds from the cameras in the club and have only just located her. It seems that he was doing all of the buying — she doesn't go to the bar once. No full facial shots there, I'm afraid."

"Oh, well, I'll take whatever you've got so far, Callum." Warren did his best to hide his disappointment.

"I've just sent you an email of some enhanced still images taken from the video footage on the door. I think you might just find them useful for identification purposes. The pictures are blurry, but they are the best we can do, I'm afraid. See what you think."

At that moment, a new mail icon popped up on Warren's desktop computer. Double-clicking, he saw that it contained several

JPEG images. Opening the first image revealed it to be a close-up of the woman's left ear. Despite the poor quality of the hugely amplified image, Warren could clearly make out the shape of her earring. A small metal trinket, in the shape of a teddy-bear. He made a quick note to have any future suspects' houses searched for just such a trinket. Two more images showed the same picture with different enhancements, adding more detail.

The next images were a close-up of her left hand. Her little finger had a gold sovereign ring on it, her ring finger was unadorned, whilst her middle finger appeared to have a simple band with a small stone embedded in it. Warren dutifully added these to his note. The presence of any one of these items of jewellery would mean nothing in court, but the presence of all three, although circumstantial, might be worth admitting as evidence.

"The final image is a beauty, in more ways than one. We discovered it quite by accident when we were enhancing her ring finger. Thought it was a shadow at first, but then we took a closer look."

Warren opened the image, then gasped loudly, his heart rate leaping.

"Er, you OK, guv?" The voice on the end of the phone sounded slightly worried.

Somehow finding his voice, Warren reassured him that he was fine. Hanging up the phone, he continued to stare at the image. He now knew exactly who the mysterious woman was, but it didn't seem possible. Everything had just got even more complicated.

* * *

Warren strode into the main office, heading for Tony Sutton's workspace. On his way he called Karen Hardwick over to join them. Gary Hastings was nowhere to be seen. With a flourish he laid out the enhanced nightclub pictures, still warm from the laser printer, on the only clear space on Sutton's desk.

"I know who the mysterious young woman is that seduced Severino."

The two officers eagerly pored over the photos, their expressions turning from excitement, to recognition, then confusion. Sutton spoke up first.

"Well, that doesn't make any sense."

Hardwick said nothing at first, but her expression spoke volumes. She too was at a loss to explain the woman's identity.

"Are we sure it's her? It could just be a coincidence." She didn't sound convinced.

"That's what I'm about to go and find out. In the meantime, I want you guys to try and come up with an explanation."

With that, Jones turned on his heel and left the two officers standing at Sutton's desk staring at each other. Sutton broke the silence first.

"Any suggestions, DC Hardwick, would be gratefully received, right about now."

Karen managed a tight smile.

"I'm just a rookie, DI Sutton. I defer to your wisdom."

"Yeah, I was afraid of that."

Chapter 50

Warren parked in the same spot as before, in the street adjacent to the White Bear. It was a little later in the day than his Tuesday visit and the pub doors were unlocked. Walking in, Warren noted the familiar smell of cigarette smoke. The room was empty, with nobody at either till.

Behind the bar, an open doorway led through to the rear of the building; cigarette smoke drifted over the threshold. Warren could hear muffled voices and what sounded like cardboard boxes being moved around.

"Hello, anybody in?" Warren called.

"Yeah, 'ang on. Hold your bleedin' horses," the wheezy voice of Larry Stribling replied loudly.

Hardly a textbook example of good customer service, Warren mused as he waited. A few seconds later, the landlord arrived, concealed from view by the three cardboard boxes of McCoys crisps he carried.

"Oh, it's you again," Stribling greeted him, unenthusiastically. Warren remembered the smouldering bar towel from his last visit and wondered if it had caught fire in the end; that would probably account for his lukewarm reception today.

"Good afternoon, Mr Stribling," Warren proclaimed, forcing

a wide smile. "I was wondering if I could ask you and your family a few more questions. It shouldn't take too long."

Stribling opened his mouth to say something, then looked around the empty bar and let the lie die on his lips. He clearly wasn't too busy to help.

"Kids are out the back." He turned and yelled through the open doorway. "Kel, Dazza, get down here. That detective's back, wants to ask some more questions."

It took a further two more attempts, before the two teenagers finally appeared. Either Dazza had bought a multi-pack of *same shit, different day* T-shirts or he was attempting to reduce his carbon footprint by wearing clothes for several days at a time. A quick whiff of sweaty teenager suggested to Warren it was the latter.

"Do you remember that girl I was asking you about? She came in here a couple of Fridays ago?"

Cautious nods.

"Could this be her?" Warren slid his mobile phone across the counter, a clear headshot on the device's large screen.

Kel and her father looked first, both nodding tentatively. "Could be, hard to tell," Stribling, admitted. His daughter was similarly unsure.

"What about you, Dazza?" Warren held his breath as the grubby teenager reached over to look at the image. He paused for a long moment. "Yeah, definitely. She was well fit."

"Any distinguishing marks or features that you can remember?" Warren continued, holding his breath, now in anticipation.

The youth continued to stare at the photo before clicking his fingers loudly. "Oh, yeah, I remember now. She was well fit, like I said, and she had a tattoo on her tit, a flower I think."

Warren resisted the urge to punch the air at the confirmation. A tattoo of a rose on her left breast; the same tattoo visible on the photos taken by the security camera in Mr G's nightclub; the same tattoo that he and Tony Sutton had seen in the interview suite on Saturday. Clara Hemmingway.

* * *

Back outside in the warm, hazy air, Warren called Sutton.

"Yeah, it was definitely her. Have you any ideas how Severino could have failed to recognise her?"

"Assuming that Severino was telling the truth about not knowing her, I'm stumped. Supposedly, the whole lab met her and they went for lunch together. I find it hard to imagine that a warm-blooded Italian like Severino could have forgotten a looker like her."

"I agree, it doesn't make any sense. Keep on checking."

"Will do, guv. Karen has some ideas that she's looking at for the moment, but she hasn't found anything yet."

"OK, I have an idea I'd like to follow up on. I'll see you back at the station later." Warren acknowledged the message and then hung up.

Climbing into his car, he headed back onto the main road. In a few minutes he had arrived at his destination.

Recognising him before he even offered his ID, the middle-aged security guard opened the double doors to the campus Security lodge and admitted him into the small control room.

"Hello again, DCI Jones. Anything we can help you with?"

Jones pulled out his mobile phone and brought up the headshot of Clara Hemmingway he'd just shown to the Striblings.

"Have any of you seen this young woman around the Biological Sciences building in the past few weeks, particularly last Friday night?"

The guard who'd let him in fished a pair of reading glasses out of a top pocket and squinted at the image. "Can't say that she looks familiar. I'll see if any of the lads recognise her." Walking towards the back of the room, he poked his head around an open door marked "Staff Only".

"Jim, Imran, come have a look at this picture."

A few seconds later a white, shaven-headed man who looked to be in his late thirties and a younger, Asian man emerged from the room, coffee cups in hand.

The first man looked carefully at the picture.

"She looks familiar... Oh, yeah, I remember her, Claire or something her name was." He passed the phone over to his younger colleague. "You remember her? Lost her handbag in a nightclub a few weeks ago."

"Oh, yeah, I remember her. Yeah, Claire or Clara or something. She turned up in tears about 1 a.m. one Friday night. She'd had a bust-up with her boyfriend or something. She stormed out of the club and left her handbag behind. Keys, wallet, phone, the lot. Bouncers wouldn't let her back in. She turned up here a bit pissed and really upset because she didn't know if her flatmate was in and didn't know where to go."

"So she came here?" Warren voiced his surprise.

"Oh aye," said the first man, the slightest twinge of a Scottish accent colouring his voice, "we get all sorts. Female students in particular are encouraged to call campus security if they are worried about their safety. Just last week, me and Imran persuaded a couple of local lover boys to leave some young ladies alone." He smiled evilly, revealing a set of suspiciously straight teeth that didn't seem to match his squashed nose.

"Yeah, they got the message," confirmed Imran with a certain amount of relish. Jones decided not to ask for details.

"So what did you do when she turned up?"

Jim shrugged. "What we usually do. We stuck her in the office with a cuppa and a box of tissues and phoned her flat to see if anybody was in. Luckily there was, so we let her finish her tea then drove her home."

"I see. Did she say anything whilst she was here?"

"Well, young Imran here would be the one to ask about that. I left, didn't want to cramp his style." He smirked.

For his part, Imran flushed slightly. "She didn't say much. She calmed down when we contacted her flatmate and then she just asked the usual questions: how much crime do we get? How long have I been doing the job?"

"It's the uniform — you know what it's like", interrupted Jim with a leer.

"I wouldn't know, I haven't worn one for years." Jones was getting a bit tired of this boorish fool. "Go on, Imran."

"Well, as I said, she was interested in what we do here and how we keep an eye on so many cameras. She asked if I could see where she worked, so I zoomed in on the Biology building."

Jones perked up slightly.

"Did she ask about the camera's coverage at all?"

Imran frowned. "No. She just wanted to see if we could peek inside the windows of the tea room. She joked that if we could she'd have to find somewhere else to skive off when she should be working, otherwise the boss might catch her on camera. I reassured her that we couldn't see around there, because the camera is at the wrong angle…" The young man suddenly stopped, paling slightly.

"Oh, shit…"

Warren smiled grimly. So Clara Hemmingway knew all about the blind spot by the side of the building.

Chapter 51

Back at the station, Warren filled in the rest of the team on what he had found out about Clara Hemmingway.

"She's definitely the mysterious woman who seduced Severino. Which means that if that's the case, she's in this right up to her neck. The question is, why didn't Severino recognise her?"

Karen Hardwick spoke up. "I have an idea. When was Hemmingway introduced to the lab? When did her affair with Tunbridge start?"

Warren answered immediately. "She started her project in November and presumably the affair started some time after that; she mentioned something about getting an extension on her essay."

"In which case, it's possible Severino never met her." Karen placed a file down that Warren recognised as Severino's personnel file. She leafed through it quickly, before stopping at a page to which she had attached a Post-it-note.

"According to this, Severino retained links with his previous research group at the University of Trieste in Italy. He popped over a couple of times a year to visit his old lab to share information on a long-standing collaboration, after which he usually delayed his flight home whilst he visited his family." She smiled. "I wonder what the odds are that one of those sabbaticals coincided with the time when Clara Hemmingway was being introduced to the lab. He might never have clapped eyes on her."

* * *

The telephone on Jones' desk rang. Picking it up, he was surprised to hear the voice of Gary Hastings on the other end.

"Sir, it's DC Hastings. Remember I interviewed the Tesco employee that claimed to have seen Clara Hemmingway on the night of Professor Tunbridge's murder?"

"Go ahead, Gary, I remember the report."

"The manager of Tesco has just called. Apparently another member of staff believes that he also saw Clara Hemmingway that night. I think you'd better hear what he has to say, sir. He's on his way in now."

"Good work, Gary. I'll be down in a moment."

There was silence at the other end of the line.

"Is there anything else?"

"Umm, yes, sir." Hastings took a deep breath. "I think I might have screwed up, sir."

Chapter 52

Jones made it downstairs to the main reception in record time. Standing in Reception was a rather morose-looking Gary Hastings. He looked even younger than normal, if that were possible, thought Warren.

"The witness is on his way in now, sir. The store manager is driving him down." A ghost of a smile flickered across the youngster's face. "Apparently police cars in the car park are bad for business."

"OK, then, let's have a quick chat. Bring me up to speed on what to expect and what it is you think you've screwed up." Jones said this last piece in an inviting tone. In his experience, those honest enough to admit their mistakes were usually wrong about the severity of the mistake, particularly younger and less experienced colleagues. And at least the kid — *detective* — had the guts to own up. Of course, if it turned out that he really had screwed up — enough, say, to cost them a prosecution — Jones would personally tear him a new arsehole...

By the time the desk sergeant let them know that the witnesses had arrived, Tony Sutton had also appeared. He too had listened as Hastings had admitted that he had forgotten to go back and pick up the breakdown of the till receipt or request the full CCTV footage of the night in question. Fortunately, when the manager had phoned beforehand, he had remembered to ask for both and the manager was bringing them with him. How significant was the mistake, wondered Jones. Depending on what this witness said and what was on the receipt and CCTV footage, it could have been either very significant or entirely trivial. And what about DC Hastings? He wouldn't lose his job over it — cock-ups happened — but the size of the blot on his record could potentially determine the course of his career for the next few years. Jones hoped for all of their sakes that the mistake was trivial. The heavy feeling in his gut predicted otherwise.

Hastings introduced Sutton and Jones to Mr Patel the store manager, who in turn introduced Aaron Jenkins. Another seventeen-year-old checkout assistant, he at least looked the right age, noted Hastings. He was short and spotty, his hair was greasy and untidy, and his dark blue Tesco T-shirt seemed to hang off his skinny frame.

Once they were settled in the interview room, Jones indicated that he should begin.

"Well, I were talking to me mate, Kevin, who does the tills. Anyhow, he said that the police had been in asking about this bird that he served on Friday night. He said that he remembered her, like, 'cause she was well fit. Anyway, I asked him what she were in trouble for and he said he didn't know, but it must have been serious, 'cause the police was after her."

He paused and glanced at both Hastings and Jones, clearly hoping for some more information that he could take back to the staff canteen. None was forthcoming.

"Anyway, he says he was unlikely to forget her, because she was wearing a dead skimpy top and he could see right down it when she bent over. Said she had a picture of a rose tattooed on her tit.

Well, I served her earlier on, like, but it was really weird because I was on the customer service desk. She come up to me with this massive trolley of shopping, all embarrassed, like, 'cause she'd forgotten her purse. She asked if I could look after her shopping whilst she nipped home to get her wallet. I said, yeah, sure thing. It's dead quiet at that time of night and she didn't have any frozen food in the trolley, so I stuck a label on it and wrote a note for whoever came in next to put it all back in an hour if she didn't return."

"And did she return?"

"Dunno. I went home about five or ten minutes later. I ain't been back in until today."

"What time did you leave?" Jones mouth was dry.

"Ten o'clock."

Ten p.m. It started to come together in Jones' mind. He turned to Patel.

"I believe that you have kindly brought in some information for us, Mr Patel."

"Yes — not sure how important it is, seeing as it's been lying around the store for the past few days." He looked pointedly at Hastings, who blushed slightly. Jones, who regarded it as *his* job to bollock sloppy officers, simply smiled politely.

"As I am sure you can imagine, Mr Patel, an investigation of this magnitude has many different threads running in parallel. Thank you for your assistance."

Patel grunted and handed over a DVD in a jewel case. Whilst Hastings went out to rustle up a TV and DVD player, Sutton, who was a surprisingly fast typist for a man with fingers like sausages, used a laptop to write up Aaron's witness statement. He also put out a call for Kevin Peterfield to be brought down to the station to sign a formal witness statement.

Eventually, Hastings arrived with a wheeled TV/DVD combo unit.

"OK, Mr Patel, so what have we got here?"

"I had one of the boys in Security retrace the young lady's steps from the moment she entered the store to when she finished shopping and left. Obviously, I have all of the raw footage as well."

No wonder he was pissed that nobody had come to pick up the footage. He'd clearly put a lot of effort into this, Jones thought. Sometimes it was easy to forget that for the most part the general public supported the police and would usually go out of their way to assist officers. He made a mental note to publicly thank Mr Patel and Tesco, at some point. Always good to foster relations with the second biggest employer in the town.

The footage started outside the store, showing Clara Hemmingway walking briskly across the car park. Pausing briefly to grab a trolley, she walked through the double doors into the store. The time stamp at the bottom of the screen clearly read 21:41h. What followed was a masterclass in speed shopping. Hemmingway raced up and down the aisles at a remarkable pace grabbing items as she went. For a cash-strapped student, she paid surprisingly little attention to the prices as she tossed food into the basket, Jones noted. As she flitted around the store, the view jumped from camera to camera. Keeping an eye on the clock at the bottom, Jones saw that it never missed a beat. Every second of Hemmingway's whereabouts in the store was accounted for. He wondered idly if Tesco used that smart CCTV that could follow individuals around the store to help track their buying habits. He decided that he'd rather not know; the whole idea was a bit creepy and Big Brother in his opinion.

Finally, Clara was done. Pushing her trolley, she didn't even head towards the tills, instead going straight to the customer service desk.

"Never even checked to see if she had her purse," murmured Sutton quietly.

There was no one at the desk, but seconds later Aaron Jenkins came into view. Even without sound, it was clear that Hemmingway was a good actress, seeming flustered and embarrassed. Jenkins for his part kept on flicking his hair and trying to maintain eye contact, clearly distracted by the good-looking young woman. Finally, he nodded and wrote something down on a piece of paper. Smiling gratefully, Hemmingway left. The time stamp on the final piece of footage as she walked through the double doors was 21:56h.

Sutton, Jones and Hastings exchanged glances. Clara had left Tesco at 21:56h. Why hadn't she mentioned that she'd had to return home for her purse?

The display went blank for a moment, before returning, this time with Clara arriving in the reception area again. The time stamp now read 22:25h. The camera view switched back to the customer service desk, Clara's trolley clearly visible to the left of the desk. A few moments after she approached the desk, one of the security guards came into view. They spoke briefly, before Clara took the trolley. Instead of heading directly to the tills, however, she pushed the trolley further into the store, before making a loop down the aisle with canned soup and exiting next to a till with no customers. She didn't add anything else to the trolley or pause to look at any of the displays.

It was clearly Kevin Peterfield waiting to serve her at the till.

The two exchanged a few pleasantries as he scanned her items. Whilst doing so she bagged them in carrier bags. Finally, they were done. Hemmingway handed over her Clubcard — Peterfield clearly glanced at the name before he scanned it — then got out her bank card and slipped it into the Chip and PIN device. The time stamp read 22:33h, the same time as that on the receipt. Pushing her trolley in front of her, now laden with white and blue plastic shopping bags, Hemmingway headed out of the exit. The time stamp read 22:34h.

Jones and Sutton looked at each other. Hemmingway had lied.

Chapter 53

Back upstairs, Jones and Sutton filled in the rest of the team on what had happened. Jones said nothing about Hastings' potential error; now was not the time or the place.

"The timing still isn't quite right for her to have murdered Tunbridge, but she definitely had enough time to get to the university and back to help Spencer hide the evidence."

Hastings groaned, looking distressed. He buried his head in his hands.

Now wasn't the time for recriminations, decided Warren. "What's done is done — we'll deal with it later. Now we have an arrest to make and I'm betting that when we find Hemmingway, we'll also find Spencer."

* * *

For the second time that day, Jones and Sutton were waiting, dressed in stab-proof vests, around the corner from a suspect's dwelling. This time, the target premises were a small, two-bedroom student flat in a converted family home. A call to the letting agency had revealed the house to be a two-floor property; the two floors shared a common hallway, but a second, internal door had been added at the end of it to split the house into two separate units. The upstairs apartment was currently empty, awaiting new students; the ground floor was occupied by Hemmingway and her flatmate, another student at the university. This time there was no back door; nevertheless two officers were hidden in the rear alleyway in case the suspects made it out of a bedroom window.

As before, the forced-entry team stood by with their two-man battering ram. Maybe it wouldn't be needed this time. Jones' radio squawked; everybody was set. With one last glance at Sutton to check he was ready, Warren set off up the short garden path. The full recycle bins in the tiny front yard confirmed that somebody had at least put the bins out in the last couple of days. The door had two doorbells, conveniently labelled A for the ground floor and B for the first floor. Warren rang both, having decided that gaining entry to the building was the first priority.

Two chimes, one higher pitched than the other, rang inside. A nice touch, it meant the occupants of the two flats could tell who was being visited. To Warren's surprise, he heard immediate movement and a second later a muffled voice, "Coming, hold on a moment." This was followed almost immediately by the metallic scratching of a door chain being applied, then the heavy click of a lock being turned. The door opened a few inches to reveal a mass of dark curly hair, framing a curious left eye. Almost certainly Hemmingway's flatmate.

Warren held up the arrest warrant. "Police. I have a warrant for the arrest of Clara Hemmingway. Please open the door."

The left eye turned from curious to shocked, then disappeared without a word as the door closed again. Immediately, there was a metallic scratching as the door chain was removed and the door opened fully.

"You're too late, Officer. She left this morning with her suitcase."

The air in the CID squad room was leaden with despair. Twice in one day the team had been pumped full of adrenaline, ready to make an arrest. Twice they had been let down. Police work, particularly crime-solving, was always a constant series of ups and downs, something that experienced officers such as Jones knew only too well. But today had been especially trying. Hemmingway had been officially added to the manhunt along with Spencer and now it was just a waiting game again.

The young woman had let them in without comment, confirming her identity as Mary Coates, Hemmingway's flatmate. She'd led Jones and Sutton into the small living room that they shared, even as other officers entered the house en masse, performing a quick room-to-room search of both apartments. Empty.

The young woman had been eager to please, more than willing to talk about Hemmingway; however, she knew little about her housemate's life and even less about her current whereabouts. As he looked about the living room, Warren felt a twinge of sympathy again for Hemmingway. The room was sparsely decorated, with a couple of small, worn couches and a cheap, old-fashioned TV hooked up to a Freeview box and a DVD player. The only personal touches to the room appeared to be a few framed photographs on the mantelpiece above the disused fireplace. Closer inspection had revealed them all to be of Coates. None seemed to be of Hemmingway.

Warren thought back to the interview with Hemmingway, earlier in the week. He remembered feeling sorry for the poor girl who had seemed so out of place. The feeling had become even stronger as he spoke to her housemate. The two girls had both been brought up in Essex, only a dozen miles from each other, yet they might as well have been from different continents. Coates' accent and precise diction spoke of expensive private schools, the pictures of her on the mantelpiece showed her on a yacht with a smiling, tanned family somewhere hot; an action shot of her jumping a fence on a chestnut-brown horse; a family Christmas with three generations smartly dressed sitting around a table groaning with festive food.

How must it have felt for Clara Hemmingway to be reminded of everything that she didn't have even as she sat in her own living room watching TV? Then Warren remembered the torn, bloody throat of Alan Tunbridge, the lifeless eyes of Mark Crawley and the tear-filled eyes of his grieving family. His sympathy evaporated instantly.

In the end, Coates could shed little light on Hemmingway's whereabouts. She'd said that she had heard her come in with somebody else early the previous evening. They had been in a rush and had gone straight to her room. She had heard drawers being opened and closed quickly, before the door to her room was slammed shut and relocked. Coates had got up to go and speak to her about a gas bill that had arrived, but Hemmingway had been flustered and in a rush, and said she'd deal with it later, before racing out of the front door.

Upon prompting, Coates had been able to remember only scant details about what Hemmingway was wearing. She'd caught a glimpse of the person with her and felt certain that it was the same man that she'd seen coming and going occasionally over the last few weeks. It was clear that Clara Hemmingway's social life held no interest for Mary Coates and they had never discussed boyfriends or significant others, but she got the impression that they were seeing each other, at least casually. Warren doubted she even knew what course her flatmate was on; nevertheless, her description of the visitor was familiar. As they had finished the interview Coates' eyes had suddenly lit up with a memory.

"I remember one evening hearing her getting ready to go out. The man was around again and he was dawdling over something. Clara sounded impatient and shouted something like, 'Come on, Tom, we're going to miss the film.'"

Sutton and Jones exchanged glances. It wouldn't stand up in court but it was good enough for them: Tom Spencer and Clara Hemmingway had been dating.

Chapter 54

Karen Hardwick sat at her desk, staring at the reams of paper in front of her. The story of what happened almost exactly a week before was coming together; she was sure of it. And so was everybody else. It needed just a few final pieces and waiting for those pieces was agonising. Around the office, workers were scratching their heads, or staring at paper in the same way she was.

The excitement of the raids on the flats of Spencer and Hemmingway had now turned to frustration as the two main suspects in both murders had vanished. It was now what the papers would breathlessly call a "manhunt". Even as she sat here, discussions were under way as to whether it was time to give up the element of surprise and release the suspects' names and photographs to the press or to hold off another twenty-four hours and perhaps catch them unawares. The fact that they had both disappeared suggested to Karen that they already assumed that they were wanted.

In the meantime, all Karen could do was wait for news, and comb through the evidence to try and work out who this mysterious fourth person was. The owner of the fourth anonymous SIM card was the biggest outstanding question at the moment and Karen felt this person could well be the key to unlock the case. But it was frustrating.

Therefore it came as something of a relief when one of the workers from Welwyn Forensics appeared in the office. A young man, he was carrying a black plastic evidence sack. It clearly held a large, flat, rectangular object of some weight.

"Anyone working the Tunbridge case? I've got his personal laptop here. We've copied his hard disk and there's no need for any physical trace analysis. Figured we may as well drop it back here since we were in the area."

Sutton raised a hand. "DCI Jones is busy at the moment. I'll sign for it." The courier wound his way across the office to Sutton's massively overloaded desk. After trying in vain to find a space to put it, he settled for the visitor's chair. Handing over a handful of sheets of paper, he asked Sutton to sign multiple times, keeping some of the sheets himself and giving the remainder to Sutton.

After the courier had left, Sutton looked around the office, clearly searching for a "volunteer". Settling on Karen, he grabbed the black bag and its associated paperwork, and carried it over to her comparatively empty desk.

With mock gravitas he started, "DC Hardwick. In light of your hard work this week, the powers that be — namely me — have decided to give you the opportunity to earn the privilege of leaving work—" he glanced at his watch "—thirty-three minutes early, thus allowing you to start your weekend celebrations in a timely manner."

Karen couldn't help but smile at Sutton's attempt to lighten the mood in the office. "I see, sir. And what would I have to do to earn the privilege?"

"Do us a favour and drop this damned laptop back at Tunbridge's, would you? We've got everything we need from it and it's getting in the bloody way. I'd do it myself, but I'm on the opposite end of town and it's almost on your way home."

Karen already had her handbag ready. "Love to, sir." It was true; she had worked hard all week. She'd been coming off the end of a five-day shift when Tunbridge had been murdered and had taken the opportunity to earn some much-needed overtime pay by working the case all week. Now she was ready for some downtime. Perhaps she'd call one of her girlfriends and go do some shopping and maybe catch a movie. She owed her best friend a phone call and then there was all that washing…

"You'll keep me posted, won't you, sir, if anything significant comes up? And if you need anything doing?"

"Of course, you've earned that much. Tell you what, give me your mobile number. I'll make sure that the guv has it as well."

The two swapped numbers and Sutton ran her quickly through the procedure for returning a victim's property. It was a bit naughty, but he pointed out that nobody would be likely to need the signed receipts any time soon, so she could file them when she came back on duty Monday morning. Karen made a mental note to file them Saturday; she was a little early in her career to be getting reprimands over sloppy file-keeping, even if it was something that nobody really cared about. Waving a general goodbye to the office, she grabbed the laptop and headed down to the car park.

The drive to Tunbridge's house was indeed almost on the way home and ten minutes later Karen was marvelling at the contrast between this wealthy, leafy suburb and the decidedly less leafy area in which her apartment block resided. She felt almost foolish for locking up her twelve-year-old Fiesta — surely her old banger would be way down the list of any potential car thief patrolling this area. Hypothetically speaking, of course, if she were a car thief, top of her wish list would be the white Porsche Boxster two doors down from the Tunbridges', or maybe the Aston Martin DB7 parked opposite. Of course, they had state-of-the-art anti-theft devices, which her Ford most certainly did not, so maybe locking her car doors was prudent, if futile.

Walking up the drive, Karen saw that Tunbridge's silver BMW was present, along with what she assumed was his wife's Ford Focus. The doorbell was answered in a few moments by a young man, who, from the description, was likely to be the Tunbridges' son. By way of greeting, Karen held up the black bag with the laptop.

"Detective Constable Karen Hardwick. I've just popped by to return your father's laptop."

"Oh, thank you, that's very good of you." He reached to take the laptop.

Karen flushed slightly in embarrassment.

"I'm sorry, Mr Tunbridge, technically it's your mother's property and so I will need her to sign for it."

"Oh, OK." He seemed slightly nonplussed. "Mum's actually having a meeting at the moment. Some friends from the university have dropped by and I think they are arranging the eulogy for Dad's funeral next week."

Karen cursed herself for not ringing ahead. Now she would have to return the laptop to the station and try again later. It was one thing to hold onto a piece of paperwork overnight, but quite another thing to hold onto a victim's property — she shuddered to think what would happen if her flat was broken into and the laptop stolen, Unlikely, yes, but still…

"All it requires really is a couple of signatures and a quick visual inspection, then it's all yours. One more thing ticked off the list." She gave her most winning smile, making it sound as if the list in question were his, not hers.

He thought for a second. "Fair enough, I'll see if she's free. Why don't you wait in her den? She's fussy about filing paperwork immediately anyway and, besides which, her den and Dad's office are usually the only places in the house with working biros."

Following Simon Tunbridge through the hallway, Karen could hear the murmur of voices in what she presumed was the living room.

It soon became clear to her why they called the professor's workspace an "office" and Mrs Tunbridge's a "den". Situated under the stairs, the room was little larger than a closet, with a small desk just large enough for Mrs Tunbridge's own laptop and a half-size filing cabinet. A couple of shelves held various office knick-knacks; a pile of books was stacked on the filing cabinet. It made sense, Karen supposed. Mrs Tunbridge was a housewife and lady of leisure, from what she'd heard, so was unlikely to spend hours in here working, just the occasional bout of household paperwork, she guessed.

Simon left and she heard him enter the living room. The voices stopped, before she heard Simon's voice and a female voice talking. The woman sounded annoyed, although Karen couldn't make out any words. Glancing around the office again, Karen's eyes were drawn to the pile of books on the filing cabinet. They seemed mostly to be well-thumbed computer manuals. She made out a few of the titles: *HTML for Dummies* and *Designing Winning Webpages*. Something tickled at the back of her mind. Hadn't DCI Jones mentioned in briefing that Mrs Tunbridge designed websites for the local Rotary Club? Looking closer, she was unable to suppress a gasp of surprise.

Hidden behind the manuals, away from prying eyes, was a black, false leather A5 binder. Embossed in gold on the spine was the current year, a small spot of something brown and crusty partially obscuring the number two. Tunbridge's missing diary!

Chapter 55

The phone rang in Jones' office. Snatching it up, he hoped it was the call he had been waiting for. "DCI Jones."

"It's Alicia Washington, Welwyn CID. PayPal just got back to us with the owner of the credit card that paid for the website you've been investigating. You aren't going to believe this."

"Try me." Warren managed to keep his tone even, resisting the urge to scream, 'Tell me, damn it!' down the phone.

"The website was paid for by a Professor Alan Tunbridge."

* * *

Karen felt her heart begin to pound and her breath caught. Reaching into her pocket, she withdrew some latex gloves. Not bothering to put them on — a little difficult to explain if she was caught — she used the edges of the gloves to slide the computer manuals fully out of the way, revealing the black organiser. The outside of the organiser was still spotted with what must be dried blood, although some effort had been made to clean the worst off. Next to the binder was a similarly stained USB memory stick.

Outside the den she could hear Simon's voice saying something to his mother, then her voice, louder and clearer, "Take your father's car — the keys are on the side. I may need mine later."

Time to call in the cavalry, Karen decided. Taking her phone from her handbag, she pressed the home key. Nothing. Oh, no, not now! The phone had turned itself off again. Swearing under her breath, Karen depressed the on button firmly. The screen lit up. Outside the small room she heard the front door open and a shout of farewell from Simon, followed by the clash of it closing again.

Although she knew it was far too soon, she glanced at the phone's screen again. It was still showing the phone manufacturer's logo. It could be another thirty seconds or more until the phone finally finished loading up its operating system then found a network signal. Assuming of course that was even possible in this little room underneath the stairs.

With that in mind, Karen turned to leave the room. Suddenly the door opened, making her jump. An attractive, middle-aged woman stood in the doorway.

"Well, what have we here?"

* * *

Tunbridge paid for the website? That hardly made sense. Why would he pay for this fake website that was then used to lure him to his death? Warren scratched his head thoughtfully. Looking around, he cast his eyes across the various pieces of paper that he'd spread out across his desk. His mind was whirring. The clue was here somewhere; he could feel it in his gut. But where? What piece of the puzzle was he missing? His gaze fell on the call list for the anonymous SIM card that they believed belonged to Clara Hemmingway. In amongst the numbers that they had identified as Tom Spencer's and Crawley's anonymous SIM cards and Severino's mobile phone was another number, again linked only to an anonymous SIM card. The call list for that SIM card showed that it had only received and sent calls to Hemmingway and Crawley's SIM card.

Who was this fourth person and what was their role in the affair? The SIM card was of course un-registered and the unique IMEI code of the handset that used the SIM was not listed on the database. If only Warren could link the number to a phone he might get somewhere. More in hope than expectation, he picked up Spencer's call log. A quick glance showed that unsurprisingly the code for his smartphone was different. Why would he have a second anonymous SIM?

Next Severino's handset. Again, no match. Then Crawley's. Nothing. Then he had a sudden thought — the IMEI code was known to be assigned to a BlackBerry smartphone. Didn't Alan Tunbridge have a BlackBerry? Warren's heart started to pound. Maybe the killers contacted Tunbridge directly? What would it mean if that had happened? His mind spun; surely that would make no sense. He riffled quickly through Tunbridge's phone records until he found the sixteen-digit code.

No match.

Of course there wasn't a match, he berated himself. The records showed that the phone had been called at 10.30 p.m. by Mark Crawley and answered in a conversation that lasted two minutes. At this time the scene would have been swarming with police and paramedics. Tunbridge's phone was in his trouser pocket; there was no way it could have been answered and a two-minute conversation held.

Holding Tunbridge's phone record in his hand, he noted how thick the stapled pile of papers was. A memory tickled the back of his mind. Simon Tunbridge talking about his father's planner and how they'd bought him the new phone at Christmas. A family plan, he'd said... Almost without conscious thought, Warren flicked the pages over to reveal the second set of calls listed; linked to her husband through a shared call plan, Mrs Annabel Tunbridge.

The numbers matched.

* * *

Karen swallowed hard, hoping her voice would sound normal. "Mrs Tunbridge, I presume?"

"Yes, my son tells me that you have some paperwork for me to sign for the return of Alan's laptop?"

"That's right. It won't take a moment." Karen's mind spun furiously; she needed to get out of the house immediately and call for back-up.

"Unfortunately, I've just realised that I left one of the sheets in the car. I'll be back in just a second." It sounded weak to Karen's ears, yet amazingly the other woman moved to the side to let her out of the room. As she did so she glanced into the den. Her sharp intake of breath showed that she realised Karen's error at the same time Karen did. With all of the fussing over her phone, Karen hadn't remembered to slide the computer manuals back to where they concealed the diary and memory stick.

Without a second thought, Karen pushed the older woman away and sprinted for the front door.

"Stop her!" bellowed Tunbridge, her voice a mixture of fear and fury. Reaching the door, Karen fumbled with the unfamiliar locks. Finally she yanked the door open and stumbled out into the daylight.

The blow to the side of her head was like an explosion. The world flared an impossibly bright white, before fading to black.

Chapter 56

Jones burst out of his office. "It was his wife all along."

Sutton spun on his chair. "Sorry?" He'd clearly been deep in thought and was struggling to change direction.

Jones cleared a space on Sutton's overflowing desktop and spread out the call-log sheets. By now, the other members of the task squad who were still present had gathered around the table, sensing a breakthrough.

"The unknown fourth SIM card that Hemmingway called on the night of the attack? The handset ID matched Annabel Tunbridge's BlackBerry smartphone. Not only that, the PayPal account that was used to pay for the fake website was paid for on Professor Tunbridge's own credit card — who else would have access to his credit card?"

Sutton was now fully up to speed, his agile mind piecing together the jigsaw puzzle and drawing conclusions almost as fast as Warren was revealing them.

"So Mrs Tunbridge decided to kill her husband before he divorced her. Spencer was the hired gun, whilst Hemmingway acted as an accomplice and set up Severino—" his face darkened "—but I still don't see what she has to gain from this. Any life insurance would now have to be split three ways — her, Spencer and Hemmingway."

"You're forgetting Crawley. We know he didn't commit suicide and his anonymous SIM card sits right in the middle of this little network of contacts. What if the original plan was for Crawley *and* Annabel Tunbridge to take over the research group and form a company to exploit Tunbridge's breakthrough? Hell, maybe she's the one that Mrs Turnbull suspected he was having an affair with? What if he started to get cold feet and was considering going to the police? Spencer and Hemmingway were in it up to their necks, but if he gave up everyone else and cut a deal, he might be able to get a conspiracy to murder charge and a sympathetic judge."

"I could see that working," Sutton started, still looking a little dubious, "but what about Spencer and Hemmingway? How could they entice them to take part, beyond simple revenge?"

"Well, I wouldn't dismiss revenge out of hand Tony, but, even so, much of the work was Spencer's. With Crawley as head of the group he'd probably pass his PhD and then end up with a job in the company, no doubt with all the usual perks. As for Hemmingway, it could just be money but she's a science student as well. Probably guaranteed employment in the new company, I would have thought. I don't think the details really matter right now. The main thing is to get an arrest warrant for Annabel Tunbridge. I just hope that she hasn't done a runner like Spencer and Hemmingway."

Suddenly, Sutton went pale. "Oh, fuck!"

Warren noted the look on his face. "What is it, Tony?"

"I asked Karen Hardwick to return Tunbridge's laptop on her way home."

* * *

In situations like this, it was better to overreact than underreact and regret it later, Warren decided. As Sutton and Gary Hastings raced for the car park he grabbed a phone and rang the main switchboard, asking for emergency assistance from any uniform patrols in the vicinity of Tunbridge's house. That done, he left the room in the steady hands of DS Kent, asking him almost as an afterthought to notify Superintendent Grayson of the break-through. As he clambered into his car and headed for the scene, he offered up a silent prayer that Karen was OK.

* * *

Gary Hastings used his knees to brace himself as Sutton threw his sporty little Audi into yet another squealing turn. Strictly speaking, this was against regulations. The car was a private vehicle without lights and siren and as such shouldn't be driven in such a manner. At this point, neither man could care less.

"Straight through to sodding voicemail again. Either she's turned it off, or that bloody handset has turned itself off. Shit, I have a spare handset at home from when my smartphone was playing up. I could have brought it in for her and then she wouldn't be in this mess—" the illogic of that statement didn't seem to register with the young detective constable "—and if I hadn't forgot to go back to Tesco for those surveillance tapes when I said I would, we could have solved this days ago."

Sutton was in no mood for Hastings' self-recriminations at this time. "Get over it, son, what's done is done. Now we need to focus on cleaning this mess up and making sure that Karen is OK. Besides which," he started, ignoring his own advice, "if anybody should be blaming themselves it's me. What the hell was I thinking sending a trainee DC off on their own to return a victim's property like she's bloody FedEx or something?"

With that, the car squealed into the road that led up to the Tunbridges' house.

"Which number is it?"

"Twenty-six — but look, there's Karen's Fiesta."

The fire-red Ford stood out like a sore thumb amongst the expensive Aston Martins and top-of-the-range BMWs. Sutton pulled up behind the Fiesta with a final squeak of his tyres. Hastings was out of the passenger seat before the handbrake had clicked fully home.

"Calm it, Constable," hissed Sutton as he joined the young man. "We don't know what we're going into. They could be sitting in the drawing room having a cup of tea for all we know. No need to make a drama unless we have to."

Gary took a couple of deep breaths and nodded. Cautiously the two men approached the house. Keeping to the edge of the driveway in an attempt to minimise their visibility, they could see that the living room was empty. As they approached the front door both men stopped at the same moment.

"Is that…?" started Hastings in a harsh whisper.

"Looks like blood," confirmed Sutton grimly, looking at the small reddish-brown patch on the top step. The front door was ajar.

Procedure at this point would have been to wait for back-up, rather than going in alone, but the voices through the hallway put paid to that.

"Stick her, she knows too much."

The two men exchanged glances; they recognised the voice. Hemmingway. And there was no more time to waste.

* * *

449

Warren pulled up behind Sutton's Audi, leaving a second set of tyre marks on the smooth tarmac of the leafy suburban street. A few seconds later a marked police Peugeot, lights flashing, made it three sets.

As the police piled out of the cars Warren spied Sutton and Hastings either side of the front door. He turned to the sergeant who'd joined him, ready to co-ordinate their assault on the building. Before he got a chance, though, all hell broke loose as Sutton reared back and planted his boot in the middle of the front door, yelling, "Police, everybody down on the floor!" The force of Sutton's kick against the unlocked door almost took it off its hinges.

"Now you know why they call him Subtle Sutton!" shouted the sergeant as they raced up the drive. Sutton and Hastings disappeared into the house. Barely a second later, Hastings re-emerged backwards and horizontally, crashing end over end down the steps. Leaping over his prone body emerged a wild-eyed Tom Spencer. Skidding slightly on the loose gravel of the drive, he raced around the side of the house. Hastings shook his head slightly, before scrambling to his feet and taking off after the fleeing student.

Warren made it to the front door, his heart sinking as he saw the prone figure of Karen Hardwick sprawled on the floor. Blood was smeared across her pale forehead. Sutton was kneeling next to her.

"She's breathing," he confirmed. Lying on the floor next to them was the still figure of Annabel Hardwick, still holding a knife. Blood was trickling from her nose and her lips were split. Sutton shrugged, a grim smile on his lips. "Self-defence."

He motioned over his shoulder. "Clara Hemmingway legged it through there. I think there's a back door through the kitchen."

"On it," confirmed the uniformed sergeant, pushing his way

through the crowd and running towards the kitchen. A wail of sirens heralded the arrival of another police car in the distance.

* * *

Hastings was sprinting flat out. Dressed as he was in trousers and smart shoes, he was nevertheless keeping up with the fleet-footed PhD student. Crossing the Tunbridges' back garden, Spencer headed for the fence, a six-foot, wooden-panelled affair. Grabbing it with both hands, he swung over it assault-course style, dropping down onto the other side. Without pausing, Hastings followed suit. Ignoring the ripping sound of his trousers, he landed clumsily in the next-door neighbour's flower bed. Scrambling back to his feet, he saw that Spencer was already halfway across the neighbour's garden and was racing for the next fence.

Forcing his legs to pound even harder, Hastings managed to gain a couple of metres before Spencer reached the next fence. This time the student misstepped slightly, stumbling on the soft soil of a vegetable patch. With less momentum behind him than he needed, he barely made it over the fence, having to scrabble with his feet and pull with his arms to complete the manoeuvre. Hastings took full advantage of the other man's error, pushing himself to reach the fence only a couple of seconds after Spencer. Learning from his predecessor's mistake, Hastings timed his strides perfectly and sailed smoothly up and over. Landing gracefully on both feet this time, he took off again, before realising that his quarry was nowhere to be seen. Barely had this registered when he felt a huge weight crash into his left-hand side.

Rolling as he'd been taught in jiu-jitsu class, Hastings struggled back to his feet, just in time to ward off a lethal snap-kick that threatened to remove his head from his shoulders. This was followed swiftly by a punch towards his face and another kick, aimed at his groin. Hastings parried all of the attacks, aware even as he did so that he was operating at the edge of his ability. He was pretty good at hand-to-hand, particularly the dirty, street-fighting style that his jitsu instructor was an expert at, but he realised that this guy was better. By quite a margin. And he had a dirty little advantage, Hastings saw, even as he realised his error, leaving his chest exposed as he sought to protect his face and his groin. The perfect target for the six-inch kitchen knife clasped in Spencer's fist.

* * *

Warren simply followed the trail of destruction. Trampled flower beds and sagging garden fences told the tale of the chase. He added even more to the story as he clumsily followed the two men. Already his chest was heaving, his legs burning as he raced to catch up. Whether he liked it or not, he was a thirty-something desk-bound pen-pusher chasing two twenty-somethings at the peak of their physical fitness. Pursuing the two men without waiting for back-up probably made him as rash as Gary Hastings, but he knew that he couldn't leave the young officer to chase the killer down on his own. Images of Tunbridge's bloodied corpse filled his mind, spurring him on as he hurled himself over the neighbour's fence. He felt something snag, couldn't be sure if it was clothing or flesh, then he was tumbling over the fence, landing face-down in the dirt.

Pulling himself to his feet, he looked on in horror as Gary Hastings desperately fought for his life against a crazed Tom

Spencer. Too winded to shout, Warren just threw himself as fast as he could towards the fighters. Suddenly he saw what Hastings plainly hadn't — the glint of metal in Spencer's right hand. Even as he opened his mouth to shout a warning he knew it was too late. Time seemed to slow, the distance between Warren and the two men becoming a yawning chasm. Warren desperately forced himself to cover the last few metres, but it was impossible. Even as his legs stretched and his arms pumped, he saw Spencer's left fist snap out in a head punch. Time was moving slowly, yet Spencer's punch was like a rocket and Warren was amazed when Hastings somehow got an arm up to block the lightning-fast blow; he was even more amazed when Hastings somehow parried an equally fast snap-kick to the groin, but of course both of those attacks, devastating as each would have been on its own, were nothing more than a distraction, a prelude to Spencer's real strategy.

The knife went into Hastings' exposed chest almost to the hilt. The effect was instantaneous; Hastings just stopped moving. His mouth opened in surprise as he fell to his knees.

Spencer stood in front of him, lost in the spectacle of yet another human being dying at his hand. He was so engrossed that he was taken unawares as Warren blind-sided him with a clumsy rugby tackle. The two men crashed into an ungainly heap. Having seen what Spencer was capable of close up, Warren had no intention of letting the man get to his feet. Before a stunned Spencer could react, Warren flipped him onto his back and straddled him, before planting a punch square on his jaw.

Or at least that was the plan. Spencer reached up, grabbing Warren's arms. Suddenly, with a squirming motion that caught the policeman by surprise, Warren felt himself being flipped. Spencer had his right arm in some sort of arm-lock, applying what seemed to be almost no pressure at all. Then, for a sickening moment, Warren thought his arm was about to be torn from its socket. The pain was intolerable and he had no choice but to allow Spencer to turn him over onto his face.

It was over, Warren realised as Spencer let go of his arm, instead wrapping both arms around Warren's head and neck in the classic chokehold. His oxygen reserves were already dangerously low from the physical exertion. He doubted he would last more than a few more seconds, even assuming that Spencer didn't just snap his spine and kill him instantly. From a distance, he could hear the crashing of more back-up on their way, but he knew that he would be dead before they arrived.

Tiny sparkling dots were starting to appear in his vision. It occurred to him that in all of this time, he had yet to hear Spencer speak.

"Why?" Somehow he managed to get his lips around that single word.

He heard a sniff, then a sobbing cry.

"It was all his fault. I'll be done for killing him, yet nobody will count the lives he destroyed. People's dreams, people's livelihoods."

Spencer's breathing was hard in Warren's ear. The greyness around the edge of his vision was starting now, but he struggled to listen. Before he died, he had to know what had gone through the man's mind. Why he thought his actions were justified.

"All I ever wanted was to be a scientist. But that bastard just couldn't stand to let anyone share the credit. He fucked me, just like he fucked Clara and made her give up that baby. He might not have killed anyone physically but if killing people's dreams can be counted as murder, he's Hannibal Fucking Lecter."

By now the greyness was complete; a rushing in his ears almost drowned out the world around him. As his vision faded to black Warren's last thought turned to Susan. Did I tell her I loved her when I left the house this morning? Suddenly that seemed the most important thing in the world.

As he faded out of consciousness Warren's last memory was of a sudden lightening sensation. Is my soul leaving my body? he thought. At the same time he became aware of a voice, slurred and muffled as if from a long way away. It sounded like Hastings.

"Take that, you prick."

Epilogue

"Come in, Warren, and sit yourself down."

It was a few days after the climax at Tunbridge's house and twenty-four hours after Warren and the other key officers involved had submitted their full written reports. The case had finally been solved, with the right people now in jail awaiting trial and enough evidence and signed confessions to all but guarantee convictions.

But it had been a messy case to say the least. Mistakes had been made, some serious, and Warren was uncomfortably aware that the very future of Middlesbury CID hung in the balance. And that worried Warren far more than he would have thought possible just a couple of weeks ago. Over the past few days he had started to see what made the little CID unit so special to people like Tony Sutton. The camaraderie within the close-knit team was remarkable — and he *was* a part of the team, he realised now. He'd taken his knocks alongside the team and earned his stripes.

He'd come to realise that the CID unit at Middlesbury was filled with good, dedicated officers. Some lacked experience, but nobody could be faulted for that; it was his job and that of other experienced colleagues to get them that experience. Most importantly, they worked as a team. Breaking up their little unit and absorbing them into the main Serious Crime Unit at Welwyn might save some money, but it would be at the cost of a valuable resource.

One of the people responsible for making that decision was the occupant of the office that Warren now sat in, Assistant Chief Constable Mohammed Naseem. He'd read all of the reports and had the facts. They had voluntarily called in the Independent Police Complaints Commission to see what could be learnt from the episode. In the meantime, though, Naseem wanted to hear the human side of the story, as he put it, straight from the horse's mouth. He wanted an honest appraisal of anything that went wrong and could be improved upon.

This case had certainly had its fair share of "learning opportunities". How many of them he could deflect onto his own broad back, Warren was unsure. Hopefully he would be allowed to issue a few slapped wrists and bollockings in the privacy of his own office, rather than having to "do it by the book" and blot the copybook of some otherwise good police officers. Those decisions would be for the future, though. For now, Naseem just wanted the story.

"First of all, how are you and your team?"

"On the mend, sir." Unconsciously, Warren touched his neck, where the bruises from Spencer's stranglehold were cycling through every colour of the rainbow. A few small cuts and nicks dotted his face from his less than graceful header into the flower bed after the second garden fence. A four-inch gash on his right calf had required stitches and a tetanus jab from where he'd snagged a rusty nail on the first fence. Aside from a slightly raspy voice caused by bruised vocal cords, Warren was in pretty good shape, all things considered, and keen to get back to work. Not least to avoid the well-meaning, but overwhelming, concern of his mother-in-law. *I think I liked her better when she despised me*, Warren thought ruefully.

"Karen Hardwick had a moderate concussion and needed a few stitches to a scalp wound, but there will be no long-term effects. She started back today, in fact, on light duties."

Naseem nodded, pleased. "And what about DC Hastings?"

Warren's expression turned sombre. "He's no longer in a critical condition, but he's still in Intensive Care. He didn't have time to put his stab vest on before he went into the house. The knife struck a rib and was deflected away from the heart, but it nicked a lung. He's due to undergo another operation tomorrow, then we'll know more. If all goes well he could be back on light duties by Christmas." Warren's voice grew quiet. "He saved my life, sir. Pulling the knife back out of a stab wound is a cardinal sin in first aid and he must have known that, but he did it anyway. I don't think I would have survived until the back-up arrived if he hadn't crawled over and stuck Spencer like he did. I can only imagine the pain he was in."

Naseem shook his head in silent respect at Hastings' bravery. "Let's hope for a full recovery, then, shall we? The service needs young officers like that — even if they make mistakes from time to time."

Warren nodded, feeling relief at the hint that Hastings' mistake with the CCTV evidence would probably be glossed over. He agreed with Naseem: the police service needed young officers like Gary Hastings. Warren just prayed that the young man agreed and was fit enough both psychologically and physically to return to duty.

"So tell me why you think this whole sordid affair took place. There are contradictory reports at the moment. Spencer, Mrs

Tunbridge and Hemmingway are all busy trying to cover their own arses and, of course, Crawley isn't here to tell his side of the tale."

Warren leaned back in his chair. "It seems that the chief architect of this whole affair was the late professor's wife, Annabel Tunbridge, and you could argue it all started nearly thirty years ago. They met and married back in the early 1980s, when she was a junior lab technician in Tunbridge's first laboratory. Screwing young women that he supervised became something of a lifetime habit, I'm afraid. Anyway, as Tunbridge's career progressed, she left her own career and became a full-time mother to their two children, following him across the Atlantic as he accepted posts in a number of US laboratories. When they came back to the UK, the kids were school age and Tunbridge was starting to make a name for himself. Although the plan had been for Annabel to go back to work and study for her own PhD, they found it impossible. Tunbridge would do secondments for months at a time in laboratories across Europe, whilst Annabel stayed at home and played housewife.

"By the time the kids were old enough for Annabel to consider going back to education, too many years had passed and the desire to go back to study just wasn't there any more. At least on the surface. I think that urge never really went away and, although she'll probably never admit it, I think she resented him for the choices they made. I can imagine that the resentment only grew as his career skyrocketed and the kids finally left home to do their own thing."

"A powerful motive, but hardly enough to commit murder over, Warren. What changed?" The chief was leaning back in his chair, clearly enjoying the tale. Rumour had it that the chief was an amateur novelist on the quiet and that when he retired, some of the many tales that he had heard on the job would be appearing in hardback — suitably fictionalised, of course. Jones hoped for at least an acknowledgement in the foreword — some royalties would be even better.

"Well, it seems that lust entered the equation. Tunbridge's philandering was an open secret around the university and in academic circles, although there is a sort of unspoken rule that 'what happens at conference, stays at conference', but it's hard to imagine that his wife didn't have at least some clue about what was going on. Anyway, it seems that life in the Tunbridge house was not at all cosy and hadn't been for some time. Tunbridge was by all accounts an arrogant egoist and something of a sociopath. I doubt he was much fun at home.

"The rumour mill had been suggesting for some time that the marriage was on the rocks. However, that was the last thing that Mrs Tunbridge wanted. A senior professor's salary isn't too bad and Tunbridge made a fair bit on the side from speaking engagements and his royalties from some early patents that he co-authored, plus she knew full well the significance of her husband's research and the last thing she would want to do is divorce him before it reached fruition."

"But surely, if she killed Tunbridge, she also killed the research so that there would be no money anyway?"

"Well, that was the beauty of it, sir. On the surface she had no motive to kill him and, if anything, plenty of reasons not to kill him. She only really piqued my interest when I learnt that Tunbridge had told others that he was considering a divorce. It seemed inconceivable that she didn't know about it, yet she made no mention of it to me and played the part of a grieving wife perfectly. Of course, that's not really a big deal, so I simply kept it in mind."

Naseem nodded. "I think that's fair, Warren. A reasonable interpretation could have been that she still loved him and the grief was genuine or that she felt his talk of divorce was just that. I think that twenty-twenty hindsight is a bit much to ask of my officers."

Warren smiled appreciatively, whilst not believing a word of it. He knew full well that the inquiry board would be demanding not only perfect twenty-twenty hindsight but retrospective clairvoyance also. Still, that was their job, he supposed.

"Anyhow, whilst she could turn a blind eye to his bed-hopping, she was herself playing a dangerous game. For the past couple of years, it seems that she and Tunbridge's experimental officer, Dr Mark Crawley, had been spending some quality time together.

"Why he and Mrs Tunbridge hooked up, we'll never know. She's still a handsome woman for her age and both had been treated badly by Tunbridge over the years. Crawley spent a lot of time dealing with the fallout from Tunbridge's lack of social graces and, whilst he would be the first to admit that he had it good career-wise with Tunbridge, he clearly hated the man. It could have been something genuine between them, or it could have been a way of figuratively screwing Tunbridge by either or both of them.

"Either way, Crawley was having troubles at home: his wife's parents are ill and he's been having problems with his kids. We also found out that they had decided to remortgage their home to have an extension done, right before the credit crunch and Mrs Crawley lost her job. With house prices falling and her parents needing care, not to mention the eldest off to university, it seems that financially Crawley was up shit creek without a paddle."

"And so they hatched their little plan?"

"Pretty much. Crawley had joked in the past that he should

461

bump Tunbridge off and take over his empire. At some point, the joke became an idea."

"I thought it was established that Crawley couldn't afford the time to set up and run his own research group, what with all that was going on in his private life?"

"We thought so too, bearing in mind what Crawley himself had told us. But when I telephoned Professor Tompkinson, he dismissed that out of hand. He pretty much ran everything anyway. Give it a couple of years and they could have suddenly announced a breakthrough and nobody would have been at all suspicious."

Naseem nodded.

"So what actually started the ball rolling?"

Warren paused thoughtfully. "We're not entirely sure what precipitated the whole thing. Tunbridge's contemplation of a divorce was probably the final trigger, but an important catalyst was Clara Hemmingway."

"Ah, I wondered when she would make an appearance."

"She appeared in November of last year when she was randomly assigned to him as a tutee to write an essay. Well, Tunbridge is something of a predator when it comes to women. He is clearly able to spot vulnerable young women and, despite appearances, Hemmingway is vulnerable. Who exploited who is a matter for debate. Tunbridge may have been the senior of the two, but Clara had been manipulating men since she was in her teens. He probably didn't stand a chance."

"So then he has his fun then dumps her?"

"Exactly. But, of course, she was pregnant and she tried to blackmail him into supporting her. The daft thing is, if he hadn't been so arrogant he could probably have bought her off, no harm done. But instead he figured he was the university's golden boy and she had more to lose than him and called her bluff."

"So instead, she did the unexpected and went to Tunbridge's wife. But Annabel Tunbridge already knew everything. She had his email password and knew all about how close he was to a lucrative breakthrough — and divorcing her. So they teamed up."

"So that accounts for Hemmingway, the wife and her lover, Crawley, so where does Tom Spencer come in?"

"Well Tunbridge had treated Spencer appallingly and was on course to pretty much end his career before it started. Mark Crawley, on the other hand, had always treated Spencer well. Add in the charms of Miss Hemmingway and his abuse of steroids and they had themselves the perfect killer."

The chief was clearly enraptured. Jones noticed that he'd diverted all his phone calls to his secretary, lest he be distracted by something as trivial as a call from the Home Secretary.

"What about this mysterious investor Priest? I get that he was fictional, but didn't Tunbridge meet him?"

"They simply paid an American exchange student that Spencer knew to approach Tunbridge during the networking sessions of a conference. A smart suit, a business card and Tunbridge's own hubris did the rest."

"Well, it's a hell of a tale, Warren. So what tripped them up?"

"Inconsistencies that seemed small in isolation but bigger when put together. Karen Hardwick was convinced that Tom Spencer's alibi just didn't make any sense. All pretty technical and entirely inconclusive, but it sent us back to look closer.

"Then there was Severino's claim to have been seduced by a woman who sounded suspiciously like Clara Hemmingway — she threw us off the track for a bit with her clever supermarket alibi, but once we discarded that it became apparent that she was in it up to her neck. In the meantime, the calls she made to

Severino as she seduced him opened the door to a network of four anonymous mobile phones, all of which were activated in the run up to the murder and which communicated solely with each other. Of course, by the time we figured this out, the two of them had disappeared into the wind.

"Their biggest miscalculation was killing Mark Crawley. At first glance it looked like a suicide — he even left a note on his computer. But the problem was that in it he took responsibility alongside Severino — which contradicted what we had already figured out. Further, it made no sense that he would happily lay the blame on Severino but try and protect the other people we knew had to be part of the conspiracy. Forensics soon figured out that the suicide and the note were both faked.

"What we now think is that Crawley had realised that the net was closing in and had gone to Annabel Tunbridge with the suggestion that the two of them confessed to being involved in the planning, then offering up Spencer and Hemmingway as scapegoats, hoping for a more lenient sentence. Forensics have since found what they think is the original version of Crawley's suicide note, which was in fact a confession to his wife and children before he handed himself in, and it seems that he and Annabel Tunbridge decided to enjoy one last night of freedom before giving themselves up.

"But in reality, Mrs Tunbridge had no intention of falling on her sword. As far as she knew, there was no evidence to link her to the murder and she was unaware that we were searching for Spencer and Hemmingway. She figured that if they could get rid of Crawley and link him to Severino, the three of them could brazen it out."

Naseem whistled. "I don't know if she was brave or foolish."

"I'd settle for arrogant, sir."

"Works for me. Is that the original note there?" He gestured at the printout in Warren's hand.

Warren nodded. "It seems that they copied and pasted chunks of this original, presumably to keep his wording and phraseology — remember he was dyslexic — then filled in the gaps themselves and hoped nobody would notice the difference." He handed over the sheet.

Deer Lizzy,

By know you will know of my arrest. I am typing this because I can't bare to look in your eyes when I tell you the truth. I am so sorry for what I did. It was a wicked thing that we planned, I can only hope that by confessing to my crime one day you and the boys will forgive me. Please now that I only did it for us. Money is so tight and with your mum and dad so ill its only going to get worse. I couldn't bear the fought that you an the boys would be made homeless.

I have been a bad husband and I know that this will all come out in the end. I had an affair with Alans wife Annabel. We both enjoyed the excitement of going behind his back and things were so stressful at home that I wanted to get away from it. I now there were times you felt the same.

I will not try and blame it all on Annabel since I am an adult and went along with it, but when Alan started talking about getting a divorce, I told her, hoping that she would join me. But Annabel instead was angry and said she had only stayed with Alan because she believed in Trident Antibacterials. Alan would discuss his ideas with her and she would help prepare his conference talks. She felt she deserved part the millions he would earn.

I am sure that you will learn all of the details from the press but I need to confess it here to you. Annabel and I plotted to steal the labs research and set up our won company. But we realised that we couldn't do it without getting rid of Alan first. So we contacted Tom Spenser and a student called Clara Hemmingway that Alan had got pregnant. Together we planned his killing.

Killing Alan was wrong, but the most wicked thing was setting up pour Antonio Severino. I want to state for the record that Antonio was entirely innocent and should be released immediately.

Yesterday I went to Annabel and we decided that it had gone far enough. She is coming around this morning and we will drive to the police station together to confess. Why the delay? Because if I have realised one thing in the past few days, it is that I love you and the boys more than life itself. I hope that by confessing my crimes I can also gain your forgiveness. This will be the last time that we are together, us and the boys. By the time I get out of prison they will probably be groan up.

I really hope you will be waiting for me when I come out.

I love you all so much,

Mark

There was a respectful silence for a few seconds.

"Do you think that this will lessen the pain of his poor wife and kids?"

Warren shrugged resignedly. "I don't know. Maybe one day, but at the moment I think they are too stunned. I went to see her yesterday and she was clearly not in the same room as me."

466

"Do you think this will be admissible in court during the trial?"

"I don't know. Probably not. The CPS are deciding if it's worth submitting. But it's really only the icing on the cake. We have plenty to charge them with regardless."

"What puzzles me is why Spencer and Hemmingway were around Tunbridge's house when you arrived. It doesn't seem to make any sense."

"Well, Spencer and Hemmingway were lying low until the shit storm died down. We've no idea what their plans were in the long run — to re-emerge and brazen it out or to run away. So ask yourself, where is the last place anyone would have expected to find them? Pretty ballsy, I agree. It also meant that Tunbridge could keep an eye on them."

"But what about her son? He met Spencer and Hemmingway at his mother's house. Was he involved?"

"Apparently not. And so what if he met them? He was already due to fly back to the States the day after the funeral. You may have noticed that I haven't yet mentioned the couple's daughter. It seems that she didn't even bother coming home for the funeral. Their son Simon has spent more time catching up with old friends than comforting his dear old mother, although he did seem genuinely shocked and upset that his father had been murdered. Apparently Tunbridge was banking on him being safely gone before we went public with any photos of the missing culprits. I guess that BBC America doesn't screen *Crimewatch* reconstructions."

Naseem shook his head. "What a messed-up family."

"You'll get no argument from me. I've often thought that what you show the world publicly is only a shadow of what you are like behind closed doors. If that's the case, then given what a nasty individual Alan Tunbridge was in public we can only imagine what was going on at home."

"I suspect you're probably right. Yet it would seem that it was Tunbridge's decision to divorce his wife that started the ball rolling."

"Yes, it's ironic that that was probably the last straw. You would think that, after all she'd put up with, a divorce would be exactly what she'd want."

The two men lapsed into a contemplative silence. Finally, Naseem spoke up. "You know, the more I learn about Tunbridge, the more I see why someone bumped him off. I hope that when I die, I'll be missed a little more than the professor."

Warren couldn't help a full-throated chuckle.

Naseem looked at him in surprise. "What's so funny?"

"Sorry, sir, it's just that I said the exact same thing to DI Tony Sutton."

"Oh? What was his response?"

"He suggested that I'd have to start working on my reputation so that everyone would love me when I go."

"I see, and did he have any suggestions?"

"He did, as a matter of fact. He suggested that I should get the first round in."

Naseem stared at him for a long moment, before looking at the clock above his desk. "Sounds good to me. There's a lovely little pub just round the corner. I'll get my coat."

Acknowledgements

They say that writing is a lonely job — but that doesn't mean you do it on your own. I will be eternally grateful for the many, many friends and colleagues who have read drafts of this book, giving invaluable feedback and encouragement in equal measure. To list all of those who had some hand in shaping the story that you hold in your hand would take up pages and I'd only embarrass myself by leaving somebody out. But keep your eyes peeled, guys, at least a few of the names in this and later books may sound familiar.

Nevertheless there are a few people I absolutely have to mention. First my parents, who are always full of encouragement for everything I do; my father proof-reads all of my novels, saving my blushes and making useful suggestions. My good friend Lawrence, whose mastery of the commenting functions in MS Word and enthusiastic use of the semi-colon is evident throughout the final manuscript. And of course my oldest friend Mark. It's always helpful for a writer to have a tame English teacher on call who can wield a red-pen...

I must also mention my favourite lawyers Dan and Caroline. Their expert knowledge forced me to rewrite several key sections of the novel, not only ensuring accuracy, but also making those scenes far more dramatic. It goes without saying that any dubious points of law or dodgy renderings of custody procedure are down to me alone.

All writers need encouragement and support and I want to say a big thank you to my creative writing tutor Danielle Jawando and all the members, past and present, who've attended her wonderful writing courses, critically feeding back on the writing I have brought to class each week. Similarly I must mention the Hertford Writers' Circle, whose monthly meetings are always a pleasure and whose encouragement and advice has been invaluable.

And last, but not least, the editorial team and staff at Carina UK and Harlequin, in particular Helen, Lucy and Victoria, for giving me this exciting opportunity.

Dear Reader,

Thank you so much for taking the time to read this book – we hope you enjoyed it! If you did, we'd be so appreciative if you left a review.

Here at HQ Digital we are dedicated to publishing fiction that will keep you turning the pages into the early hours. We publish a variety of genres, from heartwarming romance, to thrilling crime and sweeping historical fiction.

To find out more about our books, enter competitions and discover exclusive content, please join our community of readers by following us at:

 @HQDigitalUK

facebook.com/HQDigitalUK

Are you a budding writer? We're also looking for authors to join the HQ Digital family! Please submit your manuscript to:

HQDigital@harpercollins.co.uk.

Hope to hear from you soon!